INHERITANCE

MALINDA LO

A division of Hachette Children's Books

First published in Great Britain in 2014
by Hodder Children's Books

A Catalogue record for this book is available from the British Library.

ISBN: 978 1 444 91796 3

Printed and bound by CPI Group (UK) Ltd, Croydon, CR0 4YY

The paper and board used in this paperback by Hodder Children's Books are natural recyclable products made from wood grown in sustainable forests. The manufacturing processes conform to the environmental regulations of the country of origin.

Hodder Children's Books
A division of Hachette Children's Books
338 Euston Road, London NW1 3BH
An Hachette UK company

www.hachette.co.uk

To my parents,
from whom I inherited the
ability to think for myself

We care not how trifling a character may be – let it be the mere inflection of the angle of the jaw, the manner in which an insect's wing is folded, whether the skin be covered by hair or feathers – if it prevail throughout many and different species, especially those having very different habits of life, it assumes high value; for we can account for its presence in so many forms with such different habits, only by inheritance from a common parent.

– Charles Darwin, *The Origin of Species*

CHAPTER 1

The triangular spaceship hovered motionless in the sky above Reese Holloway's house, as inscrutable as a black hole. Military helicopters made large circles around the craft, the noise of their rotor blades conspicuously loud compared to the silence of the black ship.

Reese pulled her gaze away from the triangle and looked down at the crowd of reporters at the bottom of the front steps. They were as impatient as a nest full of baby birds, mouths gaping as they shouted question after question at her and David Li. His fingers squeezed hers, and through the connection that opened between them when they touched, she felt his emotions echoing her own. They both had that jittery, butterflies-in-the-stomach feeling that said: You're about to do something that could either be a huge success or a crushing defeat.

It had seemed like a good idea when they were inside: to tell the truth about what happened to them at Area 51. With the reporters clamoring outside, they had the perfect audience. If they told the world, they thought, they would be safe from their government, which had abducted and locked them in a top secret military base in the middle of nowhere, Nevada.

It didn't seem like such a good idea now that they were outside.

Across the street a line of National Guard soldiers stood with rifles in hand, blockading a vehicle that looked like it had come out of a science fiction movie. Shaped roughly like a bird, it was about the size of a city bus and black as the triangle above. What looked like wings were folded against the vehicle's muscular black walls, making it seem as if it could leap into the air at any moment. A crow had alighted on the roof, its black feathers gleaming in the August sunlight. It turned its head as if to watch the scene below, where several silver robots waited with snub-nosed weapons in their metal hands, facing the National Guard troops. The robots had humanlike bodies, but their heads had no eyes.

Reese's hand was clammy with sweat and it slipped against David's, but he tightened his grip as if he were holding on to the edge of a cliff. The reporters were a blur before her, their faces smudging into one another as waves of emotion rose up the front steps and slammed into her and David. She had experienced this unusual sensitivity to a crowd's feelings before. It had happened when she and David got off the plane at Travis Air Force Base a few hours ago, where they'd been met by a different group of reporters. She knew it must be related to her adaptation – the alien DNA that had been added to hers – but the knowledge didn't make the reality any easier to bear.

The crowd's curiosity scraped like tiny claws against her

skin. As they eyed the spaceship above, their agitation buffeted her in sharp bursts. Their emotions amplified her own nervousness. Objects in the sky weren't supposed to be as still as that black triangle, and that was the most unnerving thing of all: its perfect unnaturalness.

She swayed on her feet, nauseated by the collective anxiety, and David's fingernails dug into her hand. Maybe he wasn't holding on for himself; maybe he was trying to prevent her from falling. She was about to give in to the nausea and drag David back inside when a hand gripped her shoulder and turned her around. It was Amber. Her face was almost as pale as her short blond hair, the only color the smudge of dark pink gloss on her mouth.

David turned too. Amber had one hand on Reese's shoulder, the other on David's, and her touch seemed to push away the encroaching emotions of the crowd below. Amber gazed intently at the two of them through steady gray eyes. *Listen to me*, she told them. It didn't seem like English, exactly; it was more like she was projecting meaning without using any language at all.

Please let us help you. We can show you how to use your abilities, and we will keep you safe. Your government only seeks to use you. Please trust me.

Abruptly, Amber dropped her hands from their shoulders, and the urgent emotions of the crowd came back, pushing against Reese's spine. Amber pulled something out of her pocket and pressed it into Reese's hand. She leaned close to whisper in her ear: 'Call us when you're ready.' Reese shivered at the feel of Amber's breath on her skin, and for a split second all she was aware of was Amber's closeness, her lips a millimeter from her earlobe.

Then Amber brushed past both Reese and David and faced the reporters. 'I can't take your questions right now,' Amber said, her voice silencing the throng.

'Why not?' someone shouted.

'I'm not authorized,' Amber answered.

'Are you an alien?'

'Is your name Amber Gray? Are you the girl in the video?'

Reese saw Amber stiffen slightly, but her voice remained steady. 'I'm an Imrian. And yes, my name is Amber Gray.'

'Who are you? Why do you look like us?'

'You'll get answers soon,' Amber said.

'When?'

'Soon,' she repeated, and then she went down the steps to the sidewalk, where the robots cleared a path for her. They were called erim, Reese remembered. The reporters stayed several feet back as if they were afraid of them. Amber walked quickly through the crowd until she reached the black vehicle parked across the street. She glanced back at Reese and David before she climbed through the open hatch in the side of the vehicle. The erim followed silently. When the door closed, the crow that had been perched on top flew away, and the vehicle's wings spread out, black metal unfurling smoothly. The National Guard troops on the ground fell back as the craft lifted into the air and headed for the black triangle.

When the smaller ship disappeared inside the larger one, the reporters turned back to Reese and David. He reached for her hand once more, and like hers, his feelings were a jumble of shock and uncertainty. The reporters began to shout questions again. She briefly closed her eyes, raising her free hand to press her fingers to the bridge of her nose, and realized she was still holding the device that Amber had given her. She looked at the object in her hand. It was an ordinary cell phone.

Startled, she put it in her pocket as the reporters continued to pepper them with questions. 'Stop,' she said, but her voice was too low. 'Stop!' she cried, looking down at the assembled crowd. They fell silent, and she heard the rapid *click-click-click* of camera shutters as she and David were photographed. 'We'll take one question at a time,' she said.

There was no hesitation. A woman at the front of the pack, holding out a mini digital recorder, asked, 'Why is there a giant spaceship above your house? Is that the ship that was in the video?'

For the past five days, Reese and David had been locked in a military hospital on Area 51. They hadn't been released until a video was leaked that showed them fleeing an underground bunker in the Nevada desert, running toward a black spaceship. Amber was on the video too. Reese had seen the grainy footage only once, but the image was burned into her mind forever: Amber shoving Reese onto the ground; a bullet striking Amber, her body jerking. Reese remembered what her best friend, Julian, had told her. The media thought Amber was the hero for saving her. Reese couldn't square that with the fact that Amber had lied to her, repeatedly, about her identity.

Reese, David thought.

Hearing him think her name jolted her back into the present. The reporters were waiting for an answer. She glanced at David, and he gave her a tiny smile. She felt it inside him like the flicker of a flame in the dark. She wasn't in this alone.

'Is that the ship in the video?' the reporter asked again.

'We don't know,' Reese and David said together.

'Where did it come from? Why is it over your house?'

'We don't know,' they said again.

'Was that girl one of the aliens? Why does she look human?'

David didn't speak this time. 'Yes, she's one of the aliens,' Reese said. 'I don't know why she looks human.'

'Why are they here? Are they experimenting on humans?'

'Why did the president think they were gone? Did you see the press conference she gave an hour ago? She said the aliens had left our planet.'

'How are you connected to the aliens?'

Reese took a deep breath and interrupted the stream of questions. 'We can't answer you all at once, and we don't know much more than you. We only know what happened to us.'

'What did happen to you?'

'We were taken by government agents to a secret military base in Nevada,' David said.

'Why?'

'They wanted to figure out what kind of medical procedure had been done on us earlier this summer,' Reese said, and then realized that none of this would make sense to the assembled reporters because they didn't know about that.

'It's a long story,' David said.

'Start from the beginning. What medical procedure?'

Reese glanced sideways at David, who nodded at her. *Go ahead*. 'We had a car accident on the edge of Area 51 right after the June Disaster,' Reese said. 'David and I were in Phoenix, Arizona, for a debate tournament. We were with our coach. When all flights were grounded after those planes crashes, we decided to rent a car to drive home. Our coach died in Las Vegas during a carjacking at a gas station—'

A murmur of surprise went through the reporters, and one interrupted to ask, 'What was the name of your coach?'

'Joe Chapman,' David said. 'We left the gas station because the gunman was shooting at us, but we couldn't go back because of the roadblocks. So we kept driving.'

'That's when we had the car accident,' Reese continued. 'We didn't know we had crashed on the edge of a military base.'

'We were treated at the hospital there,' David said, 'with Imrian science.'

'You mean alien technology?'

'You could call it that,' David said. 'They've told us that we went through an adaptation procedure. They said it was to save our lives. It combined our human DNA with their Imrian DNA.'

'How were the aliens able to do this to you on a US military base?' one of the reporters asked, sounding skeptical.

'We don't think the government authorized this,' Reese said. 'In fact, we don't think the government knew what really happened to us at all. That's why we were kidnapped and taken back to Area 51 two weeks ago. Our government wanted to figure out what had been done to us.'

'You say they kidnapped you, but it sounds like they were making an effort to get to the bottom of something done to you by aliens. Shouldn't you be grateful for the government's help?'

'Government agents broke into my house and drugged me,' Reese objected. 'They took us against our will, and then they held us in an underground bunker and didn't allow us to contact anyone, not even our parents. We're not happy that the aliens did whatever they did to us, but that doesn't make what our government did right.'

Her outburst had startled the gathered reporters. One called out, 'Has the government apologized for what they did to you?'

'Senator Michaelson apologized,' Reese said. Senator Joyce Michaelson had helped get her and David out of the military facility after the video had leaked.

'We're grateful to Senator Michaelson and our families,' David added.

'And my friend Julian Arens for getting that video up,' Reese said.

'You say alien DNA was added to yours? How does the alien DNA affect you?'

Someone began to push his way through the crowd, and several reporters made irritated noises.

'We're able to heal more rapidly than normal,' Reese answered. An excited murmur traveled through the reporters.

'And we can communicate without speaking,' David said. 'Sort of like telepathy.'

Reese felt an outburst of emotion like a puff of wind in her face: shock mingled with skepticism.

'Are you able to read minds now?' a reporter shouted.

'No,' Reese said. 'It's more limited than that.'

She was struggling to find the words to explain her and David's new abilities when a man in a black suit broke free from the crowd and barreled up the steps. It was Agent Forrestal, one of the men in black who had taken them to Area 51 and brought them home earlier that day. Reese was beginning to think of Forrestal as her personal government bully.

'This press conference is over,' Agent Forrestal announced.

'What do you mean?' Reese said. 'We're just getting started.'

He ignored her and spoke loudly over the angry questions from the crowd. 'We need you to disperse right now and leave this vicinity.'

Amid shouted comments about the freedom of the press and the right to assemble, David thought to Reese: *He's shutting us down.*

'Please disperse right now,' Agent Forrestal ordered. Across the street, National Guard soldiers stood ready to move in.

'Who are you?' the reporters yelled.

Police officers began to enter the crowd, herding people away from the house, and Agent Forrestal didn't answer the question. He turned to face Reese and David. 'Let's go. Back inside,' he said grimly, and tried to push them up the stairs.

They both recoiled. 'You can't do this,' Reese protested.

'You don't understand what's going on,' Agent Forrestal said. 'This is for your own protection. Go inside right now.'

A few steps above them, Reese's parents stood in the open front doorway, David's parents right behind them. Reese saw Julian peering around her dad's arm. Agent Forrestal grasped Reese's shoulder and she jerked away.

'Don't touch my daughter,' Reese's mom snapped at the agent.

'Let's go inside, ma'am, and we can discuss this properly,' Agent Forrestal said.

Reese's mom ushered Reese and David inside, but she turned back to Agent Forrestal with an angry expression. 'No. You're not invited in.'

She slammed the door in his face and locked it.

CHAPTER 2

Reese entered her bedroom and flicked the light switch that turned on her bedside lamp. Her mom paused in the doorway behind her. 'You're sure you're all right, honey? Do you want a glass of water or something before you go to bed?'

'No, I'm fine, just tired,' Reese answered, walking over to the windows to peek through the blinds. Many of the reporters had left after Agent Forrestal ended the press conference, but they had been replaced by other onlookers who gazed up at the black triangle as if they were waiting for a divine message. She could see some of them now in the light of the streetlamp, their camera lenses pointed at the night sky.

'Okay,' her mom said. 'You know where to find me if you need anything.' She came into the room and kissed Reese on the forehead, her hand sweeping gently over Reese's hair. 'I love you.'

After her mom left, closing the door behind her, Reese sat on the edge of her bed and pulled off the shoes that the government had given her that morning. Ugly white sneakers, already scuffed along the toes. A surge of fury swept through her and she kicked them across the room. They bounced against her laundry basket. She sighed and took off the government-issue khaki pants and long-sleeved T-shirt, shoving them into her trash bin. Then she got dressed in her oldest, most comfortable pair of pajama bottoms – red-and-white plaid – and a roomy, faded Cal T-shirt and climbed into bed.

She couldn't sleep. Everything that had happened that day kept replaying through her mind. After the abrupt end of the press conference, Julian's parents had rushed over to take him home. David and his family stayed another hour or so, waiting until Agent Forrestal retreated to his tan sedan parked halfway down the block. When she hugged David goodbye in the front hall, she suddenly didn't want to let him go. Her fingers dug into David's upper back even though she was conscious of their parents waiting nearby. 'I'm sorry,' she mumbled, loosening her grip.

'It's okay,' he whispered. *I know*.

What they went through in Nevada had brought them closer together than Reese had ever anticipated. She knew David was only going to his home, but the idea of him leaving filled her with an embarrassing panic. She told herself she was being illogical – this was just some kind of posttraumatic stress thing. Besides, their parents were watching.

She pulled away before the burning behind her eyes manifested into tears. 'I'll see you soon,' she said.

He gave her a small, crooked smile. 'Definitely.'

Now Reese turned onto her side, drawing her knees up beneath the covers. David had kissed her that afternoon in this very room. The memory of it made a warm thrill snake through her, quickly followed by a surge of self-doubt. One kiss didn't necessarily mean there was going to be another – and it might not mean anything other than kissing. But she wanted it to mean something. She just wasn't sure what.

She gave up on sleeping and turned on the light again. Across the room, the red and gold paint that covered one entire wall of Reese's bedroom took on a darker, warmer hue. It was like being inside a womb: soft gold skin and streaks of bloodred. This was what she remembered of the adaptation chamber, which Amber had described as being similar to an incubator.

Reese remembered painting that wall in a possessed rush, knowing only that she needed to get this image out of her brain. She had dreamed of a pliable yellow room with bleeding walls ever since she woke up from the accident in that strange hospital in Nevada, and spilling it onto the wall seemed to be the only way to exorcise it. Maybe that had worked – she hadn't dreamed of it since she finished the painting – but she still didn't understand the full repercussions of what had been done to her in that adaptation chamber.

She climbed out of bed and pulled the khaki pants out of the trash. She had forgotten about the phone Amber had given her. *Call us when you're ready*, she had whispered in Reese's ear. Reese dug the phone out of the pocket. It was a plain gray flip-phone, the kind sold to technology-phobic senior citizens. She flipped it open; there were no messages. She looked through the contacts and found one listing: Evelyn Brand.

Dr Brand was Amber's mother, as well as the Imrian who had overseen Reese's and David's recoveries at Project Plato in

Nevada. Could Reese trust Dr Brand to tell her the truth? She was doubtful.

She put the phone down and moved to her desk, opening her laptop to go online. She needed to find out what was being reported about her and David's abduction and return. Maybe that would give her some indication of who to trust.

As soon as she logged into the Hub, news feeds from around the world showed that the entire globe was focused on the spaceship hovering over her house. *If extraterrestrials appeared over your city, would you run for your lives or run to take a photo?* one article asked. *Thousands of people have chosen the latter in the last twenty-four hours, flooding into a normally quiet neighborhood in San Francisco to catch a glimpse of the black triangle from another planet. Meanwhile, others have been stocking up on supplies and taking to the back roads – just as they did earlier this summer after the June Disaster. 'I'll be prepared,' said Tom Maynard, en route to a remote cabin near Lake Tahoe. When asked what he was preparing for, Maynard replied, 'You want to talk about terrorists? That ship is scarier than all of those birds.'*

Reese remembered the day after the planes were grounded, driving with Mr Chapman and David down highways packed with people fleeing a threat they couldn't identify. As far as she could tell, nobody had yet pinpointed the cause of that mass panic. Maybe it was only paranoia, amplified by the specter of terrorism. *At least this Tom Maynard guy has something to be afraid of*, Reese thought. The spaceship above her house was terrifying. She couldn't understand why so many people were flocking here to see it, either.

She scrolled down the screen, scanning the other news reports. Nation after nation demanded to know why the United States had concealed its cooperation with the Imria for so long. Some called for a global summit; others called for economic sanctions on the US until it explained itself. Reese and David were the subject of plenty of interest, too, with many leaders asking that they submit themselves to an international scientific board for genetic testing. And in the comments at the end of the articles, things got nasty.

Strangers writing in broken sentences mocked Reese's bedraggled appearance on television. Her hand holding with David caused commenters to speculate about their relationship. Some went so far as to guess how intimate she and David had been, writing things that made Reese cringe. Increasingly horrified but unable to stop, she kept reading as people criticized her for being too skinny, too fat, and for being desperate enough to hook up with a Chinese guy. The comments about David were equally awful. They made fun of his race, characterizing him as a nerd who only managed to land a white girl because of his new alien DNA. They called him names that Reese had never said aloud. There were some people who pushed back and flagged the worst comments as offensive, but the words that rang in Reese's mind weren't those of her supporters.

And then there were the posts about Amber. Perhaps because she had said very little and had previously been known as the heroic savior who prevented Reese from getting shot, most of the commentary about Amber was positive. But some of it was so full of lusty innuendo about what they wanted to do to that 'hot alien chick' that Reese felt as if a bucket of scum had been dumped over her head.

She could brush off some of the nastiness – these people didn't know her, and obviously some were trolls, but a few of the comments brought her up short. One person had written: There is no proof that anything these kids are saying is true. Telepathy? Fast-healing powers? These kids think they're superheroes. Someone had responded: I'll believe they're telepaths when I see scientific evidence for it. Until then, why would I believe a couple of teens? She could see how people might doubt them, since she and David had provided no evidence of what had been done to them.

Another commenter stated: I don't believe these Imrians are aliens at all. How could they be aliens when they look exactly like us? I think all the evidence points to time travelers. The Imrians must be humans from the future. Reese caught herself spending several minutes pondering the probability of time travel before she shook her head and moved on to another comment: This isn't about aliens; this is about the government trying to contain a giant secret. They've clearly been developing advanced technology, and these kids are about to blow this wide open. Why do you think that MIB stopped the press conference?

She followed a link at the end of that comment to a post titled *What is President Randall trying to hide?* She began to skim the post and then glanced at the URL: www.bin42.com. This was the site that Julian wrote for, and it had been the first to post the video of her and David fleeing the underground bunker. The site's header was an image of a green alien in a flying saucer. It didn't exactly inspire confidence in terms of reporting excellence, but she knew that Julian took it seriously, and she trusted Julian. She went back to reading the post.

WHAT IS PRESIDENT RANDALL TRYING TO HIDE?
By Jason Briggs
Posted August 7, 2014 at 7:43 PM
Tags: aliens, UFOs, conspiracy, cover-up, Reese Holloway, David Li, Elizabeth Randall

During President Randall's press conference earlier today, she stated the following:

'After the ship that you saw in the video lifted off, we have had no further contact from the Imria. At this point, we are alone, again, on our planet. So, I say this to the Imria: If you are watching, I invite you to make public contact with us. We will meet at a global summit. We will begin our relationship anew. And to my fellow Americans, I offer my heartfelt apologies. On behalf of all the administrations before mine that kept this secret from you: I am sorry. I hope we can move forward into a more truthful and open future.'

Let's take this point by point:

1. Half an hour after her press conference ended, a black triangle appeared in the skies above San Francisco and came to rest over the Noe Valley neighborhood where Reese Holloway (one of the two teens recently returned to their families from Area 51) lives. Given all the advanced technology

that the president has at her disposal, how could she not know that the Imria were still around? But let's give Randall the benefit of the doubt (for once!). The Imria obviously have even more advanced tech than we do. They could have cloaked their spacecraft after they left Area 51 and Randall might truly have had no evidence that they were still on the planet. But the question that follows is: Why did they come back?

2. Though Randall's apology might appease some people, it's hardly enough to explain the decades of silence and denial the government has perpetrated. If they've been secretly in contact with aliens since 1947 (and let's not even get into the crazy significance of that date), they can't seriously expect one tiny apology to wipe away the last 67 years of lies. If the United States government really wants its citizens to trust them, they need to do way more than offer one throwaway apology. How about starting with full disclosure about what happened at Roswell? Some things might need to remain classified, but I think it's safe for the government to admit that they covered up the truth about what happened in New Mexico. That would be a great first step toward rebuilding the American people's trust in their government.

3. Moving forward into 'a more truthful and open future' sounds good, but it won't work if the government silences key witnesses like Reese Holloway and David Li. These two may be only teenagers, but they were trying to do right by

telling the truth about what happened to them. It did not reflect well on the Randall Administration's declaration of openness to have the teens' press conference shut down by a man in black. It's imperative that Holloway and Li be given a chance to tell their story. That's why I'm inviting them to tell their story right here on Bin 42. I will do my best to make sure that their words won't be edited or censored. Reese and David: call me!

4. Finally, to determine whether Holloway and Li really do have fast-healing and telepathic abilities, they need to submit to testing by an independent board of scientists. If they do have these abilities, it is totally revolutionary, and could mean amazing advancements in medicine. While I'm sure they're not eager to become lab rats, they need to realize the incredible significance of their situation. I hope they'll let science prove to the world what they've said they can do.

There were already 138 comments at the end of the post, but Reese didn't scroll to the bottom of the screen. She saw a link in the sidebar to a video clip from the press conference, and despite the nervous twitch in her belly, she clicked on it.

There she was, standing with David on her front steps, their hands clasped. Her hair was tangled, and there were shadows under her eyes. The clothes she wore didn't fit well. The long-sleeved blue tee was lumpy on her, and the pants made her look hippy. The outfit looked better on David, but he also showed signs of exhaustion. His face was ghostly pale, and his hair had a cowlick in the back and was plastered down in front as if he had tried to tame it with water. Through her computer's speakers, she heard herself talking, and her voice sounded like a stranger's.

That was when Amber came down the stairs and turned Reese and David around. Reese couldn't see Amber's face in the video – it was obscured by the back of David's head – but she saw Amber lean into her, whispering in her ear. A moment later Amber walked around them to talk to the reporters. In comparison to Reese and David, Amber looked like a movie star. She was dressed casually in a red hoodie and jeans, but Reese knew that it didn't matter what Amber wore; what mattered was the way she wore it. She had a face that was made for the camera, with her big gray eyes and glossy lips. When she walked through the reporters toward the erim and the small craft, the cameras followed her until the craft took off. Then, with a jerk, the video turned back to Reese and David. They looked shell-shocked, and it took a minute before the press conference returned to the subject of what had happened to them.

After the video ended, Reese shut off her computer, but Amber's face lingered in her mind's eye. Reese didn't want to think about her. She was still angry about Amber's lies – angry and hurt. How could Amber expect Reese to believe her offer of help? She couldn't believe anything Amber said, even if she said it by whispering in her ear. Reese remembered lying on the beach with her, Amber's mouth against her skin, breathing her name. *All of that was a lie*, Reese told herself, shoving away the curl of desire that awoke in her. *You can't trust her. It's over. You don't feel that way anymore*. A nervous energy skittered through her limbs and she got up. She needed to get away from what people were saying online. She decided to get a drink of water.

She opened the door of her bedroom as quietly as possible and tiptoed down the stairs in the dark. The door to the guest room where her father slept was closed. In the kitchen she poured herself a glass of water from the filter and looked out the window at the backyard. Was the black triangle still out there? She opened the back door, stepping onto the brick patio in her bare feet. It was an unexpectedly clear August night, with no fog misting the air. The bricks were rough beneath her toes as she tipped her head back and stared at the dark sky. Few stars were visible, but she could see the triangular ship above, where white lights defined its three corners. It hung still and silent: a black ornament on a tree of night.

She thought about the question raised in the Bin 42 blog post. Why had the Imria returned? There was one possibility that made immediate sense to her. They came back because they wanted her and David. Why else would that ship be hovering over her house like an omen? It wasn't a comforting idea.

CHAPTER 3

Reese's parents were sitting at the kitchen table with a pile of newspapers when she came downstairs late Friday morning. 'Good morning,' her dad said.

'How'd you sleep?' her mom asked.

'Okay.' Reese went straight to the coffeemaker and poured herself a cup, adding milk. She heard the beat of rotors outside. 'Are there still helicopters up there?'

'They've been there all morning,' her dad said. 'The spaceship is still there, and people are still coming to look at it.'

She went to the back door and peered out the window. She couldn't see the black triangle from this angle, but she could see a helicopter making an arc across the sky. 'How long can they fly around up there?'

'I don't know,' her mom said, sounding resigned. 'As long as that ship is here, probably. There's nothing to stop people from coming to look, either. It's created kind of a traffic jam out front, but as long as people keep moving, the police can't force them to leave. It's a public sidewalk.'

Reese went into the living room, pulling the curtains aside a few inches to look out. The normally quiet street was choked with traffic and pedestrians. Cars moved sluggishly down the block, and the sidewalks on both sides were clogged with onlookers. Some of them were even carrying signs, as if this was a demonstration. She saw one that said WELCOME, E.T. and another that stated I ~~WANT TO~~ BELIEVE. Others weren't so friendly, declaring ALIENS GO HOME and ABDUCTEES DEMAND JUSTICE FROM ALIENS. A man carrying a sign that stated WE WANT FULL DISCLOSURE was watching the house, and when he saw Reese peeking out the window he pointed at her, his mouth opening in a shout she couldn't hear. In a wave, other pedestrians near him turned to look in the direction he was pointing, and the sound of the crowd – muffled by the closed windows – crescendoed into a dull roar. Within seconds, dozens of people were surging toward the house, cars honking as some demonstrators rushed into traffic to get a closer look at her.

She stepped back in shock and tugged the curtains closed. She couldn't sense the crowd's emotions – maybe she was far enough away that she was shielded from it – but her heart raced as she heard a police officer speaking through a bullhorn, ordering people back. Footsteps came down the hall and her mom asked, 'What's going on? I heard something.'

'I looked out the window.'

'I should have warned you not to do that.' Her mom went to the curtains and peered through a narrow slit between the drapes.

Her dad came into the living room holding the telephone.

'Reese, it's for you. It's David.'

'I didn't hear it ring,' Reese said, taking the receiver.

'We turned off the ringer. It's been ringing off the hook all morning with interview requests.'

Reese lifted the phone to her ear. 'Hey, David.'

'Hey,' David said.

'I'm taking this upstairs,' Reese said to her parents. On the way to her room she said to David, 'It's crazy out in front of my house.'

'I know. I saw it on the news.'

She entered her bedroom and nudged the door shut. 'What does it look like?'

'You're basically surrounded within a three-block radius. They're all looking at the spaceship.'

'Shit.' She climbed onto her bed and set her coffee mug on the bedside table.

'I went online to try to find out if the Imria have said anything, like whether they're going to move their spaceship, but there's no official news. Some people have some pretty insane theories though.'

'I read one last night about time travel.'

'That's a good one. Did you read about panspermia?'

'Pan what?'

'Apparently there's a theory that all life in the universe originated from one common source. Like, asteroids traveled the universe carrying life and they hit various places, including the Imrian planet and Earth, so that's why the Imria look like us.'

'That's . . . interesting. I guess that's as good a theory as any.' She remembered what typically accompanied these theories online. 'You didn't read the comments, did you?'

He didn't answer immediately.

'You did, didn't you? You shouldn't have done that.'

'Whatever, so there are trolls,' he said dismissively. 'You're not paying attention to them, are you?'

It was her turn to hesitate. She picked up the mug and took a sip of coffee.

'Reese.'

'David.'

He laughed, and it sent a tingle down her spine. She liked the sound of his laugh. She hadn't heard it in a long time.

'So that press conference didn't exactly work out the way we thought it would,' he said.

'No. Do you think we should try it again?'

'I don't know. How do we know Agent Forrestal or someone else won't shut us down again?'

'Well, this website, Bin 42, wants us to talk to them. Julian works for them.'

'That's the one that put up the video, right?'

'Yeah.'

He was silent for a second. 'We could do that.'

'What's your hesitation?'

'Well, a lot of the stuff online was talking about how there's no proof that we have these abilities. Maybe we should get some proof first.'

'How?'

'My dad says he can set up an academic review board to examine us.'

Reese remembered that David's dad was a biochemist. 'Your dad works at a pharmaceutical company in Menlo Park, doesn't he?'

'Yeah.'

'Why didn't he suggest that his company do it?'

'He doesn't want any suggestion of bias, which there would be if he was involved. He has friends at UCSF who could put together a group of scientists.'

'What do you think about the Imrian offer to help us?'

'I don't trust them. Why? Do you want to take them up on it? And what was the thing that Amber gave you, anyway?'

She glanced at the device on her desk. 'It was a cell phone. She gave us a way to call Dr Brand.' She suddenly remembered something. 'Wait, do you still have my cell phone?' While she and David were at Blue Base, someone had put a report on it that laid out the military's project to create supersoldiers with Imrian DNA. 'I gave it to you so you could read that report, remember? That is totally proof.'

David exhaled, his breath sending static over the phone. 'No, I had to leave it with my stuff and then the base exploded, so it's gone.'

'Crap.' She heard a clicking noise and checked the receiver. Julian was on call-waiting. She'd have to call him back.

'Do you not want to do this academic board testing thing?' David asked.

'I agree we need proof,' she said quickly. 'But do you think the testing is going to show us what we can do? That thing that Amber did when she touched us – how did she do that? We need to learn that.'

'I definitely don't trust Amber,' David said, and there was a sharp tone to his voice that startled Reese.

'I know,' she said hastily. 'I don't either. But how are we going to figure out exactly what we can do? The government doesn't know much about what happened to us. It would be great to have scientific proof that we're not lying, but that might not explain how we can use our abilities.'

'I tried to – to communicate with you last night.'

She was taken aback. 'You mean . . . telepathically?'

'I guess. It didn't work. I couldn't sense you at all. Not like I could when we were at Project Plato.' He paused. 'That *did* happen, right? I'm not crazy, am I? Could you hear me then?'

'Yes,' she said. 'At Plato, I could definitely hear you.' Their disembodied connection had been so strange and yet so intimate, as if their minds had met on some extra-dimensional plane. 'It's different when we touch, though.'

'Yeah. That feels more like I'm in your head. The time at Project Plato, it felt like I was talking to you on a really bizarre telephone.'

She sat up, putting her coffee down. 'Wait. Was Plato the only place it worked for you? I thought we communicated telepathically yesterday too. In my room when Amber and Julian were here. You couldn't hear me?'

He didn't answer right away. 'I don't know,' he finally said. 'I can't remember.'

There was a catch in his voice that made Reese think he was holding something back. 'What is it? If you couldn't hear me that's okay. I don't know how this works either.'

'That's not it.'

'Then what?'

His breath whooshed into the phone. 'I didn't like Amber. That's all. I was distracted by that.'

She was surprised. If he had been distracted, did that mean he was jealous? She was unexpectedly flustered. 'Oh. Um, well, we can try it again sometime when she's not around.'

'You promise?'

She could hear the smile in his voice, and heat crept up her neck. 'Yeah.'

'So . . . are you okay with my dad setting up that academic review panel thing?'

She had forgotten they were discussing scientific testing of their abilities. 'Oh, yes. That would be good.'

'Okay. Well, let me call you back after I talk to my dad about it and I have more info.'

'All right. I'll talk to you later.'

After they hung up she saw the voice-mail light blinking on the phone, and she remembered Julian. She called him back without checking the message, and he answered on the first ring.

'Dude, your house is on TV twenty-four seven!'

'I heard.' She picked up her coffee again. 'I looked outside for, like, one second and the mob started rushing toward the house.'

'It's insane,' he said, but he sounded more thrilled than scared. 'I can't believe you're back and there's a giant freaking black triangle over your neighborhood!'

'Whoa, calm down,' she said, laughing. 'This is like your dream come true, isn't it?' For as long as she could remember,

Julian had been obsessed with UFOs and aliens. He probably knew more about UFOs than most of the people outside her house.

'Well, if you hadn't been abducted and stuff, yeah.'

She smiled. 'Thanks.'

'Hey, I tried your cell first but it said the number was no longer in service.'

'Yeah, it blew up with Blue Base. Which totally sucks because it had information on it about the government's supersoldier project.'

'You have to come on Bin 42 and talk about it – about everything,' Julian said excitedly. 'David too.'

She hesitated. 'I don't know. We have to think about it.'

'What's to think about? Isn't it important to share the truth with the world? You can't let the government get away with what they did to you.'

'It was the Imria who did this to me,' Reese objected. 'They adapted me, or whatever they call it.'

'An adaptation procedure.'

'Yeah. That.'

'There's more to it than that and you know it. The government has been covering up the fact that they've been in touch with the Imria since 1947. There's definitely a cover-up going on about the June Disaster – there's still been no real explanation for why or how those birds went crazy. There's all that Project Blue Base stuff you and David found out about. That lab report you guys found proves that the government was behind the June Disaster. You have to tell the world.'

He sounded so impassioned that she knew he wasn't going to like what she was about to say. 'We have to think about it. The fact that Agent Forrestal shut us down yesterday means this is serious.'

'I never said this wasn't serious. It's totally dead serious.'

'Then you should understand we have to think carefully about the repercussions—'

'But yesterday you wanted to go public! You were all, "We'll tell the world and then nobody will control us."'

'Actually that was your idea.'

'Which you agreed with! Are you saying you don't want to tell the world anymore?'

'No. But there are a lot of things to consider. We have to prove that we have these abilities, for one thing. Nobody's going to believe us just because we say so. And we have to figure out how to use our abilities too.'

'So you'll go to the Imria, right? They did this to you, and they're offering to help you understand the adaptation procedure. Why don't you talk to them?'

'I don't exactly trust them.'

'You don't trust the government, do you?'

'No.' She scowled. 'I don't know who to trust.'

'You can trust *me*. And I'm telling you, you have to come on Bin 42 and tell your story. You have to at least give me that lab report so I can post it online.'

'That report is just a piece of paper. The government could easily say it's a fake, and who's going to believe me over the president? Did you read what people are saying about me and David online? They think we're just two dumb high school kids. We can't overturn decades of government lies just by talking to a website.'

'Change happens one person at a time,' he insisted. 'You could be that person.'

'Maybe, but one person against the entire United States government?' She remembered the National Guard troops standing across the street, the helicopters circling overhead, the police outside. The government was taking this very seriously. She hadn't realized that when she and David rushed outside to talk to the press. Now she knew enough to be scared.

'I don't think you get it.' Julian sounded frustrated. 'Do you understand how big this story is?'

She couldn't believe he had said that. 'It's not a story. It's my *life*. Did you see the soldiers outside my house?'

'Whoa, okay, I'm sorry,' Julian said quickly. 'I didn't mean it's *just* a story. I meant that it's really, super important. The US government should not be able to kidnap its citizens. You can't let them get away with that. And that's not even getting into all this crazy genetic engineering they're doing with Imrian DNA. They've been hiding this from the world for decades. That is not okay.'

'I know. I agree, and I want to make them own up to it. But I don't know the whole story yet. David and I don't know how our adaptation abilities work yet. We have a lot of things to figure out. You have to give us some time.'

Julian exhaled into the phone. 'All right.'

'Let me think about things. I'll let you know if we want to talk to Bin 42, okay?'

'Yeah.' He sounded disappointed. 'So what's up with you and David?'

She was startled by the change of subject. 'What?'

'You were making out with him yesterday. What's up with that?'

'I don't know.' She was embarrassed. 'Look, I have to pee. I'll call you later.'

'Sure.' He had a teasing tone in his voice.

'Bye, Julian,' she said, smiling.

She hung up and went to the bathroom before returning downstairs with the phone. As she passed the archway to the living room, she saw Agent Forrestal standing in one corner. She halted in surprise. Her parents were on the couch, and a strange man was seated in the leather armchair. When he realized Reese had arrived, he stood, holding a folded piece of paper in his left hand. He had short dark hair, dark eyes, and a very white smile, which he flashed at Reese as he extended his right hand to her. He was dressed in a slightly rumpled gray suit. 'Good morning, Miss Holloway. I'm Jeff Highsmith. I work with the Defense Department's Office of Public Affairs.'

She crossed her arms over her T-shirt, conscious of the fact that she was bra-less in her oldest pajamas. 'What are you doing here?' she asked.

Jeff Highsmith retracted his hand as if it was totally normal that she had refused to shake it. 'I'm here to set up some interviews for you.'

Reese glanced at her parents. Her mom had her lawyer face on: closed off and expressionless. Her dad, on the other hand, looked extremely skeptical. 'You shut down our press conference yesterday,' Reese said to Highsmith. 'Why would you want us to do interviews now?'

'We didn't feel that an impromptu press conference on your front steps was an appropriate way to present the extraordinary experiences you and your friend David have gone through. We'd like to offer you a bigger platform to tell your story to the world.'

She was suspicious. 'How big?'

'Have you heard of Sophia Curtis?'

'Of course.' Who hadn't? Sophia Curtis was a former war-zone reporter who had become a celebrity after being captured by Somali pirates during an undercover story on the trafficking of women. After her triumphant return – freed by US Navy SEALs – she launched a prime-time talk show in which she interviewed everyone from death-row inmates who claimed they were innocent to Oscar-nominated actors. She had a reputation for being fair, but more than that, she had one of the biggest audiences on television. It didn't hurt that she was gorgeous and had married one of her Navy SEAL rescuers.

'Ms Curtis is very eager to meet the both of you,' Highsmith said. 'We think it would be best if she interviewed your families as well, just to get everyone's perspectives. We'd like to do it on Monday. What do you say?'

Reese glanced at her parents. Her mom gave her a thin-lipped nod. Her dad looked irritated. 'I can't agree to anything without talking to David first,' Reese finally said.

Highsmith smiled. 'Of course. I'm visiting David and his family right after I leave here. I can give you two a little time to think it over, but we'll need your decision by two PM today so we can get things in motion.'

That was only a few hours away. She looked at Agent Forrestal, who was standing with his hands behind his back, his face blank. The rushed nature of Highsmith's plan struck Reese as particularly suspect. And why weren't her parents saying anything? She needed to talk to them alone, and it seemed that the only way to get Forrestal and Highsmith to leave was to agree to think about it. 'Fine,' she said. 'We'll let you know by two.'

'Good.' He unfolded the paper he had been holding and showed it to her. Her stomach sank as she recognized the lab report she had stolen from Blue Base the day she and David had escaped from the underground bunker. 'Before I go, you should know that I saw this on your coffee table. That's no place for a classified document like this, so I'll take it with me.'

The last time she had seen that paper was when David's dad was reading it in this room yesterday afternoon. He must have set it down, and she had completely forgotten about it. 'You can't—' she began, but he slipped the paper into his breast pocket.

'I'll do you the favor of not asking how you obtained this, and you won't be prosecuted for theft.'

Reese felt helpless, and it made her angry. Before she could say anything more her mom stood. 'We'll be in touch,' she said, the words clipped.

'Wonderful.' Highsmith pulled a business card from his pocket and handed it to Reese's mom. 'Here's where you can reach me. I'll expect your call very soon.'

'We don't have any choice,' Reese's mom said after Forrestal and Highsmith left. 'Before you came downstairs, Agent Forrestal made it pretty clear that if we don't cooperate, there will be consequences.'

Reese watched her pace back and forth in front of the curtained bay windows. 'Like what?'

'They said if you continue to reveal classified information you're in danger of being prosecuted for treason.'

The words sounded like something out of a spy movie. 'Are you serious?' Reese asked, shocked.

Her mom stopped pacing and looked at Reese, crossing her arms. Her face was drawn. 'Yes. They said you're violating the terms of the nondisclosure agreement you signed after your medical treatment back in June. I think we could have contested it in court – you're a minor – but then Highsmith saw that document on the table.'

'Cat, you're scaring her,' said Reese's dad.

'She deserves to know what she's up against.'

Rick held up his hands. 'I agree, but let's not take this to the extreme.' He looked at Reese from where he was still seated on the couch. 'I don't want you doing an interview set up by people who are clearly not looking out for your best interests.'

'If she doesn't do it, they might take her away again,' Cat said.

'You don't know that,' Rick argued.

'They said they only let her go because of the public pressure we applied—'

'And that public pressure will prevent them from taking her again.'

Cat shook her head. 'Things have changed. The Imria have come back. The government has new priorities now, and I don't think they include Reese and David.'

'Wait,' Reese interrupted. She hated it when her parents talked about her as if she wasn't in the room. 'Don't I get any say in this? What if I don't want to do this interview?'

'I don't want you to do it either,' her dad said, surprising her. It was so rare that they agreed.

Her mom let out a frustrated noise. 'Nobody *wants* this, but—'

'Why do they even want to do this interview now?' Reese asked, sitting down next to her dad. 'Yesterday they didn't want me to talk at all.'

'International pressure, I think,' her dad said. 'The United States is facing a lot of criticism from around the world about how they've been handling this Imrian situation, and it didn't look good yesterday when that agent stopped you and David from talking. I think the government wants to set you up with this interview for PR purposes, but they're going to control it the whole way. Even if you're interviewed by Sophia Curtis, I doubt they'll let you tell the truth.'

'Then what would be the point of doing the interview? We should tell our story to Bin 42—'

'No,' her mom snapped. 'You are *not* talking to that website. That would definitely put you in danger with the government, and I won't let you do that. I should have stopped you yesterday before you went outside.'

'Cat—'

She turned to her ex-husband. 'We're going to do this.

We're going to take this interview with Sophia Curtis and play along with them. I need some time to figure out what else we can do, and it can't hurt to give them something they want.'

'Mom—'

'I'm not sending her into that interview without someone to advocate for her,' Rick said, ignoring Reese's interruption.

'I'll be there,' Cat said.

'I mean a media professional,' Rick said. 'I'm going to call Diana Warner.'

'Who's that?' Cat asked.

'She's a media consultant. She'll train Reese on how to talk to Sophia. She'll go over the content of the interview in advance, and she'll be on top of Sophia's producers to make sure Reese is presented in the best possible light.'

Reese asked, 'What about David? If we do this he needs to get this training too.'

Her dad nodded. 'Sure. He's part of the deal.'

Her mom seemed doubtful. 'You think this media consultant can make any headway against Highsmith's agenda? I don't know.'

'We have to try it,' her dad said.

Her mom nudged the coffee table away from the couch and sat down on its edge, facing Reese and her dad. 'Fine. We'll hire the media consultant. Are you okay with that, honey?'

Reese glanced from her mom to her dad and crossed her arms. 'Do I have any choice?'

Her dad scooted toward her and put an arm around her shoulders. 'I know it feels like we're taking over here, but we're only trying to keep you safe.'

All of her dad opened up to her as he drew her into his embrace, and Reese was too startled to resist.

'Your mom and I – no, I shouldn't speak for her. *I* am really, really glad that you're back in one piece. I don't know what I would've done if we hadn't gotten you back, sweetie.'

Her father's interior landscape was an unsettling combination of the familiar and the strange. His physical body – the way his muscles moved, the beat of his heart – was new to her, and she almost recoiled from the intimacy of knowing him this way. But his sense of self, his consciousness: These were indelibly stamped with a deep-rooted relatedness to Reese. He was her father. As he spoke she could barely pay attention to his words, because she was so overwhelmed by his feelings. He felt guilty. Guilty for his absences over the years. Guilty that he hadn't been able to prevent what had happened to her. And he had a desperate fear that she would never forgive him.

Reese had to pull away. It was too much, and she couldn't even manage to put up her mental walls. She was shaky and sweaty as she stood up, breaking contact with her dad.

'Reese? I'm sorry if I—'

'Dad, I can't – you know I can feel how you're feeling when you touch me. Don't you?'

His face seemed to crumple. 'I – no. I didn't realize.'

She perched on the edge of the armchair, knees too wobbly to remain standing. 'Well, I can. So can David. That's what they did to us – the Imria.'

'I thought it was only between you and David,' her mom said.

'I think it works with anyone, if we're touching them.'

Her parents sat in silence for a few minutes, absorbing what she had said. She couldn't look at them – she was too conscious of her dad's feelings – but she saw her mom reach out and put a hand on her dad's knee.

'If that's true, I'm glad you felt how I was feeling,' her dad finally said. His voice was husky, and Reese didn't know what to say. Her dad didn't act like this around her. He was funny and charming on his best days, and on his worst he might be distant or cold, but he was never vulnerable. Unless she had simply never noticed before.

She got to her feet. 'I'd better call David and warn him about Highsmith,' she said, and fled the living room before her parents could respond.

CHAPTER 4

Diana Warner had dark brown hair cut just above her shoulders in expertly sculpted layers – the kind of hair you saw on female senators and businesswomen – and her red-brown lipstick was applied so flawlessly it didn't come off at all when she sipped the glass of water Reese's dad brought her. Reese soon learned that Diana did everything with the same precise, purposeful conviction. Reese suspected that her father had spent a lot of money to hire her.

She had arrived at their house on Saturday morning at ten o'clock sharp to interview Reese and her parents about what happened in the time between her abduction and her return a week and a half later. Then she drove off to do the same with David and his family, coming back a few hours later to take Reese and David shopping for clothes to wear on camera. She looked a bit breathless upon her return, and as Reese grabbed her bag to follow, Diana said, 'The crowd is feisty this afternoon. There are police outside who will escort us to my car, but why don't you pull that hood over your head? And put on some sunglasses.'

Reese's parents were standing in the hall behind her. 'Are you sure this is safe?' her mom asked.

'We'll be fine,' Diana assured her. 'We're just going to Nordstrom, and I have a driver. There's no need to worry.'

Reese doubted a hoodie and sunglasses could do much to help, but she had watched the crowd through the cracks in her blinds upstairs, and she definitely didn't want to go out there totally exposed. She tried to prepare herself for the onslaught of the crowd's emotions by imagining a brick wall around her, blocking people off. 'Let's go,' she said.

'We'll be back in a couple of hours,' Diana said, and she opened the door.

Outside, the crowd moved in a slow, continuous circle down Reese's street, around the block and back again. Reese had heard on the news that the City of San Francisco was considering what could be done to clear the neighborhood, but there was no law against walking down a public sidewalk – only against lying down on one – and none of the gawkers lay down. Diana led the way down the front steps, where two uniformed police officers were waiting for them. 'I'm parked two blocks north,' she told them.

The onlookers nearby had watched as Reese came outside, and she felt the tiny psychic jabs that accompanied their glances. She tried to focus on her imaginary wall as the cops told them to move on.

Most of the crowd was heading west to circle the neighborhood, but Reese and Diana had to go east to get to the corner, where they would turn north. They were forced to push against the tide of onlookers, and even though they had a police escort, it was slow going. Luckily, the pedestrians were so intent on keeping their eyes on the sky that most of them didn't notice it was Reese trying to walk in the opposite direction. She couldn't avoid sensing the crowd's feelings, but they weren't directed at her, and that made them easier to ignore. Their curiosity was about the thing in the sky above.

As they crossed the street at the intersection, a fake cable-car tour bus parked nearby. Usually they kept to San Francisco's tourist destinations, but since yesterday several of them had shown up in Reese's neighborhood. A group of tourists poured off the bus, jabbering excitedly and pointing at the black triangle. They swarmed around her and Diana and the cops, paying them no attention. Reese tried to avoid touching them, but she couldn't prevent them from bumping into her. Their excitement and confusion prickled all over her, and the effort to deflect their emotions made her feel like she was holding her breath underwater.

They were nearly through the crowd when someone accidentally rammed into her right shoulder. She winced and looked up to see a cardboard sign held way too close to her face. Giant block letters stated COLONIZATION IS COMING. She flinched away and tried to keep going, but the demonstrator was stuck to her. A button on his jacket had snagged on the strap of her messenger bag, and as he tried to tug himself free he saw her face. He was a boy perhaps a couple of years older than her, skinny and tall with a smattering of freckles across his face. He halted, his mouth falling open, and Reese knew that he recognized her. She froze. The crowd continued to move around them as if they were at the center of a whirlpool.

She heard the police officer ordering people out of the way, but she was transfixed by the boy's shocked gaze.

He reached out and grabbed her arm, and his emotions flooded into her: excitement fueled by adrenaline, layered over deep, dark anxiety. He was terrified of the ship, but his fear was tangled up with what Reese understood as yearning. He *wanted* the ship as much as he feared it. The end result was a tumult of feelings that made Reese dizzy.

He leaned into her space and demanded, 'What did they do to you? Are they watching you? Did they experiment on you?'

Someone knocked into the boy, unceremoniously pushing him aside, and his hand fell away from her. Freed from her connection with him, Reese reeled as he was borne away by the crowd. He kept turning back to look at her, shouting things she couldn't hear over the noise, and then in a blink he was gone.

The police officer was at her side. 'Miss Holloway, we're almost there.'

She felt his fingertips on her elbow, and she pulled away before she could sense any of his feelings. The edge of the crowd was only a few feet away and she pushed through, the memory of the boy's desperate yearning like acid in her stomach. She saw Diana waiting next to a town car with tinted windows, and someone opened the door for her. She slid into the backseat, breathless.

David was inside. He reached out as if to touch her, but he hesitated at the last second and his hand fell to the leather backseat. 'Are you okay?'

'I'm fine,' she said, but her voice shook.

The front door opened and closed as Diana Warner climbed in. 'That wasn't much fun,' Diana said grimly. She turned to the driver. 'Let's go.'

Reese reached for the seat belt as the car pulled away from the curb, trying to erase the disturbing trace of the boy's feelings from her memory.

At Nordstrom, Reese, David, and Diana were ushered into a large, private dressing room outfitted in plush couches and several three-way full-length mirrors. It was so calm in comparison to the chaotic street outside Reese's house that she felt as if she had entered an alternate dimension.

An energetic redhead named Bonnie offered them drinks as she pulled items of clothing off a rolling rack of clothes. Reese and David refused, but Diana accepted a small bottle of Perrier. Bonnie then showed Reese to a curtained dressing nook in one corner of the room, and took David to another on the far side. While Diana sat on the couch with her water, Bonnie brought Reese and David several outfits to try on.

First there were dresses for Reese: a little black one that seemed more appropriate for a formal dinner than an interview, even if it was on television. Diana nixed that one with a sharp shake of her head, saying, 'Too cocktail hour.' Next, Bonnie brought over a spaghetti-strap number with a bubble skirt in a gauzy blue-green fabric. Reese felt half-naked when she put it on, and when she came out of her curtained nook to stand in front of the mirrors, she crossed her arms over her chest. Bonnie approached her with a pair of shiny white heels and Reese stepped into them, wobbling, as David came out of his corner wearing black pants and a gray shirt with a vest and tie. He looked like he was going to a gentlemen's club – the kind with cigars and scotch – while she looked like she was going to a nightclub – the kind with a velvet rope and starlets.

'They're high school students,' Diana said, sounding cross. 'Don't dress her like an actress, and don't dress him like the 1950s. We're going for young, approachable. Genuine.'

Bonnie murmured an apology, saying she was only getting started. Reese caught David looking at her in the mirror and he grinned. *Nice dress*, he mouthed. She blushed and took off the shoes.

After that, the clothes were a little more normal. Bonnie pulled out a pair of jeans that had a price tag so high Reese couldn't believe she was allowed to try them on, and an appliquéd T-shirt that was so soft and thin Reese had to wear a tank top beneath it and a nearly see-through sweater over it. To her relief, Bonnie gave her a pair of sneakers to go with the outfit, and this time when she walked out into the dressing room, she felt much more like herself.

'That's more like it,' Diana said approvingly. 'You looked so nervous before. This suits you much better.'

David got new jeans too, as well as a long-sleeved blue-gray button-down shirt printed with faded pinstripes, worn over a black T-shirt.

'That's it,' Diana said, jumping up. She adjusted the sleeves on David's shirt, rolling them up over his forearms. 'You both look great. The audience will love you.' She pulled her phone out of the pocket of her burgundy suit jacket and snapped photos of the two of them. 'I'll e-mail them to you so you know how to dress on Monday. Now why don't you change back into your own clothes, and then come out here so we can have a chat.'

Once Reese and David had emerged from their curtained corners, Diana handed Bonnie a credit card and asked her to ring up their new outfits and give them a few minutes alone. Then she gestured for David and Reese to sit on the couch while she perched on the chair nearby.

'I've been in touch with Jeff Highsmith, and we're arranging to shoot the interview at your school,' Diana said.

'At Kennedy?' Reese said, surprised.

'Yes. It will underscore the fact that the two of you are still high school students. It was my idea, and Jeff agreed. If we play our cards right, everyone who sees the interview will adore you two.'

Reese glanced at David, who seemed a little uneasy. 'What do you mean?' he asked.

Diana smiled. 'There's more to this interview than telling the world what happened to you last week. That's certainly important, but there are other things that can influence the public's perception of you.' Diana gave them both a frank look. 'You must be aware that there's been some talk about your relationship.'

Reese stiffened.

Diana reached out and patted her on the knee. 'It's mostly harmless. But the sight of the two of you holding hands really fired up the imagination, shall we say. I'll ask Sophia to go easy on you, because you deserve your privacy. And she won't push you too far; you're both under eighteen and everybody has a soft spot for a high school romance. But you should be prepared to reveal something – you can determine what that is – about your relationship. If you're simply friends, that's fine.' Diana's smile turned mischievous. 'Although to be honest, it's going to be hard to sell that. You both have little tells that indicate something's going on.'

Tells? Reese wanted to ask what they were, but she bit her lip instead.

Diana continued: "The thing is, if there is something romantic going on, it's absolutely to your advantage. You're both attractive, smart young adults.'

Reese's face grew warm. Maybe that was a tell. She couldn't help it if she got embarrassed easily.

'You look good together. You obviously have a strong connection because of your debate team experience. And like I said, everybody loves a high school romance.' Diana leaned forward, her expression turning serious. 'You don't have to reveal everything. There's no need to do anything that makes you uncomfortable. But the two of you will need to discuss what you want to reveal, so that you're both on the same page.' Diana stood. 'Now I'm going to leave you alone while I make sure Bonnie's got everything rung up correctly. Take your time and talk about this. I'll be waiting for you outside.' She gave them a quick smile and left, shutting the door behind her.

The room seemed unnaturally quiet in her wake. When Reese shifted on her end of the couch, the slide of her jeans against the upholstery sounded as rough as sandpaper. She looked at David sideways, not quite meeting his eyes. 'So,' she said, and then didn't know what else to say.

'So,' David repeated.

Reese was nearly overcome by a desire to flee, and she dug her fingers into the edge of the couch cushion, as if to anchor herself in place. She had run away from this before. She didn't want to run anymore, but it was so hard not to fall back into old habits. If she got up right now and left, they could avoid all of this. Maybe Sophia Curtis wouldn't ask at all, and then Reese could entirely avoid the possibility that their kiss had been an anomaly. *David wouldn't do that*, she told herself. *He wouldn't kiss you if he didn't mean it*. She made herself look at him.

He smiled at her, and the corners of his eyes crinkled. 'I don't think we're just friends anymore,' he said.

Her breath got stuck in her throat. 'No?' she managed to say.

David's left hand curved over her right, his fingers gently loosening the death grip she had on the couch. 'You tell me.'

A flutter of panic rose in her. There he was, at her fingertips. Every time they touched, it never failed to shock her: the intimacy of it, the frightening yet exhilarating closeness. And he was nervous. Despite the confidence with which he spoke, she felt the tightness in his stomach, his uncertainty as he reached out to her. She turned to face him, her leg sliding up onto the couch, their hands resting together on her thigh. He was reading her – the way her body leaned toward him, the blood flushing her skin, the buzz that radiated through her from where their fingers were entwined.

'I don't think I need to tell you,' she said, and as she spoke the words out loud, wonder rose in her. This thing that had been done to them – this new sensitivity they had to each other, to the world – she was suddenly grateful for it. David could always know how she felt. She could always know how he felt. It was a gift.

'What do you want to tell Sophia Curtis?' he asked.

'I guess we can tell her the truth.'

'Maybe we should go over it, out loud.'

'Okay.' She found that she couldn't think very clearly when he was looking at her like that – especially when she was holding his hand and knew where his thoughts were heading. If she went along with it, they wouldn't be talking for much longer. That wouldn't normally be a problem, except Diana Warner was waiting for them outside and they really did need to figure this out. She pulled her hand away at the same moment that David moved back, looking flushed. 'Okay,' she said again, and scooted onto the chair that Diana had vacated. 'So, what's the story?'

He rubbed a hand over his face. 'Um. We met through debate?'

'Yeah. We were partners.'

He grinned. 'And you had an uncontrollable crush on me?'

'Hey, I'm not taking all the blame,' she said without thinking, and her cheeks burned. Why did she have to blush so easily? But David didn't seem to mind.

'Oh, I think the feeling was mutual,' he said. Even though he wasn't touching her, she could swear she felt the warm twist in his stomach as he spoke.

'Really?' she said, and then was overcome with shyness. She probably was the color of an eggplant by now.

David laughed. 'Sometimes you're a little dense, Reese. I can't believe you didn't notice.'

'Until nationals.' She made a face. 'Where I acted like a total dork.'

'Good thing I didn't give up.'

She smiled slightly. 'You're gonna spin it that way? It's sort of old-fashioned, isn't it?'

'Boy meets girl, girl rejects boy, girl dates other girl—'

'I don't want you to mention her,' Reese interrupted. David looked startled. 'I just don't want to get into it.'

'Sure. I won't mention her.'

'Thanks.' She ignored the twinge of guilt that rose in her. 'So let's just say we met through debate, we got to know each other, things happened.'

David considered her for a moment. 'Right. Things happened. We went through a traumatic experience that revealed the truth about our feelings.' He paused. 'It is the truth, isn't it?'

There was an uncharacteristic note of vulnerability in his voice, and she knew what he was really asking. He wanted to know if she honestly liked him, even after the way she had felt about Amber. They had never discussed it in detail – that would be way too weird – but he knew she had had strong feelings about Amber. For the first time, Reese realized she might have the upper hand in her relationship with David. Before, she had always thought that she was the vulnerable one, because she was the one who froze up and couldn't deal with her emotions; because David was the guy everybody liked at school, whereas she was just some girl. But whatever had transpired between her and Amber gave her the power to hurt him.

A new tenderness rose in her, and along with it came a sense of responsibility. It made her reach out and put a hand on his knee. 'I would never lie to you,' she told him softly. 'I can't, even if I tried.'

He covered her hand with his. Everything was open between them. He could see the truth.

He stood, pulling her to her feet, and when they kissed, it was sweet. Her hands slid around his back, and he was alive beneath her touch, his whole body focused on her, and she trusted him.

CHAPTER 5

Reese knocked on her mom's door. When she heard her mom's voice calling, 'Come in,' she rubbed her clammy palms against her thighs and went inside. The bedroom was empty, but she heard the sound of running water from the attached bathroom.

'Reese, is that you?'

'Yeah.' Reese closed the bedroom door and headed toward the bathroom. Her mom was washing her face at the sink.

'Your dad said he'd make pancakes this morning.'

It was Sunday morning, and the statement was so ordinary and yet so incredibly unusual – when was the last time her dad had been there to make pancakes? – that Reese temporarily froze.

Her mom turned off the tap and reached for a towel to blot away the water. 'Is something wrong?'

'No.' When her mom looked up, Reese looked away. 'I wanted to tell you something.'

'What is it?' Her mom straightened and leaned against the edge of the bathroom counter. 'You're scaring me, honey.'

Reese crossed her arms. 'It's nothing bad. I thought you should know – before we do the interview – that David and I are – we're – we're together.' Her face felt as hot as a bonfire.

Her mom's eyebrows rose, and then a smile tugged at the corners of her mouth. She hung up the towel. 'I thought you were.'

'You did?' She didn't know whether to be relieved or aghast. Was she that transparent?

'Well, I knew you liked him.'

'You *did?*' Now she was definitely aghast. 'When?'

Her mom took out a small jar of moisturizer and began to smooth the lotion over her face. 'You've had a crush on him for a while, haven't you?'

Reese sat on the edge of her mom's bed, still facing the bathroom. 'Does everybody know?'

Her mom laughed. 'I don't know about everybody, but I've noticed the way you look at him. I have to say, that's part of the reason I was so surprised about Amber.'

Reese stared down at her lap. 'Yeah. That's over.'

'I thought so,' her mom said softly. 'I'm sorry. Do you want to tell me what happened?'

Reese hadn't thought she would want to, but she found herself recounting, haltingly, how she had discovered that Amber wasn't simply a girl she met by accident but was connected to Dr Brand. How Amber had been assigned by the Imria to monitor Reese's reactions to the adaptation procedure. How their relationship had been in service to this assignment. Even though Amber had apologized and insisted her feelings for Reese had been real, that didn't change the fact that Amber had known what the Imria had done to Reese. She couldn't help thinking that if Amber had really cared for her, she would have told her the truth.

'She wants us to talk to the Imria now,' Reese said, scooting back to lean against the headboard as her mom came out of the bathroom. 'She says they want to help us, but I don't trust her.'

'I wouldn't trust her either,' her mom said. 'She lied to you and she doesn't deserve you.'

The harsh tone in her mom's voice made Reese wince. Reese had been as cruel as she could to Amber the last time she had seen her, but hearing anger directed at her by someone else made her uncomfortable. 'Mom—'

'She's a very attractive girl, and she knows it. You can't trust someone like her.'

Reese's face burned even more.

Her mom sat on the edge of the bed, facing Reese. 'She took advantage of you, and if I ever see her trying anything like that again—'

'She won't. I'm fine, Mom.' Her stomach twisted as she said the words. *I'm fine*, she told herself. Her mom's face was hard-edged with a kind of anger Reese couldn't remember seeing before.

'She'd better not,' her mom said. She ran a hand through her hair, pushing away the damp dark curls from her forehead. 'I want you to be careful, that's all. I know you had strong feelings for her, and even though I think David is a great guy, you've barely had time to deal with what happened with Amber. Are you sure you're ready to date someone else?'

Reese squirmed. 'Of course.'

Her mom gave her a look that said she knew Reese was lying. 'If he really likes you, he'll wait until you're over Amber.'

Reese's fingers clenched, crumpling the down duvet in her grip. 'I'm over her,' she insisted.

Her mom frowned. 'Are you?'

Reese looked at the bedroom window to avoid her mom's gaze. The blinds were half-closed, exposing slivers of the cloud-covered sky. 'Yes. I'm over her.'

Her mom reached out and touched Reese's foot. Reese sensed the beginnings of her mom's feelings – concern, doubt – and she pulled her foot away. 'Honey,' her mom said.

'I can handle it,' Reese snapped.

Her mom didn't speak for a minute. Reese watched a shadow move across the sky through the blinds and willed her fisted fingers to relax before they tore a hole in the duvet. 'Okay,' her mom finally said. 'Then do we need to have a talk about safety?'

Embarrassed, she drew her arms around her knees. 'No. You gave me the talk when I was twelve. I know how things work.'

'I'm sure you do,' her mom said wryly. 'But if you need anything – a trip to the doctor, whatever – come to me first.'

Reese shook her head. 'I know. Jeez, are you going to have this talk with me every time I date anyone?'

Her mom laughed and stood up. She went to the window and twisted the stick that controlled the blinds, opening them to the morning light. 'Point taken. I won't push it. And I do really like David—'

'Oh my God, what is that?' Reese cried. She jumped off the

bed and ran to join her mom at the window.

Startled, her mom moved out of the way as Reese pulled on the cord to raise the blinds.

The spaceship was moving.

Reese ran downstairs and into the kitchen, where her dad was mixing pancake batter. 'Reese?' he said, but she didn't answer. She opened the back door and went outside to look at the sky. The ship was heading north at a smooth, stately pace, and it made no sound and left no contrail.

As it headed out of sight, Reese went back inside, going into the living room to turn on the news. An image of the black spacecraft took up the whole screen as a headline crawled across the bottom: *Imrian Spaceship Moves to Angel Island*.

In a voice-over, the news anchor was reporting: '—City of San Francisco has been dealing with crowd control problems ever since the Imrian spacecraft took up position over the Noe Valley neighborhood three days ago. Today we have learned that the State of California has granted permission for the ship to land on Angel Island, which is a California state park. The park itself will be closed to tourists for the foreseeable future. The Imrian representatives on board the ship are reportedly in talks with the United Nations to meet with diplomats at the annual meeting of the General Assembly this fall.'

The black walls were a familiar sight by now: The ship was seamless and windowless, without a single distinguishing mark on its surface. Analysts had spent hours on cable news shows speculating about why the ship was so blank, with stealth being the most popular theory.

‘The crowds that have congregated daily in Noe Valley to view the spaceship are now moving with the ship as it makes its way over the city to the bay,’ the news anchor said.

The scene changed to show a helicopter’s view of the streets of Reese’s neighborhood. Thousands of people were packed onto the sidewalks, and all of them were turning en masse to watch the spaceship fly away. Their signs seemed to sag in unison, the motion of their bodies like a giant arrow pointing north. Even the cars had stopped as people climbed out to watch the flight of the Imrian craft.

‘California Governor Anthony Moreno will be giving a press conference in a few minutes to explain the state’s decision to allow the Imrian spaceship to land on state property,’ said the news anchor. ‘There is speculation that Angel Island was selected because it can be isolated, preventing large crowds from gathering there.’

Reese went to the bay windows and peeked around the edge of the curtains. The crowd was paying no attention to her house now; they were rushing in the direction of the ship. Reese heard her parents come into the living room and sit on the couch, but she couldn’t tear herself away from the window. The exodus didn’t take long. The street emptied of tourists in barely half an hour, leaving trash strewn across the road and clumped in the gutters: plastic bottles, candy wrappers, brown paper sacks greasy from the ends of burritos. It was a residential neighborhood, so there weren’t any public trash cans. Reese saw one of the neighbors across the street emerge from his garage with a broom and a trash barrel. As he began clearing the sidewalk in front of his house, she noticed a champagne-colored sedan parked nearby.

A man in a black suit was in the driver's seat.

Reese backed away from the window, letting the curtains fall shut, and sat down in the armchair. The governor's press conference was about to start, but she couldn't focus on the television. All she could think about was the man in the car across the street. The government was clearly still watching her, and it wasn't even trying to hide it anymore.

CHAPTER 6

On Monday morning, Agent Forrestal was waiting right inside Kennedy High School's front doors with the Defense Department's Jeff Highsmith.

'Good morning, Miss Holloway,' Highsmith said, smiling.

Reese hated when people called her 'miss.' She wondered when the title had lost its aura of respect; now all it did was tell her she was being patronized. 'Hey, Jeff,' she said. His smile disappeared.

Across the lobby, Reese saw Diana Warner waiting with David and his family. Reese headed across the mosaic-tiled floor to meet them, her parents following. The school smelled of industrial floor cleaner, along with that indefinable something extra – the lingering trace of thousands of students, their perfumes and deodorants and the faintly musty scent of books – that combined to create a scent that Reese would always recognize as Kennedy High. David saw her coming and stepped away from his parents to greet her with a hug.

'Hey,' he said.

'Hi.' There was no time to linger, because as soon as they

had greeted each other's parents, Diana took them to a classroom that had been taken over by the *Sophia Curtis Show*'s hair and makeup team.

As the makeup artist poked at Reese's eyes with wands and brushes, repeatedly asking her to stay still, Diana went over the plans with Reese, David, and their parents. The main interview would be shot in Mr Murray's biology classroom, and then Sophia wanted Reese and David to give her a tour of the school on camera. Reese and David were to be interviewed first, and after their portion was finished, Sophia would sit down with their parents.

'What about Highsmith?' Reese heard her mom ask.

'He'll be observing,' Diana said.

The makeup artist finished touching up Reese's lips and stood back. 'You're all set,' she said, and handed Reese a mirror.

Reese was taken aback by her own reflection. She wore makeup to debate tournaments, but she had no idea what the makeup artist had done to make her eyes look so big. They looked more greenish than usual, too, and her lips were shiny with some kind of peach-colored gloss.

'You look great,' her mom said from the makeup chair beside her.

'Thanks,' Reese said. She glanced up and saw David standing nearby, flipping through the release forms that the TV producers had given them. His hair and makeup had been finished first, but she hadn't seen him yet. The stylist had done something to his hair to tame the parts that stuck up in the wrong places, and as he read through the forms, unaware that Reese was watching him, she realized with a jolt that she was about to tell the world – on television – that she was dating him. She had known him for so long, but she didn't think she had ever seen him the way she did right then. The outfit that Diana Warner had picked did look good on him. The shirt clung to him just enough to show off his broad shoulders, and the jeans fit perfectly. The stylists had put some kind of pomade into his hair that made it seem blacker and sharper than before, emphasizing the clean line of his jaw and the angle of his eyebrows.

He looked up and caught her eye, and she realized she had been openly staring at him. Her entire body heated up and she hoped the makeup she was wearing hid the redness on her cheeks. He grinned and came over to her, leaning down to whisper, 'You look amazing.'

She was short of breath. 'Thanks.'

'David, Reese, let me introduce you to Sophia Curtis,' said Diana.

Reese scrambled to her feet. The reporter was standing nearby with a small but friendly smile on her face. 'Hello,' she said, extending her hand to Reese first.

'Hi,' Reese said. When she shook Sophia's hand, she had the briefest impression of clear, bright edges: like a cut-glass prism.

'Hi,' David said, shaking her hand as well.

'We're ready to begin,' Sophia said. 'Follow me.'

Though Diana had warned them that Jeff Highsmith would be observing, Reese hadn't realized that Agent Forrestal and another man in black would be there too. They stood right inside the door to Mr Murray's room like guards, and every time Reese glanced in their direction, they were watching her or David. Highsmith took a seat out of camera range and told Sophia Curtis to start whenever she was ready.

She asked Reese and David to begin with what had happened after they left Phoenix during the June Disaster, but as they began to talk about Project Plato, Highsmith interrupted. 'That's classified. You signed a nondisclosure agreement about your treatment there.'

Sophia smiled thinly. 'Can they talk about how they felt after they returned?'

Highsmith nodded. 'Of course.'

Reese began to tell Sophia about the rapidly healing cuts on her palms that had led her to believe something had been done to her at the military hospital, but Highsmith interrupted again. 'Do you have proof?'

Reese looked at him in surprise. 'You're asking *me* for proof? You have proof yourself – the Blue Base doctors tested us—'

'That's classified,' Highsmith said calmly. 'I'm asking if you have independent proof.'

'We're working on that,' David said. 'My father's in touch with several UCSF professors about setting up an academic board to evaluate us.'

'So you're saying no, you don't have proof,' Highsmith said.

Sophia stood up. 'Jeff, let me talk to you for a minute.'

He followed her to one corner of the biology classroom, where they turned their backs to Reese and David and huddled in front of a poster depicting the evolution of humanity, from Lucy to *Homo sapiens*. She couldn't make out what Sophia was telling him, but by the furious tones of her whispers,

Reese didn't think it was anything positive.

David nudged her with his knee, leaving it in place against her thigh. A shiver traveled through her as she registered his presence in her mind. *What do you think they're doing?* he thought.

I hope she's telling him off.

They returned a few moments later, and Sophia said, 'Let's pick up again. How did you feel when you got back to San Francisco?'

They told her about their abilities to communicate with each other mentally when they touched, and Sophia avoided the issue of proof, though she did ask David to elaborate on his father's plans to form an academic review board. When Sophia skipped over their abduction by the men in black and their time at Blue Base on Area 51, Reese knew that Highsmith had prevailed.

'One last thing,' Sophia said, flipping through her notes. 'At the press conference in front of your house, you and the Imrian girl, Amber Gray, seemed to know each other. Did you know her?'

A flash of interest crossed Highsmith's face, which made Reese immediately wary.

'I knew her,' Reese said. She didn't want to go into the details, not only because she didn't want to give Jeff any new information, but also because she wasn't comfortable telling the public that she had been in a relationship with Amber. She could already imagine the comments online.

'Did you know she's an Imrian?' Sophia asked.

'Not at first.'

'So she lied to you?'

Reese hesitated, and then wondered why she was hesitating. 'Yes.'

'Why?'

'She was sent to keep tabs on me and David.' The government already knew this, so it shouldn't be a surprise to Highsmith.

'The Imria are in discussions to speak at the United Nations next month, and they say they're here for peaceful purposes. But they lied to you and spied on you. Do you believe their motivations are peaceful?'

Sophia's characterization of the Imria – of Amber – unexpectedly stung. Reese found herself wanting to defend them, and it irritated her. 'I don't know,' she finally said. 'I hope so.'

The last portion of their interview was shot in Mr Chapman's old classroom, where the debate team met after school. Some of Mr Chapman's posters were still on the wall, and though the whiteboard had been erased, a ghostly trace of his handwriting remained in shadowed letters that could still be read: *Last debate meeting of the year: Thursday at 4 PM*.

'This was your debate coach's classroom, wasn't it?' Sophia asked.

Was. Reese wished they had never stopped at that gas station in Las Vegas.

'Yes,' David said.

Sophia asked them about Mr Chapman, and David explained how the teacher had encouraged him to join the team, and how he had paired David with Reese last year. Reese barely noticed that Sophia was nudging them toward the part of the interview she had dreaded the most.

'You sound like a good team,' Sophia said, smiling. 'And you just went through a pretty difficult situation that I think would bring a lot of friends closer together. What about you two?'

The question was phrased more delicately than Reese had expected. There was still wiggle room; they could avoid it if they wanted. Reese glanced surreptitiously at David, forgetting that the camera was trained on her. She couldn't read the expression on his face, and for a long, anxious moment, she was convinced he would deny that anything had happened between them.

'We—' As she started to speak, David reached for her hand. Startled, she sensed him right there with her. He hadn't changed his mind.

'We're together now,' he said, and a tentative smile reached his eyes.

She was certain that the makeup was doing nothing to hide the splotchy red flush on her cheeks, but somehow, she didn't care. *Yes. We are.*

While Sophia Curtis interviewed their parents in the school auditorium, Reese and David snuck up to the bell tower. It no longer had bells in it, and access was supposed to be restricted at all times, but last year someone had made a copy of the key and hidden it behind the bust of Albert Einstein outside the chemistry lab.

When they got to the statue, Reese reached into Einstein's

bronze collar and pulled out the key. At the end of the hall she unlocked the door to the tower, and she and David slipped through into the stairwell. It always felt illicit to be up here – she had accompanied Julian to smoke a few times – but there was an intoxicating edge to sneaking into the tower with David.

At the top of the stairs, sandstone archways framed a three-hundred- sixty-degree view of the city. She leaned against the waist-high wall and looked northeast at the downtown skyline. For the first time in a long time, she felt free. Nobody was watching her.

David stood beside her, his arm brushing against hers. 'I wonder who put that key behind Einstein,' he said.

'I heard it was Chris Tompkins. He stole it from the principal's office and made a copy.'

'I heard it was Jamie Yung, and *she* stole it and made a copy.'

Reese laughed, and the sound of it echoed faintly in the cupola. 'I guess we'll never know.'

'Hey, my friend Eric's having a party on Friday. You want to go?'

She looked at him in surprise. 'Like a house party?' She wasn't really friends with Eric Chung's group, and she wasn't really into house parties, either.

'Yeah.' He smiled at her, and she swore her heart skipped a beat. Who was she kidding? She would go to a party with David.

'Sure, I'll go.'

'How about I pick you up at seven?'

She gave him a puzzled look. 'But Eric lives near you. Why don't I just meet you there?'

His eyebrows rose briefly. 'Because I'm asking you on a date.'

Her stomach flipped. She felt like a dork. 'Oh, sorry. I mean, okay.'

He shook his head slightly, as if he thought she was funny, and reached out to smooth a piece of hair away from her eyes. His fingers lingered on her cheek, light as a feather. Her breath caught in her throat. And just like that, both his hands were in her hair, cupping her head, tipping her face up to his while he bent down to kiss her. His mouth was warm and firm on hers, his hands steady, but inside she felt him trembling like a butterfly on a leaf. She put her hands on his waist, drawing his body against hers. She felt the tail of his shirt hanging loose from the back of his jeans, and she ran her fingers under it and the T-shirt beneath, touching his skin. He shuddered in a long, twisting shiver that ricocheted through her, making her legs wobble. She pulled him closer so that she wouldn't fall. He pushed her gently against the wall of the tower. The ledge pressed against the middle of her back, a hard edge above which was nothing – only the air over the city. A delirious confidence filled her. If she tumbled out of the tower, she would surely float, as if she were made of cloud and sky rather than flesh and bone.

A phone rang, the unfamiliar peal echoing loudly in the tower. David was still kissing her, paying no attention to it, but she realized something was vibrating in her left front pocket. The phone that Amber had given her. 'David,' she said, breaking away from him.

'What?' He looked dazed.

She pulled out the phone. Dr Brand's name showed up on the tiny screen, and the world seemed to crash to a halt. 'It's Dr Brand,' she said, staring at the display.

'Are you going to answer that?' David asked.

She flipped the phone open with nervous hands, nearly dropping it as she lifted it to her ear. 'Hello?'

'Hello, Reese? This is Evelyn Brand.'

'Um, hi.'

'We're having a press conference on Thursday at Angel Island, and we'd like to invite you and David to come. We'll be giving tours of our ship. You can bring your parents if you'd like.'

'Thursday?' *I could see Amber again in three days*, Reese thought, and she immediately felt guilty. She turned away from David, looking down at the palm trees that marched along the Dolores Street median. 'What time? How are we supposed to get there?'

'We'll have ferries departing from Fisherman's Wharf at ten AM. Can I expect the two of you? We'd really like to have the opportunity to explain everything to you.'

Reese hesitated. David came to stand beside her. 'We'll think about it.'

'All right,' Dr Brand said. She didn't sound surprised. 'You can give me a call at this number when you decide. And, Reese, we really do hope you'll come.'

'Okay. Bye.' Reese ended the call and stared at the phone for a second before looking up at David.

'What'd she say?'

Reese relayed the invitation.

'Do you want to go?' he asked.

She put the phone back into her pocket. She knew that her reluctance to go was all about her issues with Amber, but facing that right now – with David only a couple of feet away – made panic shoot through her. 'I don't know.' She rubbed a hand over her eyes, and when her hand came away it was smeared with eye shadow. 'Crap. I have to go wash this off. Can we talk about it later?'

He seemed surprised, but he said, 'Sure. It's on Thursday, right?'

'Yeah.' She headed for the stairs, struggling to hide her sudden anxiety.

CHAPTER 7

On Wednesday Reese's new phone rang as she was pulling on her jacket.

'Oh my God, that is so loud,' Julian said.

'I just got it. I haven't fixed it yet,' Reese said, tugging it out of her pocket. It was her third phone in two months. She had lost the first during the car accident on Area 51, the second at Blue Base. Her dad had given her this one before he dropped her off at Julian's house that morning. The only people who had her number were her parents, Julian, and David. She answered the phone. 'Hey,' she said.

'Hi,' David said.

'Who is it?' Julian asked. 'We're going to be late.' They had arranged for their friend Madison to pick them up to go shopping.

'It's David,' she said to Julian. 'What's up?' she said into the phone.

Julian rolled his eyes and sat down in his desk chair.

'Did you decide whether you want to go to Angel Island tomorrow or not?' David asked. 'My parents have been asking, and I think I want to go.'

'Oh.' She was still uncertain. She wanted the information as much as David did, but the idea of seeing Amber made her nervous. 'I can't really talk right now,' she said instead of answering his question.

'Why? What's going on?' He sounded concerned.

'Nothing. I'm going shopping,' she said without thinking. *Crap*. She hadn't meant to tell him. She wanted to find something to wear for their date on Friday night, but she didn't want him to know. She worried it made her look as if she was trying too hard.

'For what?'

'For a – a thing. Julian's waiting for me. Let me call you in a couple hours, okay? We can talk then.'

'All right.'

When she hung up the phone Julian said, 'Boyfriend keeping you on a short leash?'

She gave him a pointed look. 'You did not just say that.'

He raised his hands in surrender. 'Let's go. Madison'll be mad if she gets there and we're late.'

On Monday night, after the Sophia Curtis interview, Reese had stood in front of her closet and stared morosely at her clothes, trying to figure out what she could wear to the party. She kept thinking about the people who would be there – David's friends, probably his ex-girlfriend – and how inadequate her wardrobe was. She couldn't show up at Eric Chung's house wearing jeans and a stupid T-shirt. She had called Julian.

'I don't think I'm the right person to help,' he told her.

'What do you mean? You always help me find stuff to wear.'

‘I find weird T-shirts. You’re going on a date. With a guy. I think you need girl help.’ He sounded a little annoyed, but she didn’t think to ask why.

‘You won’t go shopping with me?’ she said, feeling panicked.

‘I didn’t say that,’ Julian said, giving in. ‘Why don’t you call Mad?’

Reese went shopping with their friend Madison Pon all the time, but rarely for clothes for herself. ‘Yeah, I guess that could work.’

Madison was more than happy to help – especially once Reese revealed the reason behind her request. She then had to explain, in detail, how she and David had gotten together, although she omitted everything about Amber. Reese told herself that Amber had nothing to do with this, and it wasn’t like Madison would think to ask, but Reese still felt a little guilty about not telling her.

It was only after talking to Madison that Reese realized going shopping was more complicated than it used to be. Since her parents wouldn’t let her go anywhere on her own anymore, she told them she was spending the day at Julian’s house. Julian agreed to sneak out with her via the alley that ran behind his street, and Madison was picking them up a couple of blocks away.

She was already waiting in her lime-green VW by the time they arrived, breathless from sprinting down the alley. ‘You’re late!’ she said, but she looked more excited than upset.

Julian climbed into the backseat and said, ‘She got a call from her boyfriend.’

Madison grinned. ‘Oooh, really? What did he say?’

Reese glared at Julian and tugged her baseball cap farther down over her head. 'Nothing. Let's go – we have to be back here by four thirty.'

Madison laughed. 'All right. Let's find you an outfit for Friday night.'

Haight Street was lined with thrift stores and head shops, clumps of street kids smoking, and tourists who stopped in the middle of the sidewalk to take photos. As Reese, Julian, and Madison wove their way among pedestrians and the smell of pot smoke, Reese kept her head down and hoped that nobody would recognize her. Madison pushed open the door of a thrift shop, the bell jingling. 'Come on, let's try this one first,' she said.

Reese and Julian followed her inside. It smelled like used clothes – that combination of mothballs and other people's lives that always made Reese wonder who had worn these things before. Madison dived into the first rack, quickly flipping through blouses of every color and combination. Reese pulled off her sunglasses and wandered back to the accessories and began to dig through a pile of hats. Madison was at her elbow almost instantly.

'No,' Madison said sternly. 'Focus, Reese. You need a skirt and a top.' Madison dragged her back to the rack full of blouses and began to hold them up to Reese, while Julian looked on.

'Ew,' Reese said, pushing away an orange shirt with pink flowers on it. 'I'm not wearing that.'

'You need to have a more open mind,' Madison admonished

her, but hung up the orange shirt. 'Just try some things on and we'll see what looks good.'

Fifteen minutes later Reese was in a dressing room with an armful of shirts. The first was a clingy red tank top with lace edging that made her chest look huge. She opened the dressing room curtain and shook her head at Madison and Julian. 'This is not me.'

Madison tugged the curtain aside and gave her an appraising look. 'Wow. Yeah, not you.'

Julian poked his head over Madison's shoulder, making a face. 'Yeah, no.'

'I told you,' Reese said.

'Try on the blue one,' Madison said, pulling the curtain shut again. But the blue one was too tight; the purple too loose. As Reese struggled into a billowy white shirt with armholes in very strange places, Madison said, 'I can't believe you're dating David Li. It's so crazy.'

'Why is it crazy?' Reese said indignantly. 'I've been friends with him for a while.'

'You've been his debate partner. That's different. Besides, as long as I've known you, you've been like 'I'm not dating anyone ever!' What changed your mind?'

Amber? But Reese said, 'I don't know.'

'Hey, I'm gonna go look at the belts,' Julian called.

'Okay,' Reese and Madison said in unison. Reese finally got the white blouse on. It made her look like a cross between the Pillsbury Doughboy and – no, that was bad enough. She took it off without showing it to Madison.

She pulled on a gray flannel shirt with black piping as

Madison peeked through the curtain.

'I did not pick that shirt out for you,' Madison said.

'I know. I did.'

'It's not sexy enough.'

Reese buttoned the shirt and looked in the mirror. It fit well. 'I like it.'

'You would.' Madison pulled the curtains open and reached out to unbutton the top two buttons.

'Hey!' Reese cried.

'Cleavage,' Madison said. 'You have some. You should take advantage of it.'

'I don't have cleavage.'

'You have more than me.' Madison pointed at her size-A cups and gave herself a mournful look in the mirror. 'Guys don't like these.'

'You're not dating the right guys.'

Madison smiled. 'Yeah, probably not.' She studied Reese for a moment longer and said, 'All right, you can have the shirt. But you have to wear it with a miniskirt.'

Reese groaned.

Two shops later, they compromised on a jean skirt. It was shorter than Reese was used to, but at least it wasn't one of the plaid schoolgirl skirts that Madison kept pushing on her, and Julian approved. 'Looks good,' he said, flashing her a grin. 'Guys like skirts.'

'You're gay. How would you know?' Reese teased him.

His eyebrows rose, and he opened his mouth to say something, but then shook his head. 'I'll let you off the hook this time because we're friends. I'm gonna go look around.'

As he sauntered out of the dressing room, Madison gave Reese a questioning glance. 'What was that about?'

'I don't know,' Reese said, confused. Was she not allowed to make gay jokes anymore? Shouldn't she have more of a right now that she had dated a girl? Or was Julian pissed at her for dating David? She felt uneasy – as if she had done something wrong, but she wasn't sure what it was.

As Reese put her own clothes back on, Madison tried on a flowery summer dress. 'Reese, can you help me zip up the back?' Madison called. Reese pulled on her baseball cap and went into Madison's dressing room. Madison was waiting with the dress hanging open, and Reese's memory flashed back to that afternoon with Amber in her bedroom, trying on her red dress. Taking the dress off. Reese swallowed and zipped Madison up.

'So you and David have this mental connection now,' Madison said, looking at Reese in the mirror. 'Like telepathy? Is that true?'

'Yeah.'

'Can you tell what he's thinking when he kisses you?'

'Um, yes.'

'Really? What is that like?'

The memory of kissing David swept through her body in a dizzying wave. 'It's intense.'

Madison's eyes widened excitedly. 'I knew it. It's got to be insane. I'm so jealous!'

Reese shook her head. 'Don't be jealous. It's also kind of weird.'

'I'll take the weird,' Madison said, then examined herself in the mirror. 'What do you think of the dress?'

'It looks good on you. You should get it.'

Madison tugged at the price tag on the sleeve and shook her head. 'It's forty-eight dollars. I can't afford it. Come on, unzip me and we'll find you some shoes.'

By the time they settled on footwear, Reese was thoroughly tired of shopping. She couldn't understand how Madison could go on for hours, pawing through clothing racks like there was no tomorrow. Even Julian became bored and fidgety. 'I'm not wearing those,' Reese said over and over, as Madison presented her with heels of all kinds, followed by glossy black boots that looked like they belonged to a dominatrix.

'You're so hard to shop for!' Madison cried in frustration. They were at their fifth store, and it was almost four o'clock.

'What about these?' Reese said, pulling out a pair of chunky-heeled brown boots. They were scuffed on the toes and had metal buckles over the ankles.

'Motorcycle boots?' Madison said skeptically.

'Very dykey,' Julian observed. Reese avoided his gaze as she sat down to try them on.

'They are dykey,' Madison agreed. 'Speaking of which, did you know that Bri had a crush on you sophomore year? She's totally disappointed you're with David.'

'What?' Reese gave Madison an incredulous look. 'Briana?'

'Yes, *Briana*. Why do you think she kept trying to get you to do all those gay things with her?'

'I thought it was because she's my friend?'

'You can be so clueless sometimes, really,' Madison said severely. 'You knew, didn't you, Julian?'

'Yep.' His face was inscrutable as Reese glanced at him.

'But she never said anything about it,' Reese said, bewildered.

Madison gave her a pointed look. 'You never had any interest in dating. You made that perfectly clear. Besides, you're straight. Why would Bri bring it up if she knew you'd only reject her?' Madison caught the furtive glance between Reese and Julian and said, 'Wait. What is *up* with you two?'

Reese stood. 'Nothing.' She didn't look at Julian as she clomped over to the mirror hanging on the wall near the shoe section. 'I like them,' she announced.

'If you wear them with the jean skirt and that gray shirt you're going to look all country hoedown,' Madison warned her.

'They're motorcycle boots, not cowboy boots.' Reese pulled one off and looked at the price written on the sticker on the sole. 'And they're only twenty bucks.'

Madison regarded them dubiously. 'I guess they're all right. Kind of badass. Is that what you're going for?'

'I don't know. Is that good?' She stared at herself in the mirror. She thought she looked uncertain, not badass. And maybe messy: Loose strands of dark brown hair were escaping from the ponytail she had tucked through the back of the baseball cap.

'Sometimes,' Madison said. 'It's not a bad look for you. Just wear your hair down and put on a nice bra. David will like it.'

'A nice bra? Are you going to make me go shopping for that too?'

'I'm not going,' Julian declared.

'Don't freak out, Julian. You're on your own for that, Reese.

I don't have time. After I drop you guys off, I have to go babysit at the Chens'.'

Reese sat down to put her sneakers back on. 'I'm going to get the boots.'

'Nice,' Julian said, and when she looked over at him she saw a tiny smile cross his face. The sight of it loosened a bit of the tension inside her, though she still felt as if there was something off between them.

Madison leaned against the wall by the mirror, crossing her arms. 'Don't tell Bri I said anything, okay? I don't know if she wanted you to know.'

'Sure, I won't tell her,' Reese said.

'She's dating that girl Sara now anyway and it probably doesn't matter, but – just don't tell her I told you.'

'Yeah. I won't.' Reese picked up the boots to head to the cash register. She wondered if she should have come out to Madison. But what would be the point of that? Amber was the only girl she had ever been attracted to. Reese didn't think there would be another.

Just as the store clerk handed Reese her purchase along with a fistful of change, Madison decided to buy a pair of earrings from a rack marked 50 percent off. 'I'm going outside for a cigarette,' Julian said as Madison got in line to pay.

'Do you care if I go with him?' Reese asked Madison.

She shook her head. 'Go ahead. I'll be done in five minutes.'

Reese put on her sunglasses and picked up her bags to follow Julian outside. He walked to the edge of the sidewalk and leaned against a parking meter as he lit up. She was about to ask him about the weirdness she had sensed between them when she saw a black town car pull into the loading zone a few feet away. The rear window rolled down to reveal a middle-aged woman with dark brown hair who was looking directly at her.

'Miss Holloway?' the woman called.

'Who's that?' Julian asked.

'I have no idea,' Reese said, startled.

'Miss Holloway, do you have a moment?' the woman asked.

Reese glanced at Julian. 'I'll be right back.' He nodded and she walked over to the car. The woman was wearing a dark blue suit and looked altogether ordinary – except that she was in a shiny black town car with tinted windows, and she knew Reese's name.

'I have a message for you,' she said.

'Who are you?' Reese asked, not moving any closer to the car.

'I work for Charles Lovick,' the woman said. 'He would like to invite you and David Li to meet with him Friday evening at six o'clock, if you're interested in learning more about the Imria and what they did to you.' The woman extended a business card out the window, held between two manicured fingers with nails painted the color of pearls.

Reese stepped forward and took the card. The name *Charles Lovick* was engraved on the thick, cream-colored stock. She flipped it over, looking for some indication of who Lovick was, and on the back was a handwritten address: *88 Variety Store, Stockton Street.*

'May I tell Mr Lovick you'll be there?' the woman asked pleasantly.

'Who is he?' Reese asked.

'He'll explain on Friday. I'll tell him to expect you both.' The window began to roll up.

'Wait a minute. We don't know him. We're not going to meet with a total stranger without any other information.'

The tinted window stopped halfway up. The woman leaned closer to the open half. 'If you want to know who the Imria truly are, you'll go to the meeting. You won't be offered this opportunity again. Six o'clock on Friday. Don't forget.' The window closed and the car drove away.

A moment later Julian was at her side. 'Who was that? What happened?'

She told him and watched his eyes widen with shock.

'No way,' he said. 'Are you going?'

'I don't know. I can't believe they followed me here.' She gazed down the street as the car turned off Haight and went out of sight. 'How would they know where I am? We snuck out – I haven't seen any men in black here. And who are they, anyway?'

'They're either better at tailing you than the MIBs or you have a tracking device implanted in you.' Julian gave her a grin that quickly died as he saw the stricken look on her face. 'I didn't mean that!'

She fingered the hard edges of the business card, an unsettling dread rising in her. The Imria said they wanted to help her; the government wanted to prevent her from telling the truth; and now this Charles Lovick wanted – she didn't know what he wanted, but she was pretty sure that if it was anything innocuous, he wouldn't send a stranger in a town car to deliver the message in person. That told her that he – or his people – were following her.

Julian spouted off various theories about who Lovick might be, but she didn't pay attention. She was beginning to feel extremely pissed off. She was a citizen of the United States of America, and her very own government was making her feel like a criminal by tailing her and censoring her when she had done nothing wrong. Now this total stranger was trying to tell her what to do by ordering her to meet him as if she were his trained lapdog. It was ironic that the only people who seemed to be waiting for her to make her own decisions were those who had changed the fundamental components of who she was – her DNA – without her permission.

She had to be honest with herself. She needed the information that the Imria were offering. If she rejected it simply because she was still torn up over Amber, she would wind up hating herself for being such a wimp.

She pulled out her phone as Madison emerged from the store. 'Hey!' she called brightly. 'I'm done! Whoa, what's wrong? It looks like somebody died.'

Reese typed a text message to David as Julian gave Madison the rundown: I'm in for Angel Island. And we might have to make another stop Friday night. I'll call you when I get home.

CHAPTER 8

Fisherman's Wharf was awash with tourists dressed in shorts and T-shirts, clothing that was rarely appropriate for San Francisco in August. This Thursday morning was no exception. As Reese and her parents climbed out of the taxi they had taken from their house, she saw a family in matching khaki shorts and Disney T-shirts shivering in the cool wind from the bay. Reese hadn't been here since she was a kid, when her dad had brought his parents to view the barking sea lions lolling on their floating platforms. She remembered the briny smell of the sea: fish and salt water mingled with the warm, sugary scent of cotton candy.

They had arrived early for the ferry to Angel Island, and as they approached the dock at Pier 39, Reese saw a crowd gathered there. As they drew closer, she realized they weren't waiting to board the ferry; they were carrying signs like the demonstrators who had thronged Reese's street the week before. Her heart sank. Had they simply moved from her neighborhood to Fisherman's Wharf?

Metal barriers had been set up to keep the street and dock

area clear for pedestrians, so the demonstrators were packed close together on both sides. Police officers were stationed at regular intervals, and there was a checkpoint at the entrance to the ferry boarding area, but despite the organized security the whole place felt like it was on the brink of chaos. The demonstrators were chanting something that Reese couldn't make out yet, but they were clearly angry. The signs they held put them definitively in the anti-Imria camp: DON'T BELIEVE GOVERNMENT LIES, read one. Another declared THE BEGINNING OF THE END IS NEAR. And a whole bunch of them stated IMRIA = NEW WORLD ORDER.

Reese's parents shepherded her through the tourists and the gauntlet of protesters, but they couldn't shield her from their emotions. The concentration of their anger was like static electricity on her skin. Their chanting grew louder and clearer as she and her parents approached. 'Don't believe the lies! They're here to colonize! Protect the US border! Prevent the new world order!'

The chanting began to break up as a new cry arose from the crowd on Reese's right. She kept moving forward, head down and shoulders hunched, but out of the corner of her eye she saw the crowd roiling as if it were preparing to disgorge someone. A demonstrator yelled, 'It's her! Reese Holloway!'

The sound of her name sent a shock through her. The sensation of the crowd's anger changed; they turned their eyes to focus on her. As goose bumps rose all over her skin at the force of their attention, she began to hear words in her mind as if her brain had suddenly tuned into someone else's thoughts. *That girl – look – pushing—*

She knew instantly that the words were not the product of her own mind. They came from outside her just as the crowd's emotions did. She remembered David describing hearing voices in his head like surfing through TV channels and catching disconnected snatches of dialogue. Was this what she was experiencing now? Were her abilities changing?

She didn't like it. Even though she was outdoors, she felt as if she were in a crowded warehouse where every sound echoed, creating a cacophony of psychic noise. She wanted to shrink back, but her parents tried to hurry her along, pushing her toward the onslaught.

'We just have to get through the checkpoint,' her mom was saying.

'Traitor!' someone screamed. 'Traitor to humanity!'

Reese Holloway – traitor – traitor—

The metal barrier to Reese's right clattered over. People poured over it, rushing toward her and her parents. The police shouted at them to get back, and Reese's dad grabbed her arm, yanking her away. Her mom yelled, 'Move! Move!'

A man pushed through the mob and halted directly in front of her, blocking her way. He was breathing heavily and carrying a sign that read IMRIA = NEW WORLD ORDER, but he dropped it carelessly onto the ground as he reached for something inside his Windbreaker. Reese froze. The man's eyes were wide and crystal blue, focused on her with a piercing hatred that felt like a physical blow to her gut. He was in his twenties, with pale hair cut very close to his scalp. When his hand emerged from his jacket, he was holding a gun.

Before Reese knew what was happening, both of her parents

had knocked her flat onto the ground. Her mom's body shuddered over hers, and Reese could feel her terror, bitter and sharp. Her father threw himself over the both of them, and someone was screaming, 'He has a gun!'

Reese was immobilized beneath her parents while other people's emotions buffeted her from all sides. Anger pelted her like a sudden hailstorm while fear dragged at her limbs. She couldn't distinguish her own feelings from the others'. She could barely breathe. She heard the gunman's voice breaking through the cacophony, clear and sharp. 'You've betrayed your own kind! *Hybrid monster*.' He grunted as if someone had punched him, and she heard the sound of someone's body – his body – striking the pavement. The scrabbling, desperate sounds of a struggle reached her ears.

All she could see was the ground. The asphalt was dark gray and splotchy near her head, where something had spilled and left a stain shaped like a pear. The street shook with footsteps. Police officers were nearby, yelling for the man to drop the weapon, to lie on the ground, to put his arms behind his back. The scraping sound of metal across concrete told her that the barrier was being pushed back into place. The chanting slowly began again. *Don't believe the lies. They're here to colonize*.

It was surreal: the absurdly hilarious rhyme of the demonstrators' chant. The hard, pebbly surface of the ground, reminding her of the asphalt outside Blue Base, where the blast had thrown her into the hot desert. The immobilizing pressure of her parents' flesh and bone against her, their child. They would die for her, and she was overwhelmed by the knowledge of it, heavy as weights tied to her ankles.

Finally, when she felt as if she might be suffocated by it all, her parents helped her up, still surrounding her, still preventing her from seeing what was happening, and herded her the last fifteen feet toward the security checkpoint. Police officers in their black uniforms pushed her through the gate. The scent of the bay, salty and sour with yesterday's fish, filled her nostrils. Ahead of her the ferry to Angel Island waited like a safe house, the ramp reminding her of the ramp that had emerged from the belly of the Imrian spacecraft.

'Go, go!' her mom said, pushing her up the ramp.

Her legs wobbled as the ferry rocked in the water of the bay. They wouldn't let her look back. They pushed her inside and onto a padded, disturbingly warm seat. Her head spun from the aftermath of the attack. She was still trying to separate out her own feelings from the tangled threads of everyone else she had just encountered. There were voices all around her and inside her, and she couldn't tell them apart. Her mom was on the phone yelling at someone. Her dad spoke in hushed, urgent tones to a stranger. Someone apologized over and over. *Reese. Reese.* A person thrust a cup of water into her hands, but she pushed it away. Then her mom was seated next to her, holding the cup to her mouth. The liquid was cool against her lips, but she gagged.

'I don't want it,' she muttered.

'Honey, are you all right?' her mom asked, rubbing her hand over Reese's back. A jolt of anxiety went through Reese, and she cringed away from her mom. She pushed herself out of the seat on unsteady legs and lurched across the slanting floor of the ferry, banging into another row of seats.

The door to the deck was ahead of her, a yawning window of bright light. Her vision was blurred. She went for the door. Her dad tried to stop her, but she shook him off. 'I need some air,' she said. She stepped out onto the deck, and there was San Francisco Bay and the sky, blue and slate gray, and she sucked in a deep breath of briny, fishy air and thought it was the best-smelling thing in the world.

She leaned against the railing, staring down at the water, and breathed.

Slowly, she came back to herself. She realized that her parents were standing a few feet away, watching her. 'I'm okay,' she said to them. 'I just needed some air.'

Her mom came a step closer.

'Please don't touch me right now,' Reese said.

Her mom stopped. 'Is it your – your adaptation?'

'Yes.' She swallowed something acidic and looked toward the dock. A line of police officers blocked the bottom of the ferry ramp. Beyond them the demonstrators were a mob of signs and motion, but she couldn't see the man who had drawn the gun. 'Where's David?' she asked. 'Is he here yet?'

'No,' her mom answered.

Reese pulled her phone out of her pocket and found David's number. Her hands were shaking.

'Honey, why don't you sit down?' her dad said, trying to sound soothing.

She paid no attention to him, lifting the phone to her ear as she continued to scan the dock for any signs of David. His phone rang and rang, but he didn't answer. She hung up, feeling queasy. 'Who are those protesters? Were they in front of our house?'

'I don't know,' her mom said. 'I think some of them were, but these people are much better organized.'

'I think we should go back inside,' her dad said. He looked worried. 'I don't like being out here. We're too exposed.'

The implication of his words was clear. He thought there could be more protesters with guns. Suddenly the cool tang of the air over the bay didn't feel so good to Reese. She let her father usher her back into the ferry, where she saw several other people milling around. There were reporters holding microrecorders, photographers and video camera operators. There were a few politicians, too, recognizable by the flag pins on their lapels. Reese and her parents sat down in a row of overly soft seats on the side of the ferry farthest away from the dock, and Reese kept an eye on the main entrance. She saw Senator Michaelson come in, and her mom went over to talk to her. She saw other reporters gathering together to compare notes. A couple of police officers entered, looking frazzled. Finally, just as Reese was beginning to completely freak out, she saw David and his parents coming up the ramp.

She ran to meet him, hugging him as soon as he entered the ferry. 'Are you okay?' she asked, her voice muffled against his neck. As she held him she was nearly overwhelmed by how clearly she saw his interior landscape. Adrenaline lingered inside him like a wire still reverberating.

His arms tightened around her, relief sluicing through them both. *I'm fine*, he thought.

She pressed her hands against his back as if to make sure he hadn't sustained any wounds, and cameras flashed. They sprang apart, startled.

'This isn't a photo op,' David's mom said coolly.

The photographer backed away. 'Sorry, ma'am.'

Grace Li frowned at him and directed David and Reese away from the photographers. 'Let's go join your parents, Reese.'

As they walked across the ferry, Reese asked, 'What happened? I called your phone but you didn't answer.'

'I must not have heard it. It was so loud out there.' David's face was pale and he looked as queasy as Reese had felt when she first boarded the ferry. 'The police had to escort us from the taxi. We got a call on the way here saying there was a security situation.'

They sat down side by side, their parents taking the row ahead of them. 'There was a guy with a gun,' Reese said.

'I heard,' David said. 'I'm glad you're okay.'

Reese glanced at their parents; they were talking in low voices and occasionally looking at her and David in concern. She turned to David and whispered, 'I heard voices this time – like you described. It was so weird. I've never heard them before.'

'Really?' David grimaced. 'I think I could feel the crowd's emotions too. It made me want to throw up afterward.'

She saw their parents eyeing them and she reached for David's hand, linking her fingers with his so they could communicate without speaking out loud. His pulse was rapid, his body still hypervigilant after the experience outside. *Has it ever happened to you before?* she asked him. *Do you think our abilities are changing?*

They must be. I think it might have happened before, like when we were in front of your house at the press conference. I didn't really understand it, and maybe it was because I was holding your hand. But today it was way more intense.

I have to learn how to block the crowds or else I'm going to go crazy.

You and me both.

The ferry door clanged shut and the engine rumbled on. Reese turned her head to look out the window. The boat was leaving the dock.

CHAPTER 9

Reese didn't think she had ever been to Angel Island before. Alcatraz, yes. She remembered a school trip there in sixth grade, and the frightening dankness of the abandoned cells. She had learned about Angel Island in social studies class, how the island was once an immigration station that detained thousands of Asian immigrants – mostly Chinese – for months and sometimes years while they waited to be admitted to the United States. She couldn't decide if it was fitting or unfortunate that the Imria were now on Angel Island, decades after that immigration station had closed.

'Have you been here before?' Reese asked David as the ferry approached the dock.

'I came here last year with my Chinese school class. We visited the immigration center. It was depressing.'

'Why?'

'You can see where the immigrants wrote these poems in Chinese on the wall while they were held there. They were prisoners, basically. You can stand in the room where the men slept, and with all the writing on the wall, it's like they're still trapped there.' He paused. 'It doesn't exactly make you proud to be an American.' His words were edged with sarcasm, and she could hear the subtext clearly: *My country did that to people like me*.

Reese didn't know what to say to that. Before she and David had kissed, she had rarely thought of him as being Chinese American – he was just David – but somehow the change in their relationship caused her to recognize his racial background in a way she never had before. The comments online following their first press conference had been especially sobering – and disturbing. In the last few days when she had gone online to read the news, she had tried to resist reading the comments, but she had given in to her curiosity. She had been appalled by how casually people threw out racist comments on the Internet. David couldn't escape the fact that he was Chinese American. He was loved and gushed over by Asians, especially the Chinese, but he was also heckled and judged for being Asian. She had never anticipated that his race could come with so much baggage, and she wasn't sure what she should do about it.

David saw the pensive expression on her face and asked, 'What's wrong?' He put his hand on her knee.

She avoided his gaze and looked out the window at the approaching island. 'What you said about Angel Island made me think about those comments online. It's so awful. I didn't know people still thought that way.'

'You shouldn't read that stuff.'

'They're a bunch of assholes,' she said vehemently. 'What century do they think they're in?'

'Forget about it. There's nothing you can do.'

'But it's awful,' she said, finally looking at him. Tension radiated through him from his hand. 'Don't you want to smack them, at least?'

He smiled ruefully. 'Sometimes. But how would that improve anything? Besides, you have to look at the big picture. Those racist comments are coming from a minority of haters in the US. There are way more people on this planet who look like me than like you. I'm not going to waste my time thinking about people who hate me because I'm Asian.' His words were confident, but there was an undercurrent of anger mingled with resignation running through him, and it made frustration boil up inside Reese.

Before she could respond, the ferry came to an unexpectedly abrupt stop. David removed his hand from her knee, and she could tell that he didn't want to talk about it anymore.

'You ready?' he asked.

'Not really.' But she got up anyway and followed the others off the ferry.

It had been cool and foggy in San Francisco, but the sun was shining on Angel Island. A metal ramp led from the boat to the landing, a wide concrete expanse with an information booth to the left and a café visible down the paved road to the right. Two people in dark gray suits were waiting – a woman and a man whom Reese did not recognize – and behind them were stationed National Guard troops, weapons at the ready. When everyone had disembarked from the ferry, Reese counted about three dozen people in all, including her family and David's. For the first time in a long time, she did not see Agent

Forrestal or any other men in black. *I guess they're not invited*, she thought.

'Welcome to Angel Island,' said the woman in the gray suit. Reese guessed that she was Imrian, because she had the same quality that Reese had seen in Dr Brand and Agent Todd – a presence that made Reese feel as if she recognized them, even when she had never seen them before. Reese wondered what had happened to Agent Todd; he had vanished after the bunker at Area 51 exploded. The woman continued: 'We'll begin today with a press conference in front of the visitors' center. Afterward, we'll bring small groups of you to tour the spacecraft. Please follow me.'

It was only a few minutes' walk to the visitors' center, where folding chairs were arranged in rows on the lawn across from a two-story white building that reminded Reese of a colonial home. The lawn extended down to the cove, which was empty except for the ferry. Up front, facing the folding chairs, a podium was flanked by a dozen more chairs where several individuals were already seated. As Reese drew closer, she realized they must be the other Imria, because Amber was among them.

Disconcerted, Reese averted her eyes, and then felt self-conscious. She had known that Amber would be there; this wasn't a surprise. Reese's parents took seats in the last row, and she, David, and his parents filed in after them. Once she was seated, Reese deliberately looked at the Imria. The man and woman who had greeted them were speaking to someone else Reese recognized: Dr Brand. Most of the Imria were dressed similarly, in gray or navy suits. Some of the women wore skirts;

some did not. Amber was wearing a sleeveless charcoal-gray dress that made her look as if she was going to a business meeting. Her short blond hair was swept back, and she kept her eyes trained on her hands, folded in her lap. Reese found herself feeling slighted by the fact that Amber didn't acknowledge her, and then she was irritated by the seesaw of her own emotions.

She was relieved when a tall, dark-skinned man approached the podium, giving her something else to focus on. 'Welcome,' the man said. He had short, straight black hair, and he moved with a fluid elegance that belonged on a stage, not on a windswept beach in the middle of San Francisco Bay. 'I am Akiya Deyir, designated ambassador of the Imria, and I am very glad to convey my people's greetings to you.' His accent was slight but noticeable, giving his formal language a foreign lilt. When he said the word *Imria*, it seemed to have more syllables than the letters called for.

He continued: 'We are grateful to the state of California for allowing our ship to land here on Angel Island, where we shall remain as talks continue with the leaders of your world. We regret that our presence above the city of San Francisco has led to congestion in the streets, though we are happy that you are interested in knowing more about us. We realize that you have many questions, and we will do our best to answer them as well as we can from now on. To begin, today we are pleased to announce that we will address the nations of your planet during the General Debate at the United Nations on September fifteenth, approximately one month from now in New York City. We look forward to the opportunity to open a truly universal dialogue about cooperation between our peoples.'

As Akiya Deyir spoke, Reese began to notice the similarities between him and Dr Brand and Amber. They all had an alertness to their features, a precision to the way they moved, that made humans seem a bit sluggish in comparison.

'Twelve days ago,' Deyir said, 'when our ship touched down in Nevada, our goal was simply to retrieve the members of our Earth-based team who had been mistakenly detained by the US government.'

Reese was surprised by his explanation. The night before she and David had escaped from the underground bunker, Amber had told her that the US was going to execute her and the other Imria. Reese didn't think there had been any mistake about it, and she wondered why Akiya Deyir was spinning the story to put the US in a positive light.

'We've been working with the US government since 1947, when we first made contact with the Truman Administration and subsequently drafted the Plato Protocol, which outlined the terms of our cooperative research agreement. We've had researchers stationed in Nevada since then, but in June there was a misunderstanding between our researchers and their US counterparts. We decided that we should remove our researchers and reconsider some of the agreements we had made with the United States. However, during the retrieval operation, one of our own people, Amber Gray, was shot.'

Amber did not look up at the sound of her name. Reese wondered if Amber had been told to be as unobtrusive as possible, because it seemed abnormal for her to be so demure.

'Our first priority was making sure that Amber recovered

from her wound, so we left Earth to focus on treating her,' the ambassador said. 'You may remember that President Elizabeth Randall stated that she thought we were gone – and it's true, we were gone for a short while. However, it was always our intention to return, as we hadn't fully resolved our misunderstanding with the US government, and we also were concerned about Reese Holloway and David Li, the two teens who were detained by the government after our departure.'

Hearing Akiya Deyir say her name made Reese stiffen. She inched over in her seat so that she could touch David's arm with her own. *What do you think he means by 'misunderstanding'?* she asked him.

I think he's hiding something, David thought. *The birds, maybe?*

Because the government was using Imrian DNA on the birds?

Exactly. The government was stealing Imrian DNA and using it in a way the Imria didn't like.

'Before I address what happened to Reese and David, let me say that we Imria appreciate President Randall's offer to begin our relationship anew,' Deyir said. 'We agree that the shooting of Amber Gray was an accident and we do not intend to press charges. We also wish to begin our relationship anew, and this time, in a public manner involving all the peoples of Earth.' The ambassador paused and smiled. 'Now, allow me to introduce you to Evelyn Brand, who has been working with the United States government for almost two decades and has been our primary point of contact with your people until today. Evelyn will be explaining the details of the research she has been directing, and she will announce a special project that we hope to launch very soon.' He turned to Dr Brand as she rose. 'Evelyn?'

She took Deyir's place at the podium, and he sat down in an empty seat nearby. 'Thank you, Akiya. And thank you,' she said to the audience, 'for coming here today. I'd like to especially thank David Li and Reese Holloway and their parents for joining us. I met Reese and David through a very unfortunate situation, when their car crashed near my research facility. We Imria have a saying, *nig tukum'ta nu nig tukum'ta*, which translates roughly to 'there is no coincidence'. I'm certain that if that accident hadn't happened, I wouldn't be here today telling you about our research, which we believe will be life-changing for all of humanity.'

Reese braced herself for the wash of attention as everyone turned to look at her and David. Beside her she heard David take a quick, short breath. The Imria looked too – including, at last, Amber – but unlike the curiosity Reese felt from the humans, she sensed nothing from the Imria. The quietness of their collective gaze was somehow more unsettling than the humans' interest.

Dr Brand continued: 'Since my arrival on Earth, I have carried on the research that my predecessors began, cooperating with the United States government under the Plato Protocol. That research focuses on awakening latent abilities of the human brain. Humans and Imria are biologically similar in many ways, but humans do not possess the ability we have to share our consciousness with another. We call this *susum'urda*, and it is vital to our society.' Dr Brand pronounced the word *soo-sum oordah*. 'It allows us to have true empathy. True connection. And we would like for humanity to have this ability to connect as well.'

A reporter asked, 'How does it work? Is it like telepathy?'

'Telepathy might be your best word for the ability, but *susum'urda* – this sharing of consciousness – is not about reading someone's mind from afar. We accomplish the shared consciousness through physical touch. When your hand touches something warm, your brain is able to understand the difference in temperature. Similarly, when one Imrian touches another, they are able to understand the other's *interior* temperature, so to speak.'

David nudged Reese with his knee, and thought: *But we didn't have to be touching when we were at Plato.*

She glanced at him. *We haven't really been able to do that since then, though. Do you think that was a fluke?*

I don't know, but it doesn't sound like the Imria can do it. There's also the crowds thing. Dr Brand hasn't mentioned anything about that.

'Developing a procedure to give this ability to humans has been very difficult to do, even though we believed that humans could be perfectly capable of it if certain neural pathways were opened to allow it,' Dr Brand said. 'Some human children actually have similar abilities at birth, but because they're not developed during childhood, the brain naturally closes off those neural pathways during adolescence. It was only this past spring that we perfected what we've come to refer to as an adaptation procedure, which enables the human body to adapt to the addition of Imrian DNA. It is this DNA that opens up the neural pathways in the brain that allow for susum'urda.

After the initial procedure, in which Imrian DNA is added to human DNA, the subject is placed into an adaptation chamber. This chamber is very much like an incubator. It helps the human body to accept the Imrian DNA, and takes over regulating many common body functions during recovery.'

'Is that what happened to the teens? An adaptation?' one reporter asked.

'Yes. When David and Reese were discovered after their car accident, they were brain-dead. I knew that unless we performed the adaptation procedure on them, they would not survive.'

Reese had never heard this before. Did this mean she owed her life to the Imria? The thought didn't sit well with her.

Dr Brand continued: "The procedure put them into a healing coma for several weeks, during which the chamber – and the Imrian DNA – worked to repair their physical injuries. One positive side effect of the Imrian DNA is that it also promotes much faster healing. It was truly a last-resort effort. Had they not been on the verge of death, we would not have tried it, because at the time of their accident, the procedure was still in testing and was not one hundred percent safe.' Dr Brand smiled. 'We were overjoyed that Reese and David reacted so well to it. We are so happy to see them safe and sound today.'

Everyone turned to look at them again, but Reese noticed that Amber was the only one of the Imria without a smile on her face. She seemed pensive rather than happy.

Dr Brand said, 'I'm also very pleased to announce that we are going to make this procedure available to as many humans as we can.' A dozen questions were shouted at her all at once, and she held up her hands. 'I will answer as many of your questions as I can, and my associates will be available during your tours to take your questions as well. Additionally, information on the adaptation procedure will be provided in the précis that you'll receive later today.'

'I thought you said the procedure wasn't one hundred percent safe,' one reporter called.

Dr Brand nodded. 'It is not. I must be honest with you. We were working very hard to save Reese's and David's lives when we operated on them, and for that reason we did not record everything as precisely as we would have in a controlled environment. Therefore, we are not going to make this procedure widely available just yet. First we will issue a call for volunteer test subjects. Those subjects will need to consider the potential risks very carefully. We do anticipate that some tests will not be successful, but we hope that the number of failures will be few.'

'By "failure", what exactly do you mean?'

'I mean,' Dr Brand answered soberly, 'that we do expect some test subjects to die.'

A thrum of tension rippled through the audience. 'How many?' a reporter asked.

'We don't know. We believe the fatality rate will be low. But we cannot be sure – not until we have done more tests.' Dr Brand shifted in place and glanced at David and Reese again. 'We believe that the successful test subjects will be between the ages of thirteen and eighteen. Adolescent brains are very different than adult brains, because adult brains have become specialized. In fact, the younger the subjects are the better, but we will not undertake testing on children. That is against our principles.'

'You're going to do this to teenagers?' said an astonished journalist.

'We will only take volunteers. We believe there will be teens who are in situations where the potential for risking their lives makes sense. For example, teens who are suffering a life-threatening illness.'

'How will you find these teens?'

'We are working carefully to construct an application. We will let you know when it's ready.'

Akiya Deyir stood and Dr Brand moved aside so that he could approach the podium again. 'Thank you, Evelyn. As Evelyn said, further information about the adaptation procedure will be made available to you later today. Perhaps in the interest of time, we could move on from this subject for now. Does anyone have other questions?'

'What about Amber Gray?' one reporter asked. 'She was shot in that video, but she seems perfectly healthy now, only two weeks later. Did she use this chamber thing?'

Reese saw Amber raise her head to seek out the member of the audience who had asked the question, but it was Dr Brand who answered it.

She returned to the microphone and said, 'Our medical sciences are more advanced than yours. We operated on Amber after she was shot, but we also heal more quickly than humans. One of the prime advantages of making the adaptation procedure available to humans in the future is this lifesaving ability to heal.'

As Dr Brand sat down, Deyir asked, 'More questions?'

'In the video, it looked like Amber Gray saved Reese Holloway from getting shot, and then Amber appeared at the press conference in front of the Holloway house. What is Amber Gray's role in all this?'

Reese remembered that the press gathered here didn't know what she had told Sophia Curtis about Amber, because that interview hadn't aired yet.

'Amber is a unique member of our Earth-based team,' Deyir answered. 'She is Evelyn's daughter, and unlike the rest of us, she was born here on Earth. Her role was to contact Reese after her return from the adaptation procedure and make sure that she was healing properly. Any other questions?'

An excited murmur rose from the reporters, and one said, 'We want to hear from Amber herself. Can she tell us what she did to contact Reese? Did she see that bullet coming?'

Amber sat very still, making no move to stand. For one instant, she glanced at Reese, who tensed up.

'I'm afraid Amber will not be speaking to you today,' Deyir said with an apologetic smile. 'She has undergone a major ordeal herself, and she won't be making any public statements. Do you have any other questions?'

Reese let out her breath in relief. A buzz of frustration rose from the reporters in the audience around her, but it didn't take them long to refocus.

'You said that you had a misunderstanding with the US government. Can you say more about that?'

'I'm afraid not,' Deyir said. 'We are currently discussing the situation with your government and we don't want to disrupt that process. We'll let you know more details when we can, but I want to assure you that we believe we can move forward from this and form a solid and mutually beneficial relationship.'

'Are you behind the global phenomena of UFOs?'

'There are far too many UFOs reported for us to be the cause of them all,' Deyir answered. 'It may be that some sightings were of our ships, but I estimate that is a very small percentage.'

One of the reporters shouted out a question that caused the whole crowd to fall silent: "Why do you look like us?'

The ambassador stood still for a long moment, considering the question. 'For millennia – many more millennia than humans have known – we have been seeking answers to questions about our origins. The only thing we have learned for sure is that even we cannot know everything. We are born; we live our lives; we die. As individuals, we will never know – not truly – what we were before we were born. We cannot know if our consciousness was created during our gestation, or if it existed previously, scattered among the dust of the stars. We cannot know what happens to us after we die. There are places we are unable to walk, things we are unable to know.

'One of the things we have been unable to determine – that we will likely never be able to know – is the exact nature of how our species came into existence. We can approximate, of course. Some of your own theories about the origins of life are similar to ours. We can talk about proteins and amino acids or chemical stews or bacteria traveling the universe in asteroids. All of these – or perhaps none of these – are possibilities. What we do know from our travels throughout the universe and our research over time is that life, whenever and wherever it emerges, is always a miracle. The odds are stacked against it. Though we have found other life-forms – small, single-cellular organisms are plentiful – there are very, very few intelligent species out there. We have found evidence that others have existed, that they came into being and flourished and disappeared. We know that we are not the first, and we will not be the last. We know that life turns in a cycle, just as it does for each individual. Each species, each civilization is born, it flourishes, and it dies.'

Akiya Deyir looked out at the audience seated in front of him and smiled a thin, strange smile. 'So, the answer to your question, I'm afraid, may not be very satisfying, but it is the truth. As Evelyn said, there is no coincidence. The fact that we have found you humans; the fact that you look like us; that we could be your siblings – it is a miracle. And we are grateful for it.'

CHAPTER 10

In order to tour the Imrian ship, everyone at the press conference was divided into groups of six, and each group of six was packed into a long SUV to make the five-minute drive from the visitors' center to the landing spot. Reese, David, and their parents were ushered into the first vehicle, bypassing even Senator Michaelson, and their guide was Dr Brand. It was clear that the Imria were trying to make Reese and David feel special. Akiya Deyir greeted them personally before handing them off to Dr Brand, but Reese was wary of them both. She noticed that neither attempted to shake her or David's hand, though they did shake their parents' hands when they were offered. She didn't know what she would have done if they had tried to touch her. She was nervous about their ability to sense what she was feeling, and she wasn't sure if she could block them.

Most of the brief drive was along a wide, paved road with spectacular views of the bay on the right, but the final descent to Camp Reynolds – the abandoned nineteenth-century army post where, Dr Brand explained, there was enough room to land the large spacecraft – was down a bumpy, gravelly road that probably hadn't seen this much traffic in years. Through the SUV windows, Reese caught flashes of the giant ship in the spaces between pale yellow farmhouse-style buildings. Reese was the first to climb out of the SUV at the bottom of the road, and when she opened the door, the triangular ship was crouched on the ground scarcely fifty feet away from her. Its dull black walls rose smoothly into the sky, and even this close, she couldn't see any seams or windows. The shorter end of the triangle took up the entire width of the upper portion of the field, which sloped downhill toward the bay, and the nose of the ship pointed at the water like a giant arrow. Boarded-up, whitewashed buildings lined the left side of the field, dwarfed by the vast ship, and the juxtaposition of the nineteenth-century houses with the futuristic spacecraft was jarring. Reese felt as if she were trapped between times: the human past on the left, the alien future poised to swallow it on the right.

A ramp descended from the rear of the craft, and Dr Brand headed toward the ship. 'Please follow me,' she said.

Reese knew the media was obsessed with guessing how futuristic the spaceship would be, and Julian had pestered her with dozens of theories of his own. As she stepped onto the metal ramp, she thought, *This must be the future.* Her anticipation, though, was laced with trepidation. She also remembered the way the spaceship had moved, silent and fast, a black shark in the sky. It was frighteningly far beyond human technology, and here she was, walking deliberately into the belly of the beast.

The ramp led into a bare, utilitarian space; the floor rang

hollowly beneath Dr Brand's heels. All along the walls, clear plastic cases held silent erim, their eyeless heads unnervingly motionless. Reese felt the collective shock that passed through her and David's parents as they saw the robotic soldiers.

'Don't worry,' Dr Brand said. 'These are erim, our soldiers, but they are not active right now. They would not harm you.'

'They shot the Blue Base soldiers,' Reese blurted out. 'I saw them die.'

'They did not die,' Dr Brand said in surprise.

'I saw them get shot too,' David said.

'The weapons that the erim fire are not guns like the ones your soldiers used.' Dr Brand went to one of the cases, and when the plastic slid open, she removed the snub-nosed weapon attached to the erim's side. 'This is our equivalent of a stun gun,' Dr Brand explained. 'I cannot fire it myself. If I did, I would collapse. Only the erim can fire it because it emits a charge that disables biological organisms.'

'How long does it disable them?' David asked.

'For several hours. They would have awakened in perfect health, though they would be a bit groggy at first.'

'So the Blue Base soldiers are alive?' Reese said.

'As far as I know. They may have been injured by the explosion, but not by our erim.' Dr Brand replaced the weapon, and the door slid shut. She gestured toward the hatch in the wall that led into the interior of the ship. 'Shall we begin the tour?'

Through the hatch was a short steel corridor – an air lock, Dr Brand explained – that opened into a triangular atrium at least three stories high. Overhead, perforated steel walkways crossed the open space, creating a star pattern through which white light shone. Glass-and-steel balconies wrapped around the atrium, and on the bottom level – where Reese and the others were standing – was a floating globe that looked exactly like the Earth. It was suspended in midair with no visible support.

'This ship is built for interplanetary travel,' Dr Brand said as she crossed the atrium. 'So there are no real luxuries here; everything is made to serve a purpose. The lights here simulate sunlight, as there are no windows on this craft.' She paused next to the globe. 'This is a three-dimensional map that can show your Earth, our home planet, or anywhere else in the universe, depending on where we're traveling. Currently you see the Earth.'

Reese walked across the floor – it was covered in slate-gray tiles that absorbed the sound of their footsteps – and stared at the globe. Clouds moved slowly across the surface, and she could make out the ridges of mountains running down the spines of the continents. 'How does this work?' she asked, her voice sounding hushed in the multistory atrium. 'It's just hanging there.'

'It's a holographic projection,' Dr Brand said.

Reese caught David's eye as he followed Dr Brand across the atrium. He grinned slightly. 'Way better than three-D,' he whispered in Reese's ear as he passed her.

Dr Brand left the atrium through an archway, entering a corridor with dark, metallic walls. Tiny white lights ran along the seams at the top and bottom. They passed sealed doorways on either side, and came to another brightly lit triangular atrium that had a globe hovering in the center. 'This is our home planet,' Dr Brand said. 'Kurra.'

It was very similar to Earth, with blue oceans and white clouds, but the shapes of the landmasses were different. There were few giant continents; instead there were many smaller islands scattered across the blue.

'Here is my home island,' Dr Brand said, indicating a landmass shaped like a crescent. Several dots of light shone along the edges of the island. 'Makkas.'

'It's beautiful,' Reese's mom said.

Dr Brand smiled – a real, genuine smile – and Reese suddenly recognized Amber's face in her. 'It is,' Dr Brand said. 'At this time of year, all the flowers are in bloom, and our artisans make perfume from the blossoms to scent our homes during the rainy season.' She turned away and headed toward the corridor. 'If you'll follow me, I'll take you to the bridge first.'

They went down another corridor that ended in a locked hatch. Dr Brand pressed her hand to the door and it opened into a small, round room with matte metallic walls and a shiny black floor. Once they were all inside, the door slid shut again and the room began to rise.

'The ship has three levels,' Dr Brand explained. 'The first level is for common spaces – the dining hall, recreation areas, and the kitchen, as well as ship administration. Level two is for labs and offices. The third level contains all sleeping quarters and private spaces, but it's also where the ship's bridge is accessed. This elevator goes directly to the bridge first, and after you've seen that we'll proceed back down to the first level.'

When the elevator came to a stop, the doors slid open to reveal a triangular room with a circular table at its center. The table's surface was a hard, polished black, and above it another globe was suspended. This one showed a star system, hovering like a tiny spherical universe in midair. A man who was seated at the table slid his hand across the surface, and Reese noticed something flicker out of sight, as if a computer screen had been shut off.

'Welcome,' the man said, standing to greet them. He had light brown skin and dark hair, and he was dressed in what looked like a flight suit made out of black synthetic material that resembled scuba gear.

'This is Hirin Sagal,' Dr Brand said, 'the captain of our ship.'

'It is a pleasure to meet you,' Sagal said.

He reminded Reese of Malcolm Todd. They had similar features – sharp cheekbones and an angular jaw leading to a pointed chin.

Dr Brand went to the table and touched the surface. A light shimmered beneath her hand, and the two facing walls rippled to show the entire vista of San Francisco Bay, just like a window. 'This is an image of the view outside,' Dr Brand said.

The image was so crystal clear that Reese had to walk right up to it to convince herself it wasn't a real window made of glass. She saw sailboats on the bay, the sunlight glittering over the brownish-gray water, and Sausalito in the distance.

'Is this table a computer?' David asked.

'Yes,' Dr Brand said.

'How does it work? There are no keyboards. Is there a screen?'

The captain answered, 'The surface can become either, if you wish. But typically we issue commands to the computer via touch and neural instruction.'

'You mean through thinking?' David said.

Reese joined them at the circular table as Sagal called up a display in the surface that showed a diagram of the ship. There were tiny blips in the nose of the triangle that Reese realized must represent the eight of them in the bridge.

'It is done through thought, yes,' Dr Brand said, coming to stand beside Reese. 'Voice commands may also be used, but of course, not in English.' She said something in Imrian and the windows darkened, returning to blank metallic walls.

'The thought commands – how are they relayed to the computer?' David's father asked.

'It is similar to the way we share consciousness. The computer surface,' Dr Brand said, indicating the table, 'receives our instructions via touch.'

'If I touch the table can I make it do something?' Reese asked, leaning over the image of the ship.

Sagal stepped toward her and she withdrew her hand. 'I would not recommend it,' he said.

'It does require a certain amount of control,' Dr Brand said. 'I don't believe your thought processes are focused enough yet. Most humans have quite chaotic thought patterns because they're not accustomed to sharing them with others. But even our children, when they are young, do not have control over their thoughts, and until they learn that control, they use voice commands. A confused thought pattern simply won't work.'

'How do they learn to control their thought patterns?' Reese asked.

'We teach them,' Dr Brand said. 'And we would like to teach you as well. That is the reason we've invited you here today. After we finish our tour I'll bring you to meet the teacher who can show you how to use your adaptation.'

Despite her distrust of the Imria, Reese was intrigued. As they followed Dr Brand out of the bridge for the rest of the tour, David brushed against her. *You want to do the lessons, don't you?* he thought.

I don't know yet. Do you?

We'll see.

She caught Dr Brand's eye, and she realized that Dr Brand knew she and David were communicating with each other. She moved away from David, feeling as if she had been caught passing notes in class. 'Where are we going now?' she asked out loud.

'I thought you'd like to see our living quarters,' Dr Brand said.

The third level of the ship, beyond the bridge, had the same general layout as the first floor: long corridors lit with white lights along the seams, punctuated by the two triangular atriums. Reese reached out and touched the walls curiously; they looked like steel but felt like a dense, slightly warm plastic. The doors they passed had tiny glowing codes above them in symbols that Reese could not read. She guessed they were Imrian letters and numbers. Dr Brand stopped outside one of those doors and pressed her fingertip to a nearly hidden latch that caused the door to open with a whoosh.

Only a few of them at a time could enter the small room. When it was Reese's turn, she was captivated by the design of the compact space. She wanted to explore it slowly and figure out how each tiny shelf or folding object worked. There were panels in the wall that expanded at the touch of a finger into what appeared to be a desk. There was a bunk that descended like a Murphy bed, but Dr Brand demonstrated that it could also be made into a couch. On the wall opposite the door, a screen displayed a view of the boarded-up buildings outside. 'All the screens are calibrated to show the view as if it were seen through a real window,' Dr Brand said.

David's father was asking about the camera systems – where they were mounted, why they couldn't be seen on the outside of the ship – but Reese was more fascinated by the devices that emerged from the wall over the desk. There were numerous cubbyholes and drawers that slid out like puzzle pieces. David smiled at her as she ran her fingers along the wall, opening and closing bins and drawers. 'Having fun?' he said.

'You could be so well organized in this place,' she said, and then colored slightly when she heard what she'd said.

He laughed. 'You're a little OCD, aren't you?'

She made a face at him.

Afterward, Dr Brand took them down to the dining hall on the first level. In the center of the room, a floor-to-ceiling-length cylinder made of perforated clear plastic was full of plant life. Dr Brand explained that this cylinder was one of several that existed to help filter the air in the ship. It ran all the way up to the third level; on the second level it was in the center of a research lab; on the third it was in the captain's quarters. All around the cylinder were curved dining tables with benches affixed to the floor. Along one wall was a serving table that resembled a cafeteria-style buffet. There was no food laid out, but at one end Reese saw a coffee urn and a stack of cups, along with a sugar bowl and a carafe of what had to be cream.

'You drink coffee?' she said, surprised. It seemed so ordinary. She'd been expecting – or maybe hoping for – strange alien beverages.

Dr Brand smiled. 'I don't, personally. It's for our guests today. Would you like some?'

'Sure,' she said. The cups were a bit unusual – they were made of some kind of insulated plastic with ridged grips on the side rather than a handle – but the coffee tasted disappointingly normal.

Finally, Dr Brand took them to the front of the triangular ship, directly below the bridge. When Reese stepped through the door at the end of the corridor, she understood that this was the whole point of the tour. The room was triangular in shape, and every wall was covered with a floor-to-ceiling screen like the ones that simulated windows, but these did not display the view. They were filled with graduated blue light, dark at the bottom and pale near the ceiling. It was like being in an aquarium. In the center of the room were three seats carved out of dark wood in a shape reminiscent of ocean waves, and the person who was seated in one of them rose when Reese and David entered.

'This is Eres Tilhar,' Dr Brand said. 'Eres is an *ummi*, a teacher.'

Eres was pale-skinned and had white hair cut close to the head, like a cap of feathers. At first Reese thought that Eres was male, but as Eres approached, Reese realized she couldn't tell for sure. Eres wore a long dove-gray robe that looked like something a priest would wear, open down the front to reveal a suit similar to the captain's, except in gray. There were no lines in Eres's ageless face, but the gray eyes that studied Reese and David had a quality of experience that made it clear the teacher had not been born yesterday.

'Welcome,' Eres said. 'Evelyn has told me so much about you.' Eres's voice had the same slight accent that Akiya Deyir had; there was a softness on the Rs that reminded Reese of Spanish. Reese still could not discern Eres's gender, and that flustered her.

Eres reached out to take their hands. There was something commanding about the teacher's gesture, and Reese could not refuse. When she touched Eres's hand, all of Reese's awareness seemed to sharpen, as if the lens of her own inner eye had focused. She inhaled in surprise as Eres's consciousness directed what she could sense.

Eres's mind was like a great oak tree, ancient and broad-reaching, and Reese understood that Eres had been alive for a long time. Centuries. Visions of time passing flitted through Reese's mind: an ocean pulling grains of white sand away from an alien shore; wind scouring the surface of a mountain with stone the color of deep purple; roots burrowing through layer upon layer of moist, dark soil, shifting the earth with their slow, steady motion. And yet Reese did not feel overwhelmed by the vastness of Eres's awareness; she felt safe. Eres was a strong pilot, and Reese would not become lost when Eres was guiding her.

It was instantly clear to Reese that she had barely scratched the surface of the adaptation that the Imria had given her. The connection she had with David was only in its infancy, and in order for her to understand how to use this ability, she had to allow Eres to teach her. There was no other way, and the simplicity of her decision was a relief.

Eres let her go gently, but Reese swayed on her feet as the contact ceased. The lingering trace of Eres's touch still pulsed through her like a bright light. She saw things more clearly now. It was as if cobwebs she had never known existed had been swept from her brain. She watched a tremor pass through David's body as Eres let go of his hand too.

'It is my hope,' Eres said, 'that the two of you will return here and allow me to teach you how to use your abilities. Will you return?'

Reese didn't need to discuss it with David to know that he wanted to do this as much as she did. 'Yes,' she said.

'Yes,' David said.

Eres Tilhar did not seem surprised.

CHAPTER 11

Amber was waiting at the visitors' center when Reese, David, and their parents returned from the ship with Dr Brand. She was still sitting in the chair where she had sat during the press conference, and when she looked up, seeking out Reese, she had an anxious expression on her face. She stood, smoothing out her dress, and headed toward Reese. There were about a half dozen reporters still in the area, waiting for their turn to tour the ship, and Reese noticed them swivel around to watch as Amber approached. She was wearing black patent leather pumps with her gray sheath dress, and the heels left little holes in the lawn as she walked. Reese's chest tightened as Amber came to a stop a few feet away.

'Hi, Reese,' she said.

'Hi,' Reese said. She felt as if she were bracing herself for something bad.

Her mom touched her arm. 'Honey, we're going with Dr Brand to talk to the ferry captain about getting you and David here for those lessons, okay? We'll be back in a bit.'

'Okay,' Reese said.

'Nice to see you again, Amber,' her mom said as she was leaving.

Amber's cheeks reddened. 'Nice to see you too.'

Reese, Amber, and David stood in awkward silence as their parents left.

'So you're going to meet with Eres Tilhar?' Amber said.

'Yeah,' Reese said. She wasn't touching David but she could tell by the way he was standing, his body slightly turned away from Amber, that he wasn't eager to talk to her.

'That's good,' Amber said. 'Eres is a great teacher. I'm glad you decided to do it.'

Reese didn't say anything. She was waiting for Amber to get to the point.

'Reese, can I talk to you? Alone?' Amber smiled apologetically at David. 'Would you mind?'

David gave a brief shrug. 'It's not up to me.'

The smile on Amber's face faltered. 'Of course not. I just meant—'

'Why can't you talk to me here?' Reese asked.

'Please. Just for a few minutes. Walk with me down to the cove.' She gave Reese a pleading look.

Despite her defensiveness, Reese was curious. 'Fine,' she said finally. She glanced at David. 'I'll be right back.'

'Thank you,' Amber said, sounding grateful.

Reese started down the path toward the cove, and Amber had to hurry to keep up. 'What do you want to talk about?' Reese asked.

'I know you're still angry with me,' Amber began.

Reese shook her head. 'That's a funny way to put it.'

'You're not angry?'

'Of course I'm angry,' Reese snapped. She lowered her voice as they passed the reporters, who were still watching them. 'So what?' she added in a whisper.

'I want to apologize,' Amber said softly.

'You already did that.'

'But you don't believe me.' Amber sounded miserable.

'What does it matter if I believe you?'

A flash of desperation passed over Amber's face. 'Because we're going to have to see each other here. And I can't stand it if you hate me.'

You should have thought of that a lot earlier, Reese wanted to say, but she bit off the words and looked away. They were already at the edge of the lawn, and the asphalt path curved around the cove directly in front of them. If they turned right they'd head toward the dock, and Reese didn't want to run into her parents, so she turned left, skirting the edge of the water. Amber's heels clicked on the pavement as they walked. At the end of the path was a bench overlooking the water, and Reese sat down. They were still in full view of the visitors' center, and if she looked back she knew she'd see David waiting there. Amber sat on the other end of the bench and crossed her legs. Her shoes gleamed in the sunlight, but there was a clump of dirt on the right heel.

'I've had to lie my entire life,' Amber said quietly.

Reese kept her gaze on the water so that she didn't have to look at Amber. 'Is that an excuse?'

'No,' Amber said sharply. More softly, she continued, 'That's not what I'm saying. I'm trying to explain why I lied to you. I was born here, but for as long as I can remember, my mother warned me not to tell anyone about us. I slipped up too many times before I really understood what she meant, and we had to leave Earth for a while.'

'When?'

'I was five. We went back to Kurra for several years, until I was old enough to – to lie properly.' She paused, and Reese finally let herself look at Amber. She seemed sad, her eyes cast down to her lap. 'I went to middle school in Arizona and I didn't tell anyone who I really was. Nobody knew. It was . . . lonely.'

'You never told anyone? Not even – did you have friends?'

Amber gave Reese a tiny smile. 'Yeah. I had a best friend, but I didn't tell her. I wish I could have. I really do.'

It was said so simply, with such raw emotion, that Reese was taken aback.

'When I was fourteen, we had to go back to Kurra,' Amber continued. 'Every fifteenth birthday is sort of a big deal for us, so I stayed on Kurra until after I turned fifteen. When we returned to Earth, I went to a private school in Massachusetts. I didn't tell anyone there, either. By then it had become sort of normal for me. Like, I had this life at school, and it didn't have anything to do with my mom's work. I could pretend I was totally human, you know? Like I was actually going to apply to colleges and worry about financial aid and figure out what I wanted to major in. But none of it was real.' Amber sighed and looked out at the cove. The sunlight made her blond hair glow.

Reese wanted to be angry at her, but she found herself feeling sorry for her instead. She sounded so wistful.

‘And then when I met you, I knew I had to keep lying,’ Amber said. ‘It was understood that I would. It’s what I’ve been trained to do.’ She turned back to Reese. ‘I’m sorry. I don’t blame you for being angry with me. But I wanted to explain to you why I did what I did.’

Reese felt the tightness in her chest again, as if her heart was straining against her rib cage. ‘I told Sophia Curtis that you lied.’

Amber blinked. ‘The TV journalist?’

‘Yes. David and I had an interview with her. It airs this weekend. She asked if I knew you, and I told her that you were sent to keep an eye on us. And that you didn’t tell us who you were.’

Amber considered Reese for a minute. ‘Did you tell her anything else about us?’

Heat spread over Reese’s skin. She suddenly remembered leaning over the table at the Indian restaurant on Valencia Street, kissing Amber in full view of the other patrons. ‘No,’ Reese said, her throat feeling constricted. ‘I didn’t tell her anything else.’

Reese couldn’t read the expression on Amber’s face. Was it dismay or acceptance? All she said was “Okay.’ She lowered her gaze again, and Reese noticed she was wearing purple-gray eye shadow, the exact color of a bruise. Her lips trembled for one second, a movement so small that Reese saw it only because she was staring.

Amber said, ‘I’m really glad you’re talking to Eres Tilhar. She taught me when I was little.’

The change of subject left Reese momentarily disoriented.

One word hung in the air between them. 'She? Is Eres Tilhar a woman?'

Puzzlement flashed across Amber's face, then cleared. 'I forgot, Eres must look different to you. Eres is *ummi*, a teacher. Teachers are not male or female. They're . . . *ummi*.'

Reese thought back to her conversations with Bri last year when she had been on her gender theory kick. 'You mean she's – he's – Eres is a third gender?'

Amber seemed to struggle for a moment to find the right words. 'I guess you could say that ummi is kind of a third gender, but it's more like gender doesn't matter to ummi; it's no longer relevant to them.'

'But you called Eres "she". Should I do that too?'

'I doubt Eres cares what English pronouns you use. I used "she" because you have to use pronouns in English and it's easier to say "she" than "it", which sounds awful. Sometimes I call Eres "he", though.' Amber's forehead wrinkled in thought. 'I guess it depends on what Eres is wearing. She's not always in her *ummi* uniform.'

'Isn't that totally offensive?' Reese asked. Bri had drummed into her that she should never assume which pronoun someone preferred. 'Shouldn't you ask Eres which pronoun she or he wants to use?'

Amber seemed a little amused. 'You can ask if you want. But it's not like that. I mean, *ummi* are basically beyond that stuff. They spend their time teaching *susum'urda*, which means they're in other people's consciousness a lot. It's kind of like they've experienced so many other lives that they've become all different genders.'

Reese tried to wrap her mind around what Amber had said, but she was still fixated on how to refer to Eres Tilhar. 'So in Imrian, what pronoun do you use with Eres?'

Amber paused as if realizing something. 'Actually, in Imrian there is no *him* or *her*. The pronouns in Imrian are gender-neutral. *Ene* means *him* or *her*.'

'How do you know if you're talking about a man or a woman?'

'Usually you know who you're talking about. You use their names.'

'But if you don't know their names when you're talking about them, how do you know if they're male or female?'

Amber gave her a funny look, as if Reese wasn't getting it. 'It doesn't matter.'

Reese's forehead furrowed. 'All of you, except for Eres Tilhar, are so obviously male or female. If it doesn't matter, why don't you all look like Eres?'

Now Amber seemed perplexed. 'Eres is *ummi*; all *ummi* look sort of like her. They wear the same kind of clothes, the same – they're sort of like monks, I guess. Except they're not celibate. The rest of us wouldn't look like *ummi*; that would be like you dressing up like a priest.'

'Okay.' That part made sense to Reese. 'So the rest of the Imria – the ones who aren't *ummi* – does gender matter to them? If there's no *him* or *her* in Imrian . . . I guess I don't understand how that would work.'

Amber considered Reese for a long moment, as if trying to make up her mind about something. Finally she said, 'Well, language is only one part of this. There are other languages that also use gender-neutral pronouns – like Chinese. In spoken Chinese, there's no audible distinction between *him* and *her*. You can work around it. Does that make sense?'

'I guess.'

'Okay. So then . . .' Amber flashed her a tentative smile. 'You know that sex and gender are different things, right?'

Reese raised her eyebrows. 'You mean biological sex, like male or female, versus gender?'

'Exactly. Biologically, sex is about whether you create eggs or sperm – that's all. Gender is about everything else. The way you dress, the way you move, the way you act. Among humans, gender is usually correlated with sex, so women are supposed to look a certain way, like wear dresses and heels or whatever.'

'But there are also transgender people,' Reese said. 'And other people who don't follow those norms. It's not that simple.'

Amber nodded. 'Yes, absolutely. I'm talking about generally. Generally, humans understand gender as an expression of sex, even though that is changing in some places. But Imrians don't have a similar concept of gender.'

Reese thought about what Amber had said. One element still puzzled her. 'Is there biological sex among the Imria?'

'Oh, yes. Imrians are still male or female, in the most basic biological sense.'

'So why don't you have gender?'

Amber looked thoughtful. 'I think . . . you know, I've never explained this to anyone before. I think it's because of *susum'urda*. Male and female Imrians still have different physical bodies, and you can never escape that, but *susum'urda* allows you to see that the physical differences are really superficial when it comes to who you are as a person.'

Reese remembered what it had felt like when Eres Tilhar touched her: a kind of boundlessness. Whether or not the teacher had male or female body parts had been the farthest thing from Reese's mind. 'All right, I think I can see that,' Reese said. 'But if *susum'urda* sort of erases the importance of gender, why do you all look like men or women? Maybe you don't look like Eres Tilhar because you're not *ummi*, but you totally look gendered.' She gestured at Amber's outfit.

Amber shifted and the hem of her dress inched up. 'We're trying to make ourselves intelligible to humans.' She gave Reese a nervous smile. 'Can you imagine how weirded out all of humanity would be if you couldn't tell whether we were men or women? So we dress like human men or women. It's easier to fit in that way. Like . . . if you were going to visit a foreign country and you didn't want to stick out like an American tourist, you'd avoid wearing shorts and white sneakers.'

'What about when you're not here on Earth?'

'Well, there are definitely . . . styles of presentation. There's an Imrian word for it: *ga'emen*. I guess that's the closest we come to gender. Someone's *ga'emen* is their external identity, but it's not connected to their biological sex. It's just an external expression of their self. Like in all those movies about high schools, where people are nerds or jocks or stoners or whatever.' Amber spread her hands. 'Except *ga'emen* is a lot more complicated than that, but it's a start.'

Reese glanced at Amber; her gray eyes reflected the color of the bay. 'What would you look like if you weren't on Earth?'

Amber seemed taken aback. 'I'd look like me.'

Reese wanted to ask, *And who is that?* During their date at the Indian restaurant, they had talked about coming out and being queer. Amber had seemed very certain of who she was, but something she had just said about *susum'urda* raised a question for Reese. 'If sharing consciousness lets you see that physical differences are so minor, how come you said you don't like guys?'

Amber's cheeks turned a little pink. 'You can't escape your body. I mean, you live in it every day. And I like female bodies.' She shrugged. 'Maybe it would be different on Kurra. But I'm here, not there.' She bent down and brushed the clump of dirt off the heel of her right shoe. Amber's fingernails were painted silver, and they flashed in the sun. 'Does that make sense?' Amber asked, straightening up. 'All of it?'

There was something vulnerable in Amber's gaze, and Reese remembered the reason Amber had wanted to talk with her alone, before they had been sidetracked by Reese's questions about Eres Tilhar. Amber had tried to explain why she had lied. Reese looked away. The water of the bay sparkled beneath the cloud-scudded sky, and in the distance a ferry was chugging away from Tiburon. 'Yeah, I guess,' Reese said reluctantly. 'It's complicated.'

They sat together in silence for a long moment, and Reese felt herself tensing up, muscle by muscle, every second that Amber didn't respond. Finally Amber slid across the bench toward her. 'Reese,' Amber said gently.

Being so close to Amber set off every single alarm in Reese's body. 'What?' she said stiffly.

'I'm glad we talked. I hope – I want you to know that I'm really sorry about what happened and I just hope you don't hate me.'

Reese's heart seemed to twist inside her, as if someone were squeezing it in their fist. She looked down at the ground, at the pebbles embedded in the gray concrete, at the toe of Amber's shoe and the curve of her ankle. 'I don't hate you,' Reese said.

'You don't?' Amber's voice was tiny.

Reese turned to face her. Amber looked brittle, as if a word from Reese could shatter her. 'No. I don't hate you. But I don't trust you, either. You lied to me about a big, big thing. It's not only that you hid who you are – you hid who *I* was. You knew what had happened to me and you didn't tell me. We can't just be friends now.'

Amber went pale. 'I know. I know, I'm not saying that.'

'Good.' Reese stood up. She couldn't sit there anymore. She was brimful of anxiousness and fear and a desire to just look at Amber, and that was what frightened Reese the most. 'Then you know where we stand.' Reese forced herself to walk away, putting one foot in front of the other, leaving Amber behind.

CHAPTER 12

David arrived at Reese's house at five thirty on Friday night. When the doorbell rang, Reese was staring at her reflection in the bathroom mirror, debating whether her new outfit made her look cool or like she was trying too hard. She ran downstairs to open the front door before her parents got there. She had half expected David to be waiting on the front step with a corsage in a plastic box, and when she saw he was only holding his car keys, she was relieved. His gaze swept down her legs and back up to her face.

'Nice boots,' he said with a grin that made her feel tingly all over.

'Thanks.' She was about to leave the house when her parents came down the hall.

'Hang on, Reese. You're not even going to let us say hi to David?' her mom admonished her.

Reese sighed and stepped back, crossing her arms. 'We have to go,' she said.

Her mom's eyebrows rose. 'Oh, really?' She looked at David. 'You know you're only allowed to go to dinner and the party.

Nothing else. She needs to be back by midnight.'

David smiled a parent-friendly smile, and Reese swallowed an urgent need to giggle. 'Of course, Ms Sheridan. No problem.'

Reese's dad was right behind her mom and he added, 'Reese, you have your phone?'

'Yes, Dad.'

It had taken her quite a while to argue her way into having this night without their supervision. She had to give them the addresses of the restaurant they were going to as well as Eric Chung's house. Her winning argument, though, came from an unexpected source. After their visit to Angel Island yesterday, Agent Forrestal was waiting at Fisherman's Wharf. He told them that due to the gunman's attack, the government had decided that Reese and David would be better off with a security detail.

'You're already following us,' Reese pointed out.

'And now you'll know it's for your own safety,' Agent Forrestal said.

She wasn't happy about the development, but it did ultimately convince her parents – and David's – that they should be allowed one night without parental supervision.

She grabbed her jacket and left the house, following David down the steps to his blue Honda. As she buckled her seat belt, he started the engine and pulled away from the curb. 'They're both following us now,' he said.

She twisted around in her seat and saw two champagne-colored sedans merge into the street behind them: David's security detail, which had followed him to her house, and her own. She and David had agreed it was useless to try to prevent the men in black from tailing them to the meeting with Charles Lovick. They didn't know how, for one thing, and both of them thought it might be better if they were followed there, anyway. They had no idea what Lovick was going to do. Reese had looked him up on the Internet and learned that he was a board member at Allied Research Associates, the multinational conglomerate that owned EC&R. That was the government contractor that had managed Project Blue Base – and manufactured the listening devices Reese had found in the walls of her house. There had been little else about him online, but it had been enough to make Reese wonder if she and David were walking straight into the lion's den by going to this meeting. Nevertheless, their need to know what Lovick wanted to tell them trumped her hesitation.

The sedans followed them all the way downtown. The 88 Variety Store was on the edge of Chinatown, so David parked in the Sutter-Stockton Garage, a multistory parking structure a few blocks away. One of the sedans turned into the garage after them, but the other did not. Reese thought the men in black might wind up in the same elevator as her and David, but the doors closed before they made it.

Outside, the fog had already crept in, and the air was chilly and damp. Reese zipped up her jacket and stuffed her hands in the pockets as she and David hurried north on Stockton. The street tunneled through a hill at the end of the block, and at the mouth of the echoing tunnel, Reese and David entered the stairwell to climb up to the overpass. A gust of wind blew exhaust fumes at her, and she tried to breathe through her mouth. The stairwell was lit by fluorescent bulbs that cast the dirty corners in harsh relief. On the landing halfway up a sign read THIS AREA UNDER SURVEILLANCE. As they went up the second flight, she saw the video camera mounted on the wall above. She wondered if the men in black had access to that footage.

When they emerged from the stairwell, she gulped in a deep breath of fresh, misty air. They had to trudge uphill past the Ritz-Carlton and then go down a second flight of stairs to get to Chinatown. It was steep, but it beat walking through the tunnel itself, with its noxious air and speeding cars. She glanced over her shoulder as she and David walked, but she didn't see the men in black anywhere. She wondered if they had managed to lose them, and the idea made her uneasy. She wanted witnesses when she and David walked into the 88 Variety Store. She was relieved when they exited the second stairway and she saw one of the sedans waiting for them in a no-parking zone north of the tunnel.

'There they are,' she said.

'And there's the store,' David said.

The 88 Variety Store was wedged between an herbal shop and a store selling Chinatown knickknacks. Its sign was faded and one of the number eights was missing, leaving only a grimy outline of where it used to be. Through the single front window, Reese saw cluttered shelves lit dimly by overhead lights. She looked at David.

You ready? she asked him.

He glanced back at the sedan parked half a block away. 'Let's go,' he said, and opened the door.

It knocked against a bell as they entered, but the tinkling

sound didn't quite mask the creaking hinge. The interior of the tiny shop was crammed full of towering shelves stocked haphazardly with plastic colanders and rice bowls and pastel sponges. Reese initially thought the store was empty, but as soon as the door swung shut she heard steps behind her. She spun around to see a tall, broad-shouldered man in a suit positioning himself in front of the door. He had very short hair and his arms seemed too large for the suit, which strained against his muscles.

'Who are you?' she asked, startled.

'Mr Lovick is waiting for you in the back,' the man said. There was something about him – beyond his muscular bulk – that unnerved Reese.

'Come on,' David said, reaching for her arm. His touch startled her, sharpening the sliver of fear that had gone through her at the sight of the large man. David was freaked out too.

She didn't like turning her back on the man at the door, but she had to in order to walk down the narrow aisle toward the back of the store. There was a curtained doorway behind the counter where the cash register was located, and someone pulled the curtain aside as she and David approached. A dark-haired man in black-framed glasses, dressed in a blue oxford shirt with the collar open, stepped into the doorway. 'Come in,' he said, motioning to the room behind the curtain.

Reese and David walked into the store's back office. There were a couple of metal desks pushed against the walls, with stacks of ledgers on them. On the wall across from the curtained entryway was another door, guarded by a second burly man in a suit. In the center of the square room was a round table and four chairs. Three were empty, but a middle-aged man with steel-gray hair sat in the fourth. He was dressed in a black suit and had a hawklike nose and blue eyes that regarded the two of them coolly as they entered the room.

'Please have a seat,' he said. 'I'm Charles Lovick, and this is my colleague Alex Hernandez.' He gestured to the man in glasses, who took the chair next to Lovick.

David and Reese sat down, and Reese noticed their chairs had been placed far enough apart that she couldn't touch David without being obvious. 'What exactly do you want with us?' Reese asked, eyeing Lovick and Hernandez nervously.

A thin smile pulled up the corners of Lovick's mouth, but it wasn't friendly. 'I work for an organization called the Corporation for American Security and Sovereignty. You won't have heard of us.'

'I thought you were on the board of Allied Research Associates,' Reese said.

Lovick seemed impressed by her research. 'I am. But my work at ARA is not what brings me here tonight.'

'What do you do at this corporation?' David asked.

'What I'm about to tell you is highly classified,' Lovick said. 'It is in your best interests to repeat this information to no one.' He adjusted the cuffs of his shirt, and Reese saw the glint of gold cuff links. 'In 1947, when the Imria arrived in the United States, an organization was formed to manage our relationship with them. To make sure that our nation's engagement with the Imria remained consistent regardless of changing presidential administrations. That organization is the Corporation for American Security and Sovereignty. CASS. It is run by a board of seven individuals selected from business, defense, and the like. I joined the board of CASS twelve years ago. We oversee a variety of initiatives, including Project Blue Base, which you became familiar with last month.'

'I thought that was run by EC and R,' Reese said.

Lovick nodded. 'EC and R managed the day-to-day details of Project Blue Base, but ultimately, Blue Base reports to us. Many so-called black operations report to us, not the commander in chief. Unfortunately EC and R – and Blue Base – botched their assignment with regard to the two of you. The task force that was assigned to oversee Blue Base has been replaced. Now that the existence of the Imria has been revealed to the public, our strategy has changed, and I'd like to invite you to work with us.'

'With CASS?' David asked.

'Yes. The two of you have been treated with Imrian science without your consent. They took advantage of you, and I imagine you must have many questions about what the Imrian treatment did to you.'

'They told us it was the only way to save our lives,' Reese said.

'Do you believe them?' Lovick asked, looking directly at her.

Reese tried not to flinch. 'I don't know.'

'And what about you?' Lovick asked David.

David's shoulders stiffened. 'I don't know either.'

Lovick folded his hands on the round table. He wore a fat gold wedding band on his left hand and a black signet ring on his right. 'The Imria can be very, very convincing. When

I first decided that it was imperative that we meet, I knew that I might have a difficult time convincing you to join us. You've had a regrettable experience with Blue Base, and that must color your impression of your government and, by extension, what CASS does for your government. However, yesterday at the press conference on Angel Island, the Imria revealed something that they have kept secret from us for sixty-seven years.

'For nearly seven decades, the Imria have told us that they wanted to research ways to lengthen human lives, to help us become healthier individuals. They said they came to the United States in 1947 because we were the sole remaining stable nation on Earth after World War Two. They flattered us, and we believed them at first. But over the years, it has become increasingly clear that they have been lying about their true purpose in coming here. They have been conducting unauthorized experimentation on human subjects – including the two of you. We have never been able to determine why. Some of us believed that perhaps they were studying us in preparation for an attack.'

'Colonization?' Reese said, remembering the protesters' chants.

Lovick looked irritated. 'That is a popular theory, although I dislike the melodramatic nature of the word. Project Blue Base was one initiative aimed at defending us against a potential Imrian attack. We planned to use their biotechnology against them. And then yesterday at their press conference, they revealed their secret: their ability to share consciousness. They made it sound so wholesome, as if it were the secret to happiness.' There was a deeply sardonic tone to his words. 'Do you know what it really means?' He leaned forward. 'For one thing, adaptation, as they call it, is simply a pretty spin on what amounts to erasure. They say they want to give us this ability, but by changing us – by *adapting* us – they erase our humanity. If we become them, we lose ourselves.'

Reese hadn't thought of it like that before. She wasn't sure if she agreed with him, but his words still sent a chill through her.

'It also means that they have kept this ability of theirs secret from us for sixty-seven years,' Lovick said. 'They have lied directly to us, face-to-face, over and over again. They have told us that they are honest; that they do not keep secrets from us. And yet they clearly do.' He paused and gave each of them a penetrating glance. 'Why would they keep this ability – which they described as foundational to who they are as a people – why would they keep it a secret?'

Reese didn't have an answer for him. Dread made her stomach sink. *Do you believe him?* she thought, hoping David could hear her. *What if he's lying too?* She didn't know if David understood. All she felt was a burst of frustration, and she couldn't tell if it came from him or from within herself.

'I know that the Imria have already offered to help you learn how to use these abilities they've given you. Your *adaptation*,' Lovick continued. 'I know, also, that you have accepted their offer.'

As far as Reese knew, the Imria hadn't said anything about that publicly, so Lovick must have spies.

'But now that you know that the Imria have lied for so long

– and about such a huge thing – how can you trust them to help you?'

'We don't trust them,' Reese burst out. 'But what choice do we have? We don't know how to use this adaptation, and we need to learn how to use it. Otherwise, it's going to drive us crazy.'

Lovick nodded. 'We can also help you.'

'How?' David asked. 'You just said you didn't know about this adaptation until yesterday. How can you do anything?'

'We are not powerless,' Lovick answered smoothly. 'We have decades of our own research into the Imria that we can draw from. But what I am offering you is more than mere training. You should continue with that, because it gives you the chance to use your access to the Imria to help your fellow humans. We only ask that you share the knowledge you gain from them with us.'

'You want us to become spies for you?' Reese asked. The room was warm, and as she gave the guard a surreptitious glance, she felt a bit claustrophobic.

'*Spy* is not the right word,' Lovick objected. 'The two of you have become very important to us.'

'To CASS,' Reese clarified.

'To humanity,' Lovick said. 'You are our bridge to the Imria. You are the only ones who can show us what their sharing of consciousness really means. Is it truly a positive thing? Because it could have serious, dire consequences when it comes to security and intelligence. They may have a special word for it—'

'*Susum'urda*,' Reese said.

'Yes. Do you know what it sounds like to me? Mind reading. Consider what it could mean for an entire race to have the ability to read our minds. Consider your own lives, your families, your nation. You are the only humans who can also do this. Where do your loyalties lie? With your fellow humans, or with these extraterrestrial visitors who have lied to us for nearly seven decades about who they are?'

'What do you want us to do?' Reese asked.

'We want you to proceed with your training. Once you've begun your lessons with the Imria, you can then transmit that information to us.' He gestured to Hernandez. 'Alex Hernandez will be your contact. Beginning on Monday, he'll be teaching at your high school.'

'You'll be able to come to me with your updates at any time,' Hernandez said.

'What is your decision?' Lovick asked.

Reese met Lovick's sharp gaze, and she swallowed. She didn't like him, and she didn't trust him. If only she could touch him, then she would know what he was thinking. It was the first time she had ever thought to use her new ability that way – to purposefully violate another person's mind – and the nerves in her fingertips tingled. She knew it was wrong, but she was so tempted to do it. It would answer so many questions.

'You can't just ask us to decide like that,' David said, startling Reese. 'Can you at least give us a minute to talk about it? Alone?'

'Of course.' Lovick gestured toward the door to the shop. 'You're welcome to step outside to confer. We'll be waiting here.'

Reese got up and followed David through the curtained doorway. He looked at her and held out his hand. She took it while they moved into the narrow space behind the cash register. *We don't even have the option to say no*, Reese thought. *If Hernandez is going to be teaching at our school, he'll be watching us.*

Then we have to agree, David told her. *At least for now, until we know exactly what our adaptation is about. We don't have to tell them everything that we learn.*

You want to lie to them?

His forehead glistened with a light sheen of sweat. Everybody's lying, he thought, and now she knew that the frustration she had felt came from him. *We might as well lie too.*

Then we go with it, she thought. For now.

For now.

They returned to the back room, where Lovick and Hernandez were still seated. The gravity of what she and David were about to do began to hit home, and she rubbed her damp palms against her jean skirt. They didn't trust the Imria, but they certainly didn't trust Charles Lovick and his Corporation for American Security and Sovereignty either. They were on their own. 'Okay,' she said. She glanced at David.

He nodded. 'We'll do it.'

CHAPTER 13

The guard was still blocking the exit when Reese and David emerged from the back office and headed for the door. She was so caught up in thinking over what had just happened and how she and David were going to manage to lie to both the Imria and CASS that she barely noticed that the guard didn't move as they approached. Then he reached out and grabbed her arm.

'Hey!' she cried. His grip was tight on her, and something cold and dark seeped through his fingers into her body. She froze. He was so strong – exactly like that soldier who had manhandled her at Blue Base right before she'd had the medical exam.

This man wasn't looking at her at all. His eyes were focused on the rear of the shop, and Reese heard Lovick call out, 'They're finished. You can let them go.'

The man released her and she fell back, bumping against David. He sensed her sudden disquiet and took her hand. *What happened?*

The guard opened the door and she plunged out into the

cool evening air, her mind whirling as she plowed up the sidewalk, dragging David with her. *That guy was like the soldiers at Blue Base.*

She sensed that he wasn't entirely surprised. *I knew there was something off about them*, he told her.

She barely noticed the chilly mist on the skin of her legs as they walked through Chinatown, hand in hand. She was consumed with the realization that Lovick had Blue Base-made guards acting on his orders. She and David could try to manipulate Lovick and CASS, but the two of them were thoroughly outgunned. *How the hell are we going to pull this off?* she wondered.

'We're here,' David said, pulling her to a halt in front of a restaurant. His face was pale, and he glanced behind her down the street. She didn't have to turn around to know that he had seen the men in black's sedan. *We'll figure it out*, he told her. *One thing at a time.*

He opened the door to the restaurant, and she followed him inside. It smelled of chili peppers and garlic, and scrolls of Chinese characters hung on the walls. The hostess asked David something in Chinese, and after he responded, she showed them to a table midway down the rectangular room, dropping off two thick menus.

Reese glanced behind herself at the door. The restaurant was about half full of mostly Asian patrons, and the men in black had not followed them in. 'I'll be right back,' she said, and went to the rear of the restaurant where she saw the sign for the restroom. She had to go down a set of narrow stairs to the basement, where she found two toilets. She went into the one marked for women and took off her jacket, hanging it on the half-broken hook screwed into the wall. She unbuttoned her shirt and slid out of it, draping it over her jacket, so that she could remove the wire that was taped onto her skin. It was attached to a slim recording device clipped to the inside of her skirt. She pulled the recorder out and flipped the switch to Off, then wound the wire around the device and tucked it into her jacket's interior pocket. She put her shirt back on before taking the cell phone out of her skirt pocket to text Julian: I got it.

David looked up from the menu when she returned from the bathroom. 'Everything okay?'

'Yeah. I texted Julian.' It had been his idea to tape the meeting with Lovick – 'insurance,' he called it – and Reese had agreed immediately.

David leaned toward her and whispered, 'We can't post that online yet.'

'I know. I'm not going to give it to Julian until the right time comes.'

The waitress returned before she could say anything more. 'What would you like?' she asked.

Reese glanced down at the menu. 'Um . . .'

'This is good,' David said, flipping through the multiple pages to the noodle section and pointing out something called double-fried noodles with seafood. 'Want to share it?'

'Okay.'

David said something to the waitress in Chinese, and they had a brief discussion before she picked up the menus and left.

'What did you order?' Reese asked.

'Spicy jellyfish and soup dumplings.' He poured tea from the stainless steel pot into their two teacups.

She was still agitated from the meeting with Charles Lovick, and her leg bounced beneath the table. She glanced around the restaurant, taking in the glass-topped tables, each setting laid with a single round plate and a pair of chopsticks. A tank full of lobsters glowed near the swinging doors to the kitchen. Her dad always wanted to go out for Chinese when he visited, but they hadn't had time yet. She wondered how long he would be staying. He had been acting particularly fatherly lately, and it made her suspicious about his motives.

'Is something wrong?' David asked.

'No, sorry.' She took a sip of tea, carefully holding the cup around the rim to avoid burning her fingers. 'I was just thinking about my dad, and – we don't have to talk about it now.'

'We can if you want. What's going on?'

'My parents are divorced but my dad's been here since we got back from Nevada. I'm worried about my mom.' She picked up her chopsticks and pulled them out of the paper wrapper, breaking them apart. 'Let's not talk about that. It'll put me in a bad mood.' She and David had agreed not to discuss Lovick in public, but all she could think about was their meeting. Grasping for a new subject of conversation, she said, 'Aren't we supposed to talk about shallow things like what movie you saw recently or your favorite band?'

David grinned. 'Small talk? For a first date?'

Nerves fluttered inside her at the words *first date*. She began to fold the chopsticks wrapper into an accordion. 'Sure,' she said, trying to sound casual. 'Small talk. Have you seen any good movies lately?'

His eyebrows rose. 'Not really. I've been busy. How about you?'

'No. I was in a medically induced coma for a month and then I got abducted by the government. It totally cut into my moviegoing experiences. How about music? What's your favorite band?'

David laughed. 'Did you get these questions from a dating website or something?'

Reese squirmed. 'Uh, no. I just thought we should, you know, try to act like normal people or something.' David seemed surprised, and for a long moment of awkward silence they simply looked at each other. She was about to tell him they didn't have to act normal if he didn't want to, when he reached across the table and plucked the chopsticks wrapper out of her fingers.

'You should take up origami,' he said.

She blushed as he held up the paper with its tiny, perfect pleats. 'It's my hidden talent.'

'I like the Running Brooks,' he said.

It took her a moment to figure out what he meant. 'Oh. You mean the band?'

'Yeah. Theory's good too; he does this really cool electronic stuff with rap – you have to hear it.' He grinned. 'And I like Slick Rice, this Korean American dude who dresses like a giant nerd and raps on YouTube, but his music is awesome.'

'I don't listen to much rap,' Reese admitted. 'It's usually super sexist and gross.'

'I know. This stuff is different. It's not like that. It's political, but it's fun too. I'll make you a playlist.'

'Really?' She smiled.

The waitress arrived with the spicy jellyfish, which looked like a pile of translucent beige noodles dressed in chili sauce. Reese was a little dubious about trying it but she didn't want to seem like a dumb American in front of David, so she quickly took a large bite. The chili burned the back of her throat and her eyes widened in shock.

David laughed. 'You like it?'

'It's different,' she mumbled. It was crunchy and slippery and tasted almost entirely of the spicy, vinegary sauce. She wasn't sure if she liked it. The soup dumplings were more her style, and she scooped one up with a flat-bottomed spoon. When she bit into it, a savory broth spilled out. 'Oh my God, these are so good,' she said, burning her mouth on the crabmeat filling because she didn't want to wait for it to cool off.

'So what about you?' David said. 'What kind of music do you like?'

As they talked, Reese began to relax. She had forgotten what it was like to just hang out with David, without worrying about their bizarre new abilities or how to figure out what it all meant. She liked the way his eyes crinkled up in the corners when he smiled, his mouth curving crookedly. She couldn't remember if she had watched him this way, back when they were only debate partners. She had probably tried to avoid it, because the longer she watched him, the more the warm little glow inside her heated up. He was cute, yes. He was tall and broad-shouldered and had a great haircut and his blue shirt stretched so enticingly across his chest. But it was the interior *Davidness* about him – what could not be seen from the outside – that made her want to reach out and touch him. It was the way he laughed at her bad jokes, as if he genuinely thought she was funny; it was the focus of his attention on her, steady and deliberate; it was the fact that he had always been kind to her, even before he knew much about her.

When the noodles arrived, he served her first, cutting into the crispy noodle bed with the spoon and then lifting them onto her plate, adding stir-fried shrimp and squid and snow peas. The noodles were crunchy on the bottom and soft inside, and she decided she didn't ever want to order Chinese food without David again.

By the time they left the restaurant, she had forgotten all about the men in black who might be following them. He put his arm around her as they walked, and the heat of his body spread like warm honey through her limbs. She liked the rhythm of his paces beside her, the solid confidence in him. He didn't doubt himself. Even though Reese had always relied on herself and was wary of depending too much on others, she knew she could depend on him. It was a new feeling: a vulnerable one. To her surprise, she kind of liked it.

She took his hand as they rode the elevator up to their parking space in the garage, and in the car, she leaned over and kissed him before he started the engine. He was startled, but then he was kissing her back, his mouth firm as he cupped a hand around her face. She lost her breath. His fingers were in her hair. His consciousness seemed to open before her like a door, and he was full of heat.

'Wait,' he said, and dragged himself away. 'We have to go to the party.'

She groaned. 'Can't we skip it?'

He gave a kind of choked laugh, and she almost reached for him again, but he said, 'We'll go to the party. We don't have to stay for long.'

CHAPTER 14

Reese had grown up in San Francisco surrounded by people of all races, but she had never thought of herself as white until she walked through Eric Chung's crowded living room. It wasn't that she thought of herself as not white; she simply never thought about it. She realized that was probably the biggest sign of all that she was white.

David seemed to know everyone. As soon as they entered the house, people began to approach him – boys from the soccer team, girls who seemed to giggle in his presence, people with faces Reese recognized from school but whose names she couldn't remember. The music was loud but the voices were louder, and though she and David had tried to prepare themselves for the emotional tumult, she found it more difficult than she had expected. Everybody was excited to see David; he was their friend and they welcomed him. They were curious and a little suspicious about Reese; they wanted to know why David had brought her.

She tried to act as if she belonged there, as if it was totally normal for her to show up at a house party with David Li holding her hand. While she had gotten better at blocking the prickly sensation of people looking at her, she hadn't anticipated feeling out of place for an entirely different reason. She knew that her social circle was a lot smaller than David's – that was the way she liked it – but until tonight, she never realized how many of his friends were Asian. She was one of only a few non-Asian people at the party, and she stuck out like a sore thumb: white girl walking. It was an unfamiliar discomfort that made her feel unusually self-conscious.

As she and David left the living room and headed down the hall toward the back of the house, he turned to look at her. *You can't help who you are*, he told her. She flushed, and sensed a warm amusement in him. *You're cute when you get embarrassed*, he thought.

That made her flush deepen. 'Can we get some drinks?' she said out loud.

He smiled. 'Sure.'

They went into the kitchen, running into more of David's friends along the way, and then, finally, he handed her a plastic cup of punch. It tasted like candy: sweet and deadly. She couldn't taste the alcohol but she was 100 percent certain it was in there. A giant, empty vodka bottle stood on the counter right next to the punch bowl. David tasted his and made a face.

'I shouldn't drink anyway. I have to drive you home.' He put his cup down and picked up a can of soda instead.

She was about to do the same when a girl entered the kitchen. She had long, glossy black hair and was wearing a black minidress and shiny red heels. She shrieked when she saw David and flung herself at him.

'Oh my God, I saw you on TV!' she cried, her hands digging into his shoulders. She had red nails the same color as her shoes.

'Hey,' David said, pulling away from her gently. 'This is Reese. Reese, this is Riley.'

Riley Bennett-Huang was David's ex-girlfriend. Reese couldn't remember why David and Riley had broken up, though it had been the talk of the school last year. She stiffened as Riley's gaze raked over her. 'Hi,' Reese said, feeling like a kindergartner in comparison to Riley.

'Hi,' Riley said, and then turned back to David. 'So are you okay? I was so worried about you.'

'I'm fine,' David said.

Reese sipped her drink and studied Riley surreptitiously as she flirted with David. Riley, objectively, was gorgeous. That dress and those shoes might look trashy on someone else, but on her they looked sophisticated. Though most of the girls were dressed more casually than Riley, she seemed quite comfortable in her outfit. She had the demeanor of someone who knew when people were looking at her, and she enjoyed it. Watching her leaning into David's space, though, Reese didn't think that Riley looked like his type. She was too polished. Too fake. David seemed a little uncomfortable with her, responding to her with one-or two-word answers.

By the time David extricated himself from the conversation with Riley, Reese had drunk half her cup of punch and the kitchen was beginning to seem a bit blurry. When he grabbed Reese's free hand to pull her with him out of the kitchen, Reese saw Riley giving her a sharp, almost jealous glance. A burst of irritation went through her, and she wasn't sure if it was her emotion or David's. He led her through the back door and onto a broad deck, where clumps of people were gathered together talking and laughing. She welcomed the cool night air on her warm face. She asked David, 'Are you okay?'

'Yeah. Riley gets to me sometimes.'

'Why?' She felt an emotion pass through him like a thin wire: resistance. 'You don't have to tell me,' she said quickly.

He shook his head. 'It's okay. She's just hard to deal with when she gets like that. Pushy.' He drew her toward the edge of the deck, where they leaned against the railing. 'It's a nice night,' he said, changing the subject.

'Yeah.' The fog that had blanketed Chinatown was absent here, a benefit of San Francisco's many microclimates. 'How does Eric get away with this big of a party?' Reese asked, looking around.

'His parents are in Korea on a business trip. I don't think they care, honestly. He gets away with a lot of things.'

A guy Reese recognized from the soccer team came over to talk to David, and though he greeted her also, she didn't have much to contribute to the conversation. She continued to drink her punch as a steady stream of people came out onto the deck, several of them veering over to say hi to David. Some of them tried to talk to Reese, but she was bad at small talk; she always had been. Besides, David had slung his arm around her shoulders, probably in an effort to make her feel included – or to show that they were together – but all it did was make her feel *him*: his body, once so foreign to her but now increasingly familiar; the beat of his heart; a sense of anticipation rising between them. *We don't have to stay for long,* he had said. The punch made her pleasantly woozy, and she had to lean into David so that she didn't wobble on her feet. Her hand snaked around his waist, her fingers sliding over his hip. Heat flared inside him, and she felt a bit breathless. She finished her punch and carefully set the cup on the railing. The world seemed to tilt, and she grabbed at David.

'David,' she said. *David.*

His hand tightened on her shoulder.

I feel weird.

He pulled away briefly, and the air rushed between them, cool and refreshing. The noise of the party seemed to crescendo and she had to back away from the sound. 'I'm sorry, I think I need to go someplace quieter,' she said.

She saw concern on his face. 'Okay.' He apologized to his friends and said, 'Let's go for a walk.'

She linked her arm with his and they walked down the steps off the deck. The property was long and rectangular, and solar-powered lanterns marked the edges of a path that curved down the length of the yard. At the far end she stopped to look back. Eric's house was lit up like magic.

'Hey,' David said, brushing a lock of her hair away from her face. 'Are you all right?'

'Yeah, sorry. I think that punch must have been really strong.' Her head felt fuzzy.

'Do you need some water?'

'Maybe later.' She looked up at him. His eyes reflected the lights from the house, but most of his face was in shadow. She reached up to cup her hand around his cheek; his skin was warm. He covered her hand with his, turning her palm so that he could kiss it. It was so gentle, like a moment in a storybook. She wanted to cry.

'Are you sad?' he asked softly.

'No.' Everything inside her felt thick and heavy, all her emotions concentrated into a dense, sweet syrup. She pulled his head down to kiss him, and the moment his mouth touched hers she was overcome. All she wanted to do was kiss him. She wrapped her arms around him, pressing his body against hers. She had never imagined that kissing could be like this. Like being in his body at the same time she was in hers. She knew what he was going to do as he did it. His hands slid down her back, pulling up the fabric of her shirt. His fingers touched her skin, sending a shock through her body. He pushed her backward and she banged into something – a wall – and for a breathless second he parted from her.

'What are you doing?' she asked.

There was a door behind her. He reached around her and turned the knob. 'Privacy,' he said, and led her inside.

They were in a shed. He closed the door, but a small window near the ceiling let in light from the party at the other end of the yard. Flowerpots and buckets were stacked on the floor, and a wooden workbench was built up against the back wall. David lifted her onto the workbench, and as his hands tightened around her waist and her feet left the ground, she whispered again, 'What are you doing?' But she knew the answer.

His hands were on the warm skin of her thighs, pushing up the fabric of her skirt, and he pressed his body between her legs as he kissed her. For the first time in her life, she understood why girls wore skirts. The muddled haze in her head had changed. It was focused now on only one thing: on drawing David closer to her, on touching him. All her senses were amplified, as if the volume in her body had been turned all the way up, and she could hear nothing but the pounding of their hearts in unison. His mouth was on her neck, making her shiver. Her hands were on his back, sliding up beneath his shirt, over the curve of muscle around his spine, over his shoulder blades. The touch of her hands on his skin was like stoking a bonfire. She could feel him roaring, his body surrounding her. He kissed her again and again, hungrily, and she only wanted to drag him closer. In this space, with him, she could completely lose herself. She didn't need to exist anymore; she was merely a vessel for their connection.

Dimly, somewhere inside her, a warning bell rang. This was nothing she was ready for. It felt incredible; she was more alive than she had ever been; but who was she? She had forgotten her name. His fingers were unbuttoning her shirt, and she wanted him to do it – she yearned for him to do it – but part of her pushed back. A small, distant voice.

The last time she had been in this situation, something had gone horribly wrong.

Amber, pulling off her shirt as if she were plucking the petals from a flower. The softness of her skin, her mouth.

Abruptly, David stopped what he was doing. 'Reese,' he said, his voice thick and dark.

She remembered herself. Her eyes blinked open, and in the dim interior of the shed she saw him breathing heavily, inches from her, his hands still on her shirt. Her hands were still on his back, and she felt the confusion inside him. The sudden, unexpected questions.

She pulled her hands away. 'I'm sorry,' she whispered in horror. He had seen her memory of Amber too. 'It just happened. I don't know why.'

He stepped back. They weren't touching anymore. 'Are you still in love with her?'

There was a rushing sound in her head, as if she were holding a conch shell to her ear. 'No,' she said sharply. 'I was never in love with her.' But even as she said the words she could hear the lie in them. 'I mean, I don't think I was,' she amended, and guilt burned through her. He moved farther away, backing into a pile of ceramic pots that thunked together. She slid off the workbench, and as her feet touched the ground in her new boots, the whole world spun. She grabbed the edge of the table. She was drunk; that had to be it. That one drink – what was in it? "I didn't mean to think of her,' she said, her voice breaking. 'I swear, it was like some glitch in my brain.'

He didn't answer for a minute, and she was terrified that she had screwed this up without even meaning to. 'Maybe we need to take things a little slower,' he finally said.

His words made relief and disappointment sweep through her all at once. 'Okay. You're right.'

He took a couple of steps closer to her, and she thought he might kiss her again, but he only reached out to button up her shirt. He buttoned it all the way up, until she felt the collar closing against her neck. 'Maybe we should go home,' he said, sounding tired.

'I'm sorry,' she said again, and reached for his hand.

But he drew away. 'I know. Can you give me a minute in here alone? Wait for me outside.'

She was stunned. Unsure of what else to do, she stumbled out of the shed, leaving him inside. The night air was cool on her face and she felt like she might burst into sobs at any moment. In the distance, the lights of Eric's party still sparkled, and she heard the sounds of laughter and conversation. She and David would have to walk out of there through that party. Everyone would see that something had happened, that something was wrong. It would be the talk of the school on Monday.

The idea of facing all those curious glances galvanized her. She took a deep breath, trying to push her way through the haze of the drink and the lingering effect of making out with David. If that memory hadn't risen to the surface, they'd still be in the potting shed, and it was obvious what came next. To her shock, she discovered that part of her was grateful that the memory had stopped them. She wasn't ready, and when she was, she wasn't doing it in a potting shed.

With Amber, it had never been so all-encompassing, probably because Amber had made a point to close her mind to Reese – to 'keep things to herself,' she had said. *If I'd let you see everything, it probably would have freaked you out*, Reese remembered her saying. That was an understatement. It was like being consumed by something so primal she had no control over it. Now she felt weak-limbed and fuzzy-headed and hungover – way more hungover than one cup of punch should have made her, even if it had been strong.

And she was terrified. Was this what the adaptation

made possible? The horrifying intimacy of having someone see everything inside her, even things she didn't want to see herself?

The door to the shed opened and David came outside. They faced each other under the night sky, ignoring the chatter of the party at the other end of the yard. 'Are you okay?' David asked.

Hot tears pricked at the edges of her eyes, and she didn't move. She didn't know what to say or what to do. She wished she could go back in time – fifteen minutes was all she needed – and she wouldn't have to feel like she had betrayed David against her own will.

I don't think you betrayed me, he told her.

She looked up at him, but she couldn't read his expression in the dark. *You don't?*

No. But I think . . .

They both realized at the same instant that they weren't touching. They were communicating mentally without touching. Reese stepped back in shock. David?

I can hear you so clearly, he thought.

It's like you're in my head.

It's like we flipped a switch.

Reese's face heated up. What had done it? His hands on her thighs or the way she had kissed him? Had that delirious, drowning feeling erased the space between them?

He came toward her and reached for her hand. 'Reese,' he said out loud, breaking the taut silence. He pulled her into a delicate embrace, as if they were both made of fine china. 'It's going to be fine.'

'I hope so,' she said. Then she pulled away, letting her hand trail down his arm until their fingers were touching. Close, but not too close.

She was home by eleven thirty. David walked her up the front steps and kissed her good night, his mouth brushing over hers, light as a feather. 'I'll see you tomorrow,' he said.

David's parents had invited Reese and her family over to watch the Sophia Curtis interview when it aired on Saturday night. 'See you tomorrow,' she said, and then she unlocked the front door and went inside. She turned to peer out the window as David went down the steps to where his car was waiting on the street, the engine idling. One sedan pulled into a parking space across the street and another followed David's as he drove away.

'How was your date?' her mom asked.

Reese spun around to see her mom standing in the archway to the living room, dressed in her penguin pajamas. Her dad appeared behind her mom and added, 'You made it back early. I'm impressed.'

'It was fine. I'm going to bed.'

As she headed upstairs she heard her mom chuckling. 'All right, honey.'

In her bedroom she took off her jacket and pulled out the recording device and microphone wire, hiding it in the back of her top desk drawer. She emptied her pockets, laying her phone and wallet on the desk, and caught sight of the flip-phone Amber had given her, tucked behind the lamp. The battery had died a couple of days ago, and she had no way to charge it. She had thought about throwing it away, but that had seemed oddly personal. The flip-phone was the only link she had to Amber, even if it no longer worked. Now she opened the drawer again and shoved it in the back next to the recording device so that she didn't have to see it anymore.

She undressed, put on her pajamas, and went into the bathroom to brush her teeth. She held her long hair out of the way with one hand as she spit out the toothpaste and rinsed off the toothbrush. When she straightened up she was startled by how exhausted she looked. Her green-flecked eyes were anxious and had dark shadows beneath them. Earlier that night, before David had picked her up, she had been so worried about whether or not she looked cool enough. Now that worry seemed trivial. She had committed herself to misleading and probably double-crossing a powerful organization that had an army of supersoldiers at its command.

She clutched the edge of the counter as the reality of what she was doing struck home. If Lovick and CASS found out that she and David had recorded the meeting and planned to lie to them about what they learned from the Imria, the repercussions could be swift and deadly. She thought about her mom and dad downstairs, unaware of her intentions. She thought about the gunman at the ferry dock. It would be all too easy to arrange for an accidental shooting. Panic twisted through her gut.

There was still a chance to back out of this plan she and David had concocted. She could still do what Charles Lovick asked and make sure her parents were safe. Part of her wanted to do that; it would certainly be a lot easier. Besides, what if

Lovick was right? Had the Imria really kept their ability to share consciousness a secret for all those years? The only Imrian she had a better than passing acquaintance with was Amber, and Amber had told her she had been trained to lie. The problem was, even though her knowledge of Amber should predispose her to believe that the Imria had lied, it didn't make her believe they wanted to 'erase our humanity,' as Lovick had put it. She didn't trust the Imria – or Amber – but some instinctual part of her wanted to.

Or maybe she simply still wanted Amber.

A terrible, hot shame spread through her. She glared at herself in the mirror. *You have to stop thinking about her*, she ordered herself. *You're with David now*. You want David. And she did want him. The memory of being with him an hour ago made her ache to pick up where they had left off, even though it also scared her half to death. This thing that the Imria had done to her and David was such a frightening gift. Before it had happened, she might have thought it would be cool to have access to someone else's thoughts. Now she knew it meant that whoever she touched could know everything about her. Everything.

She splashed cold water on her face and rubbed the towel over her skin. She didn't want to think about this anymore. It was too unsettling. All she wanted to do was crawl into bed and fall asleep.

She went back into her bedroom and climbed under the covers, switching off the light. Sleep, however, was elusive. She lay curled on her side, her thoughts circling back to David and Amber. Amber and David. She tried to push Amber away, to put the memories of her in a box and lock it deep in the recesses of her mind. She reached out to David the way she had when they were in the hospital at Project Plato. She envisioned the shape of his body, the mental energy that formed the essence of who he was, but it was like groping in the dark for something that wasn't there.

Maybe he was too far away to sense her, or maybe she was too upset to focus properly. The end result was the same: She felt alone in a way she never had before she discovered this connection with him. She was in her own room, with her head on her own pillow, but she didn't feel at home.

CHAPTER 15

In the car on the way to David's house, Reese heard her mom's phone ring. 'Can you get that, Rick?' her mom said. 'It's in my purse next to your feet.'

Reese slouched in the backseat, watching the pastel buildings of Noe Valley roll past as they headed toward Woodside. Reese's dad answered the phone, and a moment later he said, 'Reese, it's for you. It's Sophia Curtis.'

Surprised, she took the phone from her dad. 'Hello?'

'Hi, Reese. It's Sophia. I'm glad I caught you before the show airs.'

Reese sat up. The woman's voice sounded oddly tense. 'What's wrong?'

'We've been cooperating with the Defense Department on our show, as you know, and I just came from a meeting with my producer. Unfortunately the DOD has forced us to change the focus of our story. You and David and your families are still in it, but we've been unable to spend as much time on your experiences in Nevada as we originally planned.'

'What do you mean?'

'We're using footage from the Imrian press conference to round out your story, and we've also done interviews with a few others – Senator Michaelson, for one. With you and David, we're focusing on how your experiences affected you personally.'

Reese did not like the sound of that. 'Does that mean you cut all the stuff we said about Blue Base?'

'I'm sorry I can't elaborate. I hope you understand that this was not my original intention, and I've been doing everything I can to tell the whole story, but this situation was beyond my control. I have to call David Li and his family now.'

'But—'

The call ended. Reese pulled the phone away from her ear and stared down at the screen. There was a photo of her on the background. She was standing in the kitchen making a face at the camera.

'What did she say?' her mom asked from the driver's seat.

'I think . . . I think she's been censored.' Reese had a dreadful suspicion about what Sophia Curtis meant by 'how your experiences affected you personally.' The show was due to air in an hour. It was too late to back out now.

'I'm calling Diana Warner,' her dad said. 'She should know what's going on.'

Reese gazed down at the photo on her mom's phone. She couldn't remember when her mom had taken it, but judging by the length of her hair it must have been at least a year ago. The thought of how different her life had been then – right before junior year, before she and David had been partnered together for debate – made her head spin. The screen darkened, obscuring the image. Feeling ill, Reese unrolled the window to gulp breaths of cool, misty air.

As the wind whipped into the backseat, her mom called, 'Honey, are you okay? Are you going to be sick?'

She swallowed, tasting something sour in the back of her throat. 'I'm fine, Mom,' she lied.

The *Sophia Curtis Show* began with Sophia spotlighted in a dark television studio, looking directly into the camera as she said, 'It's been nine days since one of the most extraordinary revelations in history: We humans are not alone in the universe. In the past week, we have struggled to make sense of the news that extraterrestrials known as the Imria have been visiting Earth since 1947 and, apparently, cooperating with a secret branch of the United States government. But while you and I – the public – have only been aware of this for a little over a week, two teenagers were swept into this incredible story two months ago during the June Disaster. Tonight, we talk to seventeen-year-old high school students Reese Holloway and David Li and find out how their experiences have changed their lives.'

As the opening credits for the program rolled, Reese glanced at David, who was seated next to her on one of the two matching couches in his living room. *Here we go*, she thought, and he gave her a tight smile. His twelve-year-old sister, Chloe, was curled in the corner of the couch beside David, biting her lip. Across the living room Reese's parents sat stiffly on the other sofa, while David's dad paced at the rear of the room. David's mom was perched on the edge of a chair they had brought in from the dining room.

The show returned to Sophia Curtis in the studio as the theme music faded. 'It all began on June nineteenth, when Reese and David were in Phoenix, Arizona, waiting to fly home to San Francisco from a debate tournament.'

The scene cut to Reese and David in Mr Murray's classroom at Kennedy High School, explaining what had happened when they left Phoenix. Reese found it disconcerting to watch herself on television. She looked much better than she had during the press conference outside her house; Sophia Curtis's hair and makeup team had turned her into a pretty girl, though her lips rarely curved into a pretty girl's smile. She seemed tense, and there was a tightness to her jaw that Reese had never seen before; it made her appear sort of angry. David looked more relaxed than she did, and from time to time he flashed a smile at Sophia, but he also seemed a bit uncomfortable. That was when Reese realized that the camera never showed Jeff Highsmith, who had been seated out of sight beside Sophia Curtis. Reese remembered him interrupting her and David repeatedly, telling them they couldn't speak about this or that. None of that made it into the interview.

After Reese and David reached the point in which they mentioned the adaptation procedure, the program switched scenes to the Imrian press conference on Angel Island. Dr Brand was shown explaining what she had done after Reese and David had their car accident. Then the show cut to the press conference on Reese's front steps, when she and David theorized that the government hadn't known what the Imria were doing.

‘When we return,’ said Sophia Curtis before the show went to commercial, ‘we’ll speak with Senator Joyce Michaelson, who helped bring Reese and David home to their families. What exactly did the government know about this adaptation procedure? Senator Michaelson explains, right after this.’

Reese’s mom let out her breath across the room. ‘Well, it’s not so bad so far.’

‘They cut out Jeff Highsmith,’ Reese said. ‘They’re not acknowledging that he was there manipulating the interview at all.’ Reese’s phone vibrated and she pulled it out of her pocket. There was a text message from Julian.

> Were you not allowed to say the
> words Area 51? Did they cut that?

She texted back: Yes.

Senator Michaelson was interviewed in her Washington, DC, office. She wore a navy blue suit and gold earrings and looked genuinely concerned as she said, ‘What happened with Reese and David was an unfortunate misunderstanding. We truly regret that. They were two teens caught in the wrong place at the wrong time, and they should never have been detained in Nevada. I’ve apologized to them directly and I want to take this moment to apologize again, on behalf of the United States government.’

Sophia asked, ‘Why were they taken from their homes in the first place?’

Senator Michaelson said, ‘I’m told we had reason to believe that they had received unauthorized medical treatment after their car accident. As you know, the teens were treated on a military base, and we were concerned that they might have adverse reactions to this treatment. They were brought back to the base for a follow-up for their own safety.'

'That is bullshit,' Reese muttered, watching the senator smoothly delivering the lies.

'Reese and David said they were taken against their will,' Sophia said. 'Why didn't the government simply ask them to come in for an exam?'

Senator Michaelson frowned. 'The men who made the decision to act in that manner have been reprimanded and placed on administrative leave pending an internal investigation. All I can say at this time is that they acted hastily and without going through the proper channels. They were concerned about the teens' safety, but they should not have done what they did. That's partly why I acted so quickly when Catherine Sheridan, Reese's mother, contacted me for help. I have two children of my own, and I can understand why Catherine was so upset.'

Reese glanced at her mother, who looked pensive. 'Do you think she's being forced to say that?' Reese asked.

'I don't know. She's obviously delivering a preapproved speech, but I don't know if she believes it.'

'Listen,' David interrupted, turning up the volume.

'– regret what happened with David and Reese, the more serious offense was done by the Imria,' Senator Michaelson said. 'They should never have performed that medical procedure on these teens – these children – without the consent of their parents. While I understand that President Randall wants a clean slate with the Imria in order to pursue peaceful talks, I believe the Imria should address the troubling fact that they essentially used these two teens as test subjects.'

The show cut to footage of Reese and David arriving at Travis Air Force Base nine days earlier, looking dazed as they descended from the airplane. 'Last Thursday, when Reese and David returned to California,' Sophia said in a voice-over, 'the Imria also returned from their five-day-long absence.' The scene changed to an overhead shot of Reese's house as she, her parents, and David's family arrived. They climbed out of their cars while reporters surrounded them. 'But when the Imrian ship reappeared above San Francisco, no explanation was immediately given for its sudden return,' Sophia said. The video switched to the black triangle hovering over the city while crowds thronged the streets below, tiny signs bobbing in a sea of people. 'As the Imrian ship flew over the Noe Valley neighborhood, perceptions of the extraterrestrial visitors began to shift from stunned curiosity to outright hostility. That hostility erupted in violence on August fourteenth, the day that the Imria first spoke to the world at a press conference on Angel Island in San Francisco Bay.'

Reese had never seen footage of the protesters at Fisherman's Wharf. Now she watched herself being herded through the roiling crowd as a man broke free, raising his hand. She flinched as she saw her parents push her onto the ground while the police moved in, circling the gunman and shoving him onto the pavement.

'What led this man, Mitchell Cole, to threaten the teens?' Sophia asked as the picture returned to the studio where she sat in a pool of light. 'What's behind his distrust of the Imria and their adaptation procedure? When we return, Mitchell Cole tells his story.'

'I had no idea she was going to talk to him,' David's mom said.

'Why is she giving him airtime?' Reese's dad asked.

Reese leaned forward, resting her elbows on her knees and dropping her head into her hands. So far the show had avoided focusing on anything too personal, but the more time that passed without Sophia mentioning Reese and David's relationship, the more anxious Reese became. Were the producers saving it for the end? David touched her, his hand sliding lightly over the small of her back. *Halfway through*, he thought.

She sensed his own tension through his touch, the acidic bubbles in his stomach and the taut muscles of his shoulders. *I wish they'd get to the end already*.

'Reese, you don't have to watch this if you don't want to,' her mom said.

Reese glanced up, surprised. She realized her mom was talking about the interview with Mitchell Cole. 'It's fine, Mom. I want to hear what he has to say.'

When the program returned from the commercial break, Sophia explained that Cole had been released on bail Friday morning, funded by members of a newly formed Ohio-based group called Americans for Humanity and Liberty. Cole joined Sophia in the studio for the interview. He was wearing a blue button-down shirt and dark pants, and his short, light hair was cut with military precision. 'I acted alone,' he said in response to her first question. 'I don't know Americans for Humanity and Liberty.' He had no discernible accent, but there was an underlying tone of contempt in his voice that made Reese bristle. 'Whoever they are, they're on the side of freedom, and I stand with them.'

'Why did you do it?' Sophia asked.

He cracked a brief, cold grin. 'Those teens are hybrids. Human-alien hybrids. They're the first of an army that the aliens are creating. That army's going to take over our country and our world. We have to put a stop to it. I know you probably think I'm crazy, but I'm not. If what I did wakes people up, then it was worth it. They're coming for us.'

'You mean the Imria?'

He shrugged. 'You want to call them that, sure. They're aliens. They've been taking people for decades, experimenting on them to create these hybrids.'

'Are you talking about alien abductions?'

'Yes.'

'Do you know anyone who has been abducted?'

'I've been abducted.' He leaned forward, stabbing his fingers into his palm as he spoke. 'They took me. They did things to me that make me wake up in the middle of the night screaming. I saw them in that press conference on the island. They act like they're trying to benefit humanity, but it's a lie. They want to change us into them. Adaptation. That's what they're calling it. It's genocide. If we don't stop them, the new world order will come, and we'll all be goners.'

Reese shrank back into the couch as Cole spoke, his pale eyes bright in the studio lights. He spoke with such paranoid conviction that even Sophia seemed taken aback. The scene cut to Sophia alone in the studio, who said, 'Cole's theories have not arisen from nowhere. They're firmly rooted in decades of conspiracy theories. In Cole's scenario, Earth's sovereign governments will be destroyed and turned into a single global totalitarian regime: a new world order. I spoke with conspiracy expert Peter Vikram, a professor of history at Harvard University, to get his perspective on Cole's theory.'

Vikram was a middle-aged South Asian man dressed in a crisp, dark purple shirt and stylish glasses. He was interviewed in his office, sitting at his desk in front of a wall of books. 'The new world order typically refers to the idea that there is a secret cabal of powerful men who wish to rule the world,' Vikram explained. 'This cabal is often believed to be comprised of businessmen, particularly Jewish bankers. In many ways it's an anti-Semitic theory. Many of those who believe in this theory fall into the category of right-wing extremists who also believe in stockpiling weapons and building secure bunkers to defend against the coming of this so-called new world order, when individual liberties will be severely curtailed. Mitchell Cole has a slightly different perspective. He's from the camp that believes that a new world order will be brought about through an alien invasion.' Vikram gave Sophia a wry smile. 'At least this version of the theory is a bit more progressive, since it's not humans of any stripe who are out to get us; it's only aliens.'

'Do you think that Cole's theory bears any weight?' Sophia asked.

Vikram grew serious again. 'If you had asked me a week ago, I would have said absolutely not. One of the things that is fascinating about conspiracy theories is the way they express anxieties about the modern-day world. They're an expression of paranoia, and a way of exercising control when one feels powerless. If you believe the world is going to hell in a handbasket, you can take steps to ensure that you survive the apocalypse by stocking up on supplies, building a safe house, et cetera. With regard to Cole's theory, we can no longer simply call him paranoid. The Imria have revealed themselves. Aliens truly do exist, and I must admit that even I have found their initial statements to be confusing and a little frightening. That changes everything.'

The next segment of the show centered on Dr Brand's explanation of the adaptation procedure, followed by interviews with a neuroscientist who had begun to go through the documentation the Imria had released on Thursday afternoon. 'I can't understand it all,' he said, 'because much of it involves science that is far more advanced than what I'm knowledgeable about. It seems as if the Imria used a viral-like vector to introduce Imrian DNA into the teens' cells. The information provided also states that the adaptation is now fully heritable – it would be passed on to children of anyone who was adapted, male or female. I'm not entirely clear on how this works, since the Imrian DNA is added to our mitochondrial DNA, which is only passed on through the mother – at least in humans. But somehow this adaptation procedure has caused the male to also be able to pass on mitochondrial DNA to his offspring.' The scientist seemed a bit awed. 'If I'm correct, this is a huge revolution in medical science.'

As the show returned to the interview with Reese and David,

explaining their ability to communicate through touch, Reese glanced at her phone to check the time. The show was almost over; there were only ten more minutes. Maybe, Reese thought hopefully, Sophia wasn't going to get into her relationship with David after all. Another text message from Julian made her phone buzz.

> I don't buy that guy's theory. Aliens
> wouldn't fly all the way here to
> destroy us.

She texted back: You trust the Imria?

On television, David's father was talking to Sophia Curtis about setting up an academic review board to test David's and Reese's abilities. Her phone vibrated again.

> If they're advanced enough to get
> here, why would they kill us?

David nudged her. *What are you doing?*

She showed him Julian's text messages and saw a skeptical expression cross David's face.

Why does he have such faith in the Imria? David thought.

He's an optimist. Although he does think the government is shady.

They're all shady.

Reese heard Chloe catch her breath, swallowing a giggle. Reese glanced at David's sister and then at the television. She froze. The scene had changed to Mr Chapman's old classroom.

She and David were looking at each other as Sophia Curtis said, '. . . would bring a lot of friends closer together. What about you two?'

The tension in Reese's face that had made her look angry was gone. Now she looked shy, and her cheeks were tinged pink.

Sitting on David's parents' couch, Reese felt the air drain from her lungs. She could barely watch the screen as David reached for her hand and said, 'We're together now.' All she could think about was how the students at school on Monday morning would react. Her internal organs seemed to shrivel up in anticipation.

'Aw, you look cute,' her mom said from across the room.

Reese was mortified. She slouched down on the sofa, wishing she could hide somewhere. What had made her think it would be a good idea to watch this with her parents?

'You both look very sweet,' David's mom said.

And David's parents! Maybe she could skip the first day of school. Or the first month.

Thankfully, the show was ending, and Sophia Curtis was delivering a closing statement that Reese couldn't hear because of the buzzing sound in her ears. All the blood must be rushing to her head in embarrassment. Her phone vibrated again. She looked down to find a short message from Julian.

LOL LOL

CHAPTER 16

Several television vans were parked outside Kennedy High School when Reese's mom dropped her off Monday morning. The front steps were crowded with students hanging out before the first bell, and some of them were being interviewed by reporters. Photographers were waiting on the sidewalk as well, long-lensed cameras in hand.

'The reporters can't follow you inside,' her mom said, reaching out to squeeze Reese's knee. A flash of encouragement came from her touch, but the knowledge that the reporters weren't allowed in didn't make Reese feel better. She knew they'd simply be lurking outside.

'Your dad's going to pick you up after school,' her mom said. 'Wait for him inside, and he'll call you when he gets here.'

'He doesn't have to pick me up. I can walk home like usual.'

'Not today. We don't know whether those protesters will be back, and I want you to be safe.'

'How long is Dad going to be here?' Reese had thought he would go back to Seattle after the Sophia Curtis interview. 'In San Francisco, I mean.'

'We haven't decided yet,' her mom said, pulling her hand away, but not before Reese glimpsed the reluctance within her.

Reese gave her mom a sharp glance. 'Is something going on?'

The expression on her mom's face was closed off. 'Nothing you need to worry about, honey. You'd better get inside. I don't want you to be late.'

Reese could tell her mom was being cagey, but it was clear she wasn't going to talk about it now. Irritation flared inside her. She hated it when her mom treated her like a kid. 'Fine,' she said, and opened the door.

'Reese—'

'I'll see you tonight, Mom.' She stepped outside.

She had intended to put up her mental walls, but the last-minute conversation with her mom had distracted her. She wasn't prepared for the force of interest that slammed into her as the reporters and students thronging the steps noticed her. Snatches of thought seemed to strike her like a rain of pebbles, and once it started, she couldn't find the mental focus necessary to shield herself.

Here – she's here – Reese – interview – Reese Holloway—

All she could do was put her head down and ignore as much as she could, keeping her gaze on the ground as she ran up the steps. When she pulled open the heavy metal door and went inside, the lobby was full of students and teachers, but she didn't see David. They had talked the night before, and he said he'd meet her in the lobby first thing.

The door slammed shut behind her. Everyone seemed to

turn toward her at once, and the volume of conversation dropped to a sudden hush. She took a deep breath, trying to calm the racing of her heart. Where was David?

Across the mosaic-tiled lobby, Reese recognized Madison squeezing her way through a clump of cheerleaders. Behind her were Bri and Robbie, and all the way in the back Reese spotted Julian's curly-haired head bobbing above the others. On the other side of the space, a knot of senior guys was standing by the trophy case near the front office, and she thought she recognized a couple of them from Eric Chung's party. But no David. She began to cross the lobby alone, deciding to go directly to her assigned locker. The students swirled around her as she walked, silent but curious. She felt the intensity of their interest in waves of heat on her skin.

She was halfway across the lobby when someone grabbed her arm. 'Reese,' David said.

She jerked in surprise. His hand slid down to hers. *Snap*. The connection between them was sharp and bright, like a lifeline to a drowning person. 'Hey,' she said. As she looked at him everyone else's emotions rolled back. Breathing room.

David was wearing a gray-and-white-striped oxford shirt with the sleeves pushed up, his shirttail hanging out of his dark jeans. He had done his hair the same way the stylist did the day of the TV shoot. He smiled at her, and she felt a little woozy inside.

What's the rush? he asked her.

I didn't see you.

I'm here.

The night before she had lain awake for hours, anxiety

making her sweat as she thought about the scrutiny she would face when she walked into Kennedy. Those who had been at Eric Chung's party on Friday night knew about her and David already, but after the Sophia Curtis interview, the whole world knew. *The whole world*.

David had tried to reassure her over the phone, but he didn't entirely get it. She wasn't upset that her relationship with David was in the open. She was happy that she was with him, and she was happy that he wanted to be with her. It was the fact that people might now be thinking about *her* that made her feel sick. She had always thought celebrities who said things like 'I'm a private person' were protesting too much, but now she understood what they meant. The idea of strangers thinking about her love life made her skin crawl. She knew what people said online; she had seen it. It made her want to hide in a hole.

Reese became aware of the fact that she was standing in the middle of the school lobby holding David's hand, and her face heated up. Whispers whirled around them, but she couldn't make out what anyone was saying.

I have to go to my locker, she thought.

I'll go with you.

They headed across the lobby together. The emotions of the gathered students hovered in the background of her consciousness like fog waiting at the top of a hill. As long as she focused on her connection with David, she could keep the fog at bay. By the time she and David crossed the whole expanse of the lobby, her friends were gathered together: Madison with an excited smile on her face; Bri looking self-conscious; Robbie dressed extra goth for the first day of school; Julian with an ironic grin as he saw her clutching David's hand. As they crowded around her and welcomed her back, she thought: *I can do this*.

They were walking down the hall toward the lockers when Reese saw a familiar man standing outside the door to Mr Chapman's old classroom, talking to the assistant principal. It was Alex Hernandez, the CASS liaison who had been at the meeting with Charles Lovick. She couldn't tell if he saw her or not; he didn't look away from his conversation with the assistant principal.

Keep going, David thought.

She passed Hernandez and tried to focus on her friends, who were teasing her about her most recent television appearance, but she couldn't help wondering if Hernandez was taking over Mr Chapman's class. Lovick hadn't specified. Mr Chapman had taught Principles of Democracy – the required social studies class for seniors – in addition to coaching the debate team. Obviously, the school district had to hire someone to replace him.

As she reached her assigned locker, she turned back to look down the hallway. Hernandez was still there, but this time he was looking directly at her. She glanced away quickly. The idea of him replacing Coach Chapman filled her with frustrated rage. She knew he had nothing to do with Mr Chapman's death, but it felt linked. If Mr Chapman hadn't died, she and David might not have crashed onto Area 51, and none of this stuff with the Imria and the government and CASS would have happened.

'Hey,' Madison said. 'What's going on, Reese? You're like in a different world or something. We have to get to class.'

David looked grim. *I saw him too*, he told Reese.

'Sorry,' Reese said to Madison. She pulled the slip of paper on which she had scribbled her new locker combination out of her pocket and turned to the lock, trying to ignore the feeling that Hernandez was watching her.

After school, Julian was waiting for Reese at her locker. 'Did you hear what happened?' he asked excitedly.

'No, what?'

'Sophia Curtis issued a statement saying that her show was reined in by network censors.'

'Really?' Reese opened her locker and began to load her backpack. 'That's – wow, when did that happen?'

'Like five minutes ago.' He leaned toward her, arms crossed, and said in a low voice, 'So you should totally come on Bin 42 now and tell your story. You need to, you know?'

She hesitated. 'I'm not sure.'

'Why not?' As the student next to her moved out of the way, Julian slid in so that he was only a foot away. 'You don't have to talk about Amber, if that's what you're worried about,' he said.

'I'm not worried about that. Besides, I'm with David now.'

His expression went blank. 'Yeah. You are.'

'Look, that's got nothing to do with this. There are other things in play.'

'Like what?' Julian asked in an intense whisper. 'The public deserves to know the truth.'

She zipped up her backpack and looked around. The hallway was scattered with students, some of them casting curious glances in their direction. She didn't want to talk about this in earshot of her classmates, but more important, she could see Mr Chapman's classroom door at the end of the hall. Alex Hernandez had indeed taken over Principles of Democracy. He had acted as if he didn't know Reese and David during class, but she was sure it was only a matter of time before he asked them for information. 'I don't think we should talk about this here,' she said to Julian.

'Fine. Come out back with me.'

'Right now?'

'What else are you doing, waiting for your boyfriend?' Julian made a face at her.

She rolled her eyes. David had soccer practice; she was not waiting for him. 'Okay.' She pulled on her backpack and closed her locker. 'But my dad's picking me up soon. I can't talk for long.'

'Your dad's still around, huh?' Julian said as they walked down the hall toward the central courtyard.

'Yeah.'

'How long's he going to be here?'

'I don't know. They won't say.'

He gave her a concerned glance. 'Are you all right with that?'

'No, but it's not like they're asking me.' She noticed several girls watching her as she and Julian passed. 'What are they looking at?' she whispered once they turned the corner.

'They're checking out their competition.'

'Competition for what?'

'Madison's right. You can be so clueless. You just took David off the market.'

'That sounds extremely crass. He's not a piece of meat.'

'I never said I was polite,' Julian quipped, and pushed open the doors to the courtyard.

It was a cool afternoon, with gray clouds covering the sky. They headed across the brick courtyard toward the athletic fields and the rickety bleachers near the concrete wall that marked the edge of school property.

'You and David should come over and I can interview you for Bin 42,' Julian said. 'We won't have to deal with network censors or commercial breaks, and you can tell the whole story, with all the details. Speaking of which, when are you going to give me that recording you made of your meeting with that Lovick guy?'

'I'm holding on to it for now.' She hadn't told Julian the details about the meeting because Lovick had warned them not to speak about it, and the Blue Base guard blocking the door had turned Lovick's warning into a threat. 'And you don't understand. It's not as simple as you think. There was a Defense Department guy there when Sophia Curtis interviewed us. He wouldn't let us talk about Area 51 or Blue Base or anything like that. In fact, you remember that document about the birds I took from Blue Base? This guy found it – we had left it in the living room like a bunch of idiots – and he took it. So I don't even have that anymore. If you start posting the quote unquote truth, they will come after you and Bin 42.'

'What are they going to do? You have freedom of speech –

it's your First Amendment right.'

'Yeah, and they have freedom of the government to do whatever they want to restrict it.' She shoved her hands into her pockets as they crossed the empty soccer field. The team hadn't arrived for practice yet.

'That's not true,' Julian objected. 'They can't shut you up, and if they try, you have every right to—'

'They *did* shut me up!'

Julian gave her a suspicious look. 'What are you not telling me? What happened at that meeting? You've never rolled over like this before.'

She scowled at the grass and didn't answer at first. She wanted to tell Julian everything. She didn't want to be cowed by Charles Lovick and his secret organization, but if she and David were really going to lie to them, it was better if nobody else knew about it.

'Reese? Come on, you can tell me.' Julian ducked beneath the bleachers, where the ground was littered with cigarettes, and dropped his backpack on a relatively clean patch of dirt. 'You can trust me,' he assured her. A few cinder blocks had been dragged beneath the bleachers to create stools, and he sat down and pulled out a pack of cigarettes, offering one to her.

Reese sat nearby and shrugged out of her backpack. 'You should really quit,' she told him, but when he cocked his head at her she took the cigarette, leaning over to light it off Julian's match. It tasted bitter and harsh, and she realized too late that her dad would smell it on her.

'So what's the big secret?' Julian pushed.

She exhaled a plume of smoke, deciding to smoke it anyway.

She didn't care what her dad thought. 'David and I need to find out what the deal is with our adaptation,' she said, avoiding Julian's question. 'So we're going to take the Imria up on their offer to train us. Our first lesson is on Saturday.'

'That's great. But that doesn't stop you from telling your story.'

She stared at the glowing end of the cigarette, picking her words carefully. 'No, it doesn't. Our abilities are only part of the story, though. We need to figure everything out before we go public, and we need to get proof.'

'You have that recording from the Lovick meeting.'

'That's one part of it. And the government is totally covering something up, but the Imria aren't telling us everything either. They're hiding stuff too.'

'They have to be hiding it for a good reason.'

She looked at Julian, her forehead furrowed. 'Why do you trust them? They're the ones who messed with me and David. They said they've been doing research on humans for decades. Aren't you worried they might not have our best interests at heart?'

Julian shook his head. 'You're not seeing the big picture.' He inhaled, and the cigarette paper crinkled into black ash.

'What's the big picture?'

He blew the smoke away from her. 'This adaptation thing that the Imria are working on could change *everything*. I read the stuff they released at their press conference. It's *amazing*. Think about what this world would be like if human beings could really do this shared consciousness thing.' He spoke with rising intensity, his body bending toward her as he gestured with his cigarette. 'Do you know why people hate each other? Because they don't understand each other. But if we could really know how other people feel – really *know* it – all that would change. It would bring humans to the next level of evolution.'

Julian's fierce belief in the adaptation procedure made Reese uncomfortable. 'Evolution's not about levels. It's not about advancing. You took bio with me; you should know that.'

'Don't get all debatey on me. Besides, I don't believe that. If the point of life isn't to become more intelligent and better adapted to your environment, what *is* the point? Just to stay in one place, reproducing yourself? That's stupid. This ability is humanity's ticket to the future.'

'You talk about it like it's some kind of superpower. But this isn't *X-Men*.'

'No duh. It's real.' He stubbed out his cigarette. 'You should know. You have this ability. You can't tell me it hasn't changed the way you see everything.'

'Honestly, it mostly freaks me out. That's why I'm agreeing to the lessons with the Imria, because until I know how this thing works in me, I don't think I can really know whether it's good or bad.' Her cigarette had burned down to the filter, and she dropped it on the ground, grinding it out with her sneaker. She felt a little nauseated from the nicotine.

'You might not know, but I do. It's good. So I want to be adapted too.'

Her head snapped up. 'What? You can't do that.'

'Why not?'

She couldn't tell if he was serious at first. 'Because it's crazy dangerous! Because you have to apply, and they're only taking teens who are on the verge of death.'

'That's what they said, but they haven't posted an application yet. Besides, they're going to need as many test subjects as possible. Why wouldn't they take a healthy volunteer? Wouldn't that be better than someone who might die?'

She gaped at him. 'You're serious.'

Anger flashed across his face. 'Of course I'm serious. I've been waiting for something like this my entire life. This is my chance to be part of something bigger than me. I'm willing to take whatever risks are involved.'

'The risk is *dying*. Don't you get that?'

'You're not dead.'

'I *was* dead!'

'You seem pretty much alive to me right now.' His expression softened. 'Look, I know it's dangerous, but I want to do this. I want to help humanity.'

'Julian—'

'It's so important, Reese. It's *so* freaking important. This adaptation procedure will change everything. Don't you see that?' He was practically crouching on his heels in his effort to persuade her.

She stared at him in dismay.

'Will you help me?' he asked. 'You know them. You can talk to Dr Brand and persuade her to take me as a volunteer.'

She was stunned. 'You want – how could you ask me to put you in that kind of danger?'

His face darkened. 'You don't get it.' Suddenly he stuck out his hand. 'Here. You have the ability. Touch me. Then you'll know why I want to do it.'

'Jules—'

'Do it.'

The desperation on his face frightened her. She didn't want to touch him. She didn't need to touch him to sense how frustrated and determined he was, or how blind he was to the potential consequences. Her phone rang, the sound pealing through the weighted space between them. She pulled it from her pocket and answered it. 'Hey, Dad.'

Julian shook his head, withdrawing his hand to take out another cigarette.

'Okay, I'll be there in a minute,' she said into the phone, and then hung up. Julian wouldn't look at her. She didn't like fighting with him. The last time they'd fought was when he was dating Sean, who had been behaving like a jerk and never doing what he said he'd do. Julian had defended him repeatedly, making excuses for him because he was in love. It had soured their friendship for weeks. 'Do you want a ride home?' Reese asked, hoping that this wouldn't turn into another of those situations.

'No.' He blew out the smoke in a long stream. 'I have to meet Bri. We're planning the first GSA meeting of the year.'

'Oh.' It was like the ground had split open between her and Julian, and she didn't know how to cross the gap.

'I'd invite you to the meeting but I don't get the impression you want to be associated with the GSA this year.'

His words stung. 'Why would you think that?'

He did look at her then, and his dark brown eyes were full

of anger. 'Why? Why don't you come out? What are you afraid of?'

Her face burned. 'I'm not *afraid* of anything. It's not relevant!'

He took another drag on his cigarette and looked past her at the soccer field. 'Your boyfriend's back.'

She felt as if he had slapped her across the face. She hoisted her backpack over her shoulders and made herself walk away before she said something she would really regret. As she crossed the edge of the soccer field she saw the boys' team running sprints. One of them slowed down, looking in her direction, and she heard the coach shouting at him to get back in line. She knew it was David, but she didn't stop.

CHAPTER 17

Every day, reporters, photographers, and demonstrators lingered outside Kennedy High School, shouting questions at Reese each time she went in or out. On Tuesday, the police set up barricades and forced most of the demonstrators across the street, where they lined the edge of Dolores Park with their signs. On Wednesday after school, Reese could see them through the library window, several dozen protesters and press crowded together behind waist-high metal railings. She was supposed to be doing her Principles of Democracy homework while she waited for David to finish soccer practice, but she kept glancing up to take stock of the signage. There were a lot of STOP COLONIZATION signs today.

She turned back to her laptop. Alex Hernandez had assigned the class what he termed a 'fun' project; he wanted them to write five-hundred-word essays on the First Amendment, discussing how it was being used in the demonstrations across the street. In the past hour, Reese hadn't gotten very far. She felt as though Hernandez was mocking her and David with the assignment. The protesters outside might be able to vocalize their beliefs, but she wasn't allowed to tell the truth about what had happened to her. She scowled at her keyboard and typed, 'The First Amendment should apply to all United States citizens, but in reality, it can be easily revoked by the government when it wants to hide the truth from the public.'

She started when someone dropped a backpack onto the table across from her. She looked up to see David wearing an old KENNEDY SOCCER T-shirt, the letters faded from too many washings. 'Hey,' he said, bending over to kiss her lightly. A warm pulse went through her, and she pulled back self-consciously.

'Hi,' she said. A couple of sophomores at the table nearby were watching them.

His hair was still damp from his post-practice shower. 'What are you working on?' he asked.

'That stupid essay for Hernandez.' He leaned over her shoulder to read the first line she had written, and she smelled something tangy and sharp, a scent she was beginning to identify with him. She scooted a little closer, her hair brushing against his cheek.

He laughed. 'You're starting off with that?'

She blew out her breath in frustration. 'No. I just can't figure out what to say.' She began to delete the sentence. 'So you're finished with practice? You're ready to go?'

'Yep.'

'Cool.' She closed her laptop and grabbed her backpack so that she could put her things away. Her parents had insisted on picking her up from school every day, making her feel like a little kid, but today they had agreed that she could go over to

David's house for dinner. He had even driven to school so they wouldn't have to deal with the Muni and the paparazzi, which seemed to come out in full force when they were together.

'I'm parked up on Twentieth Street,' David said. 'We're going to have to walk past the reporters.'

'I'm sure we'll have our little MIB escorts to protect us.'

Outside, the late afternoon sun slanted brightly down from the west, crowning the green lawn of Dolores Park in a wash of gold light. They were forced to cross the street toward the protesters and photographers, and as they stepped into the crosswalk, David reached for her hand. The tide of the crowd's mental assault lessened as she focused on David at her fingertips. She knew that photos of the two of them hand in hand would be splashed all over the Hub within minutes, but for once she didn't care. She hadn't been without adult supervision since her date with David on Friday night, and she felt a little reckless now, walking free and unchaperoned across the pockmarked grass of Dolores Park.

When she and David reached the broad meadow below the children's playground, she thought: *I'll race you to the hill.* He didn't expect it, and she took off, tightening the straps of her backpack as she began to run. The air was fresh and cool and smelled of summer, and she laughed out loud.

Reese and David spread their books and laptops open across the blue shag carpet. They were downstairs in what used to be an in-law unit; it had been converted to a large open space with a comfortable rug and slouchy sofa, a boxy old television on a stand in the corner. Reese lay on her stomach on the floor, surfing for news about the protesters on her computer and still trying to find an angle on her essay for Principles of Democracy, while David worked through a calculus problem set.

'Have you thought about what you're going to write yet?' she asked him, clicking through photos from the ferry protest.

'No. I'll do it tomorrow. This is due first.'

David sat with his back against the couch, math book propped open beside him as he scribbled numbers and symbols onto a pad of paper. He seemed fairly engrossed in his homework so Reese turned back to the Internet. She was beginning to recognize the various theories behind the signs. The STOP COLONIZATION protesters believed that the Imria were here to take over Earth via the adaptation procedure, which would turn all humans into Imrian slaves. Signs such as ABDUCTEES FOR DISCLOSURE came from groups of people who believed they had been abducted by aliens in the past. Some of these individuals claimed they recognized the Imria from their abduction experiments, while others merely wanted recognition of their traumatic experiences – along with financial remuneration. Lastly, there was a pro-Imria faction that was so enamored of the extraterrestrials that they held signs proclaiming I VOLUNTEER, in reference to the Imrian plan to seek out test subjects for the adaptation procedure. Reese wondered if Julian was going to show up at one of the demonstrations carrying a sign like that.

Thinking about their fight made her uncomfortable. He had been distant from her at school since Monday, and their friends had noticed. When they asked her what was wrong, she brushed it off as nothing important, but she was worried. Maybe she should call him, try to work things out. His last words kept ringing in her memory: *Why don't you come out? What are you afraid of?* She remembered him looking at her with a combination of disappointment and betrayal – as if she wasn't the person he thought she was.

She closed the window showing the pro-Imria protesters as if that would erase the guilty feelings simmering inside her. The window beneath it was open to a general news site, and the top headline read *Biologists Believe Imria Have Modified Their Appearances to Look Human*. She clicked on it.

LONDON – In a speech at the Royal Society for Anthropology and Archaeology, Oxford University anthropologist Daniel Green theorized that the Imria's humanlike appearance is due to calculation, not accident, as Imrian ambassador Akiya Deyir suggested earlier this month.

'Statistically speaking, it is close to impossible that life could have arisen on a different planet and produced an intelligent species that looks exactly like us,' Dr Green said. 'Because they are such an advanced civilization, however, it is possible that they have changed themselves – either through plastic surgery or other means – to resemble us.'

When asked to theorize why the Imria might have done this, Dr Green said, 'I'm speculating here, but if you were an advanced civilization making contact with a much less advanced one – and we're the less advanced civilization here

– wouldn't you make every effort to present yourself in a way that made the less advanced people comfortable?'

'Hey, what are you reading?' David asked, nudging her leg with his foot.

She glanced over her shoulder at him. 'This anthropologist thinks the Imria are changing themselves to look like us.'

He put down his math homework and lay on his stomach beside her, reading over her shoulder. He wasn't touching her, but she felt the warmth from his body all along her side.

'I guess that's a possibility,' he said skeptically.

She remembered what Amber had told her when they talked after the tour of the spaceship. She wasn't sure if she should mention Amber at all, but what she had said now seemed important. 'Amber told me the Imria purposely dress like human men and women.'

A muscle in David's jaw twitched. 'When did she tell you that?'

'When we walked down to the cove together after the press conference.' Reese looked at him, but his face was unreadable. 'We were talking about Eres Tilhar, because I didn't know if Eres was male or female. Amber said Eres is a teacher, and gender is irrelevant for them. Then she said that the Imria dress like men or women here on Earth, because they fit in better that way.'

'Interesting. What's this at the bottom?' He pointed to a link that read *Are the Imria Ancient Aliens?* He reached for her computer and clicked on the link, which led to an article with images of the Egyptian pyramids, Mayan paintings, and pictures of giant lines carved into the ground. He skimmed the article. 'Some people think aliens have been visiting Earth for thousands of years and helped the ancient Egyptians build their pyramids? That's crazy.'

She forced herself to accept the change of subject. She didn't really want to talk about Amber, either. 'Yeah, I've heard of it before. I'm not a big fan of the theory.'

'Because it makes it seem as if ancient civilizations were too stupid to figure these things out on their own?'

'Exactly. Julian's kind of into it, but even he doesn't buy some of the ancient alien theories. He does think some of it can't be explained without alien intervention, though.' She pointed at the photo of the lines carved into the mountains. 'Like this. These are in Peru, and they were made a long time ago.'

'"The Nazca lines",' David read from the caption. '"Some experts believe that these lines, created in the fifth century AD, were ancient runways used by a visiting alien civilization. Could it have been the Imria?"' He scrolled down. 'This article thinks the Imria are lying about when they first came to Earth. It says that sightings of spaceships began a long time before Roswell.'

'That part's true. People have seen UFOs forever.'

'Does Julian think the Imria got here before 1947?'

'I don't know.' She rolled onto her back, moving away from David and the laptop.

He glanced at her. 'Is something going on with you two?'

She stared at the overhead light fixture. 'We had a fight.'

'About what?'

She couldn't tell him that Julian had basically accused her of wanting to stay closeted. That was not a discussion she wanted to have with David, who clearly had issues with Amber. Instead she said, 'He wants to be adapted.'

'Seriously?'

She shifted onto her side, propping her head in her hand. 'Yeah. He says he wants to volunteer to be a test subject. I told him he's crazy.'

'Why does he want to volunteer?'

She ran her fingers through the shag carpeting. 'He thinks the adaptation procedure is this big huge thing that will change humanity for the better. He wants to be part of it. I think he's romanticizing it.'

David closed her laptop and pushed it aside, turning to face her. 'He's got a point.'

'What do you mean?'

'It *will* change humanity. If the Imria do what they say they're going to do, everything is going to change.'

She narrowed her eyes at him. 'Do you think they're some kind of savior?'

'They don't have to be saviors to change everything. You have to admit, this adaptation thing is pretty intense. Think about what the world would be like if everyone had it.'

She flopped onto her back again, avoiding his gaze. She thought about what Julian had said – that if humans had the ability to share their consciousness with others, they wouldn't be so quick to hate – and she wondered if he was being hopelessly naive. 'I don't want Julian to put himself at risk. You and I didn't have any choice in the matter – what's been done to us is done. We have to deal with the consequences. But Julian doesn't need to get involved.'

'You make it sound so grim.'

She shot him a surprised glance. 'It's not exactly a picnic. Being followed everywhere, being lied to, everybody talking shit about us on the Internet.'

'That's the public part. But think about what the adaptation has really done to us.' David reached out and touched her arm with one finger. His presence wavered into her consciousness as his finger stroked her skin. 'It's pretty amazing. Remember when we met with Eres Tilhar? I don't know what you felt, but I felt like this was the answer to everything. Eres – whether she's a woman or a man, who cares – Eres was bigger than life.'

She felt David's heartbeat quickening as he spoke. His chest tightened as he remembered what Eres had shown him. He rested his hand on her arm, and her pulse leaped in response.

'I feel like this happened to us for a reason. I know that sounds crazy, and I'm not really religious, but . . .'

'What?' she said softly. 'You can tell me.'

He gave her a quick smile. 'Karma. I think about karma, right? I don't really understand it, but I feel like there's something bigger than us. Like we pay into a central pot of goodwill or something, and we get back what we put in. That day with Eres Tilhar – that was the first time I felt like I was connected to that pot of karma.'

She grinned in spite of herself and reached for his hand. 'A pot of karma? Do you know how much I want to make jokes about Buddhist leprechauns right now?'

David's mouth curved up. 'It's a good thing I like you or I might be offended.'

'That is a good thing,' she agreed, pulling him closer.

He propped his head on his right hand as the fingers of his left laced through hers. 'What did you feel with Eres?' he asked.

She thought back to the moment in the ship with Eres Tilhar. 'It felt . . . big. Like I didn't know what the hell I was doing. It felt scary.' His body was pressed against her side now, and the warmth of him spread through her limbs. He wanted to touch her, but his hand was motionless in hers. He was holding himself back, and sensing that made her skin flush. *This feels scary too*, she thought.

She raised her right hand to his waist, where his T-shirt had pulled up. Her fingers ran over the smooth skin of his obliques, and she felt him feel it, a ripple traveling through his body. He let go of her left hand and touched the side of her face, his thumb trailing over her mouth.

Do you want me to stop? he asked. They were both nervous, remembering the overwhelming experience in the shed at the party, how frighteningly easy it was to slip over the edge. Reese told herself to focus on David. She looked up at him: his dark, half-hooded eyes; the sharp strands of his black hair angling over his forehead; the shape of his mouth, slightly open.

No, she told him. *I don't want you to stop.* He bent his head and brushed his lips against hers. Her fingers tightened around his waist, pulling him down. His leg slid over hers.

A startled shriek came from the stairs. David jerked his head up and Reese rolled away. Chloe was halfway down the stairs into the family room, her face pink. 'Dinner?' she squeaked, and then fled.

Reese sat up, her face red, and when she caught the embarrassed expression on David's face she burst into laughter. He rubbed a hand over his eyes before scrambling to his feet. 'Come on. Better my sister than my parents.'

CHAPTER 18

Their first lesson with Eres Tilhar was on Saturday. Their parents had agreed to take turns escorting them to Angel Island, and this week David's father was driving. When he picked up Reese at her house, he told her that he had arranged for them to go to UCSF Medical Center on Sunday afternoon. 'We have a preliminary team of geneticists assembled, and they need to take some samples – just blood and a buccal swab,' Winston Li said. 'Are you all right with that?'

'What are they going to do with it?' she asked.

'They'll sequence your DNA – and David's. We want to find out where your DNA differs, post-adaptation, from normal human DNA.'

Reese, seated in the backseat, touched David's shoulder in the front passenger seat. *So we're doing this?* she thought.

He turned to look at her, nodding. *I think it'll be fine. My dad knows the team.*

'Okay,' she said out loud. 'Tomorrow it is.'

Dr Brand had promised there would be guards at the ferry dock, and as they approached Reese saw hired security in black jumpsuits with guns at their hips. The protesters were still there, blockaded behind a metal barricade, and Reese eyed their signs as she and David hurried through the turnstile to the empty ferry. UNITE AGAINST THE NEW WORLD ORDER, one sign declared. Another had an alien head on it – gray skin and giant black eyes – with a circle and a diagonal slash across it.

At Angel Island, a light-skinned Imrian man with black hair met them at the dock. He introduced himself as Nura Halba and said he would be their primary liaison going forward. He looked partially Asian, and Reese wondered whether the Imria had chosen their race as well as their gender in order to be intelligible to humans. She didn't know what to think of that possibility, and she surreptitiously studied the Imrian as he drove the SUV away from the dock toward the ship. He caught a glimpse of her in the rearview mirror and asked, 'Is anything wrong?'

'No.' She looked out the window. Asking Amber about Eres Tilhar's gender was one thing – at least Reese knew Amber well enough to ask that sort of question – but she couldn't ask Nura Halba whether he had picked his race as if selecting from a menu of choices.

When they arrived at the ship, Halba escorted them down the corridors to the triangular room where they had first met Eres Tilhar. Today, two of the walls were like giant windows. Straight ahead was the beach at the edge of the field, and beyond that, sailboats bobbed on the water. Halba took David's father to meet with Dr Brand – she was going to share her research materials with him – and left David and Reese alone with the teacher.

‘Please sit,’ Eres said, and David and Reese sat down in the two empty chairs. ‘Learning *susum’urda* is a very intimate experience, and first I want to assure you that you can trust me. I won’t share anything I learn about you during our lessons with anyone else without your permission. I want you to feel free to explore your new abilities. I am only here to teach you; I am not here to judge.’ Eres sounded friendly, but Reese felt a little nervous. How much would Eres be able to know by touching them?

‘Today we’ll begin with some very basic skills,’ Eres continued. ‘The adaptation that you’ve been given is an ability that we Imria are born with. *Susum’urda* allows us to share consciousness with one another – to experience directly how others experience the world. We begin to teach our children how to manage this ability from a very early age, and the first thing we teach them is how to identify their core selves; how to situate those selves in their surroundings and to maintain that sense at all times. If you don’t maintain that sense, you are in danger of losing track of who you are when you share consciousness with another. At best, that is disorienting; at worst, it can lead to serious psychological complications.’

Disorienting, Reese thought, remembering the night in the shed with David. That was one way to describe it; another would be all-consuming.

Eres looked at Reese. ‘Have you experienced anything of that sort?’

‘Uh . . . well, David and I don’t really know how to do *susum’urda*, so it’s definitely been disorienting.’

Eres nodded slowly, but Reese could not read the expression on the *ummi*'s face. 'We Imria train from childhood how to properly manage *susum'urda*. By the time we're your age we are well-equipped to handle it. I admit I've never trained anyone of your age before.'

'Are we too old to do this?' David asked.

'I don't know. I think there is some risk involved, but of course, risk is part of everyone's life.'

Reese didn't find that comforting. 'What's risky about it?'

'You are both . . . involved romantically, is that correct?' Eres asked.

Reese blushed. 'Um . . . yeah?'

'What does that have to do with it?' David asked.

Eres sat back, hands folded. 'You both should refrain from being physically intimate before you've learned how to manage *susum'urda*.'

Eres spoke with the clinical detachment of a doctor, but Reese's face still burned.

'Okay,' David said doubtfully. 'Why?'

Eres glanced from Reese to David. 'Because the connection of *susum'urda* is very powerful. You must first learn how to be centered in your own self – your own consciousness – before you engage in physical intimacy. Otherwise you risk losing yourself in the other; you risk erasing parts of your own identity.'

'Can't you shut it off?' Reese asked, remembering what Amber had done. 'You don't always have to be doing this *susum'urda* when you touch someone, do you?'

'That's true, but neither of you are trained to do that. Neither of you can control that yet. So I must ask that you both exercise some restraint. Any questions?'

'No,' Reese and David said at the same moment. She glanced at him, and he looked about as embarrassed as she was.

'Excellent. Today we'll begin by spending some time with our selves. Every individual goes through life always already situated on a map created by his or her mind. Please close your eyes and I will show you.'

Reese reluctantly closed her eyes as Eres's soft, clear voice continued. She felt a little ridiculous. The lesson so far seemed like some kind of catechism class: a lesson in abstinence followed by prayer. This was not what she had been expecting.

'Now, look within yourself,' Eres said. 'Do you see that you have a sense of the interior of your body? The first thing you will sense are the basic needs of your physical self. Whether you are hungry. Whether you are warm or cold. Whether you are in pain.'

Reese found it difficult to focus on the sensations that Eres was talking about. Her eyelids fluttered as she struggled to keep them closed, and her muscles twitched as she tried to relax into the chair. It was made of a hard, slippery material like lacquered wood, and she was distracted by wondering what kind of tree the wood came from— or whether it was wood at all.

'Notice that you always know where your hands are. Whether your fingers are curled or straight. Notice how your body is situated in relation to the chair beneath it. You know where you are in this room. Your brain has mapped out all these details, and you are always interacting with the world. As you breathe in, you are interacting. As you sit up or lean back, you are interacting. All these signals are sent to your brain through your body. Your self – your mind – can never be separated from your physical body.'

Reese breathed in and out, feeling her lungs rising and falling. She remembered when her mom had gone through her most virulent anti-Catholic phase and brought her to a parent-child meditation retreat in Marin. Reese had squirmed on the cushion she had been told to sit on, her eyes blinking open and closed as the meditation instructor asked her to focus on her breath. This felt sort of like that: an exercise that was beyond her powers of concentration.

'Notice the details that arise in your mind. Details about where you were this morning before you came here; knowledge of where you will go when you leave. You are always situated in space, within the map of your world, but you are also always situated within the timeline of your life. On our world, we remember the first time we experience *susum'urda* with another being, usually one of our parents, who hold us in their arms and love us. For you, in your world, you may remember your first close friendship. You may remember an experience that filled you with joy. This is who you are. Only you have these experiences in this particular order.'

Unlike Eres's instructions to focus on her body, which felt like a slick rope Reese couldn't quite grasp, these instructions resonated with her. She had never thought of herself as a timeline of experiences, but it made sense to her. She saw her mother's face from above as she flew into the air on the swing set in Dolores Park, her short legs pumping into the blue sky.

She remembered her father waving at her in the Seattle airport the first time she had flown to see him after the divorce, her stomach knotted with trepidation because she was angry with him, but she still missed him. One summer night when she was twelve years old, she and Julian had snuck out of the vacation house in Guerneville and climbed down the steep steps leading to the river, where the water lapped softly at the floating dock. They swam in the dark, the full moon shining over them, while their parents' voices called from the deck of the house above.

'This is the path you will take when you share your consciousness with another person,' Eres said. 'First, you will sense their physical body, their interior experience. Then, as your own experience with *susum'urda* grows, you will be able to know their core self, how they interact with the external world. The ultimate goal is to see who they are as clearly as you see yourself. To share yourself with them as they share themselves with you. We will try that now. Please open your eyes.'

Reese blinked. The view of the bay was gone, and the walls undulated with a cool blue light. The color gave Eres's skin a faint aquamarine tinge. 'I'll begin with David,' Eres said, and extended a hand to him. 'If you feel yourself overwhelmed, you can always return to yourself. Remember your own physical experience. If you are focused on yourself, you will not sense the other person; nor will they be able to sense you except externally.'

Reese watched as he took Eres's hand. A shock seemed to pass over his face as they touched, and then his mouth went slack, his eyes glazing. Reese felt as if she were intruding on David and Eres, so she looked away. All around them, the blue walls shimmered as if sunlight were pouring through the ocean. It was peaceful and buoyant and hypnotic, this sea of blue light. After some time, she heard David catch his breath, and Eres drew back.

'Now Reese,' the teacher said, holding out a hand to her.

Eres's skin was dry and soft, and immediately Reese felt safe within the teacher's guided touch. Eres showed her the map of Reese's own physical experience at first: the path of blood in her veins, the movement of her muscles, the swelling and release of her lungs. It was strange to have someone revealing these sensations to her, as if shining a spotlight on each organ in succession. Reese had never been especially physically attuned to her body, and having Eres take her through it was almost like touring a foreign land. Then Eres expanded Reese's perception, showing her the map of her body in relation to the chair, the floor, and the room itself. After that, Eres unreeled the history of Reese's experiences, image after image, and Reese shuddered at the sensation of someone else recognizing so deeply who she was.

Now, Eres spoke in her mind, *here is who I am*.

This was like stepping through a doorway into a wilderness of such exotic beauty that Reese could barely focus.

Remember who you are. You can always return to that.

Reese focused on the feel of her own heart pumping; of her legs meeting the wooden seat. Bit by bit, as Reese remembered herself, Eres's consciousness receded until Reese was able to approach it knowing who she was.

Eres had been born long ago, and was raised by three Imrians whose faces swam in Reese's mind, at once familiar – through Eres's perspective – and strange. Eres had grown up on a world not unlike Earth, a world of oceans on which many islands floated, their mountains rising high. Reese became aware that Eres was showing her certain images, specific memories, so that she would not drown in the flood of them, because Eres had lived many human lifetimes. It was less intimate than Reese had feared it might be, perhaps because Eres was directing her progress through those memories.

Later, you will also know how to do this, Eres told her. *You will be able to order your conscious experience. You will be able to share only what you want to share, and maintain your own private conscious space if you wish.*

Understanding Eres was not like hearing David's thoughts. Reese got the impression that Eres was thinking in a language different than English, but the meaning still came through clearly.

How? Reese wondered. *How can I learn that?*

First, observe what I do as I close myself to you. This is what you will learn today.

Eres began to shut off the images that Reese could see. One by one they faded into darkness, and Reese saw how Eres was folding those images and experiences away until Reese could only see Eres with her eyes.

Eres let go of Reese's hand and smiled at her and David. 'Now the two of you will practice that with me. I will look into you, and you will close yourselves to me.'

Over and over, they did as Eres asked. It was similar to

what Reese had done instinctually when confronted by a curious crowd, but now that she knew what she was aiming for, it was easier. She wondered if this was what Amber had done every time they had touched. How had she maintained the presence of mind to do it? The only way Reese could imagine it to be possible was if Amber had never cared that much for her in the first place. Her gut clenched as the memory of Amber in her kitchen, denying that she knew Dr Brand, came back to her. The pain of learning that Amber was a liar had barely been dulled by time; it was still sharp as a razor.

You aren't focusing, Eres told her.

Reese realized that Eres had sensed everything she had thought about Amber. Her first instinct was to deny her feelings; to cover them up somehow.

You cannot lie, Eres thought. *You can close your consciousness to others, but you can never lie. Not during* susum'urda.

I was not lying, Reese objected.

Eres guided her out of susum'urda, and then Reese felt the teacher somehow compel her to open her eyes. It was like being roughly shaken awake from a deep dream state. Eres dropped Reese's hand, breaking their connection, and said, 'When you are in *susum'urda*, your body will always reveal the truth. The physical actions that occur when you experience an emotion continue regardless of whether or not you want them to.'

'What?' Reese said, confused. She was disoriented by the sudden ending of *susum'urda*, and she had the uncomfortable feeling that Eres was disappointed in her.

'When you feel fear, for example, your body undergoes a

series of physical actions. Your heart races, you might sweat, adrenaline might be released. All of these things will happen regardless of whether or not you're able to control your external reactions. You might be able to hide it externally, but it's still happening internally. You were trying to hide your emotions internally, but that is impossible. You were applying your human desire to hide your emotions, but in *susum'urda*, the person you are connected to can sense all of your internal, physical reactions. You can't hide. You can only close off the connection.'

Reese's gaze flickered self-consciously to David. He was watching the two of them with his forehead furrowed, as if he were trying to figure out what had happened. *I wasn't trying to hide*, Reese thought at Eres. The teacher did not seem to hear, so Reese tried again, not wanting to speak out loud. *I didn't realize you were seeing everything.* I wasn't ready for you to see everything.

'Do you understand what I said?' Eres asked. 'If you wish to close the connection, you may. *Susum'urda* is an intimate experience; you don't need to have that with everyone. But you must understand that you cannot lie while you are having *susum'urda*.'

Reese realized, suddenly, that Eres had not heard her thoughts. Maybe Eres couldn't hear her thoughts at all unless they were touching. Reese tried again. *Can you hear me?* But Eres's expression did not change, and Reese felt no affirmation from the teacher. 'I understand,' Reese said. 'I wasn't trying to lie. I just wasn't ready for what you were doing.'

Eres gave her a thoughtful look. 'I see. Well. I think our

lesson is finished for today. I hope you'll both remember what I told you. I look forward to next week.'

On the ferry home, Reese and David went up to the top deck, leaving David's dad down below with a tablet loaded with Dr Brand's research. Outside, the wind gusted against Reese's face as the boat left the dock. She leaned against the railing, gazing across the water at the hills of Tiburon in the distance. As David came to stand next to her, she told him, *I don't think the Imria can do what we can do. Eres Tilhar couldn't hear my thoughts when we weren't touching.*

Are you sure?

I'm sure. I tried to communicate with her this way, but Eres didn't react at all.

I tried too, but I couldn't tell for sure if Eres heard me.

Reese glanced over her shoulder; there was no one on the upper deck but her and David. 'What do you think it means if the Imria can't do this telepathic thing?' she said out loud. 'They gave us our abilities – why don't they have the same ones?'

'Maybe their DNA doesn't work in us exactly the way they thought it would. How would they know for sure, anyway? They've never been successful with this adaptation thing before us.'

Reese looked out across the water. If the adaptation procedure had changed them in a way the Imria hadn't expected, what would happen when they began adapting other human beings? "Do you think we should tell Eres about our telepathic stuff?'

'I'm not sure.'

She glanced at him. 'Why?'

'They have so much power over us. They know so much that we don't. This is the only thing they don't know.'

She thought back. 'Lovick and CASS don't know, either. They think we have the same abilities as the Imria.'

'Nobody else knows,' he said in sudden realization. 'We never told Sophia Curtis. We never got that far because Jeff Highsmith stopped us. They all think we have to be touching someone to know their thoughts.'

'We didn't tell anyone about the crowds thing either, did we?' She tried to remember what had happened the day the gunman had been arrested at Fisherman's Wharf. She had been overwhelmed by the emotions of the crowd, but she didn't think anyone had really understood why. At least, nobody but David. 'Did you tell your parents? The last time I talked to mine about our adaptation, I'm pretty sure I only told them about the touching thing.'

'No, I haven't talked to them about it since we got back from Nevada, and I couldn't figure out how to explain everything without sounding crazy, so I didn't tell them about the telepathy stuff.' His gaze on her sharpened. 'Are you sure you didn't tell anyone? Not even Julian?'

She tried to remember all the conversations she'd had with Julian about the adaptation. 'I don't know,' she admitted finally. 'I might have said something. But I think it's okay. Julian won't say anything. I know he won't.'

David nodded. 'All right. So we keep this to ourselves for now.'

A tense excitement gripped Reese. Could she and David finally have an advantage, however small? "Right. We don't tell anyone else.'

'Not until it's absolutely necessary,' David said.

The thought of what their government might do with two telepaths – even if the telepaths didn't really know what they were doing – was deeply unsettling to Reese. 'On Monday, Mr Hernandez is going to make us report in. What are we going to tell him?'

'We can tell him what Eres taught us, can't we? If we're only keeping our telepathy a secret, we might as well tell him the rest.'

'Okay. I guess that makes sense.' She turned around so that the railing was behind her and she could see Angel Island receding in the distance. Half a dozen seagulls lifted off from their perches on the pilings in the harbor, their white wings a blur of motion as they took to the air. She had gotten so used to not seeing birds around the city anymore that the sight of this flock was startling.

David said, 'And we have to agree on when to reveal it.'

'Yes,' she said, her gaze still on the flying birds.

'Reese.'

There was something in the tone of his voice that made her look at him. 'What?'

'What was that about with Eres Tilhar at the end?'

'Nothing,' she said, surprised by the change of subject. She saw a flash of disappointment in David's eyes. She rushed on: 'It was too much for me, that's all. It was too intimate. I didn't want Eres to know everything about me right away.'

He moved to stand in front of her, hands in his pockets. The wind was at her back now, and it blew her hair forward over her face. She tried to comb it back with her fingers, but it didn't stay in place. He reached out to tuck a lock behind her ear, and the trail of his fingertip over her skin made her shiver. She caught his hand in hers, and she immediately felt the tension inside him. He was anxious about what she wasn't telling him, but he didn't want to push her. She was filled with a combination of relief and shame.

He closed the space between them and kissed her gently. She wanted to pull him closer, but underneath the spark that lit inside her, she felt something else: a thin, wavering sadness. David stepped back, breaking contact, and gave her a brief, hollow smile. 'We have to restrain ourselves, right?' he said.

She stared at him, uncertain. 'Yeah,' she agreed finally. 'Right.'

CHAPTER 19

On Sunday afternoon, Reese's mom drove her to UCSF Medical Center to meet David and his dad. It was a very different experience from the exam she had received against her will at Blue Base. It took all of ten minutes. She didn't have to get undressed, and her mom stayed in the exam room with her. There was a poster of the circulatory system on the wall, like something out of a biology classroom. A nurse in blue scrubs came in to take her blood and swab the inside of her cheek with a Q-tip. She was accompanied by a gray-haired doctor who introduced himself as Dr Alan Nadler.

'How long will it take to sequence our DNA?' Reese asked after her blood was drawn.

'Not long,' Dr Nadler answered. 'It can be done in a matter of hours these days, but we'll need more time to analyze it and compare it with normal human DNA. We're hoping to work fast, but we're still in the process of assembling our team and we want to make sure nothing is contaminated. We hope to have preliminary results in a couple of weeks.' As the nurse finished up, Dr Nadler took the samples from her and placed them in a locked case. 'I'll be overseeing the process from my office here at UCSF.' He removed a card from his pocket and handed it to Reese's mom. 'You can contact me if you have any questions.'

Later that night, Reese was sitting on the couch with her laptop, reading an article about the Imria – 'Vatican Believes Imria Are Children of God' – when the landline rang in the kitchen. She heard footsteps, and then her mom's muffled voice answered the phone. Reese scrolled through the story; the pope had declared that Akiya Deyir's statements about the miraculous resemblance between humans and Imria proved that God's hand was at work. During Sunday mass in Rome earlier in the day, the pope had said, 'God is great, and there can be no greater proof of this than the fact that He has created another people also in His image.'

'Reese, do you know where Julian is?' her mom asked.

Reese looked up. Her mom was standing in the archway to the living room, phone in hand. 'No,' Reese said. 'Why?'

Her mom put the phone back to her ear. 'She doesn't know, Celeste.'

'What happened?' Reese asked.

'Julian's late,' her mom said.

Reese glanced at the time on her laptop. It was almost ten thirty. She hadn't talked to Julian since school on Friday, and even then it had been only perfunctory. They still hadn't made up from the fight they'd had earlier in the week. She had no idea where Julian could be on a Sunday night. 'It's still early,' Reese said, but her mom wasn't paying attention.

'Why don't you give him another hour or so,' she said

into the phone. 'It's not the first time he's been late.' A pause, and a worried expression crossed Cat's face. 'I know. But there are police everywhere these days – and those soldiers. I'm sure if he ran into any trouble with the protesters, you'd know by now.'

Reese closed the laptop and went to the windows, peeking through the curtains at the street below. She saw the sedan where her government agents were sitting across the street, but otherwise the block was quiet. Every once in a while protesters or tourists still swung by her house to snap photos, but the primary demonstrations took place across from Kennedy High School and at Fisherman's Wharf. The rest of the city was crawling with cops and the National Guard.

'Call me when you hear from him,' Cat said. 'I want to know as soon as you know. Bye.' The phone beeped as the call ended. 'Honey, are you sure you don't know where Julian is? He didn't tell you anything?'

'No,' Reese said. It wasn't strange for Julian to be out somewhere, but it was strange for his mom to be worried about it. That meant Julian probably wasn't answering his phone. Reese went back to the couch and opened her laptop again. The screen still showed the article about the Vatican. As her mom went back to the kitchen, Reese pulled her own phone out of her pocket. She sent Julian a message: Where are you? Your mom called my mom to find out.

While she waited for him to text her back, she opened a new tab in her browser and searched for *Corporation for American Security and Sovereignty*. She had looked it up after the meeting with Charles Lovick and had found nothing, but she wanted to try again. This time she focused her search on blogs, real-time feeds, and the news. Still nothing. As a last-ditch effort, she went to the Bin 42 forums and searched for CASS there. Several posts were returned that used the words *corporation*, *security*, or *sovereignty*, but not all at once. The closest thing she could find was a theory about something called the Majestic 12, which was a committee of twelve men supposedly formed during the Truman Administration to investigate the crash at Roswell. Unfortunately, the follow-up comments revealed that the alleged government documents that proved the existence of the Majestic 12 were now believed to be a hoax.

She closed the screen and picked up her phone again, but Julian still hadn't responded to her text.

The phone rang again after midnight. Reese had gone to bed by then, but she couldn't fall asleep. She was concocting all sorts of terrifying scenarios about Julian being picked up by CASS, or getting in trouble by challenging the anti-Imria protesters. The sound of the phone made her sit straight up. She heard a door open downstairs – her dad, probably, coming out of the guest room – and then the door across the hall as her mom ran down to the kitchen. Reese threw off her blankets and followed.

By the time she got downstairs her mom was on the phone already, a shocked expression on her face. Reese's dad was leaning against the door frame to the guest room, his arms crossed.

'But how did he get there?' her mom asked. 'It's not exactly easily accessible.' There was a pause, and Cat pushed her curly hair out of her eyes. 'I'm glad he's all right. Thanks for letting me know. Do you want me to come with you tomorrow?' She rummaged in the junk drawer and pulled out a notepad and pen. 'Yeah. Eight AM. I'll tell work I'll be in late.'

Reese crossed the kitchen, leaning over the counter to read the note her mom had scribbled down. It read *9 AM Fish Wharf*. Reese's gaze snapped to her mom, who was watching her and had one finger raised. *Wait*, she mouthed.

'I'll see you tomorrow,' her mom said, and hung up.

'What's going on?' Reese asked.

'Julian went to Angel Island.'

'Angel Island?' *Of course*. He must have tried to volunteer for the adaptation procedure. 'But how? It's not like there's a regular ferry service.'

Her mom shook her head, replacing the phone in its base. 'Celeste wasn't sure, but I think Julian hired someone. They're sending a ferry first thing in the morning, and I'm going with Celeste to pick him up and talk to Dr Brand.'

Reese's dad went over to her mom and rubbed a hand over her back. Reese tried not to stare. 'I'm glad he's all right,' he said.

'Yes, he's all right,' her mom said. 'But he's about to be grounded for the rest of his life.'

Julian obviously was not at school on Monday morning. Reese's mom had asked her not to tell anyone where he was, so when her friends wondered aloud about his absence, she didn't say a thing. It helped that they all knew she and Julian were fighting, so they didn't push her. When she saw David at lunch, though, she told him silently about Julian's Sunday night trip to Angel Island.

I'm going over to his house right after school, she thought to David. *He should be home by then. I have to find out what the hell he was thinking.*

David took a bite of his turkey sandwich. *You can't go right after school. We have to meet with Hernandez. I saw him earlier and he told me he wants us to report in today.*

She mixed up the rice and beans on her cafeteria plate. *What about soccer practice? Don't you have that?*

Yeah, but he didn't seem to care. We'll just have to make it fast.

Principles of Democracy was the last period of the day. She and David had planned what they would say, but who knew if Mr Hernandez would buy it? During class, she fidgeted in her seat, her right leg bouncing up and down as she watched Mr Hernandez drone on about the Bill of Rights. Behind him, Mr Chapman's posters depicting the Constitution and the branches of government still hung on the wall above the whiteboard. Mr Hernandez hadn't bothered to change much about the room, although Mr Chapman's personal photos had been removed. Reese kept waiting for Mr Hernandez to slip up during class, but so far he had managed to bluff his way through the lectures pretty well. Maybe CASS had hired someone to draft a bunch of lesson plans for him.

At the end of class he walked down the aisles, returning their essays on the First Amendment. As he dropped Reese's paper on her desk, he leaned over her and said in a low voice, 'I'll see you after class.'

She glanced at her essay. He had given her a C, writing, 'Interesting argument, but unsubstantiated,' in red pen. She had argued that the protesters across the street were allowed to voice their opinions because the government needed to give the public a place to vent their complaints, even if the government had no intention of bowing to demands for disclosure or anything else. 'The First Amendment,' she concluded, 'can thus also be used as a smoke screen behind which real dissent is ignored or even silenced.'

She fumed over the grade. Mr Chapman would have given her a better one. It was a well-thought-out essay, and she was sure that the only reason she had gotten a C was because Mr Hernandez didn't like her thesis. When the bell rang she took her time putting her stuff away, waiting until the room was mostly cleared. David, who sat a couple of rows away from her, turned to look at her. 'What'd you get?' he asked.

She moved into the seat next to David. 'C.'

He shook his head, a tiny smile on his face. 'I told you you should have written something else.'

I'm not changing my opinions just because our teacher is a fake, she retorted silently. She watched Mr Hernandez slide his papers into his leather briefcase, which was resting on top of his desk in the corner of the room. When the last student departed, Mr Hernandez went to the door and pushed it shut before turning to Reese and David.

'All right, let's get started.' He turned a nearby desk around to face them and sat down. Then he pulled a digital recorder from his pocket and flicked it on. 'Tell me what happened on Saturday.'

David began to relate their story, and as Reese listened, she saw Mr Hernandez's expression change from bland indifference to skepticism. She realized that David's explanation of *susum'urda* sounded strange, but the whole thing *was* strange. It was difficult to convey the quality of intimacy they had felt when Eres Tilhar touched them.

'Can you read the teacher's thoughts when she touches you?' Mr Hernandez asked.

'She guided us,' Reese said. 'We only saw what she wanted us to see.'

'So if someone were touching you, could you also do the same? Could you make them believe something about you that's false?'

'No,' Reese said. 'You can't lie. And the other person would know you were lying.'

'How?'

She tried to explain what Eres had said about the body's physical actions in response to an emotion, but either Mr Hernandez wasn't getting it or she was doing a poor job of explaining.

'This ability to share consciousness – other than you two, it only works among the Imria, right?' Mr Hernandez asked.

'Yes,' David said.

'So if you were to touch a human being, would you be able to sense their consciousness? Their thoughts?'

The question raised red flags for Reese. 'Do you want us to test it out on you?' she said before David could speak.

'Are you saying you've never tried it?' Mr Hernandez asked.

What are you trying to do? David asked Reese. *They're not going to believe that we don't know this.*

If we tell him, he'll obviously tell CASS and they'll want to use us to read other people's thoughts.

We have to focus on misleading him in one direction only. You can't throw this in too. Besides, we would know this.

Fine, she thought grumpily. Mr Hernandez was beginning to look suspicious at their long silence. *Go ahead.*

'I've done it,' David said. 'It was by accident. My mom, she – she's my mom. She hugs me. I could sense her feelings, sure, but I didn't really know what was going on. It was pretty confusing.'

'Did your mom know you were sensing her feelings?' Mr Hernandez asked.

'No. Humans can't – humans who aren't adapted can't sense that,' David asked.

Reese could practically see the gears in Mr Hernandez's brain turning as he thought about how to use their abilities for the benefit of CASS.

'You need to find out more about that,' he said. 'Next week at your lesson, ask about it.'

There was a knock on the door before Jennifer Sims, the assistant principal, opened it and poked her head inside. 'Alex? I'm sorry to interrupt—'

Mr Hernandez stood up, swiftly pocketing the recording device. 'That's all right. What can I do for you?'

'Can I speak to you?' Ms Sims asked, glancing curiously at Reese and David.

'Sure, but just for a minute. I'm in the middle of a meeting.'

'I have to get to soccer practice,' David said.

'I'll be right back,' Mr Hernandez said. 'We still have to talk about your missed assignments from last semester.'

With that, he left, following Ms Sims into the hallway. The door closed with a click, and David muttered, 'This is taking too long. My coach is gonna kill me.'

Reese slid out of her chair and ran to Mr Hernandez's desk. 'Watch the door,' she said.

'What are you doing?' David said in alarm.

At the desk, she grabbed Mr Hernandez's briefcase. 'The door,' she said again. 'Keep an eye on the window.'

There was a narrow rectangular window set in the door to the classroom, and she could see half of the back of Mr Hernandez's head. She knew she was taking a risk but she wanted to get something on him – anything – that could prove who he was. She rifled through the briefcase, finding only lecture notes and class seating charts.

'Hurry,' David said, moving toward the front of the room so he could see the window more clearly. 'I don't think he's going to take long.'

She unzipped the inner pocket of the briefcase and found a set of keys on a San Francisco trolley keychain, a flash drive, and a tablet computer. She pressed the power button but was immediately confronted with a password screen. She put it back, frustrated. Mr Hernandez didn't even have a wallet in there. She pulled the sides of the briefcase apart, scrutinizing it for any other inner pockets she hadn't seen. Next to the loops that held a few pens she found a plastic compartment made to hold business cards. She tugged out a few pieces of paper. There was a dry-cleaning receipt from a year ago, a card for an Italian restaurant in Washington, DC, and a folded piece of paper.

'I think they're wrapping up,' David said, urgency in his voice. 'She's giving him something. You'd better stop.'

Heart racing, she unfolded the paper. It was a sticker about the size of a HELLO, MY NAME IS badge, except this was a temporary ID. Under a black-and-white photo of Mr Hernandez was the name *Andrew Vargas*. There was a seal to the right of the photo, and beneath the seal it said WHITE HOUSE VISITOR PASS, VALID 1/10/13 ONLY.

'He's coming back,' David warned her.

She shoved the ID, the receipt, and the business card into her pocket and made sure the briefcase was standing upright in roughly the same spot, then raced back to her desk. David barely made it to his seat in time. The instant he sat down, the door opened and Mr Hernandez came inside. He looked irritated as he pulled out the recorder again.

'Where were we? Next weekend, you're going to ask your Imrian teacher about using your adaptation with humans.'

Reese tried not to breathe too rapidly. The pieces of paper in her pocket felt like giant rocks.

Mr Hernandez gave her a suspicious look. 'Is something wrong?'

'No,' she said quickly. 'I – we'll ask.'

'I really have to get to soccer practice,' David said. 'Is there anything else?'

Mr Hernandez went over to his desk and opened the briefcase. Reese held her breath, but he didn't seem to notice anything amiss. He returned with the small plastic device that

Reese had thought was a USB drive. He placed it squarely on David's desk. 'This is a camera.' He pointed to a tiny button on the side of the device. 'Here's the shutter.' Then he showed them a clear bump on the tip that looked like a miniature bulb. 'That's the lens. Just point and click, and make sure you're a couple of feet away from what you're photographing. We have reason to believe that the Imria have an adaptation chamber on board their ship. They've released several reports about the science involved in the adaptation procedure, but there are holes in the research. They're not revealing everything. One of the major gaps is the way the adaptation chamber actually works. Your job is to find the adaptation chamber and photograph it from as many angles as you can. Then you'll bring this camera back to me and my team will look at the photos and determine whether you need to take additional shots.'

David fingered the camera. 'But we don't know where the adaptation chamber is.'

'It's your job to find out,' Mr Hernandez said.

Reese stared at their fake teacher. 'How are we supposed to do that?'

'I suggest you start by asking them.' He leaned on the edge of the desk nearby. 'You're their first successfully adapted subjects. You have more right than anyone to view the place where you were adapted.'

'You think the adaptation chambers where they adapted us are in the ship?' she asked, surprised.

He nodded. 'There's no other place they would be.'

She swallowed. David looked unnerved. If that was true,

they had spent a lot more time in that ship than they remembered, and that disturbed her. Had Eres Tilhar visited them while they were unconscious? Had Amber?

'The General Debate of the United Nations begins on September fifteenth, exactly three weeks from today,' Mr Hernandez said. 'I'll expect you to find the adaptation chamber and bring me those photos before then.'

CHAPTER 20

Reese knocked on Julian's bedroom door, and when she heard him call 'Come in,' she opened it. He was sprawled in his beanbag chair in jeans and a black T-shirt with some kind of decal on it, his laptop open. He didn't seem surprised to see her, and she wondered if he had heard her arrive a few minutes ago. Her dad was downstairs, probably making awkward small talk with Julian's mom, who had never really liked him.

'Hey,' he said.

She closed the door and pulled out Julian's desk chair, straddling it. 'What were you doing at Angel Island?' she asked.

He closed his laptop. 'I'm fine, how are you?'

'Jules. What were you thinking?'

He set the computer on the wooden floor and looked out the bay windows, avoiding her gaze. 'I had to do it. I had to try.'

'Try *what?* Start from the beginning.'

He rubbed his hands through his curly hair, fluffing it into a puffy dark brown crown. 'I wanted to see if the Imria were what they said they were. Whether they really wanted to help humans. So I went to Angel Island and volunteered to be a test subject.' He finally looked at Reese, and his eyes seemed to glitter with excitement. 'They rejected me.'

She stared at him, her forehead furrowed. 'Thank God!' Then she narrowed her eyes at him. 'Why are you so happy about it?'

He sat up, punching the beanbag into shape behind him. 'Because if they were crazy evil colonizers, they wouldn't have rejected me. They would have taken me and done whatever tests they wanted to do. But since they didn't, this proves they're here to help us.'

She blinked. 'That is some seriously flawed logic.'

'It makes total sense.'

'No, it doesn't. All it means is that they knew who you were and they didn't want to make me mad at them. Because I would have been seriously mad if they had done anything to you.'

Anger darkened Julian's face. 'It's not always about you, Reese.'

His comment stung. 'I'm not saying it is!'

'You just said they only didn't take me because I'm *your* friend.' He jumped to his feet and began to pace in front of the windows.

He had a point, she thought, chagrined. She watched him for a moment, then asked, 'How did you get there? My mom thinks you hired someone.'

'Yeah, I hired a boat. It's crazy, the things money can buy,' he said sarcastically. His shoulders drooped a little. 'I wiped out my savings.'

'Okay, so you paid someone, but there are soldiers all over

that island. How did you get to the ship?'

He stopped pacing and pushed his hands into his pockets. He looked at her defiantly. 'Amber met me.'

She felt as if he had shoved her. 'What?'

He shrugged. 'She met me at the harbor and took me to the ship.'

'How did she even know you were there?'

'I e-mailed her.'

Reese's stomach flipped. 'Even I don't have her e-mail address. How did you get it?' His gaze shifted away from her. 'What's really going on? You didn't go there to volunteer. That's ridiculous. You knew they wouldn't take you. What were you really doing?'

He crossed the room and sat on the edge of his rumpled bed, pushing a pair of sweats out of the way. He leaned over, elbows on his knees, and looked down at the floor as he spoke. 'She e-mailed me a couple of weeks ago. Right after you and David returned from Area 51.'

Reese was shocked.

'She wanted to find out if I thought you would take her up on her offer. To let the Imria teach you guys how to use your adaptation.'

'But . . . how did she get your e-mail address?'

'I'm on the Internet. I'm listed on Bin 42. It probably wasn't that hard – it's not like I try to hide my identity. Anyway, I told her I didn't know, that she should ask you herself. But she didn't seem to want to do that. We've been e-mailing since then.' Finally he raised his head to look at her. 'She feels really bad about what happened.'

Reese stiffened. 'Did she ask you to say that?'

'No. It came up.'

'It came up? What, you and Amber are pen pals now?' She couldn't hide the bitter edge in her voice. 'Do you *like* her?'

He sat up, an incredulous expression on his face. 'Are you kidding me? I'm *your* friend. Plus I'm gay! And if you're jealous that I've been e-mailing her, you're pretty fucking gay too.'

She gaped at him. She felt as if she had walked into an inferno. Julian gave her a challenging look, as if he were daring her to contradict him. Her fingers, resting on the back of his desk chair, gripped the wood harder. Finally she said in a low, tight voice, 'Is that what this is about? Are you still pissed at me for not coming out to everyone?'

His jaw clenched. He shook his head. 'No. You can stay closeted as long as you want.'

'I'm not closeted!' she exploded. 'I don't think being gay is wrong – is that what you think I think? How could you think that? I've known you my whole life. I was there when you had your first crush on Logan Jacobsen at summer camp. I have no problems with being gay.'

Julian squirmed. 'The way you feel about me could be different than the way you feel about yourself.'

'I feel fine about myself! I don't think I'm going to hell because I liked Amber.' She lowered her voice. 'I just don't need to explain every last detail of my personal life to the public. Do you know what kind of shit they write about me and David on the Internet? Can you imagine what they would say if they knew about me and Amber? She's not even a human girl. She's an extraterrestrial.'

'Reese, I—'

'It would be insane,' she continued, ignoring him. 'The stuff they say about David is racist. Flat-out fucking racist. If they knew that I had been dating Amber, there would be no end to the crap they throw out about us. Maybe I'm being selfish for not wanting to deal with the homophobes, but think about what they would say about David, too, for dating me. I know what people think about bisexuals. That we can't make up our minds or that we're nymphomaniacs or that we're just doing it for attention. Think of what they would say if they knew I'm bisexual and that I was with an *alien*. Believe me, it fucking gives me nightmares.' She ran out of breath, face red, and glared at Julian.

He blinked at her, clearly taken aback by her rant. After a long pause, he said in a soft voice, 'So you're bisexual?'

She threw up her hands. 'Whatever. Yeah, I'm bisexual. Are you satisfied?'

He smiled slightly. 'Maybe a little.'

She groaned, laying her arms on the back of the chair and dropping her head down.

'Hey, I'm sorry. I guess I didn't think through what it might mean for you to come out like that.'

She exhaled. 'Apology accepted.'

He gave a short laugh. 'So do you still like her?'

Her head snapped up. 'No.' At the doubtful look on his face she relented. 'I don't know, okay?'

His eyes widened. 'But you're with David.'

'Yes, I know that,' she said crisply.

'Are you not over her?'

‘Why are you asking me this? Are you going to e-mail her?’

He held up his hands in submission. ‘No, no. I’m just asking as your friend. I like David. I think he’s great. But you—’ He made an apologetic face. ‘You really liked her. I could tell.’

She frowned. ‘Well, it’s over.’

‘I hate to break it to you, but that doesn’t mean your feelings are over.’ He had a wry expression on his face, and she remembered the months after he had broken up with Sean. Julian had been the one to end it, but he had moped around for weeks. She had dragged him out with Madison and Bri for a seemingly endless series of ice cream and boba tea sessions in which he sat in moody silence, only looking up when someone who resembled Sean came into the room.

Something inside her seemed to crumple at the memory of Julian dealing with his breakup. Something that she had been shoring up daily with denial and willfulness. She dropped her face into her hands. ‘I like David. I really, really like him. I don’t want to hurt him.’

‘So you do still like her,’ he said gently.

‘Maybe.’ It was the first time she had truly admitted the possibility to herself, and saying that single word out loud sent a pang through her so sharp she had to suck in her breath. ‘But I can’t,’ she said forcefully. ‘I can’t like two people at once. I won’t. Talk about stereotypes. And I haven’t even seen her in – in almost two weeks.’

‘She’s been avoiding you.’

She lowered her hands to look at him in surprise. ‘Really?’

He had moved and was now leaning against his headboard,

legs stretched out on his bed. 'I think it's hard for her to see you with David.'

'Did she tell you that?'

'Not directly. But it's obvious. Or it was obvious when I saw her last night.'

She considered him. His black T-shirt had a green alien in a spaceship printed on it, and she realized it was the logo for Bin 42. 'Hey,' she said suddenly. 'You still haven't told me what you were really doing there.' The expression on his face told her that he had been hoping she wouldn't bring it up again. 'Why were you there?'

He bent his right knee, resting his right hand on it. 'Fine. I'll tell you, but we have to come clean with each other, okay? I know you're not telling me stuff.'

'We were in a fight,' she pointed out. 'Wait, are we done with our fight?'

He grinned. 'I'm done if you're done.'

She let out her breath in relief. 'Thank God. I was getting really tired of being annoyed with you.' He threw a sock at her, and she ducked. 'Gross. How old are you, three?'

He rolled his eyes. 'So you promise to tell me what's going on for real? You still haven't given me that recording of the meeting you had with Charles Lovick.'

She hesitated. 'All right, I'll tell you what I can.'

'Reese. Everything. Am I not your best friend?'

'Of course! But I can't, Julian. I made a promise to David. Some things I can't tell you.' She waved her hands. 'But I'll tell you everything I didn't promise I wouldn't tell you.'

He finally nodded. 'I guess that's fair.'

'Good. Now tell me what the hell you were doing at Angel Island.'

He smiled. 'I went there to interview Amber for Bin 42.'

She had definitely not been expecting this. 'Seriously?'

Julian's eyebrows lifted. 'Yes, seriously. Do you not know what I've been doing for the past six months?'

'You've been doing some stuff for Bin 42, I know, but—'

'No, not "some stuff". This is major, Reese. I know you've always thought my obsession with UFOs was kind of funny, but it turns out I was *right*.' Excitement lit his face again. 'I was fucking right on, and this is the biggest story of the millennium. You think I'm going to sit back and let somebody else take it?'

She was uncomfortable. 'I didn't think it was funny.'

He gave her a pointed look. 'Well, you definitely didn't think I was going for a Pulitzer Prize or anything with my UFO blogging. I know you only agreed to start that Black Mailbox site to humor me.'

'That's not true.'

'It's totally true. I thought we were supposed to be honest with each other now.'

She tucked a strand of hair behind her ear, feeling like the worst friend in the world. 'I'm sorry.'

He shook his head. 'It doesn't matter now. The point is, this has always been what I'm interested in. And I want to break the story. Not because I'm superexcited that aliens exist – although I *am* superexcited – but because the government of this country should not be hiding this shit from us. The public deserves to know the truth, and I want to expose it.'

She shifted in her seat. 'Okay. So what did she tell you?'

'Her story, basically. Where she grew up, what happened to her after she was shot.' He saw the look on her face and raised his hands. 'She didn't say anything about you. She said you told her you hadn't said anything to the press and she didn't think your relationship was relevant.' He smiled. 'Just like you said.'

She was relieved – and ashamed of the relief. 'When are you going to post the interview?'

'Not right away. I'm working on a big feature. That's why I need you and David to sit down for an interview too. You guys are at the center of this. You have to get your story out there.'

'We already tried with Sophia Curtis, but the government shut that down,' she reminded him.

'I know. I've been in touch with Sophia Curtis.'

She was dumbfounded. 'You have?'

'Yeah. Through Keith – you know, 'Jason Briggs.' He and I have been working with Sophia; she still has the footage from your interview, and on some of it you can see Jeff Highsmith from the DOD telling you guys to stop talking. It's a gold mine.' He leaned forward, gesturing enthusiastically with his hands. 'We're building up this story piece by piece. The Amber interview is pretty awesome, because she's not talking to anybody else, and everybody wants to know about her.'

She studied him. 'Who else is involved in this investigation?'

'Just me and Keith. Sophia's giving us info but she's working independently. We haven't agreed to totally share everything.' He grinned. 'Yet. When she finds out I've got Amber on the record and if you and David agree to talk to me, I think she'll be all in.' He drew both his knees up, wrapping his arms around them loosely. 'Okay, so now it's your turn. Tell me what's been going on since the Charles Lovick meeting.'

She reached into her pocket and pulled out the pieces of paper she had taken from Mr Hernandez's briefcase. She got up and walked over to Julian, handing him the temporary ID. 'I found this in Mr Hernandez's stuff today.'

He looked at the piece of paper, puzzled. 'Isn't this our new Principles of Democracy teacher?'

'Yeah.'

'I thought his name was Hernandez, not Vargas.'

She nodded. 'That's because he's actually not a real teacher. He's been planted there to watch me and David.'

'Shit, really?' Julian climbed off his bed and went to grab his laptop from the floor.

As he opened it and plopped back down into the beanbag chair, Reese finally told him about the meeting with Charles Lovick, his Blue Base guards, and the Corporation for American Security and Sovereignty. Julian's eyes widened as she explained that CASS had been in control of American policies toward the Imria since 1947.

'Why have I never heard of them?' he asked.

'I've looked online. There's nothing about them.'

'Are you going to do what they want? How do you know if they're telling the truth?'

Reese sat on the edge of his bed. 'I don't know, but Lovick had those Blue Base guys with him. It's not like we could refuse. But we're not going to tell them everything.'

He looked up, giving her a conspiratorial grin. 'You're going to lie to them?'

'We're trying to buy time. We don't know who to trust yet. So we're going along with what CASS wants for now.' She watched Julian typing furiously into his laptop. 'What are you doing?'

'I'm looking for Andrew Vargas,' he said, gesturing to the ID. 'Where did you get that, anyway?'

'I found it in Mr Hernandez's briefcase.'

'You "found" it?'

She smiled. 'Yep. Found it.'

He laughed. 'Okay, well, look what I found.' He turned the laptop around to face her and she joined him, kneeling on the floor beside the beanbag. 'Andrew Vargas was on President Randall's re-election committee until June of this year. Looks like he left right after the June Disaster.'

She scanned the website he had found; it was a post from an anti-Randall political blog. 'Do you trust this source?'

'I can do some more digging with my contacts at Bin 42. I know some guys who work in DC. I'm going to ask about CASS too. But this post combined with the White House temporary ID and even that cleaning bill – I think Vargas-slash-Hernandez was working for Randall.'

'On his own or as part of CASS?'

'He had to be part of CASS when he was working for Randall, don't you think? There would be too many coincidences, otherwise. Besides, I don't think they'd assign him to handle a major situation like the one you and David are in if he was a new recruit. He's probably been around for a while. They have to trust him with you two.' Julian scrolled down the page. 'The real question, though, is whether Randall knew about Vargas's connection to CASS when he was working for her reelection campaign.'

She sat on the floor, crossing her legs. 'Because if the president knew . . .' She raised her gaze to Julian's. 'You think that CASS was behind her reelection campaign?'

'Maybe not *behind*, but part of?'

'I got the impression from Lovick that CASS was sort of independent of presidential administrations.'

'Then why would one of their lackeys be working for the Randall Administration?'

She looked down at the black-and-white photo of Mr Hernandez as Andrew Vargas. 'Maybe . . . maybe it's the other way around. Maybe the Randall Administration is working for CASS.' She thought about the document from the avian lab she and David had stolen from Blue Base. Blue Base – under the orders of CASS – had been genetically experimenting on birds. Those birds had been the cause of the June Disaster. 'What if President Randall is involved with CASS and their projects with the Imrian DNA? Didn't she come out of the military?'

'Yeah, that was the big thing about her campaign,' Julian said. 'First female veteran to run for president, blah blah, all the brass loved her.' He seemed to struggle to contain his excitement. 'Whoa. You think maybe Randall was involved even before she ran for office? Like, maybe CASS and Blue Base or whatever picked her to run because they knew they could get her elected, and then they'd have their figurehead as commander in chief?'

Reese paled. 'Jeez. Maybe? But even if she wasn't working for them before, she had to have known something about the birds, don't you think? She's the president. And she gave all those speeches at the beginning of the June Disaster. She visited those bird disposal facilities. She was like, "We are figuring things out, trust me." But what if she was lying the whole time?'

'We have to do more investigating,' Julian said. 'Talk to more people. You have to talk to the Imria and find out if they know anything about it. All we know for sure about the June Disaster is from that piece of paper you and David lifted from that lab, and we don't have that anymore. Yeah, Blue Base was genetically modifying birds, but the question is *why*. It's all related somehow. This thing with Mr Hernandez isn't enough. We need more.'

She folded the ID and put it back in her pocket. 'I know. I agree.' She stood. 'Let me talk to David. We'll figure something out.'

'Okay.'

'I better get back downstairs. My dad's gonna freak out if I leave him alone with your mom for too long.'

Julian scrambled to his feet. 'All right. And hey, I'm glad we talked.'

She paused halfway to the door. 'Me too.'

He came over to her and pulled her into a hug. 'I'm serious, you dork. I don't like fighting with you.'

Startled, she quickly withdrew into herself as Eres had taught her so that she couldn't sense Julian's emotions. She wouldn't invade his privacy now that she could avoid it; she owed him that much. He was tall and wiry and strong, and all she could feel was his arms around her. It felt good: normal. 'Me either,' she said, her voice muffled against his shoulder.

All of a sudden she realized the significance of what Amber had done. She had lied about a lot of things, but she had never pushed herself into Reese's consciousness, never taken advantage of her untrained mental state. She had always respected Reese's personal boundaries. Reese had never understood that until now.

CHAPTER 21

On Saturday during the ferry trip to Angel Island, Reese kept remembering what Julian had said about Amber. *She's been avoiding you.* Reese didn't see any sign of Amber during the drive to the ship, or while Nura Halba escorted them through the steel corridors to Eres Tilhar's room. As the lesson began, she tried to forget about her in order to concentrate, but she couldn't entirely erase Amber from her mind. She knew Amber must be nearby, and her unseen presence was like a phantom in the room. Reese was aware that Eres might be able to sense it in her; she only hoped the teacher wouldn't mention it out loud.

'Last time you learned how to center your attention on yourself so that you are anchored in place,' Eres said. 'Today you will learn how to maintain your position in your mental map while you connect with someone else.'

'I have a question,' Reese said, interrupting Eres in an effort to distract herself.

David shifted nearby. *What are you going to ask?* he thought.

We do have to get info for Hernandez, she reminded him.

'What is it?' Eres asked.

'With humans who aren't adapted,' Reese said, 'I know they can't do *susum'urda*, but we can still sense their emotions, right? When we touch them, I mean.'

Eres regarded the two of them with an expressionless face that nonetheless made Reese feel like she had spoken out of turn during class. After a long moment of silence, Eres said, 'Yes, you are able to sense human emotions when you touch them. I believe you've both already experienced this.'

'Yeah,' David said. 'With my parents.'

'I felt it with mine too,' Reese said.

Eres adjusted the sleeves of the gray robe as if buying time. 'It is true that humans are vulnerable to our abilities,' the teacher finally said. 'That is why we must refrain from reading their feelings without their permission.'

They seem to want us to refrain from a lot of things, David noted silently.

Reese bit her lip to hide her smile. 'So you're saying we could do it, but we shouldn't?'

The walls of the triangular room shimmered from blue to green. 'Yes,' Eres said. 'It isn't ethical to access someone's consciousness without their permission.'

'I get that,' David said. 'But are you telling me that you guys have never done that? If you're so interested in finding out about humans, wouldn't you do it?'

Eres's lips pressed together for a moment. 'It is tempting to use our abilities to understand your people, but it is wrong for us to take those liberties with people who cannot resist.'

That doesn't mean they've never done it, Reese thought.

'I see that you both doubt me,' Eres said. 'Perhaps that's because humans have a looser understanding of ethical behavior than we do.'

'That's not fair,' Reese said immediately.

'Am I incorrect?'

'You can't say that all humans do one thing or another,' Reese said. 'We're different. Some people are more ethical than others.'

Eres nodded. 'Exactly. We Imrians are not like your people in this matter. We understand it would always be wrong to cross those lines. There are very few exceptions. Parents teaching their young children, or when trying to help someone in pain, but that's all.'

'But you're fine with lying,' Reese said, more harshly than she had intended.

Eres seemed surprised. 'Lying? I think you mean with words, as I have told you that it is impossible for us to lie during *susum'urda*. Words are superficial. They are meaningless when it comes to true connection.'

'We humans only have words,' Reese said. 'Why do you think they're important to us?'

Eres's surprise seemed to deepen. 'I see that I have upset you both. I apologize. I may not understand your people as well as I should. That is another reason it is important for us to have these lessons; you can teach me as well. Shall we begin again?'

Reese and David traded brief glances. *Well, we have our information*, Reese thought. *And I bet Hernandez is gonna love it.*

'Okay,' David said aloud.

'We will review first,' Eres said. 'I'd like to make sure you're both centered in your own consciousness before we try anything else today.' Eres started with Reese this time, taking her hand and asking her to focus on herself, shutting off access to the teacher's mental space. After Eres was satisfied, the teacher turned to David and worked with him for several minutes. Reese tucked her hands beneath her thighs and tried not to stare as David's face went slack, his lips parting slightly as Eres asked him to do the same thing Reese had done.

After they were finished, Eres sat back and looked at the two of them. 'You have quite a lot of emotion inside you. It's extraordinary. You're both so different from an Imrian child. Your emotions are so unordered. It will take some practice for you to learn how to present a more ordered consciousness.'

'How are we supposed to order our feelings?' David asked. 'Don't they just exist, however they are? You can't control them.'

'It's true that feelings are uncontrollable,' Eres said, 'but emotions are not. Emotions are your brain's way of making sense of feelings.'

Reese was confused. 'What?'

'Feelings are the physical reactions your body has to something,' Eres explained. 'Perhaps English isn't the best language with which to explain this, but think of it this way: Feelings are physical sensations, like hunger or pain or pleasure. These feelings happen regardless of what you *think* of them. Emotions are the narrative your mind creates about those feelings. So if you burn your hand, you'll feel pain, but emotionally, you could be angry or embarrassed, depending on the situation. Does that make more sense?'

'I guess, yeah,' Reese said.

'I think so,' David said.

'Good. You both need to learn how to be conscious of your emotions so that you can present them in a more ordered manner to your partner – the person with whom you practice *susum'urda*. Let me show you what an ordered consciousness looks like. Reese, I'll begin with you.'

Reese took Eres's hand again and was instantly pulled into the teacher's sphere of consciousness. Every time this happened, Reese found the transition a little easier, but it was still like having the world develop an entirely new dimension. Eres's physical form receded, becoming less relevant, while the teacher's conscious self took on a strong, solid shape. Eres didn't look like a person anymore; the *ummi* had no limbs and no head, but instead was a mass of energy clearly imprinted with a recognizable identity, as deeply rooted as a tree. Eres was beautiful, but this beauty had nothing to do with physical appearance. Eres's consciousness was warmth and compassion, and Reese felt her own body inhale in relief as she experienced this connection.

Now you will see your own conscious self, Eres told her. It was as if the teacher had turned her around mentally, and now Reese was looking into a mirror. In comparison to Eres, Reese was a mess. Her consciousness took the form of a nebulous, sparking fog, loose tendrils flying everywhere the way her hair whipped in the wind. Eres began to pull at it, trying to show Reese how to shape it into some sort of order, but the closer

Eres got to various emotions, the more anxious Reese became. She didn't want Eres to find out about Hernandez and CASS. She definitely didn't want Eres to sense her mixed-up feelings about Amber. Reese's anxiety made the shape of her consciousness morph, the sparks flying off more rapidly until she was a buzzing mass of tension.

What are you afraid of? Eres asked her. *You must let me show you how to do this.*

Sweat broke out on Reese's skin, and she shook her head, but the teacher's hand still held hers tight, not letting her back out. *I can't*, Reese thought.

You must, Eres told her. *You must know yourself before you do susum'urda with anyone. Otherwise they will not be able to truly connect with you. They will only see your confusion.*

What if I don't want to do this with anyone? I'm fine the way I am.

If you were fine, you would not be so disordered. Your fear is understandable because this is so new to you, but I will not harm you. You must be open with me so that I can teach you. You need not be open with anyone else yet.

The real world swam before Reese as she blinked her eyes open. Eres was still sitting across from her, regarding her steadily, but it was too confusing to see with her physical eyes while also touching the teacher. Reese closed her eyes again. She tried to relax, to let Eres access the knot of emotions inside her, but as Eres began to lay those emotions out one after the other – anguish, longing, a bitter wash of guilt – Reese pulled her hand free, heart pounding.

'I can't,' she said out loud, her eyes wild.

'Are you okay?' David asked. He reached for her, but she shook her head and his hand hung in the air for a second, motionless, before he pulled it back. His face reddened slightly.

'I'm sorry,' Reese choked out. 'I can't do this today. I'm not ready.'

Eres sat back, the folds of the teacher's robes falling to the floor in pearlescent ripples. 'I'm sorry to have pushed you. It may take longer for you to adjust to this ability. I'll work with David for the remainder of our lesson. Would you like something to drink? Water?'

Reese shook her head, feeling as if she had narrowly escaped from a trap. She sat in silence, legs and arms crossed defensively, as Eres took David's hand and began the process with him. Out of the corner of her eye she saw him twitch from time to time, his breath accelerating and then calming. Reese dropped her gaze to the floor so that she couldn't see him anymore. She was embarrassed and disappointed in herself, and she wished there were some way she could make the time pass faster. Now that Eres had shown Reese the shape of her own consciousness, she was hyperaware of the chaotic nature of her thoughts. She bent over, clutching her head in her hands, and willed herself to breathe more slowly. Inhale, exhale. She heard David shift in his seat. She heard her own heartbeat. She gazed down at the floor, noticing every tiny, precise groove in the matte black material. There was a pattern in the floor that she had never seen before, like some kind of maze.

Finally David and Eres broke apart, and David whispered, 'That was crazy.'

Reese sat up. David's eyes seemed haunted as he looked at

her. 'You're all right?' Reese asked.

'Yeah.' *But I know why you stopped. That was intense.*

Eres stood. The lesson was over. 'It may take several weeks or months for you both to fully adjust to your abilities, especially since you're coming to this much later than an Imrian child would.' Reese moved toward the door, but Eres said, 'Reese, may I speak with you?'

Reese paused. 'Sure.'

'David, will you wait in the corridor? It will only be a moment.' After he left, Eres closed the door behind him.

'What is it?' Reese asked nervously.

'I believe that you have been trying to hide some things from me,' Eres said gently.

Reese crossed her arms. 'I'm not ready for this.'

'I know. But it serves no purpose for you to hide your emotions from yourself.'

Reese's first instinct was to deny it, to say, *I'm not hiding anything*. The words caught in her throat as she saw Eres watching her. Reese said nothing.

Eres nodded. 'You must face it. I should also tell you that I know that you and David are sharing these lessons with your teacher, the one who is a spy. And I know that you and David have abilities that differ from what we Imria have.'

Reese went pale. 'You know?'

'You cannot hide these things from me.'

'Are you going to tell?'

Eres looked disappointed. 'Everything I learn from you is learned in confidence. You must understand that. David has not tried to hide these things from me. Only you have.'

Reese colored. 'I'm sorry. I didn't know what else to do.'

'You and David must decide when you'd like to discuss these things openly. I suggest that you decide soon.'

Eres walked over to the door and opened it. David was standing on the other side, his back to the room. He spun around as the door slid open, his dark eyes seeking out Reese's face. She shoved her hands into her pockets as she exited the room.

'I will see you both next week,' said Eres. 'And, Reese, think about what I told you.'

Eres knows about Mr Hernandez, Reese thought to David as they drove back to the ferry.

Is that what Eres was talking to you about? David asked. They were sitting in the backseat of the SUV while Reese's mom made small talk with Nura Halba in the front.

Yes. Eres also knows that we have different abilities, but I don't think she knows exactly what they are.

Eres said our lessons are confidential. Do you think she'll tell the other Imria?

She said she wouldn't.

The SUV turned down the road that circled the harbor, and Reese's mom twisted in her seat to look at them. 'David, your parents know you're going to the Arenses' with us, right?'

'Yeah. They'll pick me up from there later.'

Reese and David were getting together with Julian under the pretense of working on a physics lab, but they were actually planning to record interviews for Bin 42. Reese had told David about Julian's secret investigations earlier in the week. She had thought up a whole speech to persuade David to do the interview, but he had agreed almost immediately.

'More insurance,' he said to her after school on Wednesday. 'Now that we have to deal with Hernandez, we need as much of that as we can get.'

As the SUV pulled up to the closed information booth beside the dock, David thought to Reese: *If Eres keeps our secret, that will be one reason to trust the Imria.*

Reese opened the door. *Well, it will be one reason to trust Eres.* She still wasn't ready to trust the rest of them.

CHAPTER 22

When they arrived at Julian's house, he had tacked a black cloth over the closet doors in his bedroom to create a backdrop, and he had set up a camera on a tripod. He angled several lamps straight at the backdrop and motioned for David and Reese to sit down on two crates he had arranged in front of the camera. 'I'll shoot you from the waist up,' Julian said. 'It's not fancy, but it'll work fine. I'll be behind the camera but I have a bunch of questions to ask. My voice will be edited out of the final interview, so I need you to answer the questions by restating them, if you know what I mean? Like a reality TV-style confessional.'

His questions were thorough, drawing out every last detail of their experiences beginning with the June Disaster and ending with their lessons on Angel Island. It wasn't until Reese and David began to explain the purpose of *susum'urda*, though, that she realized how little Julian – and other humans – knew about it.

'*Susum'urda* isn't about reading others' thoughts,' she said. 'It's not about getting people to reveal their secrets against their will. It's about connection.'

'What does it feel like?' Julian asked.

'It's . . . hard to explain,' Reese said, and glanced at David.

'We're not that good at it yet,' David said. 'We've really only done it with our teacher. With Eres, it's like seeing someone's interior identity. Who they actually are, beyond what they look like on the surface. It's incredible, and incredibly scary at the same time.'

'Why is it scary?' Julian asked.

'Because—' David hesitated, his gaze going beyond the camera to the UFO photos on Julian's walls. Julian waited, and when David looked back at the camera, he was focused. 'It's scary because it opens you up to someone else too. It makes you vulnerable. In order to have that connection with someone else, you have to be willing to show them who you really are.'

'What about you, Reese?' Julian prompted.

She looked at the camera self-consciously. 'For me, it's mostly just scary.'

'Why?' David asked softly.

She looked at him. His dark eyes reflected the lights that Julian had pointed at them. Reese said awkwardly, 'I'm just . . . I'm not the best when it comes to feelings and stuff.' Her emotions seemed to rear up inside her, both affirming her statement and rejecting it, and her face heated up with everything she had left unsaid. She turned to Julian, who was standing behind the camera watching her. 'Do we have to put this in the interview?' she asked.

'No, it's okay,' Julian said.

'Thanks,' Reese said, relieved. 'Could we maybe take a break?'

Julian glanced at his watch. 'Sure. My parents are going to make us come down for dinner soon anyway.'

'Great.' Reese got up. 'I'm going to the bathroom.' She fled Julian's bedroom and crossed the landing to the bathroom, locking the door behind her. There was a window in the wall that overlooked the backyard, and the sash was pushed up to let in the warm evening air. She could hear the sound of her mom's voice floating up from below, and Celeste's answering laugh. Her mom was staying for dinner, and her dad was going to show up soon too. *One big happy family*, she thought dourly.

She used the toilet even though she didn't need to and flushed, then turned on the taps to wash her hands. Her face was grim-looking in the mirror, as if she had gotten bad news and hadn't shaken it off yet. She tried to smooth out the frown that was dragging down the corners of her mouth, but her eyes still looked agitated. She felt like an idiot. David could speak so directly and honestly about *susum'urda*. He could tell the world what had happened to the two of them and make everyone believe. In comparison, she probably came off as a dork. An emotionally stunted, freaked out dork with secrets.

There was a knock on the door. 'Reese?' It was David.

'Just a minute,' she called. She dried off her hands and took a shallow breath before opening the door.

He looked concerned. 'Can I come in for a sec?'

She hadn't expected that, but she let him in. 'What's up?'

He entered the room and pushed the door shut. He had a

strange expression on his face – like he wanted to say something but wasn't sure how to word it.

'What is it?' She began to imagine all sorts of horrible possibilities. He probably thought she was ruining the interview. Or maybe he was going to – she couldn't think about it. Nervous sweat broke out on her skin.

He seemed to make up his mind. 'You sure that's all it is? That you're not good with feelings and stuff?'

Her cheeks turned pink.

'I mean—' He waved his hands as if he were trying to gather up all his thoughts into a coherent sentence. 'What happened with Eres today, and then what you said to Julian … I feel like something's wrong.' His face reddened. 'Is something wrong?'

She backed away, crossing her arms. Were they having a talk? The kind where people said, 'Can we talk about something?' but actually meant 'This isn't working out'? She scrambled for something to say to stave it off. 'I was a little overwhelmed at our lesson today, that's all. You said it yourself – it's scary.'

He nodded, but doubt was still written clearly on his face.

Her stomach sank. 'Really. There's nothing wrong.' She felt like a liar. She was a liar. She held her breath, as if that would prevent him from knowing.

His hands had been stuffed into his pockets as if to avoid touching her, but now he lifted a hand to her arms, pulling one of her hands free. She stiffened. 'Do you not want me to touch you?' he asked, his face darkening.

She forced herself to let him hold her hand, but her anxiety shivered between them like a steel sheet in a gust of wind. On the other side, she felt his mounting sadness, and she couldn't bear to feel it. Before she knew what she was doing, the words began to spill out of her. 'I don't want to do anything wrong, and I'm afraid you'll – you'll see something in me that you hate or that will make you hate me, like that night at Eric's party. I can't control what I'm thinking of, and I don't know how to deal with the fact that you can see it. I really – I really like you.' She felt as if her face were on fire, but she kept going. 'I don't want you to hate me, and yeah, I really suck at feelings and stuff. You should ask Julian! Ask anyone. I just – I wish we could be normal, you know? Like not have to do these interviews and explain everything, even though I know it's important. Nobody gets it except for us. Humans don't understand the Imria, the Imria don't understand humans, and nobody understands us. We're stuck in the middle, and we have to explain it to everyone. I know that. But I suck at talking about this stuff, and I –' She ran a hand through her hair, unable to stop talking. 'I wish we could be normal and go out without being followed, and I don't know, I wish we could make out in your car or something instead of being so *restrained* or whatever Eres wants us to be.' She finally ran out of words, halting abruptly as a smile reached David's eyes.

He laced his fingers through hers. She felt his heartbeat through his skin, a regular percussion that echoed her own.

'You can close yourself off, can't you?' he said. 'Try it.'

'You mean—'

'We can be normal for five minutes. I'll try it too.'

She sensed him folding away his consciousness, as if he were closing the panels of a puzzle box one by one. She tried to do the same thing. She focused on her own heartbeat as Eres Tilhar had taught her; she centered on her own inhalation and exhalation. She closed off the third eye that opened every time David touched her, and he bent down, letting go of her hand so he could cup her face, and kissed her. His lower lip slid across hers, slightly dry. Even though she had kissed him before, she had never kissed him without being able to sense his internal self, and he felt so different now. Separate. A physical form she did not understand. She felt inordinately clumsy, and she wondered if being divorced from his consciousness made her a bad kisser.

Had she ever noticed that he was several inches taller than her? She had to stand on her tiptoes, stretching her arms up to slip them around his neck. His upper back felt strangely unfamiliar beneath her hands, a landscape of muscle she didn't know. He pulled her closer, his hands on her waist, and she arched her back to fit against him. The heat that built inside her came slower than it had when she could also sense him, but it was unmistakable: a glowing flame that began to lick at her belly. He turned her, pushing her against the door, and in an awkward dance she moved her arms, whispering 'Let me—' And she circled her arms around his waist.

Cracks broke in her consciousness – and in his. She saw brief flashes of what he was feeling: her hair tangled in his fingers; the taste of her mouth. She shuddered as the walls of her conscious self began to crumble, and she tried to hold them up at the same time that she wanted to drink in his emotions. It didn't work.

And then David was pulling away from her even as she tried

to drag him closer. He planted his hands on the door on either side of her head and pushed back.

'I don't think that was even five minutes,' he said, breathless.

She lifted her hand to her mouth; her lips felt bruised. David's eyes were dark, his mouth red from kissing her. She felt weak. She felt exhilarated. 'Three minutes maybe.'

He laughed shortly and took a step back. She reached out, hooking a finger on his belt loop. 'David.'

He looked down at her hand, but she didn't let go. 'Yeah,' he said, his voice rough.

'I'm sorry.'

He glanced up, puzzled. 'Why?'

'Because I'm a dork,' she whispered. 'Because I can't say anything I really want to say, and I just want you to know it's because I want you to like me.'

The expression on his face softened. 'I do like you. Didn't you notice?'

She was embarrassed. 'Maybe.'

'Well, you better start noticing,' he said, but his tone was gentle. He reached behind her, and she thought he was going to kiss her again, but he was only going for the door handle. 'We should go back before Julian get suspicious.'

'He's already suspicious.'

David laughed, and for the first time all day, Reese felt like things were probably going to be all right.

After school on Monday, David and Reese told Mr Hernandez that yes, the Imria could use their abilities to sense what humans were thinking. He didn't seem to put much stock in

Eres Tilhar's statements about ethics. 'Have you gotten photos of the adaptation chamber yet?' he asked.

'We haven't been able to find the adaptation chamber,' Reese said.

'We'll get them in time,' David assured him.

They had to leave right afterward to get to David's soccer game – the first of the fall season. It was a home game, and because the opposing team was their biggest rival, Reese knew there would be a decent turnout, but she hadn't expected that having David on the team would draw so many spectators. The stands were completely filled, and Reese huddled with Madison and Julian and Bri, hoping nobody would realize she was there. David didn't even start – he'd missed too many practices that summer – but when he was substituted in midway through the second half, photographers fanned out along the sidelines and Reese felt the crowd focus on him. Their attention was so strong that she suspected David could feel it too, even out on the field. He didn't score, and sometimes she saw him turning his back to the crowd as if he were trying to shut them out.

Kennedy won 3–2, and afterward David was surrounded by press. When his coach finally extricated him, Reese saw him retreat to the locker room, white-faced. That was when the photographers noticed her, waiting near the entrance to the high school with her friends. Cameras flashed as rapidly as strobe lights, and she held up her hand to shield her eyes, but they didn't relent. Madison put an arm around her and said, 'Let's go inside.' As Julian pulled open the door, Bri shouted at the photographers, 'Leave them alone!'

Inside, the hallways echoed with distant sounds from the

boys' locker room. Reese ducked into a shadowy recess between a trophy case and the door to the computer lab. 'Thanks,' she said to Madison.

'They're so annoying,' Madison grumbled. 'Did you know they've started trying to get *me* to talk about you? I got followed home from school one day!'

'Did they? I'm sorry,' Reese said.

Madison shrugged. 'Whatever. I told them I wasn't talking.'

Julian leaned against the trophy case. 'Once they took a photo of me flipping them off. I saw it on the Hub – it got five thousand likes in ten minutes.'

Reese laughed weakly. 'You guys... thanks.'

'I don't know how you deal with it,' Bri said. 'They are relentless.'

'Come on,' Madison said. 'It's boring here. Let's go wait by the boys' locker room.'

Julian groaned.

'Shut up, you know you want to, Julian,' Madison said.

'Yeah, but I don't,' Bri objected.

'You're coming!' Madison insisted, and grabbed Bri's arm to drag her down the hall.

When the soccer team emerged from the locker room, they absorbed Reese and her friends into their big herd of soapy-smelling boys and shouted jokes, shielding her and David from the photographers waiting outside the school. They descended on a taqueria two blocks away and took up all the tables, and as Reese waited for her burrito to be made she watched David laughing with his teammates, and Bri and Julian arguing over some obscure plot point on Doctor Who, and even though she knew the press was waiting on the sidewalk, for this moment she felt safe.

There was something magical about it: this warm September night, the yellow-and-green flags fluttering from the ceiling, the salsa burning hot on her tongue, the Mexican Coke a rush of sugary sweetness. *This is normal*, she thought, and she wanted to cry.

CHAPTER 23

On Saturday, Reese's father took her and David to Angel Island. She had thought about what Eres told her at the end of their last lesson. She was determined, today, to let the teacher see everything; she wanted to know how to use this adaptive ability. She didn't expect to see Amber sitting in one of the chairs when the door to Eres's room opened.

'Good morning,' Eres said, standing up. The teacher's gray robe hung down to the floor in one long column. With white hair and a pale face, Eres was almost ghostly.

'Hi,' Amber said, standing as well. She was dressed in jeans and a baby-blue T-shirt that had MISSION stamped on it, her face bare of makeup, a lock of her hair held back with a plain clip. She looked so utterly ordinary in the triangular space with its luminous walls that Reese found it completely jarring.

'Hi,' David said warily.

'What are you doing here?' Reese asked. She had finally begun to forget about Amber – hadn't she? – and now here she was, biting her lip and looking like a nice girl. Reese's feet planted in the doorway; she couldn't move any farther into the room. She wouldn't.

'We're going to do something different today,' Eres said. 'David, I'm going to work with you individually. And, Reese, you are going to work with Amber.'

'What? Why?'

'I spoke with Amber since the last time you were here,' Eres said. 'I believe it will be helpful for you to spend some time working with her.'

Reese glanced at David. He didn't look happy. 'I don't think working with Amber will help,' Reese said to Eres.

Amber's face darkened, but she didn't speak.

'How will you know if you don't try?' Eres asked.

Reese couldn't answer the question. *I just know* sounded too much like something an impertinent kid might say, but that was the only thing Reese could come up with.

'Amber, the two of you should go somewhere private,' Eres said. 'David and I will stay here.' Eres sat down again, clearly waiting for Amber and Reese to leave.

Amber headed for the door. Reese backed away so that Amber didn't touch her when she passed. 'Come on,' Amber said, waiting in the corridor.

Reese looked at David, hoping for a way out, but his expression was guarded. He shook his head very slightly as if to say *It's your decision*, and then he sat down to face Eres. Reese realized the only options she had were to go with Amber or to throw a temper tantrum and refuse to do as Eres asked. The stern expression on Eres's face made Reese think the teacher would definitely not take kindly to the latter. So she turned away from Eres and David and stiffly followed Amber into the corridor. She wished that Amber didn't still affect her so strongly.

'Do you want to go for a walk?' Amber asked tentatively. 'We don't have to stay inside. It's a beautiful day.'

The corridor was dim and claustrophobic, and the idea of going outside seemed like a lifeline to Reese. 'Yes. Let's go outside.'

Amber led the way through the ship, and Reese kept her eyes on the floor. Amber was wearing her purple Converse sneakers. Reese flashed back to the first time she had noticed them, the day they'd had coffee at the café across from the park. She shoved the memory away angrily. *Stop it*, she told herself. *Everything is different now*.

As they exited the ship, walking down the ramp, Amber pointed at the yellow Victorian houses across the road. 'Those were the officers' quarters. There's a building up there with a sign that says 'Bake House.' Apparently the soldiers liked their fresh-baked bread.'

'How do you know that?' Reese asked.

'There's a plaque over there that explains it. This place used to be called Camp Reynolds. It was occupied by the US Army in the nineteenth century.' She started walking toward the sign and gestured at the row of whitewashed, boarded-up buildings. 'That was called Officers' Row. I guess they had a lot of officers. They used to have barracks for the ordinary soldiers across the field, but they were torn down in the 1930s.'

'Did they give you a guided tour when you landed here or something?'

'No. But there isn't much to do here, you know. During the week, I spend a lot of time walking around and reading the signs.'

They turned right at the end of the gravel road, where a sloping path led downhill past Officers' Row toward the bay. Reese glanced at Amber as they walked toward the water. 'I thought you'd have stuff to do. Like, I don't know, some high-tech spacey stuff or something.'

Amber's eyebrows rose. 'No. Hirin Sagal deals with some stuff like that. I haven't been trained in that area, so I try to keep out of his way.'

'What does everybody else do?' Reese asked, curiosity pushing aside some of her defensiveness. 'I've only seen a few of you – where is everybody?'

'Akiya Deyir is working on setting up the United Nations stuff. He has several assistants helping him, and they're always having conference calls with other nations. My mother and the others from Project Plato are putting together their research. They're going to release that at the UN, too, and a lot of it has to be translated into, well, human terms. Sometimes I help them figure out how to say things, since I grew up here. I guess I act sort of as a cultural translator.'

They had reached the end of the gravel path, and as Amber stepped onto the grass to continue toward the bay, Reese glanced back at the ship. On top of the triangular tip of the craft, a line of seagulls were perched, white feathers stark against the black ship.

'There's a little beach out here,' Amber said. 'It's nice. We can sit on the wall.'

Reese was still staring at the gulls. 'I never see birds in the city anymore, but I always see them when I come here.'

'That's probably because we don't kill them.'

Amber's words were disconcerting. Reese turned to look at her. She was waiting near the edge of the grass that overlooked the strip of sand, her face expectant. 'You want to sit?' The ghost of a grin crossed her face. 'At least it's warm today.'

Reese remembered the last time – the only time – she had gone to a beach with Amber: the cold, brisk wind at Ocean Beach ruffling over the two of them as they lay on a blanket in the shelter of a sand dune. Reese was unexpectedly flustered, and she shoved her hands into her pockets as she stepped onto the grass. 'So what else do you do here besides explain the weird customs of my people?' Reese asked. 'How much time do you spend e-mailing my best friend?'

The smile on Amber's face faltered. 'He told you.'

'Of course he told me. He's my *best friend*.'

Amber lowered herself onto the edge of the wall and gazed out at the bay. It was warm but overcast, and in the distance Reese saw a container ship moving slowly across the water. She began to think that Amber was never going to answer when she finally spoke.

'I only wanted to find out how you were feeling,' Amber said. 'Whether you were going to call us with the phone I gave you.'

Reese sat down a couple of feet away from her. The wall was rough beneath her hands. 'How did you get his e-mail address?'

'He works at that Bin 42 site. It's public info.'

'Why didn't you just ask me directly?'

Amber's face reddened, but she didn't look at Reese. 'You were so mad at me. I didn't think you'd want to talk to me. Maybe I shouldn't have e-mailed him, but I didn't know what else to do. I had to –' Her voice broke. She took a quick breath. 'I had to do it. I didn't know if I'd ever see you again.'

'You could see me here every week. You told me the day of the press conference that we were going to have to see each other, but I haven't seen you since then. You thought e-mailing Julian would be a better idea?'

Amber turned on her, gray eyes fierce. 'When I saw you at the press conference you said we couldn't be friends. You said you'd never forgive me—'

'I never said that—'

'That's what it sounded like!'

Amber's eyes were red-rimmed, and a surge of shame went through Reese, quickly followed by indignation. What did she have to be ashamed of? 'Well, maybe you were right,' Reese said angrily. 'Why should I forgive you? You might just lie to me again.'

Amber's face crumpled. She drew her feet up onto the wall and wrapped her arms around her legs, and she looked so small and fragile that Reese almost moved to comfort her. She curled her hands into fists instead.

'Yes, I lied to you,' Amber said in a low voice. 'I know I hurt you. I see that I hurt you a lot and I'm so, so sorry. But I thought it was necessary to protect you.'

'Protect me from what?'

Amber's eyes gleamed as she looked at the water. 'We were trying to keep it a secret – the fact that you and David had this procedure. Your government was suspicious already, and if they knew we were successful, they would try to take you.' Amber turned to Reese. 'They *did* try to take you. I couldn't tell you because we didn't want to put you in any more danger.'

'But you guys just released me and David to them. You gave us to those men in black, and they brought us back to San Francisco and we didn't know anything about what you did to us. Do you know how totally weird it was to be experiencing that adaptation ability without knowing what it was? We thought we were going crazy. How was that protecting us?'

Amber shook her head as if Reese wasn't getting it. 'We had to let you go. Your government suspected that we'd done something to you, but they didn't know what it was. We told them that you'd just had a car accident and you were treated for those injuries. If we hadn't released you, they would have suspected much sooner. You would never have gone home, period. You would still be stuck at Project Plato or maybe at Blue Base, being tested by the military. Your parents probably would have thought you died during that gas station explosion in Las Vegas. They would never have found you.'

Reese rubbed a hand over her face, trying to puzzle out the details of what Amber was saying. 'That's all hypothetical, but fine. Maybe it's good you gave us to the men in black, but once we were home, why did you show up? You said you were supposed to make sure I was okay. Wouldn't the government get suspicious when they saw you? Obviously they were following me.'

Amber sighed. 'They didn't know about me. I wasn't part of Project Plato. I was a secret. So really, when it came down to it,

I was the only one who could keep an eye on you in San Francisco. And I was told to not tell you what happened, because we were still trying to work out how much the government suspected. We also weren't totally sure that the procedure had worked, so we didn't think there was any use telling you until we were sure. Besides, what if I had told you who I was? Would you even have believed me? You would have thought I was insane.'

Reese sat in silence for a moment, absorbing Amber's words. 'Even if I had thought that, didn't it ever occur to you that I deserved to know? What you guys did to me and David – it changed us in ways we still don't understand. How could you justify keeping that a secret? The adaptation procedure might have saved our lives, but it also put us in the middle of some crazy chess game between the Imria and the government, and David and I aren't pawns to be moved around whenever one of you changes your mind. We're people, not test subjects. Even if it might have made sense to keep some of this a secret at the beginning, I can't understand why you didn't tell me once you started – once we started—' She still didn't know what to call it, and she made a frustrated sound. 'If you really liked me, why didn't you tell me the truth?'

Amber looked miserable. 'Maybe I was being selfish.'

Reese's forehead furrowed. 'What?'

'You have to understand: Nothing happened the way I expected. I thought it would be, I don't know, straightforward. Like I'd meet you and we'd hang out and I'd get a feel for whether you were having any symptoms of the adaptation, and that would be it. But . . .' She raised her gaze to Reese. 'I didn't expect you. The first time we met, I knew right away that I wanted to kiss you.' A faint blush colored Amber's cheeks, and despite her defensiveness, Reese felt her own face warming up in response. 'I let myself get carried away by my feelings. It was so much more fun – it made me feel so much more *alive* – to forget about who I really was and what I was supposed to be doing. I wanted to be with you and pretend like it was totally normal. I wanted to be an ordinary human girl who met another girl, and we liked each other and that was it. No complicated backstory to mess it all up.'

Amber paused, and all Reese could hear was the soft rush of waves upon the shore. 'I shouldn't have given in to what I wanted,' Amber continued. 'What I did was wrong. I know that now, and I'm so, so sorry that I hurt you. You don't know how sorry I am. But I'm not sorry that I fell in love with you.'

Reese froze. She stopped breathing; she didn't blink. The only motion inside her was the suddenly rapid pounding of her heart. Amber's eyes were shining, her expression strangely defiant, as if she wanted Reese to dare her to say it again.

'Why do you like me?' Reese finally asked. 'You barely knew me. You still barely know me.'

Amber uncoiled from where she was sitting. She turned to face Reese, one leg hanging over the edge of the wall, the other bent so that her sneakered foot rested against the inside of her thigh. 'Because there's something in you that speaks to me,' she said. 'If you want me to list the top ten reasons, I can't. I only need one reason, and that reason is that you and I work together. We work. I could feel it the first time I touched you, and I didn't need to read your mind to know it.' Her eyes glittered with unshed tears. 'I meant it when I told you I've never felt that way about anyone else before. I never have. I've been with girls I liked, you know? I was attracted to them. They were fun. But you – when I was with you I felt free. I felt . . . human.'

Amber's eyelashes were dark and wet. Her mouth was slightly open, her bare lips the color of coral, and the smudge of pink on her cheeks looked like someone had swept their thumbs over her skin before cupping her face in their hands. There was something ethereal about her at that moment, something fragile and unearthly, and for the first time, Reese saw another world in Amber's face.

'If I could go back and tell you everything at the beginning, I would. I hope that someday you'll forgive me. I just—' Amber's voice broke, and she took a quick, deep breath. 'I miss you. I miss you so much.' She reached for Reese's hand, and Reese was so stunned that she let Amber take it. Her fingers were soft and warm, and Reese felt Amber open up, as if she were making an offering of herself with no strings attached.

It was impossible for her not to look.

It was like gazing into a spiral shell, pearlescent and luminous. As Reese's resistance slowly disintegrated, she began to sense Amber's emotions rippling one into another. First there was fear: fear that made Amber's internal landscape hum with tension; fear that Reese would push her away. But as they remained connected, their fingers interlaced, Amber's fear began to recede, and gradually Reese sensed something else. It was like the sun rising over the ocean, at first only a dim glow on the horizon, then a wash of pink over the blue-gray sky, until at last a golden eye blinked open on the edge of the sea. Hope, weighted with all of Amber's mistakes and regrets and desires. Hope that Reese would forgive her, that she would let Amber in again.

It was one of the most seductive things Reese had ever felt. She couldn't help but be swayed by it, like a hummingbird drawn to the deep pink bloom of a fuchsia flower on a warm summer day. The hard-edged ache that had been buried deep within her ever since she discovered Amber had lied to her began to soften, and her eyes grew hot.

This was why Eres wanted her to talk to Amber, of course. To face this ache. Reese felt so stupid. She could never connect with another person if she didn't acknowledge this part of herself, this bruised heart. Ignoring it wouldn't make it heal, and imprisoning it behind a wall of defensiveness only served to suffocate herself. She drew in a trembling breath.

Please, Amber thought. *Please give me another chance*.

Amber reached out with her free hand and touched Reese's cheek, her fingers trailing sparks over Reese's skin. All of gravity seemed to bend toward Amber, and Reese leaned in. She was so close she could almost feel the breath from Amber's lips on hers. If she moved one more centimeter, they would be kissing.

David.

The memory of him dragged her away from Amber with a jolt. She jerked away from Amber's hand and scrambled to her feet to put distance between them.

Amber looked shocked by the sudden cessation of contact. 'What's wrong?'

Reese was horrified at herself. How could she be pulled right back in like that? 'I can't be with you,' she said, her words sounding all choked up. 'I can't.'

Hurt, plain and simple, came over Amber's face, and Reese wanted to go to her and hug her, but she didn't allow herself to move.

'Because of David,' Amber said, her voice so low that Reese almost didn't hear it.

'Yes.' Reese felt sick at what she had almost done.

Amber stood as well, but she didn't close the space between them. She looked nervous as she opened her mouth to speak, but Reese interrupted her.

'Don't say anything, please.' Reese didn't think she could resist any more of Amber's persuasion. 'I have to go back. I can't – I can't be with you. That's all.'

She turned away and started to head back up the path toward the ship. She heard Amber call her name, but she ignored it and kept walking, her legs trembling with each step. All she knew was that she had to put distance between the two of them, as much distance as possible, because she certainly didn't trust herself.

CHAPTER 24

Reese didn't go back to the ship. She couldn't face David right now, not with Amber's words still echoing in her mind. She wound up walking all the way back to the ferry, passing several armed National Guard troops on the way. She heard their walkie-talkies scratch to life behind her as they reported her whereabouts to whoever was in charge. At the harbor, two soldiers paced back and forth in front of the dock. She ignored them and sat on the bench outside the closed information booth, staring at the harbor. She kept remembering the look on Amber's face when she said she wasn't sorry she had fallen in love with Reese. The word *love* was so big, so grand. Reese didn't know if she should believe Amber. On the one hand, it would be easier if she didn't. Then she could ignore the *L* word and concentrate on being angry. On the other hand, part of Reese did want to believe her. Amber had said everything Reese had ever secretly wanted to hear, and even if the word *love* frightened Reese, she couldn't deny its allure.

But what about David? Thinking about him made a new, awful ache grow inside her, one she had never felt before. She had liked him long before she had ever met Amber. She trusted him. The way he made her feel was so different from the way Amber made her feel. With David, there was a warmth and solidity and clarity that there wasn't with Amber. David made her feel safe and respected and *happy*. Amber made her feel tormented and hungry. There shouldn't be any competition. But there was.

Half an hour later, an SUV drove up to the ferry landing and David and her father climbed out. Her dad came toward her, looking upset. 'Are you all right? Why didn't you tell us where you were going? You can't just run off like that.'

'I needed some space,' she answered, avoiding David's gaze.

'Reese, you need to tell me where you're going,' her dad admonished her.

'It's not like nobody knew. I've been watched by the National Guard the whole time.'

Her dad sat beside her, shaking his head. 'That's not the point.'

Reese surreptitiously watched David as he turned away from them to look at the harbor. 'Fine. I'm sorry,' she said. Her dad sighed, but he didn't chide her further.

On the ferry, Reese climbed the steep steps to the deck, hoping to continue avoiding David, but he followed her up. She leaned against the railing as the boat motored away from the slip, watching as the island receded.

'Reese.'

She couldn't bring herself to look at him. He was standing a foot away, and she noticed that he hadn't attempted to touch her. She didn't know what she would do if he did. She knew she could shut him out, but even the idea of it felt like a betrayal.

'Dr Brand invited us to go with them to the UN in New York,' he said.

'She did?'

'Yeah. They want us to travel with them. They're taking the ship.'

Somehow the invitation didn't surprise her. 'Do you want to go?'

'Yeah, I do. I think it's our chance to speak to both sides. They need us.'

She didn't answer. She knew she should say something, but all she could do was think to herself: *You're about to fuck this up, aren't you?* There was a strained silence. In the distance Reese heard the sound of a motorboat zipping across the water.

Finally David came to stand beside her. 'Are you going to tell me what happened with Amber?'

Reese lowered her gaze to stare at the water coursing past the ferry. 'We just . . . talked.'

'Then why are you acting so guilty?'

Her face burned. 'She's hard to deal with, okay?' Reese straightened up, shoving her hands into her pockets as she looked at him.

He studied her for a long moment. 'Yeah, I'll bet.'

The intonation behind his words was clear. He didn't believe her. She swallowed.

'Look,' he said. 'I can't help it. I don't trust her. I think she's trying to get back with you and—'

'Don't you trust me?' Reese interrupted. She heard the

accusation in her voice and she flinched. She had no right to make David shoulder the blame, and now she was accelerating straight toward disaster.

The vein in his temple throbbed. 'Yeah, I do trust you. Are you telling me I shouldn't?'

The wind blew her hair into her face and she reached up with shaking fingers to drag it away. 'No. Nothing happened. She apologized again for lying to me, that's all.'

'Do you forgive her?'

She had never heard him speak like this before, his voice low and controlled – too controlled. Her stomach lurched as the ferry crested a wave. She grabbed on to the railing. 'I don't know,' she said finally.

His expression was hard as a mask. 'She came to Eres Tilhar's room to tell us you weren't coming back.'

'She did?'

'She looked pretty upset.'

'Did she say why?'

Frustration flashed across David's face. 'No. She and Eres had a moment. They did some kind of consciousness-sharing crap and I watched her look depressed and scared, and then everybody freaked out because they had no idea where you were. And then she left. It was very dramatic. And I was scared too, because I didn't know if you'd gone somewhere on your own or if someone had taken you. And then when we find you, you won't say anything about what happened. I keep hoping you'll tell me the truth, but you don't seem to be able to talk.'

Reese wanted to shrink into nothing. She wished she could melt into the deck of the ferry and become the wood. Anything would be better than seeing David look at her as if he didn't recognize who she was anymore.

'I know you had feelings for her, and she obviously still has feelings for you.' His eyes were shadowed with something between anger and sadness. 'I just want you to be honest with me.'

Reese didn't know what to say. A thousand words were jumbled up in her head and she couldn't form a sentence out of any of them.

Gritting his teeth, David turned and headed back across the deck toward the stairs.

'David, wait!' She went after him, determined not to mess this up, not like this, and she grabbed his hand. Jealousy jolted through her, fierce and bitter, and she nearly dropped his hand in shock.

He jerked away from her. 'What?'

'You're not like that,' she said, desperation rising in her. 'You're not like this.'

'Like what?'

She pushed her hair back, her fingers digging into her scalp as she searched frantically for the right words. 'You're – you have no reason to be jealous. You're *you*. You always do the right thing. You're so put together, and you can talk about whatever happened to us when I turn into a babbling idiot, and you're – you're the good guy. I want the good guy. I want *you*.'

Something softened in his gaze, and she took that as a positive sign. She reached for him again, but his hand was a leaden weight in hers. *David*. He took a step closer to her.

'Can't you feel how I feel about you?' she asked. She raised his hand and placed it over her heart.

He lifted his other hand to her face. His fingers were warm on her cheek. He was so close to her, all he had to do was lean down a tiny bit, and he could kiss her. She put her hands on his upper arms. She wanted to tug him down to her. She wanted to close the distance between them and forget about Amber.

'Yeah, I can feel it,' he whispered.

Her fingers tightened over his biceps. *David*. He didn't move.

'But how do you feel about Amber? You need to figure that part out.' He didn't kiss her. He stepped back. 'I'm not the person you think I am,' he said, and then he turned and left her alone.

Reese and her dad had to drive David home. It was beyond awkward. As Reese's dad pulled the car away from David's house, he asked, 'Is something wrong between you two? Do you want to talk about it?'

She stared out the window at the passing houses as their car descended the hill. 'No,' she answered. She definitely didn't want to get into this with her dad. She saw him glance at her dubiously and she quickly changed the subject. 'When are you leaving?'

'Why, am I outstaying my welcome?' he said jokingly.

'I'm just wondering. Don't you have to get back to work in Seattle?'

'I'm working here. You know that. I have to fly back for a

meeting at the end of the month, but I might come back after that.'

She turned her head to look at him. 'Why?'

His eyebrows rose in surprise. 'I'm your father. After what happened to you, I want to be here for you.'

She turned back to the window. 'Oh, really,' she said, lacing the words with sarcasm.

There was a pause, and then her dad asked, 'What is the matter with you? Are you trying to start a fight?'

She shrugged, slouching down in the seat. 'Why, is there a fight we should be having?'

'Reese,' he said, sounding exasperated.

'Dad,' she mimicked. She was all prickles right now; she didn't care if she started a fight.

'You're acting like a child.'

'You guys never let me do anything on my own anymore. Maybe that's why.'

He inhaled sharply. 'Reese. I'm trying here. Are you angry with me? You have to meet me halfway.'

She didn't answer for a moment. She felt as if all her emotions were turning to stone. She asked in a bored tone of voice, 'What are you doing with Mom?'

She could sense the tension in the car ratchet up several notches as her dad said, 'What do you mean?'

She looked at him. His jaw was tight, his hands clenched over the wheel. 'I mean, are you trying to get back together with her?'

He kept his eyes on the road. 'I'm your father,' he said curtly. 'You shouldn't be speaking to me in that tone.'

‘I think you lost your parental authority when you cheated on Mom and moved out.’ Reese had argued with her father before, but she had never put this particular thought into words. Saying it out loud sent a surge of hot excitement through her, as if she were gearing up to do something reckless.

Her father’s face turned an ugly shade of red. ‘You need to tone it down. I won’t accept this from you.’

‘Won’t accept what? The truth?’ She sat up, glaring at him. ‘You never tell me the truth. What about Lydia? Are you still with her?’

Her father jammed his foot on the brake and the car jerked, the seat belt digging into her shoulder. They were at a stop sign. He turned to look at her. ‘Where did you hear about her?’ he demanded.

‘I live in the same house with Mom,’ she said coldly. ‘I can hear, you know.’

He accelerated through the intersection. ‘You’re too young to understand these things. And they’re between your mother and me and have nothing to do with you.’

His answer infuriated her, and she couldn’t seem to stop herself from pushing him further. It was as if everything she had ever wanted to tell him was waiting to spill right out of her into the space of the car, and all she had to do was let go. ‘Oh, really? Who gets to deal with the fallout when you decide you’re done with Mom again? Who? *I do*. Do you know how upset she was last time you guys broke up? It was *horrible*, Dad. You have no idea what happens because you go back up to Seattle and you don’t have to deal with it. You go back to your – to Lydia, or whoever, and you don't have any repercussions.'

'Reese, I'm warning you—'

'You don't get it!' Reese cried, anger arcing through her like lightning. 'If you love Mom, then fucking *love* her. That's the only one you get to love. You can't have your cake and eat it too.'

They had reached the house, and as soon as her dad pulled the car into the garage he said, 'You are grounded, Reese. You can't speak to me that way.'

'Whatever,' she said, opening the door. 'You can't ground me. You don't even live here.' She got out of the car and slammed the door, stalking away.

Her dad got out too. 'Reese! Come back here!'

She didn't listen to him. She just kept walking.

Her mother was waiting for her in the living room when she returned home a couple of hours later. 'Where have you been?' her mom asked, standing up. She looked tired and exasperated and upset.

'I had to get some air,' Reese said, heading for the stairs.

'Stop right there,' her mom snapped. 'I'm not finished with you.'

Reese's shoulders hunched. She turned around on the bottom step. 'Mom, I—'

'Your father told me what you said to him.'

'He deserved it.'

Her mom crossed her arms. 'He deserves your respect.'

Reese gaped at her. 'Are you serious? After what he's done

to you?'

Her mom came into the hall. 'I understand that you're being protective of me, and you know, I even appreciate that. But you don't understand the details of what's going on between your father and me, and it's not your place to manage that.'

'So tell me! Or do you want me to just wait till it's over so I can make you feel better when he leaves you again?'

Her mother flushed. 'That's enough. Go to your room. We'll discuss this when you're calmer.'

Reese made a frustrated sound and stalked up the stairs. 'Fine,' she threw back over her shoulder. 'Whatever.' She slammed her bedroom door so hard that it made the walls shake. She sat down on the edge of her bed, dropping her head into her hands, and felt as if every nerve in her body had been switched on. She was vibrating with tension, and at first she didn't realize that part of the vibration came from the phone in her jeans pocket.

She pulled it out, fearing that it was David, but to her surprise it was Bri. 'What's up?' Reese asked, answering the phone.

'Reese? It's Bri.' She sounded strangely excited.

'Yeah, what's going on?' She couldn't hide the anger in her voice, and she didn't care. It felt good.

'Um, there are these photos of you online?' Bri said hesitantly.

'This is news? There are photos all the time now.'

'These are new.'

There was something in her tone that made Reese suddenly

nervous. 'What are these photos of?' Reese went to her desk and opened her laptop.

'Well, you're with that alien chick.'

'Like during the press conference in front of my house?'

'Uh, no.' Bri paused. The computer was slowly loading. 'They're, um, you guys look a little intimate.'

'What?' Why was her computer so slow? 'Where are we?'

'Some beach somewhere? So . . . you and this alien chick?'

The laptop was finally on. Reese clicked on the Internet browser. 'What website did you see it on?'

'It's on the Hub. It just showed up like a few minutes ago.'

She went to the Hub. 'On your feed? Where?'

'Just type in your name and it'll come up.'

There it was. A somewhat grainy photo of Reese and Amber, sitting on the concrete retaining wall on the edge of Angel Island, their heads close together. Amber's hand was on her cheek. Their mouths were nearly touching. Behind them the bulk of the spaceship loomed like a giant black beast.

Reese's heart was racing. 'Shit.'

'Reese? Are you okay?' Bri asked.

Reese clicked on a thumbnail image next to the large one. It was another shot of the two of them. There was a whole series, starting with them sitting a couple of feet apart and culminating with the fuzzy, zoomed-in photo that made it look as if they were about to or had just kissed.

'Hey, I just wanted to tell you. I didn't want you to be surprised,' Bri said.

Reese took a shuddering breath. 'Yeah. Thanks.'

'Are you all right? You sound a little freaked out.'

Hysterical laughter threatened to rip out of her. 'Freaked out? Shit. *Shit.*'

'So, I gotta ask, um, did you guys hook up before? I mean, you told the news that you knew her before. When did you know her?'

Reese thought she was going to hyperventilate. The comments beneath the photos turned her stomach. There weren't many yet, but she knew this was only the beginning. *Alien hottie moves in on human girl! Guess the Chinese dude just wasn't 'enough' for her, huh? I wanna get me some of that.*

'Reese?'

She had to stop looking at this page and its comments – another three popped up that second – or she would throw up. She got up, slamming her laptop closed. 'Yeah. Yeah, I'm here,' she said. She began to pace back and forth. Her phone beeped; Julian was on call-waiting. She didn't answer, and Bri kept talking.

'I know you're not out and all, and this is probably like a giant shock to you or something. I'm really sorry. If you need to talk about it or anything, I'm here for you.' Bri laughed slightly. 'Hey, that girl's pretty hot. Congratulations?'

Reese froze in place. She had to call David. He was going to see those pictures. 'I have to go,' she said abruptly. 'I'm sorry. Thanks for telling me about the photos. I'll talk to you later.' She hung up without waiting for Bri to respond, and then she stood there with her phone in her hand, her finger poised above David's number in her address book.

She took a deep breath and hit the Call button.

CHAPTER 25

Walking into Kennedy High School on Monday morning felt like walking into a pit of vipers. Reese had already gone through the gauntlet of photographers outside on the sidewalk, shouting questions at her about her relationship with Amber, and that was bad enough. Going inside meant facing people who knew her – or thought they had known her – as well as their judgment.

The normal hum of conversation faded quickly as she came through the door. After her lessons with Eres, Reese could now sense much more clearly where the emotions fell around her. There was a lot of curiosity – which still felt like dozens of fingers jabbing at her – but layered over that was an amalgamation of distrust and, in some cases, disgust. That feeling in particular emanated from a group of kids standing by the trophy cases. David's friends. Of course his friends would hate her. The pictures made it look like she had cheated on him. She didn't see David, though, and she wasn't sure if she was glad about that or not.

He had been brief with her on the phone. She couldn't tell

if he was angry with her when she explained, haltingly, that she and Amber had been photographed together. 'We didn't do anything,' she told him. 'I left right after they took those photos.' There had been a long silence afterward. So long that she began to fear that he had hung up on her. 'Are you still there? Do you want me to come over?'

'No,' he said. 'I'll call you.'

She had kept her phone with her for the rest of the weekend, but he didn't call. Julian did, and so did Madison, but Reese didn't answer. She stayed in her room with the computer off and replayed her conversation with David on the ferry over and over in her mind, picking out every instance when she could have told him about what had happened with Amber, but chose not to. As the hours passed, dread built up inside her, layer upon layer. This was it, she thought. She had messed things up with David, just like she had feared she would, and now it was over.

As she crossed the school lobby on Monday morning, her face burned with shame. Whispers passed through the students: *Cheating little dyke. What a freak.*

At her locker, she fumbled through the combination, opening the door clumsily and nearly banging her face into it. She cursed under her breath and unloaded her backpack. She should get to class. Ignore all of these people. When she closed the locker she started at the sight of Julian, Madison, Bri, and Robbie standing right there. 'Crap, you scared me,' Reese mumbled. They all had extremely sober expressions on their faces.

'Come on,' Julian said. 'We'll walk you to class.'

A wave of gratitude swept through Reese. 'You don't have to do that.'

Robbie shrugged. 'You hooked up with some hot alien chick. Other people are just jealous.'

'I didn't hook up with her,' Reese said. 'At least, not last weekend.'

Madison's eyebrows shot up. 'When did you hook up with her?'

Reese reddened. 'Those photos are totally misleading. I would never cheat on David.' It was important that her friends understood that, and she said the words loud enough that several other students stopped to stare at her. 'I didn't,' she insisted, looking at her friends.

Julian gave her a sympathetic look and put an arm around her, ushering her down the hall as the others fell in beside them. 'Think of it this way: Now it's all out in the open. You have nothing to fear anymore.'

'Also,' Bri put in, 'you are totally coming back to the GSA.'

Reese only glimpsed David from afar at lunch, and he was surrounded by his friends, who kept shooting dark glances at her, so she didn't approach him. Her friends tried to cheer her up, but she could only manage a wan smile at their bad jokes. She couldn't avoid hearing the whispers in the hallways or feeling the waves of emotion that passed through other students when she walked past. Nobody believed that she hadn't cheated on David. The pictures were too damning. By the end of the day she had withdrawn into herself, blocking everything off so that she was enclosed in her own mental space. It wasn't comforting, though, because in her head she kept remonstrating herself for not telling David everything right away. Maybe if she had, he wouldn't have reacted this way.

During Principles of Democracy, Mr Hernandez once again told her and David to wait after class. David wouldn't look at her the whole period, and even when the room cleared out – with a few students casting curious glances their way – he continued to sit in his seat, facing forward. *David?* she thought, but he only shook his head without answering her. She hunched over in her seat and wished she could be someplace else.

Mr Hernandez closed the door. His shoes clicked across the floor as he pulled one of the desks out to face the two of them. She heard the beep as he turned on the audio recorder. 'All right,' he said. 'What happened on Saturday?'

'Dr Brand officially invited us to go to the UN with them,' David answered.

'Interesting. What did you tell her?'

'That I'd think about it.'

'I assume you're not going.'

'Of course not.' David's voice was clipped.

Have you already decided? Reese asked him silently. His answer came back shortly: *No.*

'Reese, what about you?'

'Yeah,' she agreed, still gazing down at the desk. Someone had carved *RIP MR C* into the upper right corner. 'I'm not going.' She waited for David to ask if she was lying, but he didn't.

'What about the adaptation chamber? Did you get photos?'

'Not yet,' David said. 'But I asked about it.'

Reese lifted her head now and looked at him. He hadn't told her that, and she wondered if he was fabricating this for Mr Hernandez's benefit.

'It's on the ship,' David said. 'There was no time for us to look at it, but when we go back on Saturday—'

'The General Debate begins on Monday. We need that info before then.' Mr Hernandez did not look happy.

'I know,' David said. 'You'll have it on Saturday, I promise.'

Mr Hernandez considered David for a long moment. 'You seem to have turned a corner, David. I can see that you're now fully on our side.'

'I was always on your side. On our side.'

Reese felt like she was going to be sick. *What are you doing?* she thought at David. He didn't answer her. Mr Hernandez went to his desk, where he took a large envelope out of his briefcase. He removed several glossy photos and returned to lay them on the desks in front of Reese and David. As Reese looked at the images, she began to sweat.

'As you can see, it is not only the paparazzi who are capable of photographing private moments,' Mr Hernandez said.

One of the photos showed Reese's mom at home in the kitchen. The picture had been taken through the back window. There was another photo of her dad at a restaurant. It must have been at lunch, because he was seated at a table near a window and daylight was pouring over the place setting. Her mom was seated across from him. They were holding hands.

'Saturday night, I will meet the two of you here at school,'

Mr Hernandez said. 'The front doors will be unlocked at six PM to let people in for a theatrical production. You will bring me the photos of the adaptation chamber at six fifteen. Is that clear?'

Reese looked at Mr Hernandez and made herself swallow the rage that burned in her throat. 'It's clear,' she said. She couldn't see the photos on David's desk but from the set of his shoulders, she guessed he had gotten the message too. If they didn't bring CASS what they wanted, their families would be in danger.

'Yes,' David said. 'We'll have the photos.'

Mr Hernandez nodded. 'Good. Then I'll see you tomorrow in class.'

They were dismissed. Reese stood up and saw one of the pictures in front of David before he swept them into a pile: his younger sister, Chloe, laughing. He put the photos in his backpack and headed out of the classroom. Reese turned to grab the pictures of her parents before following David into the hall.

'David!' she called. He couldn't ignore her if she spoke out loud.

He was already fifteen feet ahead of her, but he slowed, turning. 'I have to go to practice.'

'Can I talk to you?' she pleaded, hating how desperate she sounded.

'I have to go to practice,' he said again, beginning to walk backward. 'I'll call you tonight.' And then he left her standing there, the photos of her parents clutched in her hands.

* * *

Reese went to the school library, alone, to do her homework and wait for her mom to pick her up. After those pictures of her and Amber had been posted online, the paparazzi had swarmed Reese's street with their long-range cameras, and leaving the house that morning had involved Reese ducking down in the passenger seat of the car while her mom honked the horn and screamed at the photographers.

'Don't go outside until I call you,' her mom had told her right before dropping her off at school. 'I can't get there till after five but you'll just have to wait. Your dad has a meeting in Palo Alto.'

Reese had no intention of stepping outside the school's front doors until she knew her mom had arrived, but she was restless and couldn't concentrate on her homework. She thought about those pictures of her parents, together. She thought about the photos of her and Amber. Students came in and out of the library, passing her and whispering behind their hands. They didn't bother to keep their voices down, and she had to put in her earbuds so that she didn't hear them judge her. She pulled out her phone, but there were no messages. She wondered if David really was going to call her after soccer practice. With a sinking feeling, she realized she didn't believe he would.

She stared down at her physics textbook, the words blurring as her eyes grew hot. She blinked furiously. *Not here*, she told herself. If David wasn't going to call her, she would have to put herself in a place where he couldn't ignore her. They had to talk. This was all a misunderstanding. She could show him her memories of what had happened, and he would understand. He had to understand.

She glanced at the clock. It was still early, but that was good. She wouldn't miss him. She loaded up her backpack and left the library, heading downstairs toward the gym. The hallway outside the boys' locker room was empty, smelling faintly of cleaning fumes. She dropped her backpack on the floor and slid down the wall to the linoleum, drawing her knees up. She'd wait for him.

She heard the boys' soccer team approaching before she saw them. They were loud and boisterous, cracking jokes about the school they were going to play tomorrow. The double doors in the distance banged shut and then the team rounded the corner, the dozen or so boys dressed identically in maroon shorts, dirty shin guards, and gray KENNEDY SOCCER tees. They reminded her of a pack of puppies, rowdy and joyful, but as soon as they saw her their energy changed completely. They focused, becoming a coordinated group of muscle with their attention fixed on her, and in the center of them was David.

She suddenly realized this might have been a very bad idea. How could he listen to her when he was surrounded by his teammates? She pushed herself to her feet as the boys approached. David separated himself from the others and came toward her. His shirt was smeared with grass stains, his hair was damp with sweat, and his face was grimy, but the sight of him awoke a fierce ache inside her. She had never seen him this way: as someone she was on the verge of losing.

'Hey,' he said, his face expressionless.

'Hey,' she answered.

Some of his teammates continued toward the locker room, but a few hung back until David said, 'I'll be there in a minute.'

They nodded to him – brief, masculine nods that made Reese aware of exactly how far outside of his world she was at that moment – and left them alone in the hallway.

She plunged ahead before she could lose her nerve. 'I'm sorry I didn't tell you what happened from the beginning. I should have. It just freaked me out so much and I couldn't deal with it right then. I can show you what happened. Will you let me?' She held out her hand and he looked at it as if it contained a weapon. Her face burned, but she kept her hand out, her fingers curled up from her palm.

Just when she thought he was never going to accept her offer, he stepped forward. He took her hand.

She showed him everything. She made sure she left nothing out, and she was more open with him than she ever had been. In a way she felt as if she was stripping off all her clothes in the middle of the school hallway, and even though she was afraid he would hate what he saw, she did it anyway. Through his hand she sensed his emotions changing as she took him through her memories. At first he was tense and defensive, but gradually the tension was replaced with sadness. When it was over he let go of her and she whispered, 'I'm sorry.'

'I know,' he said in a low voice. 'I'm not angry that you didn't tell me. Not anymore.'

'Really?' she said hopefully. 'Then we're okay?'

He sighed. 'No.'

Her heart seemed to stop. 'What? What do you mean?'

He wouldn't meet her gaze. His eyes seemed fixed on some point over her left shoulder. 'I can't do this. I can't deal with the way people talk about us. About me.'

'You mean the assholes on the Internet? You can't listen to them. You told me that yourself.'

He shook his head. 'Not only them. People at school. Everywhere.' He finally looked at her, and he was wrecked. There was pain in his eyes, desperation in the set of his mouth. He took a step closer, lowering his voice into an intense whisper. 'Those photos made you look like a cheater, but they made me look like an idiot. And I know you have feelings for her. Even if you didn't kiss her last Saturday, you kissed her before. I *remember* how you felt about kissing her. Do you have any idea how that makes me feel?'

She flinched. 'I'm sorry,' she said again, and it sounded ridiculously inadequate – like attempting to apply a Band-Aid over a chest wound.

'I can't compete with her.' David rubbed a hand over his face and pushed his damp hair back. 'I don't want to. I shouldn't have to.'

'You're not competing with her,' she insisted. It came out sounding like a shriek. She moderated her voice. 'I want to be with *you*.'

'Yeah, you keep saying that, but you have feelings for her too.' His jaw clenched.

Heat flushed her body, and suddenly she was angry – angry at herself, angry at David, angry at Amber. 'Why can't you hear me? I have feelings for *you*. I may be the most inarticulate person on the planet when it comes to telling you how I feel, but I don't have to tell you. You *know*. I showed you everything, and you know that I want to be with you – not with her. I don't trust her. I trust you. I'm in—' She stumbled over the words and tried again. 'I'm in love with you.'

David's cheeks darkened. 'Reese . . .'

'Shouldn't the way I feel about you be more important than what other people think?' She reached for his hands. He was a mess of conflicting emotions: anguish and hope and brittle self-doubt. She had never felt him like that before, his conscious self sharp as crystal. *David*, she thought. *I'm in love with you.*

I know, he told her.

Isn't that enough?

'You're in love with her too,' he said softly. 'It's not okay with me.'

She felt like she was about to fall off a tightrope. 'Are you breaking up with me?' she asked in a small voice.

He looked somewhat startled. 'Yeah. I guess I am.'

She pulled away from him, backing up until she hit the wall, the cinder blocks cool against her sweaty palms. She was dizzy. Everything felt unreal: the glare of the fluorescent overhead lights, the shadows they cast over David's face, the dark doorway to the boys' locker room down the hall.

His cleats clicked on the floor as he shifted in place. 'It's not like I don't ever want to see you again. We have to do this – this thing on Saturday. We have to talk about all that. But maybe we should take a couple of days to think about how to handle it. Okay?'

The idea of having to continue their charade with Mr Hernandez, of taking more lessons with Eres Tilhar, of being with David when she wasn't *with* him at all – it made panic explode inside her. She couldn't do it.

'I know we can still be friends,' he was saying. 'Can't we go back to that?'

She was about to start crying at any second. 'Yeah,' she choked out. 'Of course.' And then she turned so he wouldn't see the tears spill from her eyes, and picked up her backpack and slung it awkwardly over one shoulder. She tried not to stumble as she walked away. He didn't call her back.

She pushed through the front doors of the school half-blinded by tears. She was assaulted by flashbulbs as the door slammed shut behind her.

She recoiled in shock, having forgotten that the photographers would be out there. But there were more than photographers; there were protesters. They shouted at her, their voices rising in a barrage of demands, and she remembered at that instant that she was supposed to wait inside the school for her mom's phone call. She backed away and reached for the door handle, but it wouldn't open. She tugged at it, but it didn't budge. She turned her back to the crowd and tried the other door. It was locked too.

Of course. The school doors were locked after 5:00 PM. She banged on the door frantically as the shouts of the protesters rose, but nobody came. Could they not hear her?

She turned around slowly. Down on the sidewalk, police barricades kept the people back on two sides. Paparazzi were jammed in at the front. On the right were demonstrators she vaguely recognized from the pier: men and women holding signs about the new world order. New signs had been added too, and as she read the words her stomach seemed to shrink into a tight fist.

TRAITOR.

HUMAN RACE NOT GOOD ENOUGH FOR YOU?

HOMOSEXUALS ARE POSSESSED BY ALIENS!

GOD HATES FAGS. FAGS = IMRIA. GOD HATES IMRIA.

On the left side were the Imria supporters with their WELCOME TO EARTH signs, but a new group had joined them. They waved rainbow flags and carried signs that declared GAY RIGHTS DON'T STOP WITH HUMANITY. One was done up with glitter and neon paint and stated ALIENS ARE FABULOUS!

Reese's phone rang, and she pulled it out of her pocket in relief. 'Mom, are you here?'

'I'm across the street by the café. I can't turn. There's too much police presence. Where are you?'

'I'm on the school steps. I'll come to you.' She hung up and repocketed her phone before heading down the steps. As she approached the two mobs of demonstrators their chants grew louder, but she kept her gaze straight ahead, not looking directly at anyone. She focused on herself, pushing back the waves of ferocity on the right and the pressure of curiosity on the left. She was on the sidewalk now. She only had to cross the street, passing the police who were watching her with expressionless eyes. Her mom was barely a block away, but getting to the Prius felt like navigating through a mile-long obstacle course. By the time she reached the car and slid inside, she was wired and breathless.

'Are you okay?' her mom asked, pulling the car around the corner onto Eighteenth Street.

'Yeah,' she said, still clutching her backpack. 'Some of those people are crazy.'

'You can't pay any attention to what those homophobes are saying,' her mom said grimly. 'There's nothing wrong with you. Nothing.'

Reese glanced at her mom in surprise. When they had parted that morning, they hadn't been on the best of terms; Reese knew her mom was still mad at her about the argument she'd had with her dad. Her mom's apparent change of heart startled a question out of her that she hadn't even known she wanted to ask. 'You don't think I'm a freak for dating an alien?'

Her mom shook her head decisively. 'No, honey. I don't.' Her mom pulled the car to a stop at the red light and turned to her, squeezing her knee. 'You're not a freak. You're my daughter and I love you.'

Reese hugged her backpack closer, trying to swallow the tears that kept pricking at her eyes. 'Thanks, Mom.'

Her mom sighed and turned back to the street. 'But you're still grounded for what you said to your dad.'

CHAPTER 26

Given the fact that David had just dumped her and paparazzi kept tailing her, Reese decided that being grounded wasn't the worst thing in the world. The worst thing in the world was being forced to go to school.

In the hallways, students snickered at her behind their hands. The story of David breaking up with her outside the boys' locker room had spread quicker than wildfire. 'She deserved it,' some people said loud enough for her to hear as she walked past. She tried to ignore them, but it was hard, because to some degree she agreed.

David made no attempt to talk to her about their potential trip to the UN or what they would do on Saturday when it came time to deliver those photos of the adaptation chamber to Mr Hernandez. She had no idea if David had truly asked Eres Tilhar about the chamber or if he had been lying to Mr Hernandez. She knew she should ask him. The situation with the Imria and CASS was much bigger than her breakup with David, but she couldn't bring herself to face him yet. Not when he had responded to her revelation that she was in love with him by telling her I *know*. That hurt more than anything else.

On Wednesday night she overheard her parents on the phone with David's parents, discussing Dr Brand's invitation to bring them all to New York. Reese was in the living room watching a DVD of a zombie movie instead of doing her homework, but as soon as she realized what her parents were talking about, she fled upstairs to her room. She loaded the same movie onto her laptop and plugged in her headphones so she could drown out any sound of the phone call. There was something soothing about the fake mayhem: the hordes of zombies lurching across fields and parking lots; the heroes with their makeshift weapons fighting them back. It was black-and-white, survival of the fittest. There was nothing debatable about it.

She fell asleep with the movie playing, only to awaken with a start several hours later. A high-pitched, ear-popping alarm was beeping over and over. The smoke detector. She sat up, heart pounding as she blinked in the light of her bedside lamp. Her headphones fell out of her ears, making the noise even louder. The computer screen was blank.

She smelled something burning.

She scrambled to her feet and ran to the door, pulling it open. Across the hall her mom rushed out of her room.

'Reese, are you all right?'

'I'm fine. Where's Dad?' They looked down the stairwell at the same time, and at the bottom there was an orange flickering light.

'Oh my God,' her mom said. She raced down the stairs, calling back, 'Reese, stay up there!'

Reese didn't obey. She followed and saw her father coming from the kitchen with a fire extinguisher. 'Go outside!' he cried. 'It's in the living room.' The smoke was thicker down here, and Reese covered her nose and mouth with her arm as she looked through the archway into the living room. The rug was on fire, flames billowing bright orange and sending hot, gasoline-scented fumes toward the hallway. Something glittered on the floor, and as Reese stared, transfixed by the fire, she realized it was shattered glass.

Her mom seized her by the arm and pushed her toward the front door. 'Move!'

Reese saw her dad pull the pin on the fire extinguisher and a spray of white foam launched at the flames. 'What about Dad? Is he coming?'

'He's coming,' her mom said, grabbing her purse off the hall tree. She opened the door. 'Go!' she ordered.

Outside the air was fresh and cool, and as Reese went down the front steps Agent Forrestal came barreling up. She heard her mom talking to him in frantic tones as the shrieking of the fire alarm receded. At the bottom of the steps she turned to look back at the house. Agent Forrestal had gone inside, and her mom was coming down to the street. The living room window – illuminated by the dying glow of the fire – was broken. Dread slid down her back, vicious and cold. Someone had thrown something through the window on purpose. That's what the glass on the carpet was from. *Who would do that?*

She didn't have to guess for long, because her dad and Agent Forrestal soon emerged from the house together. Her dad hurried down the steps toward her and her mom and said,

'The fire extinguisher's empty. I got most of it, but the alarm's still going off.'

Reese stared at the front door, which Agent Forrestal had pulled shut. Written in neon-green spray paint were four words: QUEER ALIEN FUCKING FREAK.

The fire department came first, their sirens and whirling lights waking up the neighbors who hadn't been disturbed by the incessant beeping of the alarm. They charged into the house in their neon-striped black coats, and then the police arrived, their sirens adding to the cacophony. All along the block, lights began to come on.

Reese stood with her mom's arm around her, feeling the cold sidewalk through her socks, trying to focus solely on herself. She couldn't handle her mom's terror and anger in addition to her own.

'Weren't you watching our house?' her mom demanded of Agent Forrestal. 'How could you let this happen?'

'It was only one guy, and he broke the window before I realized what he was doing,' the agent said.

'If it was only one guy, why didn't you catch him?' her mom pushed.

Agent Forrestal bristled. 'It's dark. He knew the neighborhood and ducked into someone's yard. And my job is to make sure Reese is safe, not chase common criminals. I couldn't leave the vicinity.'

'The police will find him,' her dad said, squeezing her mom's shoulder.

'They'd better.'

After the fire department was finished, the police did a walk-through. The first-floor bay windows were vintage single-paned glass – Reese's mom had never had the time or money to renovate – and it hadn't taken much to break one: a few fist-sized rocks hurled from the street. They found the rocks on the floor beneath the coffee table. After the window had been broken, someone had tossed a Molotov cocktail through, and it had exploded on impact. Reese's dad had put out most of the fire with the extinguisher, but the fire department had sprayed everything down anyway, so when Reese and her parents were allowed to return inside, the living room was soaked and blackened, the rug and the furniture ruined. As Reese paused in the archway, staring at the mess, she heard her mom talking to the police about hate crimes. Nobody needed to guess who the message was for.

After the police took their statements – including Agent Forrestal's vague and mostly useless description of the attacker – Reese's parents herded her into the back of the house, making her sit at the kitchen table to drink a cup of hot tea. The house smelled of smoke and gasoline and the lingering, sweet odor of the fire extinguisher chemicals, and mint tea did little to mask it. Her parents were talking in low, intense tones by the sink, acting as if she couldn't hear them. They were debating whether or not she should stay in the house.

'Where am I going to go?' she interrupted.

They turned as one to look at her. 'We're discussing that, honey,' her mom said.

'I don't want to go anywhere,' Reese said tonelessly. 'If I go somewhere, they'll win.'

Her mom crossed the kitchen and pulled out the chair next to Reese. 'Honey, I admire your courage, and I'm the first to agree that I don't want some jerkwads dictating how I live my life, but—'

'Where are you going to make me go? You want me to go to Nanna and Grandpa's? How do you know the jerkwads won't follow us there?'

'At least you won't be as accessible there.'

'They live in Mill Valley! It's just over the Golden Gate Bridge.' Anger burned through Reese. 'No. I'm not leaving. They can fuck off. I don't care if they think I'm some disgusting pervert.' Her mom sighed, reaching out to smooth away Reese's messy hair from her forehead. Reese jerked back. 'You don't have to baby me. I'm not a little kid anymore.' She stood up, her chair's legs scraping across the floor. Her color rose as she spoke, her voice growing harder-edged with every word. 'I know there are crazy people out there. It doesn't matter where I go, they follow me. They're everywhere – on our block, at school, at the ferry. Not to mention on the Internet. Have you seen the shit they say about me? I can't let them dictate what I do!'

Her mom seemed taken aback. 'I'm only trying to keep you safe, honey.'

'Yeah, well, you can't do that either,' Reese said harshly.

Her mom stood, her face flushed. 'Well, I'm going to try. You're not a little kid anymore but you're still my daughter. And you're going to go where I tell you to go.'

Reese gaped at her mom. Then she whirled on her feet and headed for the stairs.

'Come back here!'

'I'm going to my room,' Reese snapped.

'No, you're not! That's facing the street. *Get back here*.'

Reese had never heard her mom speak like that before, her voice choked with desperate terror. She turned around. 'Where do you want me to go?' she asked in a low voice.

Her mom hesitated. She glanced at Reese's dad for a split second. 'Go into the guest room,' her mom said. 'You can sleep there.'

'Fine.' Reese went to the guest room and closed the door. Then she sat down on the edge of the sofa bed, the blankets still mussed from when her father had woken up a couple of hours earlier. Her whole body shuddered as she swallowed her sobs so that her parents wouldn't hear.

Reese did not go to school on Thursday, but the news of what had happened spread quickly, because she began getting texts from her friends by midmorning. Even David called, but when she saw his picture light up her cell phone she couldn't bring herself to answer it. His voice-mail message was tentative, concerned. It made her feel even sadder.

Her mom came up with a solution that night. 'You're going to Angel Island,' she said, pulling plates out of the cabinet for the pizza she had picked up.

'Are you serious?' Reese asked. Since when had her mom decided that staying with the Imria was a good idea?

'They've invited you to go with them to the UN anyway, and it's important for you to do that. You might as well go a little early, because it's the only place I know where you'll be safe.'

'Why do you think that? You've never—'

'I've been talking to Dr Brand,' her mom said. 'She might not be a human being, but she's been honest with me throughout this entire ordeal. She showed us her research; she talked to me and David's parents about the adaptation and answered all our questions. I know you and her daughter have had issues, but Dr Brand wanted the best for you. She saved your life. If it weren't for her, you'd be dead. I trust her.'

Reese was stunned.

'I talked to her this afternoon. She agreed that you can stay on their ship, and she's sending a ferry tonight at eight o'clock. You'd better eat quickly and pack up. I'm going with you; your dad's staying here.'

'I'll get the windows repaired and put in an alarm system,' her dad said, taking a plate.

Reese turned to stare at him. 'So you're staying?'

He looked from Reese to her mother. He was obviously tired. Reese didn't know where he had been sleeping since she had taken over the guest room, and she didn't want to think about the possibilities.

'He's staying for a while,' her mom said. Her words were vague, but the look on her face as she offered her ex-husband a slice of pizza was not.

Now, that's a tell, Reese thought. She tried to focus on her dinner, but the pizza tasted like cardboard.

Nura Halba met Reese and her mom at the Angel Island harbor. It was almost dark by the time the ferry had arrived, and going to the island without David had felt strange to Reese. She knew she needed to talk to David soon – her move to the ship changed everything with regard to Mr Hernandez and CASS – but she told herself she'd call him tomorrow. One more night wouldn't make a difference, and maybe in the morning she'd have a better idea of what she wanted to do. Right now, everything was a jumbled, confusing mess in her head, and the only thing she could think about was the fact that she and Amber were going to be sleeping under the same roof tonight.

The rooms that Nura Halba took them to were in the living quarters on the third level of the spacecraft. 'Your door is programmed to recognize you,' he explained after Reese pressed her palm to the black glass plate in the center of hers. 'You don't need a key.' Inside, on the wall across from the door, was a screen that showed the dark hillside of eucalyptus trees outside. 'You can adjust the view with the touch screen here,' he said, showing her a smooth glass surface beneath the screen. 'It is done by thought, but if you have trouble with it, you can use voice commands. I've had it modified to understand simple English words. You can turn the screen off or dim the lights by commanding it to do so.' Reese and her mom shared a tiny, efficient bathroom between their rooms, and Halba explained that they were welcome to help themselves to food in the dining hall on the first level. 'There will be breakfast available in the morning. If you need any assistance, don't hesitate to let me know.' He showed them how to contact him through a device near the door.

When he left, Reese's mom said, 'I'm going to give your dad a call to tell him we're all settled in. Do you need anything?'

'No. I'm kind of tired. I might just go to sleep.'

Her mom kissed her on the forehead as if she were a six-year-old. Reese smelled the scent of her lotion and she wanted to curl up in her arms and pretend like everything was completely normal, but she didn't let herself give in.

'All right,' her mom said. 'Good night, honey.'

'Good night.'

After her mom left, Reese changed into her pajamas and lay down on the bunk, staring up at the ceiling. The overhead lights glowed warm and golden. 'Turn off the lights,' she said out loud, feeling a little ridiculous as she did so. The lights dimmed immediately so that the only illumination came from the screen depicting the hill outside. It was peaceful to watch night fall over the eucalyptus grove, and when she could no longer make out the shapes of the trees in the dark, she turned off the screens. The room was plunged into blackness.

As she closed her eyes, she wondered where Amber's room was. Did Amber know she was here? She rolled onto her side, pulling the blanket over herself. She wondered, too, if the adaptation chamber was really in this spaceship. Had she slept within these walls before? The thought was perversely comforting, and she fell asleep remembering the cocoon of red and gold around her, soft and warm as her mother's embrace.

CHAPTER 27

Reese's phone pealed, the screen lighting up the dark room. She sat up, disoriented, and grabbed the vibrating device from where she had stowed it on a shelf near her bunk. It was David. She answered the phone, heart racing from her abrupt awakening, and croaked, 'Hello?'

'Hey, are you coming to school today?'

He sounded wide awake, and she pulled the phone away from her ear to check the time. It was nine fifteen in the morning. She fumbled for the light switch and then realized there wasn't one. 'Lights,' she said groggily, and heard David's tinny voice coming from the phone. She raised it to her ear again as the overheads glowed on. 'Sorry, I didn't hear you. What's going on?'

'I looked for you at school but I couldn't find you. Are you still at home?'

She blinked. 'I'm on Angel Island.'

A beat. 'Why?'

'My mom thought I'd be safer here.' Reese rubbed a hand over her eyes, trying to wake herself up. She pushed the pillow against the wall and leaned back. 'Aren't you in school?' At nine fifteen, he should be in the middle of second period already.

'Yeah, I snuck out for a minute. I got some news from my dad. The scientists who are analyzing our DNA – they have an initial assessment. They think we're descended from the Imria.'

She stared at the close weave of the blue-gray blanket over her legs. It had a meticulously repeated diamond pattern. 'What?'

'They think humans evolved from the Imria. My dad says they can trace this back through our mitochondrial DNA – it's the same way anthropologists have been figuring out how humans evolved. They thought we were descended from a common ancestor in Africa, but apparently our DNA says we came from the Imria.'

Reese was wide awake now. 'Are they sure? They could figure this out just from our DNA?'

'They also had a sample from Dr Brand. She gave one to my dad – he never told me this. But with the Imrian sample and ours, yeah, they're pretty sure. I think they want to do more analyzing, and they're not going public with this yet, but it kind of explains a lot, doesn't it? Why we look like them.'

'But Akiya Deyir said they didn't know why—'

'Obviously he was lying. And you know what? Lovick had to be lying too. CASS has had access to Imrian DNA for years. They have to know too.'

She wrapped her arms around her knees. She was cold. 'So Charles Lovick and Akiya Deyir were both lying.'

'But Dr Brand wanted us to know. Why else would she have given that sample to my dad?'

Reese's mind raced. 'Do you think there's some kind of disagreement among the Imria? I mean, if Dr Brand wanted us to know but Akiya Deyir didn't . . .'

'Yeah. I don't know what's going on with them. If you're on the ship now, you need to find out. Talk to Dr Brand.'

'Okay, I'll try.' Her shoulders were stiff with tension. 'But what are we going to do about Mr Hernandez? I know the Imria haven't exactly been telling us the whole truth, but I don't trust CASS at all. You can't go to that meeting with Mr Hernandez tomorrow night.'

'If I don't go – you saw the photos he had. And what about you? Have you decided not to go?'

'My mom won't let me leave this place until after she thinks our house is secure. I can't go even if I wanted to, but I don't want to. I don't want to help CASS do whatever shady thing they're planning.'

David's voice dropped. 'My family, Reese. I can't leave them.'

'Then bring them here,' she said impulsively. 'Just bring them all.'

'To the ship?'

'Yes. Bring your parents and your sister. CASS can't get to them here.'

'I'll have to tell them why.'

'So tell them.' She was tired of lying; the idea of simply telling the truth was a seductive novelty.

He was silent for a moment. 'So you want to just throw in

with the Imria. We rely on them for everything.'

'No. We rely on each other. You're supposed to be here tomorrow for another lesson with Eres anyway, and the UN thing is on Monday. You should stay here tomorrow night, because if you go back, you'll have to go to the meeting with Hernandez, or else CASS will move in. At least if you stay here, we'll be able to talk to Dr Brand together. We'll get them to tell us everything. We'll figure it out together.'

She realized this was the first time she had talked to David since he broke up with her in the school hallway on Monday. She had avoided him all week, not even returning his texts after he heard about the attack on her house, because she had been so embarrassed by the breakup. Now that seemed like a million years ago. She was glad David had called this morning while she was asleep, because that was probably the only reason she had answered the phone – she hadn't been awake enough to be self-conscious. She slid to the edge of the bed and threw off the blanket, swinging her legs off the bunk. The matte black floor warmed beneath the soles of her feet, as if the material was made to sense her presence. David still hadn't answered, and the silence on the other end of the phone worried her.

'Please,' she said. She didn't care anymore if she sounded like a dork. The only thing that mattered was keeping him safe. 'I don't want anything to happen to you. Just come here.' Her heartbeat thudded in her ears as she waited for him to respond.

Finally he said, 'All right.'

'Thank you,' she said, relieved.

After they hung up, she held the phone in the palm of her

hand for a long moment. She took a deep breath before calling her home number. 'Hi, Dad,' she said when he answered. 'Look, you need to pack a suitcase.'

It was past ten o'clock by the time Reese made it down to the dining hall for breakfast. She didn't expect to find anyone there, but the room wasn't empty. Amber was seated at the curved table closest to the plant-filled cylinder, a laptop open in front of her. She didn't look up when the doors slid open; she was too absorbed in whatever she was reading on the computer.

Reese knew she should say something, but it was the first time she had seen Amber since the disastrous afternoon on the beach. She was wearing a faded green T-shirt, and her blond hair was messy, as if she had just woken up. Reese wanted to be angry at Amber for trying to kiss her last Saturday, but it was hard to be mad at someone who had only done what she knew you wanted. Amber had made a mistake, but so had Reese. Did that make them even now? Reese wasn't sure.

'Hi,' Reese said out loud.

Amber glanced up and looked rattled to see her. 'Hi.' She gestured at the buffet area. 'There's breakfast over there.'

Reese walked over to the buffet. She heard Amber slide something across the table – a bowl or a cup – and the clink of a spoon against ceramic. As Reese assessed the remaining breakfast options, she felt Amber's gaze on her back like the brush of feathers against her skin, even though she had no idea whether Amber was actually looking. On the buffet table was yogurt, fruit, and granola; bread and various spreads in small jars; a coffee urn; and dishes and utensils. At the end of the table, almost like an afterthought, was a box of Cheerios. Reese spooned strawberries and yogurt into a bowl and made herself a cup of coffee. She added milk and stirred it slowly, wondering whether the Imria always ate ordinary American food, and then she realized she was delaying the inevitable. She picked up her bowl and went to sit across from Amber.

'There's usually more food, but it's getting late,' Amber said.

'It's fine,' Reese said, taking a sip of the coffee. It wasn't bad. 'Where's your mom? I thought she was with you.'

'She went for a hike. She left me a note.' The floor-to-ceiling screens on the wall showed the view outside: the grassy field and the hill of eucalyptus trees, a hazy sky above. Reese wondered where her mom had gone. When she returned, Reese would have to tell her that she had persuaded her dad to come to the ship on Saturday, and she would have to tell her why. She wasn't looking forward to the conversation in which she confessed that she had been deceiving a secret organization that had been surveilling her and her parents for weeks.

Amber closed the lid of the laptop and folded her arms on the table, pushing her own bowl out of the way. Reese saw a few Cheerios floating in the milk at the bottom. 'I saw the photos,' Amber said in a soft voice. There was a vertical line in the middle of her forehead, a groove of worry in her skin. 'I didn't know there would be photographers out there. If I had, I wouldn't have suggested we go to the beach. I'm sure you didn't want to be outed that way.'

Reese was midway through a bite of yogurt and strawberries, and the yogurt suddenly tasted sour. She swallowed it with some difficulty and reached for her coffee.

'Are you okay? I read about what happened at your house. It sounded . . . awful.'

'I'm fine,' Reese said, though her stomach had clenched when Amber said the word *awful*. 'Nobody was hurt.'

Amber's expression, which had been grave, became apologetic. 'I know it doesn't help that I'm not human. I'm sorry to put you through that.'

Reese's eyebrows rose slightly. 'You didn't. It's not your fault the world is full of assholes.'

Amber almost smiled. 'I'm glad you're all right.'

'I am. Thanks.' Reese nudged the strawberries in her bowl with her spoon. 'And you shouldn't read that stuff. They don't know you. They're just being jerks.'

Amber's eyes lit up, and now she did smile. 'Oh, I know they don't know me. The stuff they write about me is hilarious. The speculation alone! Do you know how much money I could make if I would just pose for *Playboy*?'

Reese nearly choked on her spoonful of yogurt.

Amber leaned forward, a mischievous gleam in her eyes. 'That's all they want – to know exactly how alien I am. Maybe I should do it and get some tentacle prosthetics or something.'

'You don't find this insulting?' Reese said, amazed.

Amber shrugged, lifting one shoulder fluidly. 'Not really. It's just ignorance. I am insulted by the fact that the masses seem to think I'm stupid. You think it's because of the blond? Maybe I should dye my hair black. I think I'd get more respect as a brunette.'

Reese laughed. 'I like the blond.'

Amber grinned. 'I know.'

Reese felt her face warming up and she busied herself with her breakfast, even though she could barely taste it anymore. What was it with people saying *I know* in response to things? To change the subject, she asked, 'Why are you using a laptop? Don't you have more advanced computers or whatever?'

'It's easier to use human technology to access the Internet. It's built for it, you know?'

'That makes sense.'

'Hey,' Amber said, her tone turning serious again. 'I really hope those pictures didn't screw things up with David. Was he upset?'

Reese's spoon clattered against the bowl. 'Upset? He broke up with me.'

Shock flashed across Amber's face. 'What? I'm so sorry. Do you want me to tell him nothing happened?'

'No,' Reese said sharply. 'I think it's best if you guys never talk to each other about it.'

Amber flushed. 'Oh. Does he hate me?'

'I don't know.' It felt wrong to discuss this with Amber – as if she were betraying David all over again. 'I don't want to talk about it.'

Amber's gaze lowered. 'Okay.' Her cheeks were tinged pink, and she looked worn out and sad. That made Reese ache as if it were all her fault.

Reese pushed her bowl away and said, 'Can I ask you something?'

Amber looked up. 'Sure, what?'

Reese almost winced at the hope in Amber's eyes. 'Is the adaptation chamber in this ship?'

Amber was clearly surprised by the question. 'Yeah, why?'

It's that easy, Reese thought. She could have asked about this weeks ago. 'I want to see it. Will you show it to me?'

Amber seemed uncomfortable. 'I don't know if I should do that.'

'Why not? I was in it, wasn't I? I have as much right to see it as anyone. More.'

Amber considered her for a moment, then glanced around the empty dining hall. 'Okay. I can bring you when you're finished with your breakfast.'

Reese took another sip of her coffee and said, 'I'm done. I'm not hungry.'

Amber bit her lip. 'All right.' She stood. 'Let's go.'

Reese followed Amber out of the dining hall. They walked down a corridor that Reese had never noticed before, and paused in front of a door with a plaque on it that Reese could not read. When Amber touched the plaque, the door slid open to reveal a room with three large, clear tanks on the floor. Two of them were empty, but the third contained a thick, gel-like substance that glowed with a faint blue luminescence. Inside the tank, suspended in the gel, was an oval pod the length of a human body.

Reese crossed the floor toward the pod. The walls of it were made of a material with a golden sheen that looked smooth and hard as an eggshell, but Reese knew it was pliable. She recognized it. She remembered being cocooned in this device, a gelatinous liquid cradling her, making her feel weightless.

The smooth, curved walls had sealed shut around her until all she could see was the red-veined golden interior. Had she been in this very chamber? She raised her hand to touch the edge of the tank, and then halted. Her skin crawled. 'Is there someone inside?'

'No,' Amber said. She walked around to the other side of the tank. 'It's empty. This one is set up because we're testing it.'

Reese reached out to touch the tank. It was cool and hard, and a buzz of electricity swept across her skin. 'Was I in one of these?'

Amber nodded reluctantly. 'Yes.'

'Which one?'

'You were in this tank, but I don't know if you were in this particular chamber. They've all been removed for cleaning and stuff, so I'm not sure which one was put back in for the test.'

Reese stared down at the pod through the glass walls of the tank. She remembered the slow, underwater-like beep from her dream. 'What happened the night of the accident? Did you guys bring me to this ship? How did I get to Project Plato?'

'I wasn't there, but from what I've been told, the military found you and David. There are security sensors all around Area 51, and when you guys crashed, you tripped a lot of alarms. The military didn't want to bring you underground, so they took you to Project Plato. My mom was working. When she saw how seriously you were injured, she knew you'd need the adaptation chamber. She did the surgery at Project Plato, but she also called the ship. Right before dawn, the ship came and they transferred you and David into the chambers. The military didn't know. They were dealing with the June Disaster that week – a lot of protocols were skipped over or ignored because of the fallout from that.'

The gel surrounding the chamber had tiny bubbles in it. Reese asked, 'So why did they move us back to Project Plato? Why didn't they just let us wake up on the ship?'

'They had to move you. There were records that put you and David at Plato the night that you crashed. My mom had to account for your whereabouts to the military liaisons. You couldn't just disappear after getting that medical treatment.'

Reese spread her fingers over the glass of the tank. Her hand cast a faint shadow over the pod. 'Didn't they – the military or whatever – realize that David and I weren't there? They never checked our rooms?'

Amber came closer, brushing against the opposite side of the tank, and Reese glanced up to see the vertical line in Amber's forehead again. 'You have to understand, things really were messed up with the June Disaster. It was literally a disaster for your government. They were involved in this giant cover-up operation that involved a zillion different components – rerouting traffic, the Internet, clean-up crews – and they let things slide at Plato. They didn't have time to check up on two random kids who'd had a car accident. It didn't seem relevant to them. By the time they sent someone to check, my mom had transferred the two of you back to Project Plato. You were still unconscious.'

Amber's words slid like ice down Reese's back. 'What do you know about the cover-up?' she asked.

'I don't know the specifics,' Amber said quickly.

'Was it about the birds?'

'Yes.'

'What did the government do to those birds? And why?'

'I don't know. I just know that your military was doing these crazy experiments on livestock – birds and other animals too – using Imrian DNA. My mom might know more about it. But after the planes started crashing, they had to cover up the fact that it was their failed experimentation that made those birds attack the planes. All that confusion saved your life.'

Reese felt sick to her stomach. 'My life isn't worth the lives of the two thousand people who died in those plane crashes.'

Amber seemed upset. Her fingers gripped the edge of the tank. 'Why not? You're exactly what we've been working so long to create. You and David, both of you.'

'David and I were in a car accident. An *accident*. We could have been anybody.'

Amber's eyes were hard and bright. She leaned over the tank toward Reese. 'There are no coincidences.'

Reese's eyes narrowed at her. 'Your mom said that at the press conference. What's that supposed to mean?'

'*Nig tukum'ta nu nig tukum'ta*,' Amber said in Imrian. 'There is no coincidence. It means that you're alive for a reason. My people have been working on this adaptation procedure for a really long time. Everything that happened to put you and David in that car in Nevada on that night in June – the debate tournament, your government's secret project with the birds, the plane crashes – it all points to you and David. You two were meant to have this procedure. You two survived it, and now you're here. Alive. You're important.'

Reese shook her head, a fuzzy panic coming over her. 'No.'

She backed away from the adaptation chamber. 'Maybe your people don't think there's such a thing as coincidence, but I'm not Imrian. I'm human. And to me, this is all just one big giant accident, and now I'm here in the middle of something I never chose to be involved with, and—'

'Choice has nothing to do with it,' Amber cut in.

'We are not getting into some debate about free will right now,' Reese snapped.

'That's not what I'm doing!'

'Maybe we're having a cultural difference, then.' Reese crossed her arms and stood her ground. 'Just tell me one thing. If David and I are so important to you guys, when are you going to tell us the truth about who you are?'

Amber took a step back. Her hands left condensation marks on the tank, like the handprints of someone trying to escape. 'What do you mean?'

'David called me this morning and said his dad got the results back from the preliminary tests on our DNA. He said the results show that we – humans – are descended from the Imria.'

Amber's face went pale.

'Is that true?' Reese asked.

'I don't think it's my place to say.'

Reese stared at her, dumbfounded. 'It's not your place?'

Amber gave Reese an anguished look. 'It's not like I don't want to tell you, but Akiya Deyir made me promise – I mean, I messed everything up with you. They don't trust me anymore. They want me to do what I'm supposed to do and shut up. I can't tell you.'

Amber's words echoed in the quiet of the lab. Reese's shoulders slumped in disappointment. Amber had been so forthcoming today that Reese thought – she had hoped – that the time for secrets was behind them.

'I'm sorry,' Amber said. 'I'll ask my mom—'

'Amber, please,' Reese said in a low voice. 'This is so important. Can't you tell me the truth?'

Amber's gaze faltered, her eyes flickering toward the door. Reese heard the whisper of Amber's breath as she inhaled and exhaled. Finally, after what seemed like forever, Amber said, 'Okay. I'll tell you, but not here. They could come in at any minute. We have to go somewhere else.'

CHAPTER 28

Amber's room was only a few doors down from the one Reese had been assigned. It had the same layout as Reese's, but it was obvious that Amber had lived there for a lot longer – and she was much messier. Makeup and jewelry were scattered all over a shelf near her bed. Clothes peeked out from drawers in the corner. The bunk was unmade, the pillows pushed haphazardly against the wall. As the door closed behind Reese, Amber pulled a chair from the corner beyond the end of the bunk.

'Have a seat,' Amber said. She pushed aside the blankets on the bed and sat down, scooting up so that her back was against the wall.

Reese lowered herself into the chair and looked at Amber.

'Here's the thing,' Amber said. 'We do want to help you – I mean the Imria want to help humanity. That is totally our number one goal.'

'But?' Reese prompted.

'There's no but. I want you to keep that in mind.'

'Why?'

'Because what I'm about to tell you might make you doubt

that.' Amber paused. 'So, David's dad is right – sort of. Humans are descended from us, in a way. We've been coming to your planet for a long time.'

'How long?'

'We first discovered Earth about two million years ago.'

'Two *million?*'

'Um, yeah. Humans didn't really exist back then. We – the Imria – were in a period of exploration at that time. We were trying to figure out how to deal with environmental changes on our own world, and we were sending out lots of probes across the galaxy to look for intelligent life. Earth was an amazing discovery. There were no humans, like I said, but there were plenty of species who seemed like they might develop into intelligent life. So we sort of helped a few of those species along, just to see what would happen.'

Reese's mouth fell open.

Amber rushed on, waving her hands. 'It was an experiment, and it wasn't well thought out. Communication was very slow back then. It took forever for the explorers who discovered Earth to get in touch with our home planet, Kurra. The experimentation on Earth was never authorized by our leaders, and by the time they learned about it, it was kind of a done deal. So then we couldn't exactly abandon Earth. We had a responsibility to make sure we hadn't completely messed things up with the species we'd modified. Eventually it became obvious that one species in particular was evolving differently than the others, and that it was going to become the most intelligent species on Earth. That species became *Homo sapiens*.'

'How many times did you guys . . . modify us?'

Amber looked uncomfortable. 'I'm not sure. The historical records are really complicated and really old, and honestly, even our historians aren't entirely sure. We're talking about millions of years here. But after a while, we stopped intervening. Humans were obviously doing fine, and most of us didn't want to interfere anymore. A lot of us didn't think we had any business messing around with your societies, especially because humans at the time couldn't always understand who we were. Sometimes humans thought we were . . . well, gods.'

'You mean those ancient alien shows are right?' Reese said in disbelief.

Amber made a face. 'Not entirely. A lot of that stuff is bullshit. But . . . some ancient human societies thought we were gods. Not all of them. Some humans understood exactly what we were. It's the same as it is now – or the way it was before we revealed ourselves last month. Some people totally believed in extraterrestrials, while others thought the people who believed in them were crazy. Anyway, my people decided it was best to leave you guys alone and wait until your societies developed the technology to be on equal footing with us.' Amber took a deep breath. 'But a few things happened to change our minds.'

'Wait a minute,' Reese said, backtracking to make sure she understood everything. 'You said the Imria came here two million years ago and found some species that you experimented on. So basically, you *made* us look like you?'

Amber hesitated. 'Um, yes.'

'Are you saying that you created us?'

‘Not exactly. Some species that could have evolved on their own already existed, but we pushed certain species in a different direction, one that wound up as *Homo sapiens*.’

‘And if you hadn’t done that, humans might not exist in the way we do today.’

‘Right.’

Reese rubbed a hand over her forehead. ‘Okay. So you said you guys left the planet. Why did you return?’

‘For a couple of reasons. Our birth rates are really, really low. It’s not that we’re infertile. It doesn’t really matter if we’re fertile, because we use artificial wombs. They’re a lot like the adaptation chamber, actually. But even though we can have children, our birth rates keep declining. So, many Imrians have begun to believe that humanity – that your people are our best hope of surviving. That’s the first reason we decided to come back to Earth – to support humanity, to make sure you all survive.’

‘But humans aren’t dying out. Don’t we have a problem with overpopulation?’

Amber gave Reese a nervous smile. ‘Yeah, that’s one of your problems. In the first half of the twentieth century, the United States developed the atomic bomb. We didn’t want you guys to destroy yourselves. That’s why we made contact with your government after the end of World War Two. We wanted to steer you away from nuclear weapons, and we also wanted to figure out why you guys had never evolved our ability of *susum’urda*. That’s really central to our society, and all our leaders thought it was important for humans to be able to do it – if humans were going to be the future of the Imria. That’s what Project Plato was really for, at least on our end: to research human biology and develop a way to give you that ability. Now that you and David have shown that the adaptation chamber works, we want to share it with the rest of humanity. That's what Akiya Deyir is here to do, to start the process of spreading this ability throughout humanity.'

Amber fell silent, and at first Reese simply stared at her. Everything that Amber said was so mind-boggling that Reese could barely keep it all straight. Finally Reese asked, 'Is Akiya Deyir going to tell this whole story at the UN? The fact that you guys manipulated us like guinea pigs for millions of years?'

Amber winced. 'I don't know. It's really complicated.' She crossed her legs and leaned forward. 'If they go public about it, it completely upends your belief systems. Practically every single religious system. Evolutionary theory – at least as it applies to humans – is wrong. Some Imrians think it would be better if we start implementing the adaptation procedure first, so that humans can better understand why we did what we did.'

'What is there to understand?' Reese said, disgusted. 'You guys treated us like lab rats. I think humans can understand that. Clearly we are descended from you.'

Amber sighed and shifted in place. She was wearing faded jeans that had a hole in one knee, and she hooked a finger in the hole and pulled at the threads as she spoke. 'I get that. I do. But a lot of the Imria aren't ready to face what would happen if they told humanity the whole truth right now. They believe that they created humans, and humans are their responsibility

– their children. They think this adaptation procedure is going to help you grow up or something.'

Reese watched the hole enlarge. The skin of Amber's knee peeked through. 'You keep talking about the Imria as if you aren't one. Are you saying you don't buy their argument?'

Amber stopped messing with the hole and leaned back against the wall. 'Not completely. I was born here; I grew up here. Sometimes I feel more like a human than an Imrian. I see what they mean, but I'm not sure they're right.'

'Your mom doesn't think they're right either.'

Amber's eyebrows drew together. 'How do you know that?'

'She gave an Imrian DNA sample to David's dad. That's how we found out that humans are descended from the Imria. We wouldn't have known if she hadn't done that.'

'Yeah. Well, there's been some disagreement among the Imria here about what to do. My mom – obviously she decided to do something about it.' A strange expression passed over Amber's face, as if she were realizing something.

'What is it?' Reese asked.

'Nothing.' Amber gave Reese a small smile. 'So, that's about it. That's everything, I swear.'

Reese shook her head in frustration. 'That's not everything. You guys need to tell the truth.'

'I can't convince them,' Amber insisted. 'They don't listen to me anymore.'

'Then let me talk to your mom. David and I both need to talk to her – and to Akiya Deyir.' Amber looked doubtful, and Reese moved to sit on the edge of Amber's bed, facing her. 'You can't let them go through with this lie. Even if it did work, and somehow the scientific board that David's dad put together decides to sit on their research – which I seriously doubt will happen – our abilities aren't—' Reese cut herself off. She had promised David that she wouldn't tell anyone about their abilities without discussing it with him first, and she had almost spilled it all to Amber.

'Aren't what?' Amber prompted.

Reese didn't bother to invent a lie. Everything was going to come out tomorrow anyway. 'I can't tell you right now. I promised David. Could you ask your mom and Akiya Deyir to talk to us? Tomorrow, after David gets here.'

'I can't guarantee they'll listen to you even if they talk to you,' Amber warned her.

'They'll listen,' Reese said, sounding more confident than she felt.

Amber said reluctantly, 'Okay. I'll ask.'

CHAPTER 29

Reese spent the rest of the day trying to do her homework and failing miserably. When her mom returned from her hike, they went downstairs for lunch and discovered that the dining hall was empty. 'Your dad called and said he's coming tomorrow,' her mom said as they assembled sandwiches from the tray of cold cuts. 'What's going on?'

'It'll be safer here,' Reese said.

Her mom gave her a pointed look. 'Safer?'

The conversation about CASS and the threats went about as well as Reese expected. Her mom exploded at her, completely freaked out by the fact that Reese had been putting herself in so much danger. 'We weren't in danger,' Reese protested. 'There's no real danger until – until tomorrow night.'

'Oh, that's supposed to make it okay?'

'I'm sorry, but there wasn't any other way.'

'How about you tell me about these things? Have you learned nothing from what happened to you earlier this summer?'

'Yes, I have learned!' Reese cried. 'I've learned that I have to figure out what the fuck is going on before I say anything to anybody. That is what I learned. And we're fine. You and I are fine, and David's fine, and Dad's going to be fine too – because I didn't say anything.'

Her mom fumed. 'You will tell me everything from now on.'

'Tomorrow,' Reese said, picking up her sandwich. 'Once everyone is here – David's family too – we will tell you all everything. I promise.' She knew she was taking a risk by talking to her mom like that, but she couldn't think of any other way to do it. She wanted her mom to accept the fact that she was in control of this situation – even if she secretly worried that she wasn't.

Her mom silently watched her eat. Reese saw the way her mom's jaw had clenched, and she knew her mom was spinning through various counterarguments in her mind, trying to punch holes in her plan or find a way to pull the whole story out of her right now. To her credit, her mom finally said, 'Tomorrow. You promise.'

'Yes,' Reese said quickly. 'I promise.'

Nura Halba appeared midway through lunch, and Reese pulled him aside to ask if there was room for David's family and her dad to stay on board for the next several days. He was taken aback, but he said he would find out. They didn't see him again until dinner, when once more he was the only Imrian to join them in the dining hall. 'Evelyn sends her apologies,' Halba said. 'But it's fine for your father and for David's family to stay with us. We'll all fly to New York on Sunday.'

'Where is everyone?' Reese's mom asked. 'I hope we haven't frightened them all away.'

Halba gave her a strained smile. 'Oh, no. They're in meetings, preparing for the UN.'

Even Amber? Reese wanted to ask, but didn't. She ate the roast chicken and potatoes that had been left out for them, and wondered whether the mysterious, invisible Imrian chef was making food that was especially intended to be intelligible to humans.

After dinner, Reese and her mom went back up to their rooms. The ship felt empty and lonely. Before they parted, her mom said, 'It might be nice to have your dad and David's family here. It feels sort of abandoned, doesn't it?'

'Yeah.'

Her mom opened the door to her room. 'I have to work on a case tonight, but if you need anything, you know where I am. What are you going to do?'

Reese shrugged. 'I'm still not done with my English homework. I have to read *The Sun Also Rises*.'

Her mom nodded. 'I never liked that book.'

Reese smiled. 'Why not?'

'I thought it was boring.' Her mom made a face at her and then went into her room. 'Good luck.'

In her own room, Reese lay down on her bunk and opened *The Sun Also Rises*, but perhaps her mom's words had biased her; she thought it was boring too. She kept picking up her phone and checking if she had any messages, but nobody had texted. She thought about calling Julian to see what he was doing with the interview footage of her and David, but then she remembered he was finally finished being grounded after his secret trip to Angel Island, and he had a date – his first date in forever, with a guy he had met online. He would be annoyed if she called to interrupt him because she was bored.

The knock on her door was soft, and she wasn't sure she had heard it at first. It sounded again, and then she heard Amber's voice: 'Reese?'

She sat up, *The Sun Also Rises* sliding to the floor with a dull thunk. She bent over to pick it up before she went to open the door.

Amber had changed clothes. She was wearing tight black jeans tucked into scuffed ankle boots, and a loose white T-shirt with a big black flower on it. 'You don't have to get up to open the door,' she said with a smile. 'You can just say 'open.''

Reese stepped back and dropped the book on the shelf by the bunk. 'I didn't know.'

'Can I come in?'

'Sure. Did you talk to Akiya Deyir?'

Amber entered the room; the door slid shut behind her quietly. 'Yeah. Sorry I missed dinner. Everybody had to discuss it – my mom, Hirin Sagal, Eres Tilhar, everyone.' Amber pulled the chair out from the corner and sat down, crossing her legs. She was wearing eyeliner; it was smudged slightly in the corners.

Reese perched on her bunk, feeling inexplicably nervous. 'What did they say?'

'They're willing to talk to you and David tomorrow afternoon.'

'That's great.'

'And then I think Akiya will want to check in with home – with our leaders on Kurra.'

‘Oh. What do you think they’ll say?’

Amber shook her head. ‘I don’t know. But Eres is on your side. And my mother. And me.’

Reese fidgeted with the hem of the blanket. ‘Thanks.’

Amber smiled a little sadly. ‘It’s the least I can do.’

‘Were they mad at you for telling me the truth?’

‘I don’t think Akiya gets mad. But let’s just say I don’t think they’re going to give me any more assignments.’ Her gaze flickered to Reese. ‘I don’t mean that—’

‘It’s fine. I know what you mean.’ Silence fell between them, thick and heavy. Amber looked away, studying her fingernails. They were painted black.

‘I’m sorry,’ Amber said, her voice barely audible.

Reese’s fingers dug into the edge of the bunk. ‘You don’t have to apologize anymore.’ There was something in the slump of Amber’s shoulders that unexpectedly reminded Reese of Amber’s body collapsing against hers in Nevada, the pain from her gunshot wound dragging her down onto the rocky desert ground. ‘Amber,’ Reese said. Her name was soft on her lips.

Amber looked up, a guarded expression on her face. ‘What?’

‘In Nevada, when the bunker was about to explode and we were running toward the ship – this ship – did you know those soldiers were aiming for me? Did you know they were trying to shoot me?’

Amber regarded her for a long moment. Reese forced herself to not look away. She wanted to know. Amber finally said, ‘You mean did I purposely try to save you?’

Reese’s mouth went dry. ‘Yeah.’

Amber’s lips were shining in the warm glow of the lights. ‘I didn't know if they were going to shoot you. I only knew that if I could do something to prevent you from getting shot, I was going to do it. It wasn't like there was a lot of time for thought. I just did it. That's how I do almost everything.' Amber's mouth twisted in a thin, self-hating smile. 'That's my biggest flaw.'

Reese's heartbeat thudded inside her. 'It's not a flaw.'

'No? Tell that to my mother.'

Reese's mouth twitched. 'So your mom doesn't approve?'

Amber choked on a laugh. 'No,' she said, shaking her head. 'She really doesn't approve. Although given what she did with that DNA, it's not like she should be judging.'

Reese was transfixed by the expression on Amber's face: her self-deprecating smile, her bright gray eyes. For a moment it was like being suspended in time – just the two of them in this room, divorced from everything that had come before, poised on the brink of what might come after. Reese wanted to freeze this instant, to linger in it. And for several breaths, Amber didn't move.

When Amber slid to the floor, kneeling in front of the bunk between Reese's legs, Reese didn't try to resist. She had known what was coming. Amber's hands, cool and dry, reached for hers. Inside, Amber was a whirlpool of longing. 'Can't we start over?' she whispered.

There was nothing stopping her. Nothing at all. She could try to stifle the desire that bloomed inside her. She could make the decision to never set it free again. Or she could give in. She watched Amber's mouth tremble. She saw the rise and fall of Amber's chest as she waited, her fingers curling through Reese's, knotting them together.

Kissing Amber was like falling down the rabbit hole. Reese could barely believe she was doing it again. Amber's mouth was so familiar to her, the shape of her lips soft and warm against her own, but there was more this time. There was all of Amber behind it: the tide of her emotions dragging at Reese the way the ocean waves suck the sand out from under your feet. Memories of Reese from before, images flashing past like an old home movie. There they were in the park, on the swing set at night, momentum making her stomach flip as her whole body lit up from the kiss.

Amber rose. Reese scooted back on the bunk and Amber climbed up, straddling her lap and cupping Reese's head in her hands. Reese couldn't breathe. She didn't want to breathe. She only wanted to touch her, and she pulled Amber closer, her hands gliding over Amber's back. The T-shirt slipped off her shoulder, and Reese's fingers slid beneath the strap of Amber's black bra, her skin silky. Reese knew that Amber had put these clothes on for her, that she had come to her room hoping for this moment, and the knowledge made her dizzy, as if everything was spinning around the two of them. Amber buried her fingers in Reese's hair and whispered, 'Of course I hoped. I've always hoped.'

Reese drew her close and kissed her again. With David, it had felt as if they were careening out of control every time they kissed, because neither of them knew how to drive this connection between them. It was frightening in its headiness. With Amber, it was different. Amber clearly had done this before, and even as Reese felt the rising heat inside Amber, her increasing focus on the shrinking space between them, Reese did not feel afraid. She felt intoxicated: held between Amber's hands, pressed against her body. But beneath the luxurious slide of desire, she felt a keen, persistent ache. Even if she was in love with Amber, that didn't stop her from being in love with David.

Amber pulled away, stroking Reese's hair back from her face, and whispered, 'I don't care. I don't care.'

Reese looked into Amber's eyes and said, 'But I do.'

'It doesn't matter,' Amber insisted. 'You can love him too.'

'How would that be okay?' Reese asked, bewildered. 'You would start to resent me.'

Amber shook her head. 'I wouldn't. You don't understand. It's not like you have a limited supply of love. You can love more than one person at once.'

Reese flushed. 'But that's not fair to either of you.'

'It's not fair to shut yourself off. That's what's unfair. To know that you have these feelings and then deny them.'

'I'm not denying them!' Reese's hands had come to rest on Amber's thighs, and she pushed her back.

Amber looked hurt. She climbed off Reese's lap and sat against the wall at the head of the bed, drawing her knees up defensively. The laces of her right boot had come undone.

Reese missed her instantly. 'I can't be with you if I still want to be with him,' she said miserably. 'I can't be with either one of you.' As she said the words she realized this was the solution she had been looking for: a way out of the quagmire of being in love with two people at the same time. She wished the solution didn't make her feel like digging her own heart out of her chest.

A teardrop trickled down Amber's cheek and into the corner of her mouth. 'That's a really limited way to think about it.'

Reese groaned. 'It's reality. Why don't you get that?'

Amber's expression hardened. 'I do get that you think that way. I'm saying you don't have to.'

'What do you mean?'

Amber wiped the tear away roughly, smearing her eyeliner across her cheek. 'I mean you could date both of us.'

Reese stared at her in astonishment. 'At the same time?'

'Not at the same time,' Amber said, as if Reese were being dense. 'I'm not that into guys. Although David is cute, but—'

'No,' Reese said. For a second a kind of awful hope had burned in her, but she stomped on it with both feet. 'How would that even work? Like I see you one week and I see him the next?'

Amber leaned her head against the wall. 'Maybe. It's not that unusual. Not for us.'

Reese was confused. 'For us? You mean for the Imria?'

Amber nodded.

Reese's eyes widened. 'Well, it's pretty unusual for humans.'

'That's because humans are jealous all the time,' Amber said, sounding frustrated. 'They don't have any idea what their partners are thinking because they can't do *susum'urda*. So of course they're jealous.' She leaned forward, one leg sliding over the edge of the bed. 'But you and David don't have to be jealous. You have the ability now.'

Reese took a shallow breath. Her pulse was still thrumming within her from kissing Amber. She could still feel her, ghostlike, beneath her hands. 'I really don't think David would go for it.'

Amber scooted toward her, but she didn't touch her. 'Have you asked him?'

'I don't have to ask him to know that he doesn't want to have anything to do with you.'

Amber didn't flinch. She only shook her head. 'He doesn't know me.'

Reese had to admire Amber's self-confidence. She said gently, 'I don't think he wants to know you.'

Amber sighed. 'We don't have to be *friends*. Besides, if he really loves you, and this is what you want, he'll try.'

Reese gave Amber a challenging look. 'If I love him, and I know that he doesn't want this, I won't ask him.'

Amber raised an eyebrow. 'If I love you, I won't stop trying.'

Reese flushed. 'Are we going to do this all night?'

Amber cocked her head. 'We could.'

Reese moved to the edge of the bunk. 'No. I'm sorry. This isn't going to work.'

Amber reached out and touched Reese's arm. Reese looked back at her. 'Reese,' Amber said. She was all longing, warm and waiting for her right there. Reese couldn't hide her feelings either, and she no longer felt the need to. Amber knew. Amber had always known.

So Reese said the only thing she could think of to shut this down. 'My mom is in the next room.'

Amber gave a short laugh, but her fingers didn't move. 'The door locks.'

Reese shook her head, smiling involuntarily. She got off

the bunk, and Amber's hand fell away. 'We can't, okay? I can't. I'm sorry.'

Amber stared at her, and slowly her expression turned inward. 'Okay.' She climbed off the bed and stood up, moving toward the door.

Reese felt as if she had kicked a puppy. 'Amber.'

Amber looked at her, but her face was closed off now, distant. The black smudge on her cheek looked like a bruise. 'What?'

Reese opened one of the cabinets in the wall and pulled out a T-shirt. She went to Amber and lifted the cloth to her face to wipe away the smeared eyeliner. Amber's eyes glistened. 'I'll see you tomorrow,' Reese said.

Amber nodded. She raised her hand to open the door, but at the last second she turned back to press a kiss to Reese's surprised mouth. 'I told you,' she whispered. 'I won't give up.' Then the door slid open and Amber left.

After midnight, Reese called Julian.

He answered on the second ring. 'Hi.' He sounded wide awake. 'What's up?'

'How was your date?' She was lying in the dark in her room, the light from her phone casting a ghostly pall over her bunk.

'It was fine. I got back an hour ago. Can't sleep so I'm working on the video footage for Bin 42.'

'What was his name again?'

'Evan.' He filled her in on their date. They had gone to see *Butterfly at Midnight*, an indie film about a painter obsessed with finding an elusive black butterfly. Julian described it as 'pretentious but at least the painter was hot'. Afterward, he and Evan had gone to the diner across from the movie theater to have coffee.

'Did you kiss him?' she asked.

'No. He was cute, but he seemed a little too self-absorbed. He kept talking about how he's going to shoot his own independent film this winter, but honestly, I was bored.'

'I thought you liked the moody artistic type.'

'I thought I did too. Maybe I was corrupted by hanging out with the soccer team last week. They do have really good abs.'

She laughed. 'True.'

'Hey, what's up with you? Why are you calling me so late?'

'What's that thing where you're in a relationship with more than one person at a time?'

'Polyamory?' He sounded confused.

'Yeah. Amber thinks we should – we should do that. Me and her and David.'

'Are you serious?'

She told him what had happened, brushing over the more intimate details. 'I told her I can't. And even if I could, David won't.'

'Have you asked him?'

'No! He wouldn't do it, anyway. He hates Amber, and he doesn't like me enough to try to get over that.'

'That doesn't make any sense. If he hates Amber, doesn't that mean he's really into you?'

She blew out her breath. 'I told him I was in love with him, and he said "I know".'

Julian broke into laughter. 'He Han Solo'd you.'

'He what?'

'He Han Solo'd you. You know, in *The Empire Strikes Back* right before Han's about to be frozen in carbonite, Princess Leia says, 'I love you,' and Han Solo says, 'I know.' You've seen it.'

She clutched the phone tighter. 'I don't remember that.'

'Good thing you have me as your friend, then.' She heard the smile in his voice. 'Come on, it's kind of funny, isn't it?'

'I think your definition of "funny" is different than mine,' she said sarcastically.

'It doesn't mean he doesn't like you. It just means he wasn't ready to say it.'

'Yeah, well, it doesn't matter anymore. He broke up with me, and I told Amber I couldn't be with her, so we're all on our own now. Nobody has to say anything to anybody anymore.' She sounded bitter.

'I do know one person who's poly,' Julian offered.

'I'm not poly.'

'I know, I'm just saying I know one person. He's a friend of a friend, so I don't know him well, but there are also a lot of gay guys who are in open relationships.'

'How is that different from being poly? Wait, I don't care, I'm not doing that either.'

'Why not? Six months ago you weren't even wanting to date anyone, and now you're like, no, I'm monogamy only?'

'No, I'm going back to not dating,' Reese said sourly. 'I was right – it is too much drama.'

He laughed. 'Okay, okay. Well, you want something to take your mind off the drama?'

'Yes,' she said quickly.

'We heard from Sophia Curtis. We're on. She's giving us her footage, and she told us that she's looking into the connection with Mr Hernandez aka Vargas, the guy who was working for President Randall. Sophia says she found something that draws a clear line between the president and CASS, dating back to her time in the military, which we've never been able to verify before.'

'That's great. When are you going to release the info?'

'Not till after the UN thing. I'm really hoping one of our informants will come through with more info on the birds by then too.'

'Amber told me the government was behind the birds. Actually she said the government was doing genetic experimentation on all sorts of livestock using Imrian DNA. But the birds went crazy, and that's why the government had to cover it up.'

'Really? Can you get her on the record?'

'She said she didn't know that much about it but her mom might know more. Dr Brand.'

'Will you ask her?'

'I can try, but I don't know if Dr Brand will go on the record with Bin 42. Regardless, I learned something seriously crazy today.' She thought back through what Amber had told her about the Imria. 'I can't tell you everything right now, but I'll call you as soon as I know I can tell you.'

'Dude, tell me now!' he said, excited.

'I can't. It's too huge. But look – I never gave you the recording of the meeting with Charles Lovick. It's in the back of the top desk drawer in my room. You should go over to my house tomorrow morning as early as you can, because my dad's going to be leaving around ten. He'll let you in; you should take it.'

'Sure. But what's the news about? Can't you give me a hint?'

She took a deep breath. 'It's about who we are. Who the Imria are. It changes everything.'

He let out a frustrated groan. 'I can't believe you're leading me on like this!'

'I'm sorry. I shouldn't have mentioned it. I just wanted you to know something's coming. I'll call you as soon as I can – Monday at the latest.'

'Okay, fine. But I better get the exclusive – don't talk to anyone else.'

'I won't,' she promised. 'I should try to get some sleep. You be careful tomorrow.' She had a sudden burst of worry for him. She didn't think CASS was keeping an eye on Julian, but she had no real way to know.

'I'll be fine. You be careful too. I'm sure it's gonna be dangerous, being trapped in a spaceship with two hot people who are both in love with you.'

'Oh my God, shut up. Good night, Julian.'

'Good night, Reese. Sleep tight.'

She hung up the phone, smiling in spite of herself.

CHAPTER 30

Reese thought she had prepared herself to see David on Saturday, but when he emerged from the ferry, she realized she was fooling herself. He was the first off the ramp, followed by his sister, his parents, and Reese's dad.

'Welcome,' Nura Halba said, stepping forward to help them with their luggage.

Reese wished she had waited back at the ship, because now she had to greet David in front of their families, and this was the first time she had seen him since before the attack on her house. She didn't expect him to drop his backpack and duffel bag on the ground and pull her into a hug.

'Hi,' he said.

'Hi,' she mumbled into his shoulder. Her hands slipped tentatively around his back. She smelled the faint tang of his hair product layered over the scent of his shirt. Fresh laundry.

I'm glad you're not hurt, he told her.

She tried to prevent herself from sinking too deeply into him as they touched. She wanted to let herself go, but she was acutely aware of the fact that they weren't together anymore.

She let herself feel his relief that she was unharmed, but nothing more. She knew he was holding back too, and the sensation of his carefulness – as if he were tiptoeing around the edges of her consciousness – made her feel so awfully distant from him, even though the whole length of her body was pressed against him.

She pulled back before she got carried away. 'I have so much to tell you,' she said.

He smiled faintly. 'Okay.'

For a moment, Reese thought she saw something in his brown eyes that made her heartbeat quicken, but then she noticed Chloe in the background, watching surreptitiously. Reese lowered her gaze self-consciously. Out of the corner of her eye she saw their parents loading the bags into the SUV.

'We should go,' he said.

'Yeah.' She followed him toward the vehicle, where she greeted their parents.

At the ship, Nura Halba escorted them to their rooms on the third level. Chloe was wide-eyed and a little frightened; Reese heard her quick intake of breath as they passed through the atriums with their floating globes. When they arrived in the living quarters, Reese's mom came out to meet them. There was a second round of greeting and hugging as everyone jostled through the corridor. Reese waited until they were all settled into their rooms and beginning to unpack before she pulled David aside.

'Can we talk for a minute?' she asked. She heard Chloe's excited voice floating down the corridor as Halba explained how the voice-operated commands worked.

'Sure. You want to come in?' He gestured to his room and they went inside, closing the door. The space was identical to hers, but with a view of the whitewashed officers' quarters instead of the hillside. She still thought the boarded-up buildings were a little creepy.

'There's something else you should know,' she began. She had planned this part out. David was standing beside his bunk, one hand on his duffel, and she crossed the room and reached out to touch his arm, her fingertips grazing his bare skin. She sensed defensiveness in him like a rapidly rising shield, and she knew he thought she was going to tell him that she and Amber were together again. *It's not that. I told Amber I can't be with her either*.

David's surprise was palpable. *Really?*

Yes. And then she admitted: *I do have feelings for her, but I also still have feelings for you. There's no other way to deal with it. It's over*. 'I want to move on from this,' she said out loud. Her voice sounded remarkably steady. 'We have to work together, you and me and maybe even Amber. All of this—' She gestured at the ship around them. 'It's important. It's more important than us. I know I hurt you and I'm sorry. I didn't want to but I screwed up. You said that you hoped we could be friends again and at first I didn't think I could do it, but—' She realized that her fingers had slipped down his arm and he was holding her hand now, and it almost undid her.

'We never stopped being friends,' he said when she didn't continue.

She squeezed his hand. His fingers were warm and strong in hers. She felt regret like a shadow stretching between them, but at the same time, she felt his love. It was clear and startling: a gift she had yearned for but never expected to receive. She couldn't understand how she could be so happy and so sad at the same time. When he let go of her hand, she missed him.

'Tell me what Amber told you about the Imria,' he said, unzipping his duffel.

The abrupt change of subject felt almost like a rejection, but she knew it wasn't. It was David trying to do what she asked: to move on. She had known that talking to him wouldn't miraculously erase all the hurt, but the reality was harder to bear than she had anticipated. It was going to take time for them to figure out how to make their friendship work again, when they both knew they wanted more.

'Okay,' she said, and as he unpacked, she told him everything.

Eres Tilhar began the day's lesson by walking David and Reese through the mapping practice again. Reese was beginning to be able to shape her own consciousness into more of a contained presence; she was no longer a mass of conflicting emotions.

When they finished, Eres said, 'There is much improvement. I am very glad to see that. At this point we can continue with the same practice – that is what we would normally do – but because you'll be meeting with Akiya Deyir this afternoon, I want to ask you: Is there anything you'd like to tell me?'

Reese tucked her hands beneath her thighs and glanced sideways at David. They had discussed this earlier; today was the day. *Go ahead*, she told him.

'We know you've already guessed,' David said to Eres. 'Today we're ready to talk about it.'

Eres nodded. 'Good.'

They took turns explaining to Eres about their ability to speak to each other telepathically. They told the teacher how crowds affected them, how sometimes they sensed not only waves of emotion but snatches of thought, and how their abilities had developed differently in each of them.

'To be clear: Reese, first you only sensed emotions, while David, you only heard broken thoughts?' Eres asked.

'Right,' David said. 'But we can do both now.'

'Why do you think it happened that way?' Reese asked.

'It may simply be the way the adaptation affected you. We didn't think it had been completely effective in David at first. We'd have to do more testing before we know for sure. Tell me more about how it feels when you sense a crowd's emotions or thoughts.'

'It can be really confusing and overwhelming,' Reese said. 'These lessons have helped. I try to block them out now – the crowds.'

'And how close to the crowd are you when this happens?' Eres asked.

'I think we have to be pretty close,' David said.

'Yeah,' Reese said. 'I couldn't sense them when I was inside my house and they were in the street.'

'What about your telepathic communication? You said you first discovered this when you were at Project Plato, separated. Have you communicated that way since then?'

'No,' David said. 'We tried, but it hasn't worked.'

'We've had to be able to see each other to communicate that way,' Reese said.

The teacher regarded the two of them thoughtfully. 'I see. Perhaps it has something to do with your level of mental focus. You may have been more desperate to reach out to each other when you were at Plato. That situation could have forced you to focus your consciousness in a way you haven't done since then.'

'Maybe,' Reese said. 'It was a pretty intense experience.'

'Do you think we could do it again?' David asked.

'There's no reason why not. If you could communicate from a distance before, I think you'll be able to do it again. I do believe it will require practice on your part. Have you been able to hear the thoughts of any other humans? Or Imria?'

'No,' Reese said.

'Only in crowds, and that's not the same at all,' David said.

'David and I are the only two humans who have gone through the adaptation procedure, so maybe that's why?' Reese said. 'Maybe if you adapted other humans, we'd be able to hear their thoughts too.'

'Perhaps,' Eres said. 'The crowd sensing is interesting. How big do the crowds need to be?'

'I'm not sure,' Reese said. She and David had never formally tested their abilities; they had only muddled through on their own, trying to avoid becoming overwhelmed.

'These things occur when you are not touching another person, right?' Eres asked. 'This is not *susum'urda* – not the way I've been teaching you.'

'No, it's not *susum'urda*,' David said. 'That sort of makes sense to me now. But this other stuff . . . it still feels random. Like I don't really know how it works.'

'Why do you think we can do it?' Reese asked. 'You can't do it, can you?'

'No. None of the Imria have this ability. *Susum'urda* is predicated on physical connection. This is certainly different.'

'So this wasn't meant to be part of the adaptation,' David said.

'No.' Eres looked pensive. 'I suppose we could have suspected this was possible. There have always been humans who exhibited signs of being able to do things like this. You've called them psychics or mystics. And telepathy has always been a source of fascination for your people. It would make sense that humans were fascinated by it because some of you have been able to do it.'

Reese was skeptical. 'So the adaptation procedure has turned us into psychics?'

'Not exactly. For a long time, we attempted to analyze the DNA of so-called psychic humans and compare it to our own, to determine why certain genes were turned on and others weren't, but it was very slow, painstaking work. Those psychic abilities turned out to be mutations that were usually irreproducible in offspring – or at least so random in occurrence that it was impossible to predict. Our scientists stopped testing psychics decades ago, believing that those psychic skills were side effects of the fact that humans did have the ability to share consciousness in their genes, but that ability was never properly developed. The adaptation procedure was supposed to correct that. It was supposed to awaken your latent abilities and to make them heritable so that they will be passed on to your descendants. Apparently the adaptation procedure has awakened abilities we did not expect.' Eres leaned forward. 'Will you show me how it works?' The teacher extended a hand to Reese.

'How?' Reese asked, confused.

'Take my hand, and David can send you a thought. Allow me to experience it as it happens to you.'

Reese glanced at David, who nodded. She took Eres's hand and immediately felt the focus of the teacher's attention like a lens trained on her. Reese took a breath. *David?* She sensed Eres in the background of her consciousness like a shadow presence.

Yes, David thought. *I'm right here.*

Eres's consciousness seemed to flash in surprise. *Again*, Eres told her.

Got any other thoughts? Reese asked David.

What should I say? Testing, testing?

Reese smiled. *Ten four.*

Eres dropped Reese's hand and said, 'I have never encountered that before.' The teacher sounded unusually breathless. 'This afternoon when we meet with Akiya Deyir and the others – you will tell them, won't you?'

'We were planning to,' David said.

'Good. They should know. It is right that they learn it from the two of you.' Eres studied them, as if seeing them for the first time.

Reese shifted uncomfortably. 'Is it totally weird?' she asked.

The teacher looked astonished. 'It is not weird. It is . . . beyond what we had ever dreamed of. I only hope that Akiya agrees.'

CHAPTER 31

Akiya Deyir's offices were on the second level of the ship, and as Reese stepped into the foyer, she felt as if she were truly entering another world. The wall screens depicted a landscape that Reese knew must be Kurra. There was a cliff of red-and-purple rocks angling over an aquamarine sea. Buildings that resembled crystal formations clung to the top of the cliff, some of them secured by steel wires that looked like cobwebs. The ocean waves moved below, licking against the base of the cliffs, and as the water turned, it changed color, showing a flash of gold beneath the aquamarine.

The door slid shut behind them and someone called, 'Please come in.'

Reese and David followed the sound of the voice through the open doorway in the foyer and into the main office. It was a wide room with screens that ran the length of the longest wall, showing a forest of trees with black trunks and moving, bluish-green leaves. At one end of the room was a curved, glossy black desk, behind which a display cabinet held various items suspended on wires. Reese saw stones or jewels of different colors; a sphere that looked like a miniature planet; and a black statue that resembled the fertility goddesses that had been carved by ancient humans, with a round belly and heavy breasts. In the center of the room was a long, oval table made of the same glossy black material as the desk. Four people were seated already: Akiya Deyir, Dr Brand, Eres Tilhar, and Amber. Two black chairs, carved to resemble waves like the ones in Eres's room, remained empty.

Akiya Deyir gestured to the chairs. 'Please sit,' he said. He was as elegant as Reese remembered from the press conference, but today he was dressed in clothing that was clearly not from Earth. He wore a jacket made of deep violet cloth; it had narrow lapels and long, billowing tails, almost like a gown. He had dark blue trousers on that made Reese think of jodhpurs, tucked into shiny boots of the same color with a stripe of silver running up the side. It was an ensemble that Reese might expect on a Japanese pop star, but there was nothing frivolous about the ambassador. As Reese sat down, she surreptitiously studied Deyir's dark, smooth skin. He was so extraordinary looking, like a film star from the 1930s, all cheekbones and shadows. She wondered if his beauty was natural, or if he – or his parents – had engineered it.

'I've been informed that you both know about our long history with your people,' Deyir said. 'And that you are concerned about the fact that we have not yet revealed this. While I understand your concern, the two of you are not qualified to make that decision. You do not have the benefit of the full context of our situation.' Deyir's tone was mild, but there was an authority to his presence that did not invite challenge. 'Your people – humanity – are our greatest concern. We did not always feel that way, it is true. Many hundreds of thousands of years ago, my people were careless. We had great scientific knowledge and we had great ambition, and that combination resulted in many mistakes. We were never violent; that was not our pleasure. We have been, always, connected to each other through *susum'urda*. What we wanted was to create life. To create intelligence. Unfortunately, our eagerness to create life was not tempered by consideration for the responsibility that would bestow upon us.'

There was a hypnotic quality to Deyir's voice, and though dozens of questions raced through Reese's mind, she did not ask them. She watched him speak, transfixed by the movements of his mouth and the fluid gestures of his long-fingered hands.

'We were much younger then, and less experienced. We only thought: Look at this new world – Earth – and see how similar it is to ours. Look at these creatures here; they could become us. We were enraptured with that idea. Our science, however, was not perfect. We had not created humans from nothing; we changed what already existed. That meant that humans did not turn out exactly the way we had hoped. Your people could not share consciousness. You were fixated on violence, on war. We did not know what to do, and to our great disgrace, we simply abandoned you. We thought: Humans can find their way out of this on their own; we have interfered too much.

'But we could not entirely leave you behind. We watched as your populations grew and your technology developed. We came to understand that you are our greatest responsibility.

We were poor creators; poor guardians of what we made. We cannot allow you to destroy your planet and to destroy yourselves. That is why we have returned. We have come here to correct the mistakes we made before it is too late. The adaptation procedure, which Evelyn developed with her team, is finally a success. Our goal is to adapt all of humanity, bit by bit, using this procedure. There are many of you now, and we cannot adapt all of you; that is why the adaptation is heritable. Your children will inherit the same abilities, and your children's children will as well. Over several generations, humanity will become what we had initially intended. You will become true Imrians.'

That is exactly what Charles Lovick told us, David thought to Reese. *Akiya Deyir is just putting a different spin on it*.

The ambassador sat back, crossing his legs. The silver on his boots gleamed. 'In order to implement our plan we have moved cautiously. That is why we haven't yet revealed all of this to your people. The two of you are different now. Because you've been adapted, you are more like us. You are better able to understand us. Humans who haven't been adapted will not have your ability to empathize with us. They need to be adapted first; that's why we haven't told them.' He paused, his eyes flickering toward Dr Brand. 'I understand that Evelyn has given a sample of Imrian DNA to your human scientists, and they have questioned how closely we are related.'

'It's not a question,' David said. 'They know.'

Deyir nodded. 'You will need to ask them to refrain from sharing their knowledge. It is in your best interests to delay this. To give your fellow humans time to accept us.'

Reese finally spoke out loud: "But you're wrong.' Deyir's gaze turned to her, and she straightened up, clutching the edges of the slippery black chair as she faced him. 'We aren't true Imrians. What you've done to me and David— it's not what you expected.'

'What do you mean?' Dr Brand asked. Both she and Amber looked startled.

Reese suddenly felt the weight of what she and David were about to do. There was no one else here to speak for humanity. It was their responsibility: hers and David's. At that moment, she saw her future stretching out before her. She had never given much thought to what she would do with her life; maybe she'd go to journalism school, or maybe she'd become a lawyer. She hadn't had to decide yet, and now she knew she never would. The decision had been made for her.

She remembered her conversation with Amber about coincidence. *Choice has nothing to do with it*, Amber had told her, and Reese hadn't understood then. Now she did. She was in this position, and it was a privileged one. She had told her mother that she wasn't a child anymore. The only option was to take the responsibility that had been given to her, even if she hadn't wanted it to begin with. To refuse would be an insult not only to humanity but to herself.

'What you did to us changed us, but not into Imrians,' she said to the ambassador. 'We have other abilities now.' She looked at David, and he began to explain what they could do.

When he was finished, Dr Brand said, 'We can't be sure that other humans will also have your abilities.'

'You can't be sure they won't,' Reese said.

Dr Brand smiled as if Reese had said exactly what she wanted. 'That's true.' She turned to Deyir. 'We must reconsider our plans. You must contact home and tell them.'

Deyir had listened to David, Reese, and Dr Brand without interrupting. Now he turned to Eres. 'What is your opinion?'

'Their abilities need further study,' Eres answered. 'We don't know exactly what they can do yet, but the telepathy alone is extraordinary. At the very least, I think we do need to discuss changing the implementation of our plan.'

Deyir looked at Reese and David, his expression sober. 'This does change things, but I cannot see the utility of modifying our plan. If anything, we should be even more cautious now about revealing your abilities. I know that your government will be especially interested in using your abilities for their gain, not for the advancement of humanity.'

'But that's why you need to tell the whole truth,' Reese said. She couldn't see why Deyir wasn't grasping this. 'The more people who know, the more difficult it will be for the government to take advantage of it. The problem is in keeping things secret, not in telling the truth.'

'Besides, it's not your job to manage the way humanity deals with this,' David put in.

'It *is* our job,' Deyir said. 'We have failed you. It is our task to right your course.'

This was the first time Reese had heard him speak with such emotion, and it surprised her.

'No, it's not,' David said. 'Maybe you were there at the beginning, however many thousands of years ago, but you left. We kept on without you.'

'Humanity's problems are humanity's problems,' Reese said. 'It's our job to fix our own problems. You can offer support, but if you secretly try to turn us all into Imrians – which isn't going to work anyway because apparently the adaptation procedure doesn't turn us into Imrians – you'll be exactly what all those freaked-out protesters say you are: colonizers.'

'I don't think you understand,' Deyir said.

'No, *you* don't understand,' Reese insisted, growing increasingly frustrated. 'You can't just come here and say, 'Oops, we fucked up a million years ago, let us fix things.' You may have had a hand in creating us, but we have been doing fine here this whole time. We have created our own cultures and our own technologies. Your plan doesn't take account of that. Your plan just says humans need to be changed, so we'll change them without their permission.'

'Humans might not be able to do *susum'urda*,' David said, 'but we're not idiots. We've managed to survive this long without your abilities. We're not going to roll over and say, 'Sure, adapt us, we don't know any better.''

'Besides, the truth will come out,' Reese said. 'It always does. If you don't tell the truth from the beginning, you're just asking for a war. You said yourself that humans are prone to violence. Don't you see what you could be starting?'

For the first time since they arrived in his office, Akiya Deyir seemed rattled. Amber leaned forward and said, 'She's right. David's right too. I don't think humanity is going to go for it. You can't just expect them to fall in line. They don't know us. We're strangers to them, and we've already started off on the wrong foot by lying about who we are.'

'You have to tell the truth on Monday at the UN,' David said.

'If you really want us to change, you have to change too,' Reese said. 'You have to start treating us as your equals.'

Deyir's gaze flickered around the table. His face gave away nothing. Finally he said, 'I'll think about what you've told me. That's all I can promise you. I'll think about it.'

CHAPTER 32

When David and Reese returned to the living quarters after their meeting with Akiya Deyir, the door to Reese's mom's room was open. Reese paused in front of her own room and asked David, 'What are you up to now?' She was anxious and impatient, and she wished that Deyir had given them a more concrete answer.

'Homework?' he said, grimacing. 'How long do you think it's going to take for him to decide?'

'I hope not too long.'

Reese's mom came out of her room, followed by her dad. 'While you're waiting,' her mom said, 'I think it's time for you two to come clean about everything.'

David gave Reese's parents a nervous grin. 'Hi, Ms Sheridan.' He paused as Reese's dad's name seemed to escape him, but was saved when his own parents came into the corridor too. Reese had the distinct impression that the four adults had been waiting to ambush them.

'Why don't you all come into our room,' David's mom suggested. 'We have a little more space.' Reese glanced at

David. *We do have to tell them about our abilities, and your dad has more info about the test results, right?*

Yeah. I guess now's as good a time as any.

Beats doing homework?

David smiled slightly. 'Okay,' he said out loud, and walked down the corridor toward his parents' quarters. Reese and her parents followed.

At 6:15 PM, Reese was seated in the dining hall with David and their families, eating a perfectly acceptable but rather boring meal of chicken, salad, and crusty bread that seemed as if it had been ordered out of a nearby Whole Foods. 'I apologize for the absence of my colleagues,' Nura Halba said as he sat down with them in the nearly deserted room. 'They are in discussions, and I believe they will be there all night.'

Dealing with what we told them, Reese thought. She took a sip of her water and pushed the cherry tomatoes around on her plate. She wondered how long it would take Mr Hernandez to figure out that neither she nor David was coming to their meeting.

'That's fine,' her mom said. 'We're grateful that you've allowed us to stay here on such short notice.'

Halba smiled, and he looked more Asian than ever. Reese still hadn't figured out how she could broach that subject with any of the Imria. 'Tomorrow night we'll have a proper dinner,' he said. 'Everyone on board will come. It will be a belated welcome banquet.'

'Will there be actual Imrian food?' Reese asked.

Halba seemed amused by her question. 'Well, we do have to

buy local. We can't bring fresh groceries all the way from Kurra, but yes, we'll have some Imrian-style dishes.'

The door slid open and Amber came into the dining hall alone. She gave them a smile before she went to serve herself from the dishes on the buffet. Reese glanced across the table at David. He had tensed up every time Amber was nearby, and tonight was no different. *She got out of the meeting*, he thought. *Do you think it's over?*

I don't know, Reese told him. When Amber came to the table, she slid into an empty seat at the end next to Halba. 'Hi,' she said to everyone. 'I don't think I've met you all?' After the introductions, Halba excused himself, leaving a gap at the table where he had been sitting next to David. Amber did not move over to close up the space, and Reese saw David turn away from her slightly while he spoke to his sister in low tones.

'Amber,' Reese said, 'are they still in their meeting?'

Amber glanced up from her meal. 'Yeah. They have to talk to Kurra, and there's sort of a time lag. It's going to take a while.'

Reese knew David was listening, even though he was pretending not to. She could feel it across the table, his attentiveness like a charged webbing between them. She had never been able to sense his emotions so acutely when they weren't touching, and she knew it was because Amber put him on edge.

'What do you think they'll decide?' Reese asked.

'I don't know,' Amber said. 'I hope they listen to you guys.'

Chloe suddenly burst out, 'I don't want to do that. I'm bored.'

Everybody turned to look at the twelve-year-old, who was glaring at her mother. Grace Li frowned at her daughter. 'I'm sorry. I told you that we would be here for a few days and you should bring some things to read. Maybe your brother can play a game with you?'

Even David seemed a little annoyed, but he said, 'Sure. What do you want to play, Chloe?'

Chloe rolled her eyes with such vehemence that Reese thought they might pop out of their sockets. 'He doesn't want to play a game, Mom.'

Reese swallowed a laugh at Chloe's sarcastic tone. Amber leaned over the table so she could see David's little sister and asked, 'Do you want to watch a movie or something?'

Chloe realized that everybody was looking at her, and her face turned red. She didn't seem to be able to speak anymore.

Grace said, 'That's nice of you, but you don't need to go out of your way.'

Amber looked surprised. 'Oh! No, I mean, I can just set up the screens over there to play a movie if you want. We can get whatever's online.'

'Anything?' Chloe said, sounding doubtful.

'Sure.' Amber glanced at Chloe's parents. 'Well, anything your parents say is okay.' She got up and went over to the screens that showed the view outside. The sky was darkening toward twilight, and across the field the eucalyptus trees moved in a gentle breeze. Amber touched the wall and the screens went black. A moment later she had pulled up an Internet movie rental site.

'You can get that here?' Chloe said, scrambling out of her seat.

'Of course. What do you want to see?'

David's parents traded wry glances, and Grace stood. 'I'd better make sure she doesn't pick something she's not allowed to watch.'

Chloe chose *Blue Moon*, a movie about a high school cheerleader-turned-werewolf-hunter who falls in love with both the leader of the pack and the high school football star. Reese finished her dinner as Amber set up a viewing area in front of the screen. She did something that caused some of the tables to lower into the floor out of the way, and then dragged some cushions into the dining hall, returning several times with blankets and pillows. By the time she was finished, Chloe was chattering with Amber about the actor who played the alpha werewolf.

The parents left as the movie began. 'We're going for a walk,' Reese's mom said, dropping a hand on her shoulder. 'Call us if you need anything.'

'I will.' Reese pushed her plate aside and looked at David. 'What are you gonna do?'

He made a face. 'I don't really want to watch that movie, but I'm supposed to stay with Chloe.'

'Oh.' Reese glanced over at his sister; she was reclining in a mound of pillows as the movie began. Amber was walking toward the door behind the buffet that led into what Reese assumed was the kitchen. 'It could be worse,' Reese said to David. 'At least it's not vampires?'

He briefly grinned. 'I don't mind vampires.'

She smiled at him. 'Good to know.'

Amber emerged from the kitchen carrying four bowls, spoons, and a quart of ice cream. She set it all down on the table near Reese. 'Want some?' she asked, peeling off the lid.

'What kind is it?' Reese asked.

'Salted caramel from Mitchell's.' Amber began to scoop some into a bowl and called over her shoulder, 'Chloe, you want some ice cream?'

'Yes!' Chloe replied.

Amber glanced sideways at David but didn't say anything to him as she prepared a bowl for his sister. As she carried it over to Chloe, Reese picked up a spoon for a taste. 'Wow, this is good,' she said, and reached for the scoop. 'David, you should have some.'

When Amber returned, she eyed Reese's bowl. 'You took a lot.'

'You don't like to share?' Reese said.

Amber gave her a look that made Reese blush, but she didn't respond aloud. Instead, she scooped ice cream into two bowls and slid one across the table to David. 'You'll love it, I promise,' she told him. Then she went to put the ice cream back in the freezer.

Reese ate her ice cream in silence. David didn't touch his. Amber emerged from the kitchen, grabbed her bowl, and went to join Chloe in the nest of pillows to watch the cheerleader-werewolf-hunter discover that she had been chosen to lead a ragtag group of fellow students in battle. Reese could still sense David's resistance, as if his hackles had been raised. She didn't know what to do about it. *We can leave*, she told him. *I'm sure they'll be okay*.

I'm fine.

Over on the cushions, Chloe and Amber burst into giggles. David's gaze flickered toward the corner of the room where the girls were sprawled in front of the big screen.

Your ice cream's melting, Reese thought at David.

He looked at the bowl that Amber had set near him. Chloe giggled again, and Amber whispered something back. David picked up the spoon.

Reese asked, *Do you want to go watch over there? It'll be more comfortable*.

He shrugged. *Go ahead*.

Reese went over to the corner to rearrange some of the pillows, pulling them slightly apart from Chloe and Amber in case David changed his mind. She made herself comfortable and focused on the movie while she finished her ice cream. A few minutes later David joined them, dropping down beside her. 'Next time we are not watching a chick flick,' he said.

Chloe squealed. 'It's not a chick flick! There are werewolves! And fighting!'

Her point was lost when the cheerleader-werewolf-hunter kissed the pack leader. 'See?' David said, pointing with his spoon.

Amber laughed. Chloe gave him a dirty look. 'Fine, next time you pick.'

'Good,' he said.

Reese reached out and touched his elbow. Thank you.

The tension inside him was still there, but it had lessened. *You owe me*, he told her.

For what?

For making me watch this movie.

She smiled.

Sunday dragged by, as if every minute before the summit was weighted. Reese felt as though she was going crazy with impatience.

After breakfast, she called Julian to tell him the whole story as she had promised she would. He was so shocked that he didn't speak for what seemed like an entire minute. Then he asked her to say it all again so he could record it. When they finished talking, Reese went to look for David, only to run into him leaving the ship with her dad. They were both dressed to work out, and she asked in surprise, 'What are you guys doing?'

'We're going for a run,' her dad answered. 'You want to come?'

'Uh, no. Have fun.' She watched them leave together, feeling weird about the whole thing.

It's just running, David assured her as he stepped into the elevator.

She retreated to her room and stared at the screens depicting the field outside. She wanted to know what her dad was saying to David. She wondered what Amber was doing. She worried about whether Julian was going to be assaulted by CASS goons, and she texted him to find out if he was all right. The fourth time she texted him he replied: Dude I'll call you if I'm abducted.

Lunch brought a brief moment of excitement when Dr Brand joined them, but when Reese asked whether Akiya Deyir had made any decisions, Dr Brand only said, 'He's still thinking about it.'

All afternoon Reese pretended to do her homework, while David and Chloe sprawled nearby in the heap of cushions that had been left in the dining hall after their movie night. Finally, an hour before dinner, Nura Halba asked them to leave the room while they prepared for the meal. 'Should we get dressed up?' Chloe asked excitedly.

'Only if you wish to,' Halba said. 'It's not formal.'

Reese stood in front of her narrow closet for half an hour, trying to decide if she should wear the single skirt suit she had brought to wear to the United Nations. At the last minute she only changed her shirt, swapping her old blue tee for the new one that Diana Warner had helped pick out at Nordstrom. She heard her mom knocking on the door and opened it to find everyone already assembled in the corridor: David, dressed in an untucked black oxford shirt and jeans; her parents, looking disturbingly like a couple; David's parents waiting with Chloe, who had put on a pink skirt and white blouse.

'Okay,' Reese's mom said with a nervous smile. 'Let's go.'

In the dining hall, every Imrian on the ship was waiting. Reese was startled when the door slid open and she saw all two dozen of them standing there, dressed in strange clothing that Reese knew had not originated on Earth. For the first time, they weren't wearing their intelligible-to-humanity outfits, and Reese now understood why they had done so in the first place. Some were dressed as colorfully as Akiya Deyir had been the day before in his violet coat; others wore garments that seemed made out of metal mesh or other synthetic fabrics that rippled like feathers when they moved. Only Amber and Dr Brand were dressed like humans, and in comparison to the other Imria, they almost looked plain.

The meal began with small dishes of pickled berries that resembled cherries but tasted like olives. 'We brought these from Kurra,' Nura Halba explained. He was seated with Reese and the other humans, and Reese wondered if he was growing tired of acting as their interpreter. 'They're traditionally offered at the beginning of every ceremonial meal. They're called *buru*.'

The *buru* were followed by sliced cabbage and carrots served in a cold, tangy broth. After that, platters of grilled squid were brought out, speckled with remnants of charred chilies. Whole sea bass were served too, and Halba filleted them at their table, removing the heads and stripping away the delicate bones before plating portions with a bit of bright green, garlicky sauce on the side. The final course was a sweet, many-layered pastry that reminded Reese of baklava, except this was filled with something that tasted like red bean paste.

At the end of the meal, Akiya Deyir stood while servers walked around the dining hall, placing small glass cups shaped like eggs before each person and filling them from black pitchers. Reese sniffed hers; it smelled like wine. Halba said, 'It's called *kurun*. It's drunk at the end of the meal as a toast.'

'Tonight we would like to welcome our guests to our home, temporary though it may be,' Deyir said. He was wearing a crimson tunic that flowed into long tails like his jacket, with trousers the color of steel. The sleeves of his tunic extended over his hands like petals, and he wore a ring that resembled a vine on his left hand. '*Nu nig tukum'ta*. It is no coincidence you are here; we are glad of your company.' He raised his small glass of kurun and said, 'Welcome. *Sude silim*. A blessing and a greeting.' All the Imria stood, and Reese scrambled to stand with them. They said in unison, '*Sude silim*,' and then sipped from their cups.

Reese followed their example, lifting her glass to her lips. The *kurun* was sour and lukewarm, and not anything she would ever want to drink on a regular basis, but as it left an unexpectedly hot trail down her throat, she felt as if it had marked her internally. She was no longer entirely human, and the taste of it was like fire in her stomach.

CHAPTER 33

Liftoff was scheduled for midnight. 'We don't want to draw too much attention to ourselves,' Nura Halba had said at dinner, but Reese suspected the state of California had asked them to travel at night in order to prevent a massive crowd from gathering to watch the launch.

The ship would fly at a much higher altitude than commercial airplanes, but it would not leave Earth's orbit. The entire trip would last about two and a half hours, and when they arrived in New York they would take up a position over New York Harbor, where they would remain for the duration of the weeklong General Debate. Their lander would ferry them to and from the United Nations headquarters on the East Side.

The Imria did not linger in the dining hall for long after dinner. Reese imagined they still had plenty of business to attend to before morning. Amber was the only Imrian who stayed behind.

Reese knew it wouldn't be like a rocket ship taking off from a launchpad, but she had thought it would be a bigger deal than it turned out to be. The only audible indication that the ship was lifting off was a low rumble. Amber adjusted the lights and the screens so they could see the night outside. The ship seemed to levitate off the ground, silent and steady as a well-oiled elevator. As the island fell away beneath them, Reese saw the lights of San Francisco across the black swath of the bay, and then the lights vanished as the ship was engulfed in a cloud bank.

Reese glanced at her watch. It was just after midnight. In nine hours, Akiya Deyir was scheduled to speak at the United Nations. She hoped he would be telling the truth.

Reese slept fitfully after takeoff, waking as dawn broke through the screens in her room to reveal New York Harbor below the ship. She scrambled toward the screens as if they were real windows, staring down at the water and the Statue of Liberty and the toothy skyline of Manhattan. Helicopters were circling the ship, and while some of them bore news channel logos, others were sleek and black, and she knew they were from the military.

She dressed in her debate suit: knee-length navy blue skirt, white blouse, and jacket. It only survived midway through breakfast, because she spilled strawberry jam all over the skirt at the sight of David entering the dining hall in his suit and tie. She hadn't seen him so dressed up since the national tournament in June, and his appearance made her feel like she was jolting backward through time. Unfortunately, her skirt was ruined, and she had to go back up to her room and put on a pair of black pants. She hoped nobody would notice that the color didn't match her jacket.

All of the Imria going to the UN had put on their made-on-Earth clothes. Akiya Deyir was wearing a tailored black suit with a white silk handkerchief peeking from the breast pocket, making him look more like a film star than ever. Amber wore a black cap-sleeved dress with a fitted skirt and a narrow, patent-leather belt that matched her shoes. Reese recognized the shoes from the day of the press conference.

The Imria had received authorization for only one parent each to accompany Reese and David to the UN, and Reese's mom and David's dad were chosen to do the honors. They followed Nura Halba into the cargo bay on the first level, where two landers were parked. He directed them to climb into the larger one. Reese buckled herself in and held her breath as the ship opened in midair and the lander hovered up, rocking slightly before it accelerated out of the craft. She saw the steely color of the water below and the blue sky all around them, and she felt as if she were living in the future. Then the military helicopters fell in on both sides of the lander, and she was sucked right back into the present.

Reese had never seen so much security in her life. Police officers and squad cars lined the East Side of New York as the lander descended into the barricaded plaza in front of the United Nations. As they exited the lander, they were greeted by officials in suits and eyed by soldiers carrying machine guns. They were given badges on lanyards with their photos already laminated onto them, then escorted through a security tent where they had to walk through body scanning machines and be patted down for weapons.

The interior of the United Nations building looked like it had come straight out of the 1950s. In the multistory lobby, stacks of curved balconies overlooked a long, switchback staircase. As they were ushered past the stairs toward a bank of elevators, Reese glimpsed the press waiting behind ropes on the other side of the lobby, cameras flashing. She had put up her mental defenses as soon as she had stepped off the lander, but some of the curiosity still leaked through.

'After you, miss,' said one of their escorts, gesturing toward the elevator.

She turned away from the photographers and stepped in. The elevator operator held the doors until they had all crammed inside, and then he pressed the button to take them upstairs.

The General Assembly Hall was packed. Reese hadn't realized that she would be seated up front, and as she was led into one of the reserved sections on the right side of the central podium, she found it difficult to look at the audience. There were too many of them, and they were all staring directly at her – or at least it felt that way. She sank into her seat, closing her eyes as the waves of their interest surged over her. David, who sat beside her, reached for her hand. He was as overwhelmed as she was, but it was easier to face it together. After several minutes the audience quieted, and a man stepped up to the microphone to introduce Akiya Deyir. Reese felt the audience turn their attention away from her, and she allowed herself to open her eyes.

Akiya Deyir didn't look nervous at all as he approached the

podium. The General Assembly Hall was completely silent as he took out his notes. Reese felt the weight of the hush on her skin like a layer of static.

'Good morning,' Deyir said. 'Thank you for welcoming me and my fellow Imrians to the United Nations. We are eager to open the dialogue between our people. In fact, we have been waiting for this day for many, many generations.' He paused, glancing at Reese and David. The whole General Assembly glanced with him, and for a moment Reese couldn't breathe.

'One month ago,' he continued, 'when I first spoke to your reporters at Angel Island, I told you that we did not know all the details about our origins. This is true. We do not know where we come from. But I misled you on another subject: the origin of humanity.'

The mood in the hall became palpably more tense. Reese saw the ambassador betray the first sign of his own strain, as he gripped the edge of the podium with both of his elegant hands.

'We Imrians are an old people. We have lived for many millennia, and some of our beliefs are so deeply ingrained that it has been extremely difficult to recognize that they are wrong. I must thank your children, Reese Holloway and David Li, for showing me that we must change the way we have thought of you. For too long we have considered you, humanity, to be our responsibility, but now I realize that we have been acting out of guilt, and that guilt has blinded us to who you are. Your scientists have spent decades trying to uncover the origin of your species, and today I must tell you that they have been... misled by us.' A ripple of shock rolled through the assembly hall. 'We Imria first came to this planet millions of years ago. We were a younger people then, and we thought we had all the power of science at our disposal, and we exercised that power by creating you in our own image. That is why we are so similar. Because we made you to look like us.'

The hairs on Reese's arms rose at the sensation of utter astonishment that swept through the General Assembly Hall.

'Our belief in our own power, however, was arrogant,' Deyir continued. 'We brought your species into existence, but we did not succeed in the most important way. As we told you a month ago, the foundation stone of Imrian society is our ability to share consciousness with one another: *susum'urda*. It makes us who we are. From the day we are born, we are connected intimately with our loved ones, and this is the reason that we have survived for so many millions of years. But we failed to give you this ability, and because of that, you grew into a very different kind of people. Because you cannot share consciousness with one another, you have had to create societies different from ours. We thought your lack of *susum'urda* made you a violent people, prone to attack rather than to love, and we wanted to correct this. In many ways, we saw you as our greatest mistake.'

A murmur rose in the hall, accompanied by waves of stunned disbelief and the beginnings of indignation. Akiya Deyir raised his voice.

'That is why we returned to your planet in the early nineteen hundreds: To find a way to right this wrong; to bring you the most wondrous aspect of our civilization. We thought of this as the next stage in humanity's evolution. We called it an adaptation. Our research encountered many roadblocks. We had been absent from your planet for too long, and human beings have changed since the last time we intervened in your evolution. But we were overjoyed this past summer when our adaptation procedure was successfully implemented in two of your children. We thought this meant that the time had finally come for us to share this ability with the rest of you: to adapt all of humanity. We wanted to bring you into the Imrian family; to make you, finally, the people you were meant to be.

'Two days ago, I learned that Reese and David have adapted far beyond what we initially intended. They are now capable of *susum'urda*, but they are capable of more than that. They can not only share consciousness; they have true telepathic abilities. We do not know if all human beings who undergo the adaptation procedure will develop these same abilities, but we do know one thing: It is time for us to stop intervening without your full cooperation. We Imria are not the future of your species. We may be where you came from, but David and Reese are where you're going. They are the future of both our peoples. I come here today on behalf of all the Imria to ask your forgiveness for what we have done and what we have left undone. I hope that we can move forward into a new age. Together.'

CHAPTER 34

'Reese, wait!'

Amber's voice made Reese turn around halfway into the elevator to the parking garage. Amber was running across the landing outside the General Assembly Hall. The elevator door began to close and Reese put her hand out to stop it.

'Amber's coming,' she said over her shoulder. Her mom, David, his dad, and Nura Halba were already inside. They were heading to the Waldorf for a special luncheon and had to take a car to get there. The elevator operator pressed his finger on a button to hold the doors.

'She's supposed to go with Evelyn and the others,' Halba said, poking his head out to look.

Amber arrived a few seconds later. 'Thanks. They told me I should go with you. They were held up by the press.'

'Do you know how long they'll be delayed?' Halba asked.

Amber stepped inside. 'No. There were a lot of reporters, though.'

'Are you ready, sir?' the elevator operator asked.

'Yes, thanks,' Halba replied, and the doors slid shut. Reese was glad she hadn't been required to stay for the press conference. The response to Akiya Deyir's speech had been chaos, with half the audience frozen by shock and the other half shouting a hundred questions at once. She had no idea how the Imria were going to deal with this, and though she knew she would have a part to play for the rest of her life, she was grateful for the temporary reprieve.

When the elevator came to a stop, they trooped out into the garage. It smelled faintly of gasoline fumes, and the fluorescent bulbs overhead gave the space a garish cast. As Halba went to request their vehicle from the valet, Reese asked Amber, 'Why can't we take the lander?'

'There's nowhere to park it at the hotel,' Amber said. 'We couldn't get a permit.'

'You have to get a permit to park a spaceship?' David asked.

Amber shrugged lightly. 'We're trying to play by the rules.'

I wouldn't have picked parking in New York as the right time to start, David thought to Reese.

Me neither.

David's fingers worked at the knot of his tie, loosening it. 'So what happens after lunch?' he asked, changing the subject.

'Meetings with diplomats, receptions, that sort of thing,' Amber said.

'Are we supposed to go to them?' Reese asked.

'Some, I think,' Amber said.

A limousine pulled up to the valet booth, and the driver jumped out to open the door. Nura Halba called them toward the vehicle, and Reese, David, and Amber turned to follow Reese's mom and David's dad into the limo. In the distance

Reese heard a screeching noise, like brakes slammed on too sharply. She stopped, looking in the direction of the sound.

An explosion split the air like a whip crack through the stillness. The ground rocked.

Amber stumbled on her heels, falling against Reese as Reese banged into David. He grabbed her arm, saying, 'What the hell?'

Sirens began to wail as emergency strobe lights flashed to life, sending bursts of white through the garage. Reese spun around, but she couldn't see where the explosion had come from.

Her mom scrambled out of the limo, screaming, 'Reese!' David's dad was right behind her as a black-and-white police van careened through the parking garage straight at the limo.

'Mom!' she cried, starting toward the car.

David's hand was still on her arm and he jerked her to a stop. 'Get back!' he shouted, pulling Reese with him toward the elevator. She grabbed Amber, dragging her with them as David cried, 'Dad, get away from the car!'

The van turned at the last possible second, barely grazing the limo's front fender as Nura Halba, Reese's mom, and David's dad dived for the ground. The back of the van opened and several men in SWAT uniforms swarmed out. Relieved, Reese moved toward them. One of the men came directly for her and grasped her arm.

That was when she knew.

Inside the man was a cold, hard void, and she froze as she realized who he was – who they all were. They were from Blue Base, just like Lovick's bodyguards. The man who had grabbed her bent her arms behind her back as easily as she might break a toothpick. With a ratcheting sound, her wrists were bound with a plastic strip, and the man half carried, half pushed her toward the van. To her left she saw David trying to struggle, but it was useless. He was shoved inside the van too, and deposited onto the bench across from her. A soldier inside the van covered her mouth with a strip of tape, then patted her down and pulled out her cell phone and handed it off to another soldier. It happened so fast that she hadn't even had time to scream.

The soldiers began to climb back into the van, falling into place silently and efficiently. Reese heard Amber cry out in pain, and a moment later she was pushed into the van too. She had a red welt across her face, and her eyes were bright and angry. The soldier who had thrust her inside pulled the door shut while another bound and gagged her.

'Who's this? We already have two of them,' barked the soldier next to Reese.

'The orders say "all the teenagers",' said the soldier who had taken Amber. 'Here's the third.'

'Fuck it, take her too,' the first soldier said. He smacked on the metal grate between the rear of the van and the driver's cab. 'Let's go!'

They roared out of the parking garage, the wheels squealing. Reese's stomach lurched as she banged into the soldier beside her. She recoiled from the dense compactness of his body, all muscle and adrenaline, and the acidity in her stomach threatened to rise into her throat. She choked it down, trying to inhale through her nose, but the tape over her mouth magnified the false sensation that she couldn't breathe. A buzzing sound filled her ears as her panic crested. She thought she was about to faint and she looked across the van at David, his face swimming in her vision. Then someone pulled a hood over her head, and she couldn't even see.

She screamed through the tape, but it came out as a desperate gurgle. The van took a curve so quickly she slid onto one of the soldier's laps. 'Sit up,' he growled, pushing her away.

She sat up, her limbs trembling. She focused on breathing through her nose and through the black material of the hood over her head. The air was warm and smelled of sweat and the soldiers' sour, metallic odor. She strained against the tie around her wrists; it cut into her skin like a knife.

Reese.

She froze.

Reese, are you hurt?

David. Relief flooded through her. *No, I'm okay. Are you?*

No. I'm fine. Don't panic.

She choked on a hysterical laugh, the tape an impenetrable barrier against her lips. *Don't panic?* The soldiers around them were silent. She could hear them breathing like well-oiled machines. In, out, in, out. Beyond that she heard the rough inhale of someone trying to breathe through a mask. *Amber?* But though she focused as intently as she could, she was unable to sense Amber at all.

I can't talk to Amber, she thought to David. *Can you?*

No. Did you feel these soldiers?

Yeah, like pits of nothing. Fear shuddered through her. *They're from Blue Base.*

They had to be sent by Charles Lovick, since we obviously didn't give Mr Hernandez the info they wanted.

Something beeped loudly, and Reese recognized the lead soldier's voice as he said, 'Retriever one, we have the quarry.'

A scratchy sound followed, and Reese realized the soldier was speaking on a walkie-talkie. A woman's voice came through. 'Base six. Exercise option one-zero-four. Repeat, option one-zero-four.'

'Roger that.'

'Report when finalized.'

She heard the crunch of a lock being opened. Someone asked, 'Why one-zero-four? They can't do anything.'

'We don't ask questions. We follow orders.'

A soldier pulled her away from the wall. His touch made her cringe. There was something disturbing about him that went beyond the dense weight of his body – something unstable. Without warning, a sharp needle plunged into her shoulder, and she yelped. The drug flooded into her bloodstream in a thick, numbing rush, and then she blacked out.

CHAPTER 35

Reese woke up slowly. She was lying on her stomach, her hands still bound behind her back, her cheek pressed against something hard and gritty. Her head was cloudy with the remnants of the drug they had injected into her, and her mouth tasted foul. She tried to lick her lips but the tape was still covering them.

That jolted her into blinking her eyes open, panic arcing through her as she wriggled against the restraints binding her wrists. Her cheek scraped against a dirt floor. Wherever she was, it was dark, but the hood had been removed. She inhaled through her nose, sucking in several deep breaths. She smelled dust and mold and something pungent – the scent of old chemicals.

Footsteps sounded above.

She tried to roll onto her back but her shoulder got in the way, grinding painfully into the ground. She scooted onto her side as well as she could, using her legs to turn herself, and angled her head toward the ceiling. There were several cracks of light in the middle of the roof. As the footsteps returned, she realized she was seeing floorboards. She must be in a basement somewhere. That explained the odor of mildew and closed-up spaces.

A voice called, 'I'm going to check on them.'

'Take the drugs,' someone else said.

A door opened, spilling light into the basement. Reese froze, closing her eyes. The only thing she could think to do was play dead.

The man came down the stairs. Reese heard a click, and then light glowed through her eyelids. He had turned on an overhead bulb. His boots scuffed across the floor and paused. She heard a muffled whimper. Amber.

'You awake yet?' the man said in a low voice. There was a soft thump, and Amber cried out.

Fear lanced white-hot through the lingering haze in Reese's mind. The man laughed.

'Aliens,' he muttered. 'Too bad they don't all look like you.'

Upstairs a door slammed. The sound of men's voices floated down the stairs. 'Why's the door open?' someone asked.

'Wilson's giving them another dose.'

'Aw, shit. I wanted to see them awake.'

'Why?'

Another man laughed. 'Why do you think?'

They came down the stairs, their footsteps loud and carefree. Reese held herself as perfectly still as she could, trying to pretend she was the dirt floor itself. Her heart was beating so loudly she was terrified they would notice her twitching.

A pair of footsteps came closer to her. Paused. A man said, 'What about this one? This is the human chick, right?'

He grabbed Reese's shoulder and pulled her onto her back, causing her to land on her wrists and elbows. Pain spiked up her arms and her head spun from the sudden movement. She forced her body to remain limp on the ground even as her upper arms burned from being twisted in a direction they didn't want to go. 'She's still out,' the man said, sounding disappointed.

'Forget about her. This one's awake.'

There was a ripping sound, and suddenly Amber screamed, 'Don't touch her! Don't you fucking touch her!'

A thunk, brutal and hard. Amber made a guttural noise.

'Shut up or we'll tape you again.'

Sweat broke out on Reese's skin. She heard the sound of Amber's ragged breath across the room.

Footsteps shuffled across the dirt. 'Maybe she likes to be gagged,' said one man. The others laughed.

Reese concentrated on breathing. They wouldn't do anything to Amber, would they? Her brain was so foggy that part of her felt as if she must be dreaming this.

'Let's take a look at you. Just how alien are you?'

A snicker went through the men again. Desperately, Reese tried to figure out how many there were. Three? Four? She opened her eyes a sliver. The basement leaped into view, the overhead light seeming bright as a mini sun. It made her head pound. She winced and then froze, but she soon realized none of the men was looking in her direction at all. They were the soldiers from the van, and they were all on the other side of the basement standing in front of Amber, their backs to Reese. She couldn't see Amber clearly, but she did see something move through the men's legs.

'Nice shoes,' one of the soldiers said.

'Who's looking at her shoes? You got something you wanna tell us, Carter?' More laughter.

Reese's gaze darted around the basement, searching frantically for something, anything she could use to get away from this place. She saw David lying in a heap in another corner, face-down and turned away from her. She couldn't tell if he was awake or not. *David?* she thought, but her head throbbed when she tried to communicate with him. It felt as if a thick, cloaking blanket had been tossed over her mind, muffling her ability to project her thoughts. She couldn't focus enough to be sure that he had heard her.

Reese looked back at the soldiers. She was afraid to watch but too terrified to look away. The men moved slightly and Amber came into view through a narrow gap between two legs. She was huddled on her side, knees bent, her dress hitched up to her thighs.

'Open up, Blondie,' one of the soldiers said. Reese thought it was Carter.

'Get away from me,' Amber hissed, pushing herself away from them until she struck the wall.

'There's nowhere for you to go,' Carter said.

'I thought your people were *friendly*,' said another soldier. That got a big laugh.

'Not to assholes,' Amber spit out.

'Oooh, she's got some fire in her,' one soldier said, and then he stepped forward and smacked her. 'Shut up.'

'Now, here's how we're gonna do this,' said Carter, who was

obviously the leader. 'Wilson, go upstairs and shut the door.'

'Why?' said Wilson. Reese remembered that he had been the first one down here. 'What sorta shit you thinking of pulling? You know Torres ain't gonna stand for that.'

'Torres ain't here,' Carter growled. 'Go upstairs and shut the door.'

Wilson glared at the other soldier, but Reese saw him make the decision to give in. He was outnumbered. There was one of him and three of them, and if they were all Blue Base soldiers, he had no chance, even if he was one too. He gave the other soldiers a disgusted look and stomped up the stairs.

'Aiiight,' said Carter, clapping his hands together. 'Come on, E.T. Let's see what you got.'

One of the men bent down to grab Amber's ankle and she kicked him, the heel of her shoe digging into his arm. He grunted in shock and cursed before yanking her shoe off and throwing it out of the way. Reese watched it spin across the floor, black patent leather still shining in the light of the bare bulb. She thought she was going to vomit.

Amber was screaming now, loudly, cursing at them over and over. The men laughed as they pulled off her other shoe and held her legs down.

Reese took a deep breath. She opened her eyes fully, and with a groan, she lurched onto her side and scrambled to her knees. Her muscles were sluggish and she still couldn't think clearly, but she knew she had to do something. Before she had a chance, someone came running out of nowhere and rammed into one of the soldiers.

It was David. She heard the thud of his head meeting the

hard muscle of the soldier's body, and the surprised *oof* as the man swayed on his feet.

'What the—'

David rammed himself into another soldier. It was like tossing pebbles at a brick wall, but the soldiers were initially so startled that he at least got them to move away from Amber.

'You awake, chinky?' one of the soldiers snarled. He grabbed David and slammed him against the wall, and Reese felt the impact like a physical blow to her stomach.

The pain seemed to clear her head – and David's. She became briefly aware of him struggling through the remnants of the sedative to tell her something, but his thoughts slid away before she could grasp them. She saw David's head lolling against his shoulder, his chest heaving. The soldiers turned in unison to face him. He met Reese's gaze from across the room and shook his head slightly. She felt him urging her to stay put in a fierce wave of *Don't move*. Then one of the soldiers punched him in the face. Blood spattered across the dirt floor.

'Maybe the boy just wants his turn,' said Carter.

David launched himself, battered face and all, directly at the soldier. The man caught him as if he was plucking a ball out of the air and threw him against the floor. David made a sound between a yelp and a muffled scream. Reese felt his pain burst through him like an electric shock, and then he went unconscious.

Reese got to her feet just as Amber did. They saw each other across the space of the basement, and at the same time, they both ran at the soldier who had thrown David to the floor. But it was pointless. One of the men grabbed Reese and said, 'Look who's awake.' She cried out against the tape over her mouth as he jerked her arms back. Amber shrieked as another soldier caught her.

The door at the top of the stairs crashed open. A woman's voice called down, 'What the hell is going on down there?'

The man who was holding Reese spun around to face the stairs, bringing her with him. A woman in fatigues came down. She had black hair pulled into a tight bun at the nape of her neck and a scowl on her face that could choke someone twenty feet away.

'The kids are awake,' said the soldier who had punched David.

'Yeah? Did you wake them by beating them up?' the woman asked.

'We were just having some fun,' said the man holding Reese.

'They're not for your fun,' the woman said coldly. 'Do you know what would happen if they got damaged?'

'They're supposed to heal fast,' said the soldier holding Amber. 'We wouldn't hurt 'em. We were just checking out the alien chick.'

The woman glared at him. 'Put them down and drug them up and don't ever do this again. Do you understand?'

'Yes, ma'am,' they all said in unison.

Reese was deposited back into her corner. David was dragged over to another. Amber was taken back to her wall and she slid down to the floor. One of the soldiers opened a case that Reese hadn't noticed before. He pulled out a hypodermic needle.

She squirmed, moaning against the tape. She didn't want to

be put under again. She didn't know what the soldiers would do to them while they were unconscious.

The woman took the needle from the soldier and came over to Reese, squatting beside her. She had brown skin and full lips and dark eyes that seemed to burn with a frightening fever. 'Shut up,' she said. And then she plunged the needle into Reese's shoulder.

CHAPTER 36

Voices trickled through the floorboards. Reese tried to listen but her brain wouldn't focus.

'. . . handoff was supposed to happen yesterday,' a man said.

'What's the delay?' a different man asked.

'We're waiting for Randall to make up her mind,' said the first person.

'That's what happens when the president's a woman. Can't make up her fucking mind.'

'Shut up,' said a woman's voice. A thud.

'Jesus, Torres.'

Reese blinked in the dark. She was facing the center of the basement. The slivers of light that shone through the floorboards above weren't enough to cut the gloom, but they gave her an idea of where she was.

'They should be awake again.' The voice came from a woman, but it wasn't the woman who had come downstairs before.

'We'll go down and check.' That was the woman from

before. It had to be Torres.

'You want me to go?' Reese thought the man speaking was Wilson.

'No,' said Torres. 'You stay up here and keep an eye on the boys. I don't want them near the kids again. Griffin and I will go.'

The door opened and Reese lay still, her pulse speeding up as Torres and Griffin came downstairs. Reese heard a clunk as a box was set on the ground. The needles. A couple more thumps sounded like plastic bottles. Reese heard the women walk away from her; they were checking on Amber or David first.

'They must have really clocked him,' Griffin said. 'His face is still bruised and he's still out.'

'We don't know how fast they heal,' Torres said.

'I should examine him. You can't just give a kid a concussion and then dope him up and expect him to be okay.'

'Go ahead. I'll check the others.'

Reese listened to Torres walk across the basement. She heard a moan from Amber. 'This one's almost up,' Torres said. Her footsteps came over to Reese, and a moment later Reese felt the woman nudge her shoulder. 'How about you?'

Reese held still for a moment, trying to stretch her consciousness toward Torres. But the woman was barely touching her, and Reese's brain was still so fuzzy from the drugs that all she got was a vague sensation of hardness, like a shell. She opened her eyes. Torres was looking directly at her.

'I knew you were awake,' Torres said. 'Dinnertime.' She pulled Reese up to a seated position as easily as if Reese weighed nothing. 'I'm gonna take off the tape, but if you make any noise, I'll put it right back on. Understand?'

Reese nodded, and Torres ripped off the tape. Reese let out a short cry of pain. Torres considered Reese.

'I'm gonna cut your hands free so you can feed yourself. You aren't gonna do anything else.'

Reese shook her head. Her lips were cracked and dry. 'Water?'

'I got that too.' Torres turned Reese around. Reese heard the flick of a pocketknife, and then the plastic bindings were gone.

Her arms ached as she brought her hands in front of herself. Torres opened a water bottle and held it up to Reese's mouth. She reached for it with numb hands, trying to hold it in place. The liquid sloshed over her chin but it was the best thing she had ever tasted in her entire life. She sucked at the bottle greedily, swallowing as much as she could. When she was finished, her hands were tingling, the blood surging into her fingers.

Torres unwrapped an energy bar and handed it to her. 'Eat up,' she said, and then went across the room to Amber.

Reese ate the bar. It tasted like plastic coated with peanut butter, but she wasn't about to complain. Even though it smelled disgusting, her stomach still growled. Torres had left the water bottle with her, and when she was finished inhaling the energy bar she picked it up and drank the last few drops, holding her head back to drain it. The food and water pushed away some of the fog in her mind, and she watched as Torres gave Amber the same treatment. David was still being examined by Griffin and hadn't moved.

Torres glanced across the basement at Reese. 'You finished?'

'Yeah,' Reese said hoarsely.

Amber's face was in shadow but she said, 'Reese? Are you okay?'

'Shut up,' Torres said almost automatically. 'Eat your dinner.'

'I'm fine,' Reese said anyway.

Torres crossed the room in a flash, leaning over her. 'I said no talking.' Torres pulled a plastic strip from a receptacle on her belt. 'Hold up your hands.'

'Wait,' Reese said, desperation spiking in her. 'Please. I have to – let me go to the bathroom. Please.'

Torres's expression gave nothing away, and Reese didn't think she would say yes. But at the last second she nodded shortly. 'Fine. I'll take you.' She glanced over her shoulder. 'Griffin, you got it under control?'

'Yeah. This one's gonna be out for a while longer. I'll watch E.T.'

'All right.' Torres reached for Reese's arm and hauled her to her feet. She wobbled. 'No funny business, Holloway.'

The sound of her last name startled her. 'I know,' she said quickly. Torres led her toward the steps, keeping a viselike grip on her arm. Reese stumbled up the stairs, nauseated from having eaten the energy bar too quickly, and Torres's consciousness began to seep through her hand into Reese.

Torres didn't feel exactly like the male Blue Base soldiers. Reese remembered the sensation of something being off about them, as if their brains were so wired for combat readiness that they were unable to manage ordinary thought patterns. Torres had the same dense physical interior landscape, as if her muscles were made of Kevlar and her bones out of steel, but the feeling of wrongness was different. Unlike the chaotic consciousness of the male soldiers, Torres's brain was sharp as a blade, but it didn't feel normal. It felt speedy. Too fast for her own good.

Reese didn't have time to dwell on it. Torres pushed her up the stairs into the kitchen, a 1980s time warp with stained linoleum on the floor, a rickety wooden table, and appliances that didn't look like they had worked in years. All the windows had their curtains drawn, and the lack of light behind them made Reese believe it was nighttime. Wilson, who was standing at the back door with a machine gun in his hands, was surprised to see them. Torres said nothing to him and only propelled Reese through the kitchen into a dimly lit hallway, where she nudged open a door with the toe of her boot.

Torres came into the bathroom too. She let Reese go, but stood with her back to the door. 'Do your business,' Torres ordered.

Reese's face reddened, but she didn't bother to ask for privacy. She went to the toilet and did what she had to do. 'What day is it?' she asked. 'How long was I out?'

'I told you no talking,' Torres growled.

Reese flushed the toilet and glanced at Torres out of the corner of her eye. She was hardened, but she didn't look too much older than Reese. Maybe she was in her twenties. Reese wondered how Torres had gotten to her position. The men were clearly afraid of her. Reese figured she should probably be afraid of her too, but she couldn't forget that Torres had been the one to stop the soldiers from assaulting them.

Reese turned on the sink and found a bar of yellowing soap on the counter. She washed her hands, running her fingers tentatively over the welts from the plastic restraints. Above the sink, the mirror on the wall was cracked. Her face was sickly pale, her hair tangled, her eyes bloodshot. There was a raw red line in a rectangular shape around her mouth where the tape had been ripped off. She saw Torres watching her.

'It's Tuesday night,' Torres said.

Reese briefly caught Torres's eye in the mirror. Why had she answered? Reese rinsed the soap off her hands while she worked out what exactly that meant. She, David, and Amber had been taken from the UN on Monday just before noon. They had been gone for thirty-six hours by now. There was no sound of traffic outside, so Reese doubted they were still in New York City. Maybe Torres had mixed feelings about taking them – or at least about keeping them here, wherever they were. She decided to push her luck.

'Where are we?' Reese asked.

'Doesn't matter.'

There was a rusty towel ring dangling empty on the wall near the sink, but no towels in sight. Reese flicked the water from her hands. 'You're from Blue Base,' Reese said.

Torres reached for her and spun her around, her fingers digging into Reese's shoulder bones. Reese swallowed a cry of pain as Torres glared at her. 'No. Talking.'

Even though Eres Tilhar had told Reese it was against Imrian ethics to access someone else's consciousness without their permission, she decided this situation was an exception. She kept her gaze on Torres's face as she reached out with her mind. She wasn't sure what she was looking for, but she knew she had to make use of every advantage she had. Torres and the other Blue Base soldiers obviously had been genetically modified, but they hadn't been through the Imrian adaptation chamber. Reese didn't think that Torres would be able to sense her mental intrusion.

'So you know about Blue Base. You think you know it all, don't you?' Torres said, considering her.

'No,' Reese said. There was definitely something different about Torres. She might not be as unhinged as the other soldiers, but she seemed more dangerous. Like a shark, all teeth and instinct.

'You tell me something, Holloway,' Torres said in a low, threatening voice. 'You tell me: What did you get done to your head that I didn't get done to mine? Why are you so precious that I have to babysit a squad of muscle heads to bring you in? What did they do to you?'

'They – the Imria adapted me,' Reese stammered. 'They gave me their DNA.'

'I got that DNA too.'

'You got it from the military. Not the Imria.'

'What does that matter? Same DNA. But you're nothing like me.' Torres sounded disgusted and let go of her, giving her a little shove.

Reese fell back against the sink. Torres's grip had been so tight that it seemed to have left a phantom handprint on her shoulder. She reached up to rub the bruised area, wincing. Her eyes darted behind Torres to the closed door. There was no way she'd be able to get past the soldier. 'Maybe it's the same DNA, but I don't think the military knows how to use it,' she said, trying to buy time while she figured out what to do. 'You guys – you and the other soldiers – you don't feel right.'

'We don't *feel right*? We can run faster, sleep less, and shoot better than any *normal* human being. We don't *feel right* because we're different.' Torres leaned closer to Reese. 'I know why they made me the way they did. I was recruited out of nothing. I probably would've been in prison by now if I hadn't joined up. But I wasn't born stupid. They made me into a killer, and I'm doing that fine. Way better than those dumbasses they want me to order around. I can take all of them, every single one of those shit-for-brains fucktards the military calls supersoldiers. But why do they want you? You can't do shit. I could snap you with my little finger.'

Torres's words were harsh, but there was an edge of desperation to her words that Reese didn't understand. 'The adaptation procedure isn't supposed to make us into killers,' Reese said. 'The point of it is to help us communicate better. To share our – our thoughts and emotions.'

Torres nodded. 'That freaky mind meldy thing they talk about in the news. Yeah. What good is that?'

Reese gaped at her. 'What good is it to be a killer?'

Torres's face darkened and Reese thought she was going to hit her. Instead she grabbed a fistful of Reese's hair, jerking her head back so she was forced to meet her gaze. 'You can do that mind meld thing, can't you?' Torres said. Tears blinded Reese's eyes as Torres's fingers tightened on her hair. She was so close that Reese could smell the sourness of the soldier's breath. 'So you do it. You do it and you tell me what's the deal with me. What the fuck is going on with me? Tell me.' Torres's dark eyes gleamed with a manic energy.

'Okay, I'll do it,' Reese choked out. 'Just let me go. I can't do it if you're holding me like that.'

With a sound of disgust, Torres dropped her. Reese took a shaking, relieved breath, rubbing a damp hand over her scalp where Torres had held her motionless.

'We don't have all night,' Torres snapped.

Reese blinked back her tears. She didn't think Torres would be sympathetic. 'I have to touch you,' she said bluntly.

Torres seemed taken aback. 'Where?'

'Just give me your hand.' Torres looked at her suspiciously, and all the fear and panic inside Reese exploded into impatience. 'Do you want me to do it or not?' she demanded.

Torres hesitated for a second. Then she held her hand out as if offering it to Reese to shake. 'Do it.'

The soldier's palm was calloused, her fingertips rough. Reese wasn't sure if she'd be able to sense anything at all; Torres had been mostly unreadable before, beyond a general sensation of predatory skill. And even if she could gain access to Torres's consciousness, that wouldn't necessarily explain what her 'deal' was. Reese only hoped she could sense something that would give her a clue about what Torres wanted to hear – and then Reese planned to tell her precisely that.

She concentrated, beginning with her sense of herself as Eres Tilhar had taught her. Those lessons seemed an eternity ago, but as she laid out the map of her consciousness, situating herself physically within her mind and within this space – this bathroom, in this house, standing a foot away from Torres – Eres's instructions came to her clear and strong. Reese was *here*. She took a deep breath, grounding herself, feeling the hard edge of the sink behind her, smelling the foul scent of a bathroom that hadn't been cleaned in forever. She was unexpectedly grateful that Torres had grabbed her hair, because the throbbing pain on her scalp showed her the precise limits of her physical self.

When she was satisfied that she knew where she was, she opened herself to Torres's mind. The soldier was tense, and at first all Reese could feel was that tension. Muscle and bone, dense and powerful, built for exactly what Torres had said: killing. Behind that physical barrier, Torres's consciousness confronted Reese like a blank wall. As Reese mentally circled the wall, she sensed Torres's emotions slowly shifting like tectonic plates grinding into new positions. And as the woman's internal landscape shifted, Reese glimpsed memories that Torres didn't know how to conceal. They were dark and brutal, and Reese clung to her own identity, trying to shield herself from the images' assault so they wouldn't overwhelm her.

The dirty line where a wall met the filthy floor. The flickering light of a television casting shadows over something she didn't want to see. The recoil of a gun in her hand as tin cans flew off the edge of a fence. Someone's birthday. Off-key singing, a candle that wouldn't blow out. A dusty backyard at midnight, yellow light leaching out from a curtained window. A boy. A little boy with a bruised face and a cut lip, who said, *Don't go*.

Then Reese recognized the Nevada desert: hot sun on brown dirt and rocks. Running for miles with nowhere to go. Men and women beside her in matching fatigues, every one of them watching her warily as she sprinted, one foot after the other, wishing she could outrun this place, this thing they had done to her. The memory skipped, and Reese saw Torres's hands holding a soldier down beneath muddy water, cutting off the pulse in his throat. His esophagus collapsed beneath Torres's fingers, and she rocked back on her heels, feeling as if an animal had clawed its way out of her body.

Reese recoiled from Torres's consciousness. In front of her Torres was watching her intently, hopefully, and Reese said, 'Wait. Almost.' She forced herself to go back in because she knew she was close. It was there, nearly buried beneath all those black memories, beneath the armor of Torres's anger and cunning. It was in the rapid pulse of her heart, the speed with which her blood pumped through her body, the iron of her muscles and sinews. Reese understood her deal.

'You're dying, aren't you?' Reese whispered. Torres's body was burning up her physical energy at a rate that Reese couldn't believe. She couldn't replenish herself fast enough. Inside Torres's body, Reese felt the decay eating away at her, like a corpse rotting into the ground.

Torres's face was grim. She didn't seem surprised. 'This thing they did to me is going to kill me?'

Cold sweat trickled down Reese's back. 'You don't have to die,' she said, grasping at straws. 'The Imria – they can save you.' She had no idea if it was true or not, but it was the only thing she could think of.

Reese sensed a spark of hope flare within the soldier, but it was extinguished before it had a chance to burst into flame.

Torres jerked her hand away from Reese. 'You're lying. Don't lie to me.'

'I'm not lying,' Reese insisted. 'Help us get back to the Imria and we'll ask them. They have really advanced science—'

'As advanced as the shit the military stole to fix me up? I don't think I want any more of that science.'

'The military screwed up. The Imria won't. I swear. They didn't screw up with me.' For the first time since she had woken up in that hospital after the car accident, Reese realized it was true. The Imria hadn't screwed up with her. The thought was so startling that it sent a shudder through her body.

Torres stared at her long and hard. Her face was expressionless, but Reese knew the soldier was spinning through every possible option to keep herself alive. Finally she leaned close, her breath hot on Reese's ear. 'If I leave, they'll take my kid. It's too late for me. I'm in too deep. You better not say shit about what you just told me. You say anything and I'll come and kill you myself.'

Ice went down Reese's back. 'I won't say anything, I swear.'

Torres drew back. 'Give me your hands.'

Her heart pounding, Reese held them out, wondering if Torres was going to ask her to look again, but instead Torres pulled out a plastic restraint. The efficient jerk of the plastic against her already sore wrists drove a gasp out of Reese.

'Back downstairs,' Torres said, opening the door. 'No funny business, Holloway.'

Reese didn't resist as Torres pushed her out of the bathroom. At least her hands were in front of her this time.

CHAPTER 37

Griffin was a medic. Reese couldn't tell whether she had been genetically modified like the other soldiers because she didn't touch Reese, but there was something horribly wrong with Griffin's right hand. It looked as if it had been cut off, leaving the blunt stump of her forearm behind. Out of that stump grew three fingers, nailless and limp. Griffin used her left hand to raise the needle to Reese's shoulder and caught Reese's eye.

'What're you lookin' at?' she said in a rough voice.

'Nothing,' Reese said, averting her gaze. 'Please don't give me any more drugs. They're messing me up.'

'That's the point.' But Griffin paused and squirted some of the liquid out of the syringe before she plunged the needle into Reese's arm.

It was still dark in the basement when Reese awoke. She heard the sound of breathing from the other side of the room. David and Amber. She tried to focus her mind, to seek out David. She was still foggy from the drug, but it wasn't as bad as the first time she woke up. *David?* There was no response, and she thought he must still be unconscious.

Reese scooted back until she bumped against the wall, and then pushed herself into a seated position. Her back hurt, her shoulders hurt, and her hands were numb from the restraints, but it felt better to sit up. She stiffened as footsteps sounded above.

Torres's voice filtered through the floorboards. 'Orders came in. We'll move them after dark.'

'Who's taking point?' Wilson asked.

'You'll drive. Carter'll sit in the back to keep an eye on them. The rest of us will go separately in the truck, and the agent will follow you.'

'You're leaving them with just Carter?'

'You think he can't handle three drugged-out teenagers?'

'No, ma'am. I mean, of course he can.'

There was a long pause, and Reese got the impression that Torres was speaking more quietly, but she couldn't make out a single word.

'I'll go check the vehicles,' Wilson said.

'You do that,' Torres said.

Reese heard the back door open and close. A chair dragged across the kitchen floor. Then nothing.

Reese.

Her head snapped in David's direction. *David? Are you awake?* She got to her feet, her knees wobbling.

I'm awake.

She walked toward him carefully, trying to remember where he was in the dark basement. When her foot nudged David's back she knelt down, her bound hands touching his shoulders and neck. He moved slightly. 'Are you okay?' she whispered.

He felt groggy inside, and beyond that there was pain in his jaw from where the soldier had struck him.

'I'm okay,' he said, wincing as he tried to roll over.

She helped him to sit up.

'Did they hurt you?' he asked.

'No. That woman, Torres, she stopped them.'

'Is Amber okay?'

'I think so. She's still asleep.'

'How long have we been down here? We have to—'

'Shh.' Reese heard footsteps again and they both froze. *Have the drugs worn off enough that you can hear me clearly?* she asked him silently.

I think so.

The footsteps faded away. *Then listen.* She told him what she had heard right before he woke up. *We have to get away from them. When they move us, that will be our best chance.*

You think we can get past Carter?

We don't have a choice.

When Torres, Griffin, and Wilson came downstairs a few hours later, Reese was back in her designated corner. Amber had woken up only a few minutes before, and Reese had wanted to check on her, but there was no time. Wilson pulled David to his feet, and Griffin went to Amber. 'Where's your shoes, E.T.?' Griffin asked.

Torres found one and then the other, kicking them over to Amber. 'Put them back on,' she said before going to Reese and yanking her up. 'Time to move.'

Griffin and Wilson went upstairs first, pushing their charges ahead of them. Torres drew Reese close and whispered in her ear, 'Wilson will stop the vehicle. He'll give you ten minutes. If you can deal with Carter and the special agent, you're out. *You owe me*. Diego Luis Torres. Children's Home of Los Angeles. Don't forget.' She shoved Reese toward the stairs.

Stunned, Reese began to climb, Torres's words echoing in her brain. *You owe me*. Torres was going to give them a chance.

She didn't have long to be happy about it. Outside, it was nighttime and it smelled like the middle of nowhere: dirt and grass and nothing. A bare bulb over the kitchen door revealed a farmhouse with dingy, peeling siding. Several vehicles were parked on the concrete driveway. One was an army truck, and Reese saw movement in the back that made her suspect several of the Blue Base soldiers were inside. The second vehicle was a champagne-colored sedan, the same model as the one used by Agent Forrestal in San Francisco. She wasn't surprised to see a man in black leaning against the side of it. The third was a blue van, the kind that paranoid parents on television always pointed to and said, 'Don't ever get into one of those.' Next to the van was the soldier who was going to escort them. Reese recognized him immediately as one of the men who had threatened Amber and beat up David. Carter.

Reese watched David and Amber climb into the van ahead of her. When she passed Carter, she saw a gun at his waist as well as what looked like a couple of blades. She began to think that Torres's offer of help – if that's what it was – left a lot to be desired.

The interior of the van had two benches in it, just like the SWAT vehicle they had arrived in. David and Amber sat down next to each other, and before Reese had a chance to say a thing, Carter said, 'Other side, lezzy.'

Reese hesitated. He shoved her. She almost went sprawling but managed to find her balance at the last second. She sat down across from Amber, her heart pounding.

'Watch it, Carter,' Torres said. 'They have a scratch on them when they arrive and I'll cut off your balls.'

'Yes, ma'am,' Carter said, sounding as grouchy as he could without pissing her off. 'Ain't Griffin gonna dope 'em up?'

'They've been doped too many times. We do it again and they might die. You saying you can't handle three skinny teenagers, two of 'em girls?'

Carter's shoulders stiffened. 'No, ma'am.'

'You'll get a message when we have the location specifics.'

'Yes, ma'am.' Carter climbed in and sat down next to Reese. She inched as far away from him as she could.

Torres looked into the van, her gaze pausing on Reese. 'All right. See you later, kids.' She slammed the van doors shut, and they were in the dark until Carter reached past Reese to bang on the panel separating the cab from the back.

'Lights, Wilson,' he called.

A moment later a dome light snapped on. Reese heard the van's driver-side door close, and then the engine turned on. As the van started to move, she looked at Amber. Her hair was matted on one side with dirt, there was a dull bruise on her cheek, and her wrists were bound together in her lap. Dirt from the basement floor was smeared all over her knees and shins. She gave Reese a pointed stare, her jaw clenched tight, as if to say *We have to get out of here*.

Reese nodded very slightly – she didn't want Carter to notice – and glanced at David. She was vaguely surprised to see that he was still wearing his tie. It hung askew from his loosened collar, now soiled with the blood that had trickled down from his face. There was a black stain on his cheek from his nose to his mouth, and even though Reese knew he healed quickly, the sight of it made her stomach lurch. His eyes turned to hers briefly.

Carter's watching me, he thought.

Torres is helping us, she told him. He kept the surprise from his face. *She said the van will stop, but we have to get out on our own. We have to take out Carter and the man in black following us.*

Shit.

They rode in silence for a while as they tried to come up with a plan. Reese knew that the three of them would have to work together, but even if they all attacked Carter at the same time, it still seemed like a long shot. The man was big and solid and bristling with weapons, and he wasn't going to be nice to them. And then if they did get past Carter, there was the special agent to contend with.

I have to get Carter's gun, she told David. *That's the only way.*

David's gaze lowered. Reese guessed he was trying to assess the soldier's weapons. Finally he thought: *I'll kick him.*

What? That's not gonna do much.

I'll kick him in the face. When he's distracted, grab the gun.

She stretched her wrists against the plastic restraint. *We need to cut these off.*

We'll take his knives too.

What about Amber? You need to tell her. There was no way for

Reese to communicate with Amber when the whole width of the van was between them, but David was sitting only a few inches away from her. She sensed David's dismay as he realized this, and for a second his eyes flickered toward Reese.

Okay, he thought. She saw him begin to move incrementally closer to Amber.

It seemed to take forever, because Carter was keeping his eyes on both David and Amber, but when the van turned a corner, David used the momentum to slide up next to her. After they rounded the bend, Reese saw that his leg was pressed against Amber's, and she was keeping a carefully blank face.

A beeping sound came from Carter, and Reese watched out of the corner of her eye as he removed a device from his pocket. It looked like a cell phone, although it was encased in some kind of thick, protective covering. He pressed something on the screen and then held it up to his ear.

'Wilson, we have the location,' Carter said.

Wilson's voice could be heard through the phone, tinny and unclear.

'Christ, you gotta be kidding me,' Carter said, disgruntled. 'Fine. Five minutes.'

I told her, David thought to Reese.

She glanced at Amber, whose face was slightly flushed, her eyes lowered.

She's in?

Of course she's in. David seemed a little rattled, and Reese wondered what else he and Amber had communicated, but this was definitely not the time to ask him.

Carter slid the phone into a holster on his hip next to one

of his knives, and Reese tried to visualize where his gun was. It was on his right hip, next to her. The phone was toward the front, and the blades and an extra ammunition clip were attached on his left. Thinking about how she could grab the gun made nervous sweat break out on her skin. She had gone shooting with her mom once before, when a particularly nasty case had terrified her into believing she needed to teach Reese how to handle a gun. Reese had thought her mom was crazy at the time, but in retrospect, maybe her mom had done her a favor. They had gone to a police shooting range and her mom's friend Jose Gutierrez had walked her through the whole thing: loading the clip, the stance she should take, how to aim. The only thing she remembered clearly now was that the handgun scared her half to death the first time she shot it, the kick jerking her arms back so that the bullet completely missed the target. She was no expert on guns, but Carter's weapon didn't look that different from the one she had shot. She desperately hoped it wasn't. She was grateful that he wasn't carrying a machine gun.

The van began to slow down, and Reese tensed up. She looked at Amber and David. They tried to appear relaxed, but she could tell they had noticed too.

You ready? David asked.

No, Reese thought.

The van pulled to a stop. Reese thought her heart was going to jump right out of her chest, and nothing had even happened yet.

On my count, David told her. *One, two—*

She was definitely not ready. David leaned back against the

van wall and kicked Carter straight in the face with both feet, shoving the soldier's nose back. Blood spurted from his nostrils as he let out a guttural cry, and David kicked him again before he could recover. Reese heard the awful crunch of cartilage as Carter's nose broke.

Reese lurched at the soldier, her bound hands extended to tug the gun out of its holster. To her utter shock, she got to it before Carter noticed her. The gun was heavy and cold and she scrambled to her feet, trying to point it at him. He lunged at her, blood pouring down his face, and managed to shove her backward into the rear wall. Her head slammed into the steel.

'Wilson!' he shouted. 'Wilson, get in here!'

David was on his feet trying to drag Carter away from Reese, who had backed up into the corner, but the soldier threw him off like a fly. David smashed into the doors. In the second that Carter was distracted, Reese raised the gun, bracing herself as she aimed for his leg. She squeezed the trigger just as Amber seemed to come out of nowhere and plunged the heel of her shoe into Carter's neck. The noise of the gunshot was so loud in the enclosed space of the van that Reese's ears began to ring. Carter collapsed, screaming. The bullet had torn into his stomach, and Amber was standing above him with her shoe still in her hand, blood dripping from the heel and onto a horrible-looking gash on Carter's neck.

'Oh my God,' Amber cried, face white. 'You shot him. You shot him!'

'Are you okay?' Reese asked, appalled by how close Amber had come to the bullet. 'I didn't know you were going to do that – I could have shot you!'

'I'm okay,' Amber said, although she looked like she was about to pass out. She dropped the shoe, and it bounced off Carter's twitching body and onto the metal floor of the van. She backed away, bumping into David, who was trying to unlock the van doors.

Reese pushed herself to her feet and edged around Carter. His eyes had rolled back in their sockets, and he seemed to be on the verge of falling unconscious. The doors opened and Reese felt the night air blowing into the vehicle. She noticed that one of the knives on Carter's belt was gone – David must have grabbed it somehow – but the phone was still there. Before she could second-guess herself, she knelt down and pulled it off his belt, juggling it in her bound hands with the gun, and jumped out of the van.

A car's headlights nearly blinded her. The vehicle screeched to a halt a few feet away, and the door opened. Reese raised her hands, squinting into the glare, and pointed the gun at the man in black.

CHAPTER 38

'Put the gun down!' the agent ordered.

She didn't budge, though her hands trembled. Beside her Amber was breathing rapidly. Reese couldn't see David. *David? Where are you?* She began to edge over to the right, trying to get out of the headlight beams.

'Stop moving and put the gun down,' the agent yelled. He was a black shadow pointing at her. She knew he was holding a gun too.

'No,' she said. 'We're leaving.' Her hands were slippery with sweat and she thought about dropping Carter's phone, but she wanted it. Evidence. She pressed the device against the weapon and let her finger hover over the trigger.

'You don't know what you're doing,' the agent said.

She took another step to the right. The headlights were no longer directly in front of her, and she saw the gleam of his weapon lit up on one side. 'How do you know that?' she demanded, fear and anger bursting out of her. 'I shot that guy.' She thought again: *David? Where are you?*

I'm here.

His presence in her mind made everything around her snap into focus. It was like being at the eye doctor's office and having the proper lens slide into place, and what had previously been a blur was now crystal clear. Reese was near the edge of the road, the van doors gaping open behind her. Amber was to her left, still trapped in the beams of the agent's headlights. David had somehow snuck behind the sedan and was creeping up behind the man in black. He had a rock in his hands. She knew what he was going to do.

'Put the weapon down and we can make sure you aren't prosecuted for that,' the agent said.

David smashed the rock into the back of the agent's head. The man lurched, letting out a surprised grunt. David struck him again,. and the agent collapsed against the side of the car, sliding down to the ground. David threw the rock away and pulled the agent's gun from his limp hands. 'Come on, we have to get out of here.'

'Should we take the car?' Reese asked, gesturing at the sedan.

'It's probably got a tracking device in it,' Amber said. They all froze as a sound came from the front of the van. Wilson. Reese didn't know what kind of deal Torres had struck with Wilson to persuade him to give them ten minutes, but the time would be up soon if it wasn't already. She didn't want to stick around to deal with Wilson if he decided he had to get out of the van.

A crescent moon was rising in the east, sending a dim light over a field of knee-high grass that stretched away from the road. 'Across the field,' Reese said. 'Let's go.'

The grass crunched as they sprinted through it, the sound of their footsteps thumping dully on the earth. Reese was wearing flats, and as she ran her shoes slid across the uneven ground, nearly tripping her several times. She soon realized she had it easy, because Amber had been forced to pull off her other shoe and was now running barefoot. She began to slow down, wincing as she ran. Reese glanced behind them, but she couldn't see anyone following, and she hadn't heard the van's engine start up again.

The ground began to slope down, and in the distance Reese saw the glint of water. She still gripped the gun and the phone in her bound hands as she tried to avoid tumbling down the hill in her slippery shoes. David slowed as he approached the edge of the creek and turned back to wait for Reese and Amber. He put the gun he had been holding on the ground and pulled something out of his pocket: one of Carter's knives. 'Come here,' he said, flicking open the blade.

Reese held out her hands and he sliced through the plastic restraint. She put Carter's gun down and pocketed the phone before taking the knife to cut David free.

'What is that?' David asked, nodding at the phone.

'I took Carter's phone for evidence.'

'Turn it off,' Amber said as she scrambled down the slope. 'Turn it off now. They could be using it to track us.'

Reese felt as if a bucket of cold water had been dumped on her. She pulled out the phone and scrutinized it in the dim moonlight. 'I can't find the power button.'

David sliced off Amber's wrist restraints as she said, 'Give it to me.' Reese handed it over. Amber inspected it up close, and then she pressed her fingertip into the back of the phone and removed the thick exterior case. The device beeped.

'What are you doing?' David asked.

'Taking out the battery.' Amber pulled it out and gave it to Reese. The screen of the phone flashed once and then died.

'I'm sorry,' Reese said. 'I just wanted some evidence – I didn't think—' She squeezed the battery.

'It's okay,' Amber said, sounding tired. 'It was smart to take it for later.'

'We don't know if they could track us with it,' David said, rubbing a hand over his forehead.

'Well, now they can't,' Amber said. 'Hopefully. We ready to go?'

'Yeah,' David said, picking up the agent's gun.

'Wait,' Reese said. She pocketed the disassembled phone and took off her jacket. 'Give me the knife.' When David gave it to her, she poked the tip of the blade through the seams, detaching the sleeves and handing them to Amber. 'Wrap these around your feet.'

'I don't think that's going to work,' Amber said dubiously, but she took the two sleeves anyway and wound them around her feet, flinching as she did so.

Reese handed the knife back to David and glanced up the hill behind them, then across the creek. 'It's not that deep, is it?'

'You want to cross it?' David asked.

'Where else are we going to go?' Reese slid her arms through the now-sleeveless jacket and picked up Carter's gun from the ground.

'Let's just do it,' Amber said. 'The farther we can get the better. We'll just keep running east toward the moon so we don't go in circles.' She finished wrapping her feet. 'Sorry about ruining your jacket.'

'It's okay. Sorry you ruined your shoes.'

Amber let out a choked laugh. 'I'm not.'

The creek was only a few feet deep in the middle. Mud squished beneath their feet as they waded across. They clambered out onto the opposite bank and started up the hill. When they reached the crest, they stopped to look across another field of grass.

Reese saw a single light in the distance. 'Do you think that's a house?'

'Maybe,' Amber said.

They began to walk toward it. Reese kept listening for any sounds of pursuit, but the night was quiet, with only the faint whisper of the cool wind blowing through the grasses. By the time they reached the edge of the field, the moon was straight overhead, and Reese guessed they had been walking for at least an hour or two. The light she had seen from the riverbank did come from a house; they could see the outline of its roof against the night sky. As they drew closer she saw it was an exterior light attached to a carport, where a dirty white truck was parked. They halted about a hundred feet from the edge of the field and the house.

'Do you think we should just go knock on the door?' Reese whispered.

'It's the middle of the night, I don't know,' Amber said.

The sound of a car engine could be heard in the distance,

and a moment later headlights came toward the carport. 'Get down,' David said, crouching onto the ground. Reese and Amber dropped onto the dirt.

'Maybe it's just some guy coming home late,' Reese said.

The vehicle pulled up to the carport. It was a black-and-white police car.

'Or maybe not,' Amber said.

The engine shut off and the driver's-side door opened. The police officer climbed out. Reese peeked through strands of grass, her chin digging into the ground, and watched the man walk up to the farmhouse. He pressed his fingers against what Reese guessed was a doorbell. When there was no response, he knocked. The sound was small under the vast night sky, like a pin tapping against glass. He stood there for several minutes, pressing the doorbell and knocking, before the door finally opened. A man in boxer shorts and a white T-shirt came out onto the concrete front step.

They couldn't hear the conversation clearly, but they saw the police officer show his identification. The man scratched his head and eventually let the cop into the house. The lights went on room by room.

'Are they searching the place?' David whispered.

'Looks like it,' Reese said.

'Do you think they're looking for us?' Amber asked.

Reese watched the house with growing anxiety. Eventually the lights began to go off, and the front door opened. The officer handed the man a business card before returning to his car. As he drove away, the man closed the front door.

'I think we should keep moving,' David said. 'If they're

looking for us, we can't stay here.'

'But if that cop was looking for us, then he's already checked this place,' Reese said. 'So isn't it safe for us to stay?'

'What are we going to do?' David asked. 'Wait in the field? It's dark now, but when the sun rises we'll be totally obvious.'

'Do you guys know what day it is? Or what night?' Amber asked.

'I think it's Wednesday night,' Reese said. 'When Torres took me to the bathroom she told me it was Tuesday. I don't think it's been more than a day since then.'

'So the guy in the house is going to have to go to work in the morning,' Amber said. 'We should wait till he leaves and then go into his house and call for help on his phone.'

'What if he has a wife or kids or something?' David asked.

'I don't think he does,' Amber said. 'There are no toys in the yard, so probably no kids. And there's only one car. When the lights went on in the house we didn't see anybody else getting up. I think it's just him.'

Reese stared across the field, trying to figure out what the bulky shapes were in the dark. One of them looked like a pile of hay bales. 'Let's go over there,' she said, pointing at the rectangular shapes. 'Maybe we can hide behind those and keep an eye on the house.'

'All right. I guess we can try it,' David said.

They got to their feet and crossed the rest of the field as quietly as they could. It was indeed a pile of hay bales, and Reese realized they must have been running through hay fields earlier. The bales were stacked five feet thick and ten feet high, although the back row was lower. They moved a few of the bales from the rear to create a second low wall to hide behind, hoping that the homeowner wouldn't notice a difference from the front. If they peeked over the low wall of hay they could glimpse the light from the carport. Reese tucked Carter's gun between two hay bales and saw David do the same with the agent's weapon.

As they huddled on the ground in the corner behind the hay, cold seeped through the thin fabric of Reese's pants and she shivered, struck by a wave of exhaustion. Amber was shivering too, her bare arms wrapped around her knees. 'Are your feet okay?' Reese whispered.

'They hurt, but I'll be fine.'

David pulled off his jacket and held it out to Amber. 'Here. You're cold.'

She didn't take it at first, and Reese didn't need to be touching Amber to know that she was surprised by the offer. 'Thanks,' she said after a moment, and took the jacket.

They sat in silence for a while with Reese between David and Amber. Reese heard David lean back against the hay bales. A chilly breeze whistled through the air, ruffling her hair. She realized they were all keeping a careful amount of distance between one another, and it made her heart sink. She drew her knees up, trying to quell the shaking in her body as the aftereffects of what they had done flooded through her. She had shot a man. She didn't know if he was alive or dead. They had fled across a field in the middle of the night and now they were hiding out in order to break into someone's house in the morning. She shuddered again.

David reached out and touched her arm. *Come here.*

He pulled her over to him, putting his arm around her, and after her initial surprise, she let herself lean into him. He was warmer than her, and she felt the steady thump of his heartbeat beneath her cheek while his hand stroked her shoulder. His body buzzed with relief and exhaustion, and she sensed the ache of a bruise on his back from where he had been thrown against the van door.

It's okay, he told her, and his hand sought out the lump on the back of her head, touching it delicately.

She winced and he lowered his hand to her shoulder again, drawing her closer. She wanted to stay there, but it wasn't fair to Amber, and she began to pull away.

Don't, he thought, and then he made a suggestion.

She was taken aback. *I can't.*

You can.

She sensed him withdrawing from her mentally, closing off his consciousness until she was unable to sense anything more than his physical self. It felt almost alien to be like this with him: her body curled into his, her face against his chest, with no connection to his thoughts. She knew why he had withdrawn from her, and yet she couldn't bring herself to follow through on what he suggested. She stayed there, motionless, feeling the rapid flutter of her own heartbeat as she told herself she could do it.

She took a deep breath and closed herself off too. She focused on the pain in her head from where she had hit the back of the van. She focused on the chill on her skin from the cool wind. She focused, and then she reached for Amber.

Amber was shivering beneath David's jacket, and Reese

shifted so that she could put an arm around her. Amber pulled her legs up and tucked herself against Reese, her hair tickling Reese's chin. She drew in a long, quivering breath, as if she were about to cry, and then she exhaled. Slowly, Reese relaxed. She was a lot warmer now. Although she had fully disconnected mentally from both David and Amber, she somehow felt closer to them than she ever had before. As they waited for the sun to rise, she closed her eyes. Tears streaked down her cheeks, and she felt the night air blow gently over her damp face.

CHAPTER 39

When Reese's eyes opened, Amber was gone and the sky was lightening. Reese was still curled in the crook of David's arm, and she felt his lungs rising and falling beneath her cheek. She sat up carefully, trying not to wake him, and looked for Amber.

She was crouched behind one of the hay bales nearby, peering at the house. In the early morning light, Reese saw the blood and dirt caked over Amber's feet, which were still poorly wrapped in the sleeves from her jacket.

'Oh my God, does that hurt?' Reese whispered, crawling over to her.

Amber glanced at her feet and shrugged. 'A little.'

'We have to get that cleaned up.'

Amber smiled slightly. 'Later.' She nodded toward the house. 'I think he's up. I saw a light go on a while ago.'

As Reese watched, another window lit up on the ground floor. Through the mini-blinds, she saw the edge of a refrigerator. 'Have you seen anyone else?'

'No. It's still just the one guy.'

Reese backed away and leaned against the hay. David

stirred, blinking his eyes. The dried blood on his face and neck was cracking. She grimaced. 'Are you all right? That doesn't look so good.'

David sat up, raising his right hand to his face. His hand was covered with dried blood too, and he froze as he saw it.

'Did you hurt your hand?' Reese asked. She reached for it, studying his palm for wounds, and felt him twitch at her touch.

'No,' he said.

She lifted her gaze to his eyes and realized the blood was from the agent's head. David pulled his hand away, looking a little sick.

The sound of a door slamming startled them all. They crawled over to the lower hay bale and peeked over the edge. The kitchen light had gone off, and they saw the homeowner, now dressed in jeans and a sweatshirt and carrying a lunch box and a hard hat, heading to his truck. The engine rumbled and a moment later he pulled out of the carport, heading down the dirt driveway. They waited until the sound of the truck had completely faded away, and then they waited a bit longer, worried that he might have forgotten something and would come back. Finally Reese whispered, 'I think we should go in.' She pulled the gun from its hiding place nearby, and Amber recoiled from her.

'Be careful with that,' Amber said.

'I am.' Reese ejected the clip and counted five bullets before pushing it back into place.

'Do you know how to use that?' Amber asked warily.

'You pull the trigger,' Reese said.

Amber raised an eyebrow. 'Oh really.'

David picked up the agent's gun and got to his feet. 'Let's go,' he said.

'Shit, I forgot you had one too,' Amber said.

'I don't think we should leave them behind,' David said.

Amber eyed his bloody fingers and said, 'You two scare me.' She carefully stood up, barely flinching as she walked around the stacked hay bales and headed for the house.

The front door was locked, and the front window – through which Reese could see a sparsely furnished living room – was locked too. They went to the rear of the house, looking for an easier way in, and found a back door with a square window in it. Reese looked from Amber to David. 'Are we really going to break into this house?'

He shrugged. 'Or we could keep walking and hope someone takes us in?'

She shook her head at him. 'Funny.'

Amber had already begun to look for something to use to break the glass. She returned a minute later with a fist-sized rock. 'Get out of the way,' she said. When they were all a decent distance from the door, she hurled the rock at the glass. It shattered, and the rock dropped through into the house. 'Give me your jacket,' Amber said to Reese.

Reese took it off and handed it over. Amber walked to the door, edging carefully around the fragments of glass that had fallen outside, and wrapped the remains of the jacket over her hand to knock a few more shards out of the window. Then she gingerly reached inside and unlocked the door, pushing it open. 'Voilà,' she said.

'We scare *you*?' Reese said.

Amber shook out the ruined jacket and held it out to Reese. 'I never said it was a bad thing.'

The house was clearly a bachelor's residence. The back door opened into a mudroom that was empty except for an extra pair of work boots and a puffy winter coat. They passed a bathroom with a sink strewn with men's shaving equipment, and a bedroom with an unmade bed and a dresser with several drawers hanging open. They proceeded into the kitchen, which had the remains of someone's breakfast sitting on the counter: a cereal bowl with an inch of milk in the bottom next to a box of Frosted Flakes. There was a stack of mail on the round kitchen table in the corner. Reese laid Carter's gun on the table and shuffled through the envelopes. 'Hey, we're in Ohio,' she said. 'The guy who lives here is named Carl Baldwin.' A cordless phone was lying nearby, and David set the agent's gun down to pick up the phone.

'Wait a second,' Reese said. 'Who are you calling? Don't you think our parents' lines will be tapped by now? The Blue Base people have to be looking for us.'

Amber held out her hand. 'Let me call Malcolm Todd.'

'Agent Todd?' Reese said in surprise. 'Where is he?'

'He's not really an agent, and he had to go undercover. He leaked the video, you know. The one of me getting shot. So after that he couldn't exactly go back to work for your government.'

'Really?' David said. 'So he's been hiding out ever since then?'

'Sort of. He's been waiting for the call to go back home, but the ship hasn't been able to leave Earth yet. So he went underground.'

'Is he near here?' Reese asked.

'I don't know where he is, but he can contact the ship securely, and they can get here. Give me one of those envelopes with the address on it.'

Reese handed her an electric bill, and David gave her the phone. Amber dialed a number from memory. It rang for what seemed like a long time, but finally she said, 'Hello?' After a brief pause, she began to speak into the phone in Imrian. Reese had never heard more than a few words in the language, and hearing Amber speak it was startling. Even though she knew Amber was Imrian, Reese had always thought of her as being American. Of course, Reese realized, she wasn't. Amber's whole body language changed when she spoke Imrian; she seemed to stand up straighter, and the tone of her voice lowered. The language sounded liquid, with multiple syllables rolled together in soft *R*s and breathy *H*s. After a few minutes of conversation Amber read out the address on the electric bill, and then concluded the call.

'What did he say?' Reese asked.

Amber put the phone down. 'They're coming. He said to be ready in a few hours and to wait outside.'

'Did he say anything about our parents?' David asked.

'They're okay. He's been in touch with the ship since we were taken, and they're all safe.' Amber rubbed a hand over her eyes. 'I need to use the bathroom to wash off my feet and stuff. Do you guys need it first? I might be a while.'

David glanced at Reese. 'Go ahead,' he said. 'I'll wait.'

'Thanks,' Reese said. 'I'll be quick.'

The bathroom was about a thousand times cleaner than the

one in the farmhouse where they had been held prisoner. As Reese washed up in the sink, the water ran brown down the drain. She felt filthy all over. Dirt from the basement was crusted over her previously white shirt, and dirt from the field was smeared all over her pants. She found rusty spatters of dried liquid on her knuckles, and she scraped at them with damp fingernails, hoping it wasn't Carter's blood from when she had shot him.

She thought she was going to be sick.

She moved to the toilet, flipping up the seat, and gasped raggedly as she bent over. Droplets of water plummeted from her chin into the toilet bowl. *I shot a man*, she thought. Last night it had happened so fast she hadn't had time to think. She had no love for Carter, but she hadn't wanted to kill him either. What would happen to her if he was dead? Would she be tried for murder? The thoughts made her head spin. She remembered the agent saying he could make sure she wasn't prosecuted for what she had done. David had smashed his head in with a rock.

'Oh God,' she muttered.

She had to kneel on the floor. Her hands gripped the edge of the toilet bowl and she tried to breathe regularly. *One thing at a time*, she told herself. First things first: get out of Carl Baldwin's house.

When her stomach stopped lurching, she got up. Her hands shook as she finger-combed her hair away from her face. It didn't look good, but it helped a little. She looked less like an escaped lunatic, and more like the average juvenile delinquent who had gone running in dress clothes across a field in the middle of the night. She sighed, dried her hands on Carl Baldwin's towel, and went back to the kitchen.

David and Amber were looking at each other with extremely weird expressions on their faces. They spun around when she returned, and she realized she had been gone for a while. 'What's going on?' she asked warily.

'I have to pee,' David said, brushing past her.

Amber went to the refrigerator and opened the door, peering inside. 'I'm starving.'

Reese followed her. 'Amber.'

'Hey look, Carl's got some mac-and-cheese leftovers. Do you think he'd care if we ate them?' Amber held up a casserole dish half full of macaroni and cheese.

'What were you guys talking about?' Reese asked.

Amber didn't look at her. 'It's between me and David, okay? Do you want some mac and cheese?' She put the casserole in the microwave and searched the drawers until she found forks. She laid them on the counter and began to open the cabinets. She took down two glasses and filled them with water from the tap. 'Here,' she said, putting one on the counter in front of Reese. 'You must be thirsty.'

Reese took it, studying Amber's suspiciously calm face. Reese drank the water. When the microwave dinged, Amber took the casserole out and set it on the counter between them, then forked up a mouthful. Her eyes closed when she tasted her first bite.

'Oh my God, Carl Baldwin is a great cook,' Amber said, quickly taking another bite.

'Really?' Reese put down her water glass and tried the

macaroni and cheese. It was salty and creamy, and she tasted the unmistakable tang of blue cheese. 'Wow.' Reese took a bigger bite.

By the time David returned a few minutes later, they had eaten almost all of it. 'I'm sorry,' Amber said apologetically. 'Look, there's still a little left.' She grabbed another fork and gave it to him.

'Thanks,' David said dryly.

Amber flashed him a brief smile, which made Reese's suspicion return. What had happened between them when she was in the bathroom?

'I'm gonna go wash up,' Amber said, avoiding Reese's questioning gaze. She put down her fork and hightailed it out of the kitchen.

David was opening the cabinets, and Reese asked, 'What are you looking for?'

'Water glasses?'

She pointed to the cabinet to the left of the stove. As he filled a glass at the sink she said, 'You should eat the rest of the mac and cheese. I think there's bread and stuff too if you want a sandwich.' She noticed that he had washed the blood off his face and hand, but some still remained beneath his chin. She pulled a paper towel off the roll and dampened it beneath the faucet. 'You missed a spot,' she said, and dabbed at the dried blood on his neck. The towel came away red. She stepped back. His tie was crooked, and now the collar of his shirt was wet as well as stained. 'You kind of look like a refugee from a postapocalyptic debate tournament,' she said, smiling.

He laughed. 'I think we lost.'

She shook her head. 'They haven't finished judging yet.'

He reached for her hand, pulling the stained paper towel out of her grasp before he linked his fingers with hers. 'We have to talk.'

She stiffened. 'About what?'

'Amber talked to me.'

Reese's stomach dropped. 'Oh God.'

He almost smiled. 'Reese—'

'I told her it wouldn't work,' she said. He wouldn't let go of her hand, and she knew he was feeling everything she was: the sharp acceleration of her heart; the fear that he would be insulted; the mortification that Amber had been the one to broach the subject of the three of them.

'I know,' he said.

'I don't want to put you through that. It's not fair. Amber's not thinking clearly. I mean, we're not Imrians, we're—' She stopped. He wasn't insulted or angry. In fact, she sensed something else entirely, but it confused her.

'What are we?' he asked softly.

The tips of David's black hair were wet from the bathroom sink. His brown eyes were focused intently on her, and she could sense all of him through the touch of his fingers: whole, separate, his consciousness an entire world apart from hers.

Before the adaptation, she had never known the way someone else felt – not truly. She could guess. She was usually bad at that, or at least she thought she was. She had a hard enough time figuring out what she was feeling herself, and now, standing in Carl Baldwin's kitchen in the middle of Ohio, she realized that was why she had been so scared of getting involved with anyone. It wasn't about being afraid of being hurt. It was about being afraid of the inchoate heart of herself. If she wasn't sure of herself – if she couldn't predict how she was going to feel from one moment to the next – how could she be in a relationship with anyone else?

That night in Phoenix last June, when David walked her back to her room and almost kissed her, her emotions had risen up in an unexpected tidal wave of fear and self-doubt, and she had had no idea what to do about them except shove them – and him – away. She wasn't going to do that again. Now she was different. Now she *knew* what David was feeling, and by opening up to his consciousness, she saw the way he saw her. He didn't think she was a tangled mess of conflicting emotions to be avoided at all costs. He thought she was complicated and beautiful and stubborn, and he loved it all, and she whispered, 'I don't know what we are, but I know I love you.'

She slid her arms around him and nestled her face in the hollow between his neck and shoulder and took a long, shuddering breath. He squeezed her tighter and said, 'I love you too.'

She smiled, hiding it against his shoulder, but she knew he couldn't mistake the warmth that flared in her. She wanted to stand there forever, feeling the steady rhythm of his heart next to hers.

It was much too soon when he said gently, 'We do need to talk about that other thing.'

She disentangled herself from him and he backed away, putting a couple of feet between them. 'Okay,' she said nervously.

He reached for his water glass and took a drink first. His cheeks were a little pink. 'So, Amber suggested that, um, you could date both of us.'

'Yeah, but—'

'Let me just say this. I know you told her I wouldn't go for it. She told me that too. And you were probably right. I was—' He hesitated, rubbing his hand through his hair so that it stood straight up. 'I was really jealous before. I didn't like her because I knew how much you liked her, and I couldn't get past the fact that other people would see you with her and judge me for being – not enough, or something.' The pink spots on his cheeks darkened. 'The day we broke up, you said that the way you felt about me should be more important than what other people thought. I couldn't hear that then. I was too jealous. But now ...' He looked at her, and it was obvious how difficult it was for him to say these things. She wanted to reach for him, to tell him he didn't have to say another word, but as she stepped forward he shook his head.

'You were right,' he said. 'The way you feel is way more important than how other people think about me and you. And I know how you feel about me. I *know*.'

'I know,' she said, the words thick in her throat.

He took a quick breath. 'I know how you feel about me, and I know how you feel about her, and ...' He hesitated. 'I know how she feels about you, and I don't want to be the reason you don't get to feel that. But most of all, I don't want to have to pretend that I don't love you.'

Reese was astonished. 'What are you saying?' she whispered. Every nerve in her body seemed to tremble.

He was backed up against the counter, arms crossed. 'I'm saying we can try. If you want to date us both, we can try.'

She stared at his flushed face. She saw the tension in his shoulders. 'Are you sure?'

He looked uncomfortable. 'Yeah, I'm sure. Do you want to do that?'

'I don't – I mean – maybe?' It was so hard for her to say yes. It still seemed like an impossibility. 'I don't know how it would work,' she said, waving her hands.

'We'd have to talk about that.'

She groaned. 'Oh God, I hate talking.'

One corner of his mouth curved up. 'I'd say we could not talk, but I think it would be better if we said these things out loud.'

She almost said *Why?* The word was on the tip of her tongue, but she bit it back. She knew the answer. Saying it out loud made it real in a way that *susum'urda* never would – not for her and David. They might be different now, but they had been born human, and they could never completely leave that identity behind. 'Okay,' she said. All her disparate emotions seemed to coalesce. She knew what she wanted, and now that she had made the decision, the words came easily to her – as if they had always been there in the background, waiting. 'We'll talk about it. I want to be with you, and I want to be with her, and I want to try to make it work.' Her legs wobbled as she moved toward him and reached for his hands. 'Now can I kiss you?'

She felt the imprint of his smile on her mouth as his hands moved around her waist, the connection opening up between the two of them as she pulled him closer: all of him tangled with all of her, and she wasn't confused, not one tiny bit.

Amber wasn't in the bathroom anymore. 'Amber?' Reese called.

'I'm in here,' Amber said from the bedroom.

Reese went into Carl Baldwin's bedroom and saw Amber picking through what appeared to be his sock drawer. 'What are you doing?'

Amber pulled out a pair of white tube socks. 'I can't fit into any of his shoes, but I'm not walking around barefoot anymore.' She sat on the edge of the bed and unrolled the socks, giving them a dubious look. 'I guess they're clean enough.'

'You just ran through two dirty fields in bare feet and you're worried about the cleanliness of these socks?' Reese said, laughing.

Amber arched an eyebrow at her. 'You're in a good mood.' She crossed her right ankle over her left knee and studied the sole of her foot. It was still red and scarred, but the skin no longer appeared to be broken. Amber slid the sock on. 'Did you talk to David?'

Reese leaned against the dresser. 'Yeah.'

Amber glanced up and then back down at her foot, a faint pink stain on her cheeks. 'So?'

'When you first suggested this – last Friday on the ship – you said it wasn't unusual for Imrians to be in relationships of more than two people.'

Amber seemed surprised that Reese was bringing this up. 'Yeah, so?'

'Is it normal?'

Amber pulled on the second tube sock. They came all the way up over her knees, and she tugged the hem of her dress down so that it looked like she was wearing thick white tights. 'It's not uncommon. I have three parents.'

Reese's jaw dropped. 'You mean, Dr Brand is in a – a—'

'I prefer to not think of my mother too closely in this situation,' Amber said dryly. 'But I do have two fathers. They're back home.'

'Really?'

Amber smiled. 'Really. I think you'd like them.'

Curiosity overcame Reese's self-consciousness. 'How does that work with, um, you said the Imria use an artificial womb? Is only one of them your biological father?'

'No, they're both my biological fathers.' At Reese's look of confusion, she elaborated. 'You always need an egg to begin with, and then genes from all parents involved are added in during conception. It's like genetic engineering, I guess.'

'So they picked who you would look like and everything?'

'Well, you can't actually know that for sure, but . . . sort of. I guess I'd say that Imrian children are deliberately created.' Amber crossed her legs. 'But let's not get off track. You talked about it with David? What did you decide?'

Amber was trying to sound nonchalant, but Reese heard the anxiousness in her voice. Her dress was smudged with dirt and the right cap sleeve had a rip in it. She must have tried to wash off her face in the bathroom, but traces of eyeliner remained, and her hair was wet.

'You said that you liked me because I made you feel human,' Reese said, thinking back to that afternoon on the beach at

Angel Island. 'But humans ... we don't normally do this. We have a hard enough time being with one other person, much less two. I know there are people who can do it. But I've never thought I could be one of them. I never thought about it, period. It's scary, you know?'

'What scares you the most?' Amber asked.

'I'm scared that we're going to screw it up,' Reese said frankly. 'That I'm going to hurt one of you, or that it's just going to be too complicated. And if I start thinking about what might happen when other people – the public – find out, I might have a panic attack. I've never done anything remotely like this before. Before I met you, I didn't think I'd ever want to date anyone.'

'Really?' Amber said, surprised. 'You never told me that.'

'Would it have mattered if I did? I don't think you would have paid any attention.'

A wry smile crossed Amber's face. 'Probably not.' A cautious hope seemed to dawn in her eyes. 'But does this mean that you want to now? Date people?'

Reese knelt on the floor in front of her and threaded her fingers through Amber's. 'No,' Reese said, and Amber's eyes sparkled as she sensed Reese's feelings spilling through her. 'I don't want to date people. I want to date you, and I want to date David.'

Amber looked as if she could hardly believe what Reese had said. 'Really?'

Reese smiled. 'Really.'

Amber lifted a hand to Reese's face, her fingertips tracing Reese's cheek, and Reese felt the joy that rose inside Amber, warm as her skin and sweet as the taste of her mouth. Amber put her arms around Reese's neck and kissed her, murmuring, 'I love you.'

Reese couldn't resist. She pulled back an inch and said, 'I know.'

Amber's fingers, twined in Reese's hair, tightened abruptly. 'You did not just say that.'

'Ow,' Reese said, laughing. She pulled Amber off the bed and onto her lap, and as they kissed, Reese told her: *I love you, I love you, I love you.*

That's better, Amber thought, and Reese ran her hands up Amber's thighs and felt as if she were floating.

CHAPTER 40

They left a note for Carl Baldwin. Amber found a pen in the kitchen's junk drawer and flipped over the electric bill to write on it.

Dear Carl Baldwin,

We're really sorry for breaking into your house. We didn't have any other choice. We'll send you money to cover the damaged window. Also we're sorry for eating your macaroni and cheese and for taking a pair of your socks. You're a really good cook.

Sincerely,
Amber Gray, Reese Holloway, and David Li

Amber left the note in the middle of the table, weighted down with a fork, and then scribbled Carl Baldwin's address on a pizza menu and gave it to Reese. 'I don't have any pockets,' Amber said at Reese's questioning glance. She had given David's jacket back to him.

‘Oh.’ Reese pocketed the address. ‘Ready to go?’

‘Don’t forget your guns,’ Amber said as she headed for the back door.

David looked amused. He picked up the agent’s gun from the counter and Reese grabbed Carter’s weapon from the table, and they followed Amber out of the house.

The black triangle was far above them in the sky, but its sharp edges were clearly distinguishable. A small dot emerged from the ship and descended toward the field. As it approached, Reese recognized it as the lander, wings extended. It touched down behind the stack of hay bales, and when the door opened, their parents ran out to meet them.

Reese’s mom hugged her so tightly that Reese squeaked. ‘Are you all right? Did they hurt you? What happened? Why do you have a gun?’ her mom demanded all at once. She only let her go when Reese’s dad stepped in to hug her too.

Reese saw Malcolm Todd standing beside the lander’s hatch. He caught Reese’s eye and nodded toward the craft. ‘We should go,’ Reese said, pulling away from her parents. ‘We’ll explain everything when we get back to the ship.’

Returning to the black triangle felt like arriving at a safe house. Reese had never been so relieved to walk down those corridors before. Everyone was gathered in the dining hall – even Akiya Deyir – where stained coffee cups were scattered all over the tables, and the screens on the walls showed several different television stations at once. The fancy headline at the bottom of one network’s broadcast, decorated with the crosshairs of a rifle scope, read: *HOSTAGE SITUATION*. The moving text below stated: *Hunt continues for three missing teenagers taken hostage by AHL militia during botched UN bombing.*

'What's going on?' Reese asked. 'What's the AHL militia?'

Akiya Deyir answered, 'Americans for Humanity and Liberty. That's the name of an anti-Imrian group – the same one that posted bail for the man who tried to shoot you at Fisherman's Wharf.'

'But they didn't kidnap us,' David said. 'Blue Base soldiers did.'

'There's a cover-up in process,' Dr Brand explained. 'AHL supposedly bombed the United Nations the day you were taken.'

'Was that the noise we heard in the parking garage?' Reese asked.

'Maybe,' Dr Brand answered. 'It wasn't a very successful bombing. There wasn't much damage, but the UN was evacuated and the General Assembly was interrupted. But shortly afterward, AHL – which does model itself on a citizens' militia group – took credit for abducting you.'

'We think that AHL might have actually pulled off the bombing,' Todd said. 'It was a bit clumsy, and they would have needed inside assistance, but it does line up with their anti-UN stance.'

Reese watched another of the TV stations, on which photos of her, David, and Amber were shown while an anchorwoman spoke. The volume had been turned off but the closed-captioning at the bottom of the screen read: *FBI officials declined to release details on whether they have any leads, but one anonymous agent reportedly claims that the search is fruitless. Imrian ambassador Akiya Deyir has offered assistance to locate the teenagers, but so far the Randall Administration has not issued a public response.*

Deyir, who had seen where Reese's gaze went, said, 'That was right before we heard from Malcolm. President Randall still hasn't spoken.'

'President Randall ordered the kidnapping,' Reese said.

Everyone in the room stared at her. 'What?' Dr Brand said.

'Are you sure?' the ambassador asked.

'Yes, I heard them talking about it.' Reese thought back to the voices she had heard through the floorboards. 'The soldiers said the president couldn't make up her mind about what to do with us because she's a woman. I totally remember that.'

Amber asked, 'Wait, what exactly is the official story?'

Dr Brand answered, 'The news is reporting that the AHL militia group bombed the UN as a cover to abduct the three of you. They're supposedly holding you hostage.'

'What for?' Amber asked.

Todd shrugged. 'The theory is that they'll ask us – the Imria – for money. It doesn't make a lot of sense, and basically shows that the Randall Administration is engaging in another cover-up without thinking through the details.'

'So what's the true story?' Reese's mom asked. 'This is all very confusing. Why would the president want to kidnap you three?'

Reese turned to her mom. 'She's still trying to hide what happened during the June Disaster. It all goes back to those birds.'

'It goes back well before that,' Todd said.

'We need to release the news that you've been found,' Dr

Brand said. 'We have to put an end to this fake hostage story – not to mention the fake search for you three.'

'Yeah,' Reese agreed. 'We should do all that, but first we need to go to Los Angeles.'

'Why?' Deyir asked.

'Diego Luis Torres,' Reese said. 'I owe someone a favor.'

CHAPTER 41

Los Angeles Times
October 18, 2014
GENETICALLY MODIFIED SOLDIER FOUND DEAD
By Anthony Krause

LOS ANGELES – The body of a 23-year-old woman identified as Daniela Torres was found dead in downtown Los Angeles on Thursday. Autopsy results from the remains have not been made available to the public, but an unnamed source from the Los Angeles County Department of the Coroner said that the body held traces of Imrian DNA.

Imrian spokesperson Nura Halba said that Daniela Torres has never undergone Imrian treatment or received an adaptation procedure. 'We believe Ms Torres was part of a United States military research initiative that used Imrian DNA to create so-called supersoldiers,' Mr Halba said in an interview. He declined to elaborate, citing ongoing legal proceedings.

According to unreleased findings from a joint investigation undertaken by journalist Sophia Curtis and citizen journalist website Bin 42 that were previewed by the *Los Angeles Times*, the initiative's goal was to create genetically modified soldiers with enhanced strength and endurance. The Pentagon has denied any knowledge of Ms Torres and has obtained an injunction from the United States District Court, Northern District of California, to restrict publication of the investigation, citing national security concerns. Currently, the decision is under appeal in the Ninth District Court of Appeals, and is expected to be appealed to the Supreme Court.

In an unusual coincidence, adoption proceedings for Ms Torres's 7-year-old son, Diego Luis Torres, were filed the same week that Ms Torres's body was discovered. Catherine Sheridan and Richard Holloway, parents of the adapted human teenager Reese Holloway, are attempting to adopt Diego Torres, who until recently was a resident at the Children's Home of Los Angeles. Ms Sheridan, an assistant district attorney in San Francisco, and Mr Holloway, an Internet entrepreneur, have refused to comment on their adoption proceedings.

CHAPTER 42

www.bin42.com
THE TRUTH
By Julian Arens, Jason Briggs, and Sophia Curtis
Posted November 17, 2014 at 6:00 AM
Tags: Amber Gray, Blue Base, conspiracies, David Li, Elizabeth Randall, extraterrestrials, Imria, June Disaster, Project Plato, Reese Holloway, Roswell, truth

Yesterday, the United States Supreme Court issued a historic decision in Bin 42's favor, stating that the Pentagon's concerns for national security are outweighed by public interest and the importance of the First Amendment. We at Bin 42, along with Sophia Curtis, who has assisted us in this investigation, applaud the Supreme Court's decision to overturn 67 years of secrecy regarding the most important discovery in all of human history. We thank our supporters, including the Foundation for Universal Rights, the Full Disclosure Project, and the Imria, for supporting our legal battle and making sure that the public is now able to hear the truth, the whole truth, and nothing but the truth.

Out of the Cold War

The story of Imrian engagement with the United States began in 1947, when an Imrian craft landed near Roswell, New Mexico, with the express goal of making contact with the US. Although the Imria had been coming to Earth for millions of years, this was their first official contact with a human government. According to Imrian Ambassador Akiya Deyir, the Imria chose to make contact with the US rather than other nations because of its role in World War II, including its development of nuclear weapons. The Imria wished to prevent further nuclear proliferation, and they believed that direct cooperation with the US would be the best method of doing this, particularly in light of the postwar geopolitical situation, which left much of the globe unstable or in reconstruction.

The US, which was engaged in the beginnings of the Cold War, chose to keep its contact with the Imria secret. To that end, the Plato Protocol established a secret research agreement between the US and the Imria. The Imria offered to help the US military develop lifesaving biotechnology, while the US government agreed to provide the Imria with human research subjects. Neither side disclosed their actual plans: The Imria wished to develop an adaptation procedure to adapt humans into Imrians, while the US military planned to use Imrian science and DNA to create supersoldiers.

In order to manage the Imrian-American relationship, the US formed a highly classified nongovernmental organization known as the Corporation for American Security and Sovereignty. Like the Federal Reserve Bank, CASS was not an official government entity, but its job was to represent the federal government in order to ensure consistent leadership across and outside successive presidential administrations.

American Military Supremacy

For decades, CASS managed Project Plato and other classified military projects that arose out of Plato, often violating the Plato Protocol in order to obtain Imrian DNA and biotechnology. CASS justified these violations under the goal of maintaining American military supremacy during the Cold War and later in the face of rising global terrorism.

CASS launched several military initiatives, including most notably Project Blue Base and Project Blackbird. The goal of Project Blue Base was to create genetically enhanced operatives, or soldiers, using Imrian DNA. These soldiers would be faster, stronger, and smarter than ordinary human soldiers – or at least that was what military scientists promised. In reality, Blue Base soldiers' bodies were often unable to process the Imrian DNA they were given. In some cases, these soldiers suffered severe mental illnesses and psychotic episodes; in other cases, they died of immunodeficiency diseases at accelerated rates.

Project Blackbird also utilized Imrian DNA, although in this case the goal was not to modify humans but to gather intelligence. Imrian investigations into American thefts of Imrian technology showed that many animals were genetically altered in attempts to render them capable of following precise human commands. The most promising results arose from genetically modifying birds, which military intelligence planned to use as biological surveillance tools, essentially replacing aerial reconnaissance aircraft. These birds, which were implanted with cameras, would be trained to fly over enemy territory. The first wide-ranging test of Project Blackbird was authorized by President Elizabeth Randall in May 2014 and began the following month.

This test released a large number of genetically modified birds, which had been ordered to fly in a loop across the United States with their embedded cameras recording the entire journey. The birds did not respond well to the test. In early June, reports were received at Project Blackbird headquarters at Area 51 in Nevada indicating that some birds had deviated from their flight patterns, with some attacking small planes. On June 14, 2012, those attacks became widespread as genetically modified birds began to lead flocks of non-genetically modified birds in suicidal assaults on commercial aircraft. The subsequent accidents became known as the June Disaster.

As the extent of the June Disaster became apparent, President Randall authorized a full cover-up of the government-created tragedy. She ordered all crashed airplanes to be cleaned up under classified procedures, with all bird remains destroyed in order to suppress any evidence of the genetic experimentation. In addition, President Randall authorized closures of various public highways and the Internet in order to prevent citizens from observing the results of these plane crashes.

During the widespread confusion caused by the June Disaster, human teenagers David Li and Reese Holloway suffered a near-fatal car accident on Area 51. Their adaptation at the hands of Imrian scientist Evelyn Brand of Project Plato has been extensively documented elsewhere. It should be noted that it was due to the massive government cover-up of the June Disaster, however, that the Imria were able to secretly adapt Holloway and Li in the first place.

In an attempt to recover Holloway and Li for military testing, CASS authorized the abduction of the two teenagers from their San Francisco homes in July 2014. Their release from Area 51 following the leak of the video showing the Imrian spacecraft resulted in further complications for the Randall Administration, as it became obvious that the two teens planned to reveal what they had learned during the time they were held at Blue Base, including evidence that the June

Disaster was related to genetically modified birds created by the US military. Plans were then set in motion to kidnap the teens once again, this time permanently.

Although the Randall Administration has denied any involvement in ordering the abduction of the teens, evidence obtained by Holloway and Li show that Blue Base soldiers were clearly behind their kidnapping from the United Nations. Bin 42 has learned that Congress will launch an investigation into the Randall Administration's role not only in the abductions of these teenagers but in the cover-up of the June Disaster, beginning next week.

June 2015

CHAPTER 43

Amber's door slid open and Reese leaned into the room. 'What's taking you so long?' she asked.

Amber was sitting on the edge of her bed, lacing up a pair of knee-high black combat boots. 'These,' she said.

Reese came inside, the door whooshing closed behind her, and picked up the pink dress hanging over the back of a chair. 'This is going to get all wrinkled.'

'It's been there for five minutes,' Amber protested. 'Here, give it to me.' She stood, reaching for the dress she had just worn at the departure ceremony, and hung it in the narrow closet. The pink edge of it peeked out when she shut the door.

After months of preparation, the Imria were finally returning to Kurra, along with Reese, David, Julian, and several other human ambassadors. In May, the six-month-long Congressional investigation into President Randall had resulted in her impeachment, with Vice President Huntington stepping in to take her place.

Reese sat in the chair and watched while Amber returned to lacing the boots. 'Are those new?'

'Yeah. Somebody sent them to me.' Amber seemed pleased. 'Ever since they started that photo blog of my outfits I keep getting really awesome stuff.' Amber had developed a particularly enthusiastic following after her interview went live on Bin 42 last fall, with adoring fans documenting her every move.

As Amber tied the laces into a bow, Reese asked, 'Are you going to send them a photo of this outfit?'

'Maybe.' Amber was wearing black leggings and an artfully ripped vintage T-shirt over a blue tank top. 'Do you think I should?'

'Why not? I like the boots.'

'Me too. I feel prepared for anything in them. Kidnapping, assault, running through hay fields.' She stretched her legs out to examine the boots. 'If only they didn't take so long to put on.'

'That's why I came to get you. Everybody's ready for the launch.'

'I'm almost done.' Amber went to the mirror on the back of the closet door and made a couple of adjustments to her short blond hair. She picked up a tube of lip gloss and raised the wand to her mouth, spreading the dark pink gloss over her bottom lip in a quick, sweeping motion. She pressed her lips together, then ran the wand over her upper lip and studied her reflection carefully. She caught Reese staring at her in the glass. 'What?' Amber said. 'Does it look bad?'

'No,' Reese said, smiling slightly. Amber shot her a playful look, and if they weren't already late, Reese would have kissed all that lip gloss right off. 'Let's go,' Reese said, standing to open the door.

'Okay, I'm ready.' Amber grabbed her hand as they left together.

'I can't believe we're finally leaving,' Reese said.

'You're going to love it. Except there's no ice cream on Kurra. That is truly tragic.'

'With a zillion years of technological expertise, you guys haven't engineered ice cream over there?'

The third level corridor was empty; everyone was already downstairs in the dining hall, which had been set up to view the liftoff.

'It's not the same,' Amber said. 'There are no cows.'

'You could import some,' Reese suggested as they waited for the elevator. 'Or bring in some cow fetuses and birth them on Kurra.'

Amber shook her head. 'It'll disturb the ecosystem. I made Mom get a few gallons from Mitchell's but it's not going to last.'

They entered the elevator, and Amber circled her arms around Reese's waist. 'So you're staying for the whole year?'

'Yeah. We just confirmed it today.' Reese, David, and Julian had all deferred their freshman year of college to stay on Kurra and learn the language. It had taken months of discussion before their families all agreed, and Reese had pulled a lot of strings to persuade Akiya Deyir that Julian should be permitted to join them. It was Julian's work for Bin 42 that finally convinced the ambassador, and while Julian was on Kurra, he would continue to report on his experiences for the public back on Earth.

Bringing Julian on board, though, had been less difficult for

Reese than navigating the last nine months with David and Amber. It had been complicated from the start, because even if David hadn't wanted to be jealous, it didn't mean he wasn't. Amber presented a whole different set of issues, because although she could touch Reese and know her feelings, she had a hard time understanding David's struggles. Amber and David mostly avoided being alone together, and though they were polite to each other when they were in larger groups, they weren't friends. Reese felt as if she was constantly translating for the two of them. In her darker moments, when none of them seemed to understand one another even though they could have practiced susum'urda together and known the others' emotions intimately, Reese thought it would be easier if they gave up this relationship entirely. The only thing stopping her from calling it off was the knowledge that it would make them all equally miserable.

Ultimately, it was going through the experience of having their relationship revealed to the public that brought them closer together. They had managed to keep things quiet until December, when one of Reese's and David's classmates— they never knew who – leaked the story to the press. Reese had known it would get out eventually, and she hadn't wanted to lie about it, but she wished there had been more time for the three of them to work things out in private.

The weekend after the news broke, they met in Amber's room at the Imrian ship on Angel Island and talked about how to deal with the fallout. There had been so much immediate judgment, so much snide commentary and innuendo – along with disconcertingly vocal support from the tiny polyamorous community – that it felt like being thrust into the center of a tornado. For the first time since they took shelter in Carl Baldwin's house, being alone together felt safe.

Watching Amber and David face each other in person after months of careful distance, Reese realized she had to stop protecting them. She had been willing – even eager – to be the buffer between them, but now she saw that she had only made things more awkward. Though Amber and David had spent little time together, they knew each other intimately through Reese's emotions. That created a disconnect that could only be mended by getting to know one another the old-fashioned way. That weekend in December, Reese asked them, for the first time, to talk to each other, and she left them alone to do it.

Things improved after that, little by little. When the possibility of spending a year on Kurra – where plural relationships were normal – was raised, Reese knew they had to go. They might be able to figure it out on their own here on Earth, but it could only be easier if they were in a place where nobody thought their arrangement was unusual.

'I'm glad it worked out,' Amber said, smiling at her as the elevator descended.

Reese leaned in, the tip of her nose touching Amber's. 'Me too.'

When the door opened, a boy squealed, 'Cat sent me to get you!'

Reese pulled away from Amber. 'Hi, D.' She bent down to smile at Diego, ruffling his black hair. He was still dressed in his departure ceremony outfit, a kid-sized gray suit with a mini blue necktie.

'Come on, you guys are late,' Diego said, grabbing Reese's hand to drag her down the corridor.

Amber laughed and followed.

The first time Reese had seen Diego, in the orphanage in Los Angeles, he had been silent and terrified. At first he refused to speak at all, and meeting him had made Reese understand, in a way she never had before, how significant it was that she could touch him and know what scared him. Perhaps because of that, Reese had been the first person Diego had spoken to. He still didn't allow most people near him, but he liked Reese's parents, and he had completely latched on to Julian. One day, Reese knew, she would have to tell him about his mother, and she wasn't sure how she was going to do that. She still remembered Torres's emotions so clearly – her pain and loss, coupled with the sheer edge of her deadliness – and she saw the soldier's face in Diego's. To some degree, she felt responsible for Torres's death, even though she knew the soldier's days had been numbered long before she helped Reese, Amber, and David escape. To Reese's surprise, her mom had recognized that when Reese brought up the possibility of adopting Diego.

'Taking care of her son won't bring her back,' her mom said.

'I can't leave him there without any sort of connection to her,' Reese insisted. She was stuck, though. If her mom didn't agree to help with the adoption, Diego would have to stay at the Children's Home for now. The state of California would never allow an unemployed teenager to adopt a kid.

A few days later, her mom told her that she and Reese's dad

had decided to try to adopt Diego. That was how Reese learned that her parents were back together.

'I'm willing to give him another chance,' her mom said when they were alone in the kitchen of their home in Noe Valley. The house had new front windows and a new alarm system, and her dad had moved his things into her mom's room. 'I want you to try to give him another chance too.'

'But what if it doesn't work?' Reese asked, an unsettling mixture of hope and fear sparking inside her.

'Honey, you can never know. I can't predict the future. I only know that it feels right to try again.'

Reese couldn't object, because she understood what her mom meant. And even though she had her issues with her dad, she couldn't deny there was part of her that had always wished they could be together again as a family. With the addition of Diego, it was like a new beginning for all of them.

Diego ran down the corridor, tugging at Reese's hand so that she had to jog to keep up with him. 'Come on!' he urged her.

In the dining hall, the tables were gone and chairs were lined up to face the floor-to-ceiling screens. They showed the view of the eucalyptus trees outside, and to the left, Reese saw the sparkle of the bay. Everyone in the ship except the captain and his assistants had come down for the liftoff. She saw Akiya Deyir, Nura Halba, Eres Tilhar, and Malcolm Todd. She saw the nervous-looking delegates from the newly formed Council of Earth Nations, who would be establishing the first human embassy on Kurra. And she saw Dr Brand talking to David's parents, with her own parents nearby. Their families would only be going to Kurra for a month. They would return to Earth on a different ship with another group of Imrian representatives who would continue readying the adaptation procedure while Reese, David, and Julian stayed behind. Up front, in the corner of the room, David waved to her. He was sitting with his sister, Chloe, and Julian.

Diego let go of Reese's hand so that he could rush over to Julian, yelling, 'I found her! Can we go now?' Julian laughed and tackled Diego onto the floor, tickling him until the boy shrieked with laughter.

'You ready?' Reese asked Julian.

'I've been waiting for this my entire life,' Julian said, a smile splitting his face from ear to ear. 'You have no idea how ready I am.'

Julian dragged Diego upright as Reese sat on the floor next to them. David was behind her, and Amber took the seat beside David. That wouldn't have happened a couple of months ago, and Reese felt a surge of happiness inside her. Maybe all this really would work out. She leaned back against David's legs and sensed his anticipation in a warm glow between them.

Akiya Deyir came to the front of the room and stood before the screens, raising his hands for quiet. 'I've just heard from Hirin Sagal, and we are ready for takeoff. I suggest you all find a seat. It should be a smooth liftoff but just in case, you might not want to stand until you've gotten your space legs.' Some of the humans laughed nervously, and Akiya Deyir added, 'Don't worry. We are very much looking forward to bringing you to our home.'

A scattering of applause followed as he sat down, and then

Reese felt the ship's engines hum on, a slight rumble shaking the floor. Diego squealed. Reese sat forward, her arms wrapped around her knees, and gazed at the screens as the ship lifted from the ground. A murmur of excitement went through the dining hall. They rose over the lawn of Camp Reynolds and the whitewashed officers' quarters, and as the ship turned, Reese saw the strip of beach where she and Amber had been photographed that day in August. They had walked down there again after returning from Ohio, and flipped off all the paparazzi who lurked in boats on the bay. The memory of that made Reese grin, and she looked over her shoulder at Amber, whose legs were crossed in her big black boots. She was watching the view with something like sadness.

'Hey,' Reese said, tapping the toe of Amber's boot.

She glanced at Reese and slid off the chair to sit beside her. 'What?'

'It's amazing,' Reese said, turning back to the screens. Amber leaned against Reese, and Reese put an arm around her. She realized that the sadness she had seen on Amber's face was about leaving Earth. 'We'll come back,' Reese said, surprised.

'I know. But it's my home too, you know. I get homesick when I leave.'

Far below, the steely water of the bay was dotted with sailboats and yachts and fleets of ferries that had been reserved for tourists to watch the liftoff. The edge of Angel Island, like an irregularly shaped starfish, came into view, and across the water the hills of Tiburon and Sausalito were speckled with houses. Then the Golden Gate Bridge sliced across the water, its crimson cables stretching over the mouth of the bay. To the south, past the rock of Alcatraz, Reese saw the city of San Francisco, and she imagined the crowds gathered in the Marina, cameras and binoculars pointed at the black triangle cutting across the sky. In the distance the Pacific Ocean curved away in an endless dark blue, marking the edge of the horizon and the edge of the Earth itself.

David put his hand on her shoulder and she leaned back, reaching up to clasp his fingers in hers. Here we go, he thought, and she and Amber and David all held their breath as the ship ascended and the Earth dropped away beneath them. It was graceful as a dancer, the clouds like veils. As North America receded and the blackness of space began to envelop the planet, Reese gazed at her world in wonder.

It glowed from the reflected light of the sun, but it seemed lit from within, as if every life on the planet gave off a luminescence that together created an ethereal lantern in the dark. The ship slowly turned away from Earth, and a sigh went through the room as the blue-and-white sphere disappeared from view. Then they were facing the stars: masses and masses of stars scattered in a carpet of diamonds for them to walk on.

ACKNOWLEDGEMENTS

Thanks to my agent, Laura Langlie, for all her support in this project. Thanks to my editor, Kate Sullivan, for her spot-on comments and brilliant advice on how to make this book work. Thanks to everyone at Little, Brown Books for Young Readers for bringing *Adaptation* and *Inheritance* into the world, including library marketing mavens Zoe Luderitz and Victoria Stapleton; eagle-eyed production editor Barbara Bakowski; and designer Alison Impey for the fantastic covers. Thanks to my good friend and critique partner, Cindy Pon, who pushed me to answer every single question (at least in my head). Thanks to Casa Mexico Retreat for helping me hammer out the shape of this book: Paolo Bacigalupi, Holly Black, Cassandra Clare, and Sarah Rees Brennan. Thanks once again to my friend Dr Vincent Smith for providing me with fancy medical jargon. Though I'm sure Antonio Damasio did not intend for his book to be used this way, I must acknowledge how useful his *Self Comes to Mind: Constructing the Conscious Brain* was to me in thinking about consciousness. All errors, science or plot-related, are mine. And thanks to my partner, Amy Lovell, for supporting me through another crazy writing year.

CINDERELLA AS YOU'VE NEVER KNOWN HER

Alone with the sheer misery of her stepmother's cruelty, greed and ambition in preparing her two charmless daughters for presentation at court, orphaned Ash befriends a fairy – a mysterious, handsome man who grants her wishes and restores hope to Ash's life – even though she knows there will be a price to pay.

But then Ash meets Kaisa, a huntress employed by the king, and it is Kaisa who truly awakens Ash's desires for both love and self-respect.

Ash is a fairytale like no other...

978 0 340 99837 4 PBK 978 1 444 90371 3 eBook

"BEAUTIFULLY WRITTEN... SENSUAL AND EVOCATIVE... A SOPHISTICATED FAIRY-TALE FOR OLDER READERS"
Booktrust

WWW.HODDERCHILDRENS.CO.UK